THE TIGER'S IMPERIUM

The Stiger Chronicles
Originally published as
Chronicles of an Imperial Legionary Officer

Book 6

THE TIGER'S IMPERIUM

BY
MARC ALAN EDELHEIT

This book is a work of fiction. Names, characters, places, and incidents are either the product of the author's imagination or are used fictitiously. Any resemblance to actual persons, living or dead, or to actual events or locales is entirely coincidental.

The Tiger's Imperium Book 6: The Stiger Chronicles. *Originally published as The Tiger's Imperium Book Six: Chronicles of an Imperial Legionary Officer.*
First Edition

I wish to thank my agent, Andrea Hurst, for her invaluable support and assistance. I would also like to thank my beta readers, who suffered through several early drafts. My betas: Jon Cockes, Nicolas Weiss, Melinda Vallem, Paul Klebaur, James Doak, David Cheever, Bruce Heaven, Erin Penny, April Faas, Rodney Gigone, Tim Adams, Paul Bersoux, Phillip Broom, David Houston, Sheldon Levy, Michael Hetts, Walker Graham, Bill Schnippert, Jan McClintock, Jonathan Parkin, Spencer Morris, Jimmy McAfee, Rusty Juban, Joel M. Rainey, Jeremy Craig, Nathan Halliday, Ed Speight, Joseph Hall, Michael Berry, Tom Trudeau, Sally Tingley-Walker, James H. Bjorum, Franklin Johnson, Marshall Clowers. I would also like to take a moment to thank my loving wife who sacrificed many an evening and weekends to allow me to work on my writing.
Editing Assistance by Hannah Streetman, Audrey Mackaman, Brandon Purcell
Cover Art by Piero Mng (Gianpiero Mangialardi)
Cover Formatting by Telemachus Press
Agented by Andrea Hurst & Associates, LLC
http://maenovels.com/

A Ranger's Tale
Book 1: **Eli**
Book 2: **By Bow, Daggers & Sword**
Book 3: **Lutha Nyx (Coming 2023)**

The Way of Legend: With Quincy J. Allen
Book One: **Reclaiming Honor**
Book Two: **Forging Destiny**
Book Three: **Paladin's Light**

SCI-FI
Born of Ash
Book One: **Fallen Empire**
Book Two: **Infinity Control**
Book Three: **Rising Phoenix (Coming 2024)**

Guardians of the Dark
Book One: **Off Midway Station (Coming 2024)**

NONFICTION
Every Writer's Dream: The Insider's Path to an Indie Bestseller

Author's Note

Writing The Tiger's Imperium has been a labor of love and a joy. I am excited to share this next action-packed and exciting chapter in The Last War Universe. It is my sincere hope that you love it as I do.

I also want to take a moment to thank you for reading and keeping me employed as a full-time writer. For those of you who reach out to me on Facebook, Twitter, or by email, I simply cannot express how humbling it is, as an author, to have my work so appreciated and loved. From the bottom of my heart... *thank you.*

Reviews keep me motivated and also help to drive sales. I make a point to read each and every one, so please continue to post them.

You can reach out and connect with me on:
Facebook: Marc Edelheit Author
Facebook Group: MAE Fantasy & SciFi Lounge
Twitter: Marc Edelheit Author
Instagram: Marc Edelheit Author
Amazon Author Central: Marc Edelheit Author
Newsletter: You may wish to sign up by visiting my website www.maenovels.com

Again, I hope you enjoy The Tiger's Imperium and would like to offer a sincere thank you for your purchase and support.

Best regards,
Marc Alan Edelheit, your author and tour guide to the worlds of Tannis and Istros

EXCERPT FROM THELIUS'S HISTORIES, THE MAL'ZEELAN EMPIRE, VOLUME 3, BOOK 2.

The Mal'Zeelan Imperial Legion
Pre-Emperor Midisian Reformation

The imperial legion was a formation that numbered, when at full strength, 5,500 to 6,000 men. The legion was composed of heavy infantry recruited exclusively from the citizens of the empire. Slaves and non-citizens were prohibited from serving. The legion was divided into ten cohorts of 480 men, with First Cohort, being an overstrength unit, numbering around a thousand. A legion usually included a mix of engineers, surgeons, and various support staff. Legions were always accompanied by allied auxiliary formations, ranging from cavalry to various forms of light infantry. The imperial legion was commanded by a legate (general).

The basic unit of the legion was the century, numbering eighty men in strength. There were six centuries in a cohort. A centurion (basic officer) commanded the century. The centurion was supported by an optio (equivalent of a corporal) who handled minor administrative duties. Both had to be capable of reading and performing basic math.

Note: Very rarely were legions ever maintained at full strength. This was due primarily to the following reasons: retirement, death, disability, budget shortages (graft), and the slow stream of replacements.

The most famous legion was the Thirteenth, commanded by Legate ...

Post-Emperor Midisian Reformation

Emperor Midiuses's reforms were focused on streamlining the legions and cutting cost through the elimination of at least half of the officer corps per legion, amongst other changes.

The basic unit of the legion became the company, numbering around 200 men in strength. There were ten twenty-man files per company. A captain commanded the company. The captain was supported by a lieutenant, two sergeants, and a corporal per file.

TABLE OF CONTENTS

CONTINENT OF ILOSTA
WORLD OF ISTROS

CARTOGRAPHER:
PIERO MING

EASTERN OCEAN

NORTHERN REACH

ELVYN LANDS

EARTOL
MALHARA

KINGDOM OF THE RIVAN

FORESTS OF ARAITH

MOGVI ZEITH

SERTAL ZEITH

THE WILDS

BARRENS

NUANIA ICA

MALIZEIAN EMPIRE

KINGDOM OF TARGEL

OCCUPIED SOUTHERN PROVINCES

INDEPENDENT KINGDOMS

NARIGANLIA

CYPHAN CONFEDERACY

URA STEPPE

CHAPTER ONE

Stiger bent down, grabbed a battered stool, and pulled it across the floor away from the window, to the middle of the room. Hundreds of people, mostly civilians... the half-starved scarecrows of Lorium, stood outside on the street. They wanted a glimpse of their savior, their liberator and new emperor.

His mind kept returning to Taha'Leeth, fighting for her life outside the city. He should be there with her. He hated that he couldn't be, just as he disliked the new role he'd been thrust into, one he had not asked for.

Not too long ago, the Stiger name had lost much of its luster, becoming quite tarnished. His family name was synonymous with rebellion and betrayal. Stiger had come of age living in disgrace, a near outcast, excluded from polite society. And when he had joined the legion, his peers, fellow officers, and noblemen had done their best to shun him. They had made it known he was not even welcome to serve the empire he loved.

Almost for as long as he could remember, people had either shuddered in fear at the mere mention of his name or cursed it. And now... they clamored around for a look at him, hailed him as their savior, a true hero of the empire and a desperate hope for the future.

"How things have changed," Stiger said quietly.

1

Resisting a groan, he sat down. He had been worn down by the events of the last few weeks and months. He had not only pushed himself hard, but the legion too and then some. The last day and a half, starting with the assassination attempt and culminating with the battle against the Cyphan Confederacy, had been not just harrowing, but simply exhausting. Then there had come the unexpected shock of what had occurred a little over an hour before in a crypt turned sick house.

If he was being honest with himself, Stiger was feeling somewhat overwhelmed by the turn events had taken. The emperor, Tioclesion, his one-time childhood friend, was dead. Stiger himself had been designated his heir. In the burned-out remnants of Lorium, he was now the emperor. Just the thought of it sounded ridiculous, so unreal...unbelievable. A Stiger as emperor? Seriously...the world must have truly gone mad.

It was an honor, to be certain, but one he had never sought. His first instinct had been to refuse it. He wanted someone else to bear the heavy burden that came with the crown of wreaths and the curule chair. But...deep down, he knew he could not turn away this honor, no matter how dubious. He would not give up the imperium he had been granted. To do so would be foolish and incredibly shortsighted.

The High Father had set him down this path and made him his Champion. Who else could do what needed doing? Worse, if some other fool was named emperor, they might actively work against him and hinder what must be done.

The thought of being the emperor made him thoroughly sick to his stomach, as if he had eaten undercooked meat. Despite that, Stiger simply could not and would not take the chance of trusting the responsibility to someone else. No, he must take hold of the reins of power. There was just too much at stake.

And that was the rub of it all. Whether he liked it or not, he had to assume the mantle of the emperor, along with all the responsibilities and headaches that came with the title. The Cyphan had to be stopped, for they could not be allowed to open the World Gate. If they did, it would mean the end of the empire he loved.

Worse, darkness, like a veil, would fall over Istros. And so, he had to own being the emperor, accept the burden, bear it…no matter how onerous. Stiger clenched a fist. There would be no half measures. He could afford none, and that meant he had to be utterly ruthless in achieving his goals, which began first with securing his hold over the empire. Then, and only then, could he focus his attention on the true enemy, the Cyphan.

"Very nice establishment, sir," Centurion Ruga said as he entered the room, making a show of gazing around. Except for a handful of stools, any furniture that had once graced the room was now gone. "Grand, sir…just grand. I must say, I approve of your choice for a throne room. Sends a humble message to the common man, it does, sir. A right man of the people you are."

Fighting a scowl and rubbing his jaw, Stiger, looked over at the centurion and held the other's gaze for a long moment. "I am so glad you approve, Centurion, so very glad. It just makes my day. You have no idea how much it pleases me to have your approval."

Ruga actually grinned. It wasn't a large smile by any measure, but it was there just the same. He, like Tiro, enjoyed occasionally teasing his commanding officer. Stiger did not mind much, for it wasn't done in a mean-spirited or disrespectful manner. In fact, he permitted it because he felt it kept him grounded and attuned to the rank and file. Stiger often found nuggets of wisdom in Ruga's jests, and he'd learned to take them seriously.

"A lovely establishment, sir," Ruga said. "It's just a shame the ladies are long gone, a tragedy really."

They were in what had been, up until the siege of the city, a house of ill repute. It was one of the few buildings that had escaped destruction caused by the long siege the city had endured. The room was dingy and smelled of must, sweat, and too many unclean bodies.

Judging from the layer of dust and grime on the floor, it had not been cleaned for some time. Stiger did not care, though. All he wanted was a few minutes of peace to recover from the shock of what had happened ... to regain his balance and to plan. He would confer directly with Eli, Treim, and Aetius. Then, like a juggernaut, he would push on down the path he had chosen. And nothing would stand in his way.

"I've placed our men about the building, sir," Ruga said, turning professional. "There are two entrances, one to the front and another to the rear. Three men will guard each entrance."

"What about the rest of your men?" Stiger asked, for Ruga had brought a total of twenty men.

"I will stand them down, sir." Ruga pointed to the back of the room. Along the wall, a narrow staircase led up to the second floor. It was one of two staircases in the building. "There are six small rooms on the second floor. My boys will operate in shifts of two watches. Colonel Aetius offered me ten additional men. I accepted. He went to see that they get organized and said he'd be back in a moment."

"Very good." Stiger gave an absent nod as his thoughts traveled back to his childhood friend. He had left General

Treim and Father Restus with the late emperor's body. To them would fall the responsibility of caring for Tioclesion, seeing that the remains were ritually prepared for funeral rites. That would include making a wax mask for the family's personal shrine so that Tioclesion could be honored by those generations yet to come.

According to imperial custom, in two days' time, there would be a funeral. The emperor's body would be burned. His ashes would be collected and then, along with the mask, be transported back to the capital.

Stiger looked up as Eli entered the room, his boots thunking on the floorboards. The elf glanced briefly around, and his nose twitched at the smell. Without a word, he set his bow in the corner by the door, leaning it against the wall. His leather-wrapped bundle of arrows and pack he set down next to the bow, before giving a slight yawn.

"All I ever wanted was to be a soldier," Stiger said to Eli. "Emperor? Me? Can you believe that?"

"We don't always get what we want, sir," Ruga said, before Eli could speak. "Sometimes we get what we deserve."

"Ruga, you just have a natural way with words," Eli said as he looked at Stiger. "Don't you think, Ben? He's a regular ... what do you people call it ... um ... wordsmith." The elf shook his finger at Ruga. "You are a very witty man."

"I think the centurion is pushing his luck," Stiger said, with a meaningful glance shot to Ruga.

"I would never push my luck, sir." Ruga seemed scandalized.

"Oh really," Stiger said.

"You know," Eli said, "about a hundred years ago ... maybe it was two hundred now that I think on it, I ..."

"Two hundred years?" Ruga exclaimed, turning an astonished expression on the elf. "Really?"

"I am pretty sure it was two hundred years," Eli said. "Sometimes the years kind of become a blur. Anyway, where was I? Oh yes, I once met a wordsmith. He was quite a refined human, very educated and well-read. He was so gifted at weaving words together that it was almost mesmerizing. Sometimes, he spoke so eloquently, his words did not make sense to others, myself included. He was that good. Though to be honest, some thought him slightly mad. His name was Livserus. Good gods, I've not thought on him in years." The elf looked over at the centurion before looking at Stiger. "I spent several months with that fascinating man. Though he did not provide as much excitement as you, Ben." The elf turned his gaze back upon the centurion. "Thank you, Ruga, for jagging my memory."

"Jogging," Stiger corrected. "Is there a point to this story?"

"No," Eli said. "I was simply sharing."

Colonel Aetius appeared in the doorway, forestalling any further conversation.

"I'm sorry we could not do better, Imperator," Aetius said, looking around with distaste. "This is one of the few buildings that is structurally sound and not being used to house the sick or injured. Up until a half hour ago, it was a praetorian command post, for their portion of the wall."

"It'll do," Stiger said, glancing about once again. There were a number of closed doors that led off of the common room. Above each doorway was a tile mosaic, depicting a man and woman engaging in a sexual act. Each mosaic detailed a different position. The mosaics clearly indicated the services which could be purchased at the establishment. Behind him, a staircase led to the second floor. There was another set of stairs by the entrance. "It's ironic, really. My first throne room is a whorehouse. And here my father thought I would never amount to much."

Eli opened a door and looked inside. "There's a cot." He glanced back at Stiger. "If you don't mind ... I believe I will take a nap."

"A nap?" Of all the things Eli could have said, Stiger was surprised by that. He had wanted his friend's perspective and counsel. "You want to take a nap? Now? Are you serious?"

"It was one long and difficult march from Vrell," Eli said, "followed up by a battle that, by all rights, we should not have won. You found enough excitement to last any High Born for a lifetime. And, if I might be honest ... well, knowing you ..." Eli let out a tired breath. "You're just getting started. So, if you don't mind, I am going to catch up on some sleep." The elf yawned again. "Surely you can spare me for a few hours."

Stiger was at an absolute loss. He was about to protest, then gave a shrug of his shoulders. There would be plenty of time for them to talk later. If Eli wanted a nap, he had more than earned one. With that, Eli closed the door behind him.

"Praetorians, you say, sir?" Ruga said to Aetius.

"The emperor's personal guard," the colonel confirmed.

Ruga looked over at Stiger. "I would have expected it to be cleaner, sir, praetorians occupying this place and all. I may be a simple valley centurion, but even I've heard of the praetorians."

Ruga did have a point, Stiger decided. It spoke to the quality of the emperor's guard, or perhaps lack of it. Then again, the city had undergone a horrific siege, where it would have been difficult to maintain standards. Perhaps he was judging them too harshly. But then again, the praetorians were known for being pompous, spoiled toy soldiers who excelled at pushing the civilians around in the capital. Amongst the regular legions, it was believed they lacked a true ability to stand in line against a determined foe.

"We will find you something better soon enough." Aetius stepped fully into the room. His gaze was focused wholly on Stiger. It was deep, penetrating. "I have men looking over the city for something more suitable."

"There's no need for that," Stiger said. "Once the army comes up, I will move out of here and back into a tent. With any luck, the vanguard will arrive tomorrow morning."

"A tent, Imperator?" Aetius seemed surprised. "Surely we can do better for you."

"A tent will do." Stiger said this more harshly than he intended, as he felt a sudden stab of anguish, so strong it was almost physical, as if he'd been cut in battle. His last tent had burned the night before the big battle. He and Taha'Leeth had been attacked...ambushed by elves, her own people. His love...his wife...had been badly injured and brought to the doorstep of death. He could still feel her warm blood on his hands, see her pale face and well remembered the helpless feeling he had felt and the murderous rage that had followed. Even now, she was fighting for her life.

When he had left for the city, this trip to Lorium to meet with his emperor, she had yet to regain consciousness. To say he was worried for Taha'Leeth and the child she carried...his child, was an understatement. Stiger bitterly resented every moment he spent in Lorium and not by her side. He had a feeling duty would soon draw him farther away.

"Your father was very interested in your career," Aetius said, pulling Stiger back to the present. "Regularly, he wrote both the general and myself for updates."

Stiger looked up at that, noting the change in subject…the focus on his father. Marcus Stiger was reportedly in command of the legions guarding the capital. At least Menos had told him so, and Stiger had no reason to doubt the noctalum. He might occasionally mislead, but he never lied.

That his father had been placed in command of the defense of the capital was another incredible occurrence and told him just how desperate the senate had become. It was also a complication. Stiger had no idea how his father would respond to what had happened here in Lorium, nor his brother Max, the favored son. Then what Aetius had said hit him.

Aetius studied his reaction to the news. "You didn't know, did you?" His question was more of a statement.

"No." Stiger shook his head. He knew he should not be shocked that his father had inquired. Marcus Stiger would have expected his son to bring the family honor and prestige through service. It was only natural that he would write, and yet Stiger found it surprised him all the same. "I did not."

Actius ran a finger against his chin as he moved over to one of the small, almost tiny windows that lined the left wall. The shutters that had once been in place had been removed, torn from their hinges, likely for firewood once the siege got going in earnest.

The colonel glanced out at the crowd. They were alternating between singing and chanting of some kind that Stiger could not quite hear clearly.

"We did not part on the best of terms," Stiger admitted.

"I know." Aetius turned around. "Yet, I believe he is proud of the man you grew into. And now that you are emperor…I am sure his pride in your achievements will know no bounds."

Stiger found that difficult to believe. "I will be upstaging the old man. I can only imagine what he'll think of that and how he will react."

"Upstaging…" Aetius scowled. "I seriously doubt he will see it that way. You are emperor now, and not the first in your family either. That is, if I recall my history correctly."

"Emperor," Stiger said quietly, testing the word out as he looked down at the dirty wood-planked floor under his boots. He turned his gaze up to meet Aetius's. "He will have to swear loyalty to his son. Can you guarantee he will do that?"

"Guarantee?" Aetius said. "With your father, I can guarantee nothing. He answered directly to Tioclesion and the senate. One thing I know is that you are his son. A man takes pride in his children. Marcus Stiger is no exception."

Stiger was still not convinced. His father was a complicated man, and their relationship had been strained, frosty even, for years. It had been that way ever since the civil war that had seen the death of Stiger's mother and sister. In over a decade, they had only exchanged a letter or two at most, and nothing other than family business was discussed.

"We both know my family has enemies in the capital," Stiger said, after a moment's thought. It was time to push Aetius a bit. "The only reason they tapped my father to command is because he is the best general the senate has and Treim was trapped here in Lorium. They are desperate men. They may have tolerated him, but there are many who will not accept a Stiger in the curule chair. The emperor can declare me his heir, but the senate can easily enough give the honor to someone else. You know that, just as I know that."

Aetius suddenly looked uncomfortable. He held his hands out to either side. "I'm just a lowly staff officer."

"There is something else we both know." Stiger placed both palms above his knees and leaned forward, the stool creaking. "You are no such thing. Don't even bother trying to deny it."

Aetius did not reply. The man's eyes, however, remained fixed upon Stiger. He was clearly wondering how much Stiger knew, which was much.

"You are from a good house and well-connected." Stiger came to his feet and walked slowly to the window himself. It was so small it could hardly be called a window at all. A five-year-old child would have difficulty wiggling through.

The singing outside had intensified. The interior of the room was darkened. Only a couple of hanging lamps had been lit. With the brightness of the day, he doubted anyone could see him as he gazed outward.

The crowd had grown. There were now several thousand people gathered in the street. They were singing one of the High Father's holy hymns, "The Blessing of Deliverance." Stiger could see several priests leading them. Everyone seemed to be in a sort of religious fervor.

After a few more heartbeats of watching, he turned back to Aetius and locked gazes with the colonel.

"You served two masters, General Treim and the emperor. There is no point in denying it. I know who you really are ... especially after the affair in Thresh. I never said anything to you about knowing. There was no need."

"And what do you think I am?"

Stiger refused to be drawn into a game. "After what happened all those years ago, on that gods-forsaken island, Desindra figured she owed me."

"She told you the truth." One of the colonel's eyebrows rose slightly. "Didn't she?"

Stiger gave a nod.

"I should have expected it," Aetius said. "You and she have a unique relationship."

"I did save her life."

"And she saved yours," Aetius said, "Eli too."

"I almost did not come back from that mission you and Treim sent me on," Stiger said. "It got a little desperate."

Aetius's expression suddenly became irritated. "That little princess has a big mouth. She causes me no end of trouble."

"You probably should not have married her, then," Stiger said.

"The problem with me is I love playing with fire. And besides, when you showed up with her, she literally threw herself at my feet. How could I have said no?"

"I don't think Desindra ever threw herself at anyone's feet," Stiger said, amused by such a thought. "She's too strong-willed for that."

"Too true."

"You served the previous emperor in the same capacity that you did Tioclesion," Stiger said as a statement, returning to the matter at hand.

"We all serve the emperor," Aetius replied carefully.

"I very much doubt that we all serve in the manner you do."

Aetius did not reply. Out of the corner of his eye, Stiger saw Ruga quietly watching the two of them verbally spar. The centurion was nothing if not smart. It was one of the reasons Stiger kept him around. It was a risk having Ruga present for this conversation, but the centurion needed to know that Aetius was no simple senior officer. There was more to the man than met the eye.

"In my presence, I expect you to speak plainly," Stiger said as he moved back to the stool and sat down. "I will never begrudge anyone honesty."

"As you command, Imperator," Aetius said.

"Now," Stiger said, "give me your thoughts on how my ascension to the throne will be received...bluntly, if you will."

"Since you insist." Aetius placed both hands before him, interlocking his fingers. "It will be a blow to learn the emperor has died. People will be generally saddened, for he was quite popular, if an ineffectual leader. As you are no doubt aware, perceptions don't always match reality." Aetius paused for a moment, as if gathering his thoughts. His gaze flicked to Ruga and then back to Stiger. "At the same time, your victory over the confederacy and your ascension to the throne will quickly overshadow the emperor's death. There will be great celebration amongst the masses. The mob will almost certainly view you as their savior and blessed of the gods."

Aetius fell silent for a moment. Stiger waited, for he knew the man had more to say.

"The Stiger name, despite its recent tarnishing, runs deep and strong amongst the populace. Your family is known for the fine officers it produces for the empire, loyalty, dedication, sacrifice, and service." Aetius paused a moment, almost dramatically. "There have been few successes of late. None, actually, until you came along. The news has been grim. You will be the hero of the year, perhaps even the decade."

"But?" Stiger asked, for there surely was a "but."

"There will be strong resistance to your ascension by some in the nobility. That will run deeply to the senate itself. If not handled properly, the empire could see itself involved in yet another destructive civil war."

"With the confederacy moving up the coast and at the empire's throat?" Stiger felt his frustration increase. He slapped a palm down on his thigh. "A civil war would be madness. Surely the fools in the senate can see that. A blind man could spot it a mile away."

"Not for those who crave power," Aetius said. "And we both know there are such men in the senate. No matter how desperate they actually are, they will see such a struggle against our enemy differently. Remember, Mal'Zeel has never fallen. The walls of the city are strong and no enemy has ever in our history breached them. That's what they know... that and their own lust for imperium. When such things are certain, why entrust power to a whelp of a Stiger?"

"They've clearly not seen dragons at work," Stiger said.

"No," Aetius said, "they have not. Even after the detailed reports dispatched to the senate of the destruction of Tioclesion's army, there will still be some who believe dragons do not exist. They will say that they were just an excuse for failure on the battlefield, incompetence in command, made up for convenience sake. Worse, some will listen and allow themselves to be swayed."

"Fools." Stiger shook his head in disgust. He slapped his thigh again. "A bloody civil war. I tell you, there is no time for that."

"Then we will need to work doubly hard to keep it from happening," Aetius said. "Won't we?"

"I'm sure you will find a way to charm them, sir," Ruga said, speaking up. "Make them see reason, even if it's at the point of a spear."

Aetius shot the centurion an unhappy look that said he should know his place.

Stiger turned his attention to Ruga, who abruptly looked the soul of innocence. It was time to send the centurion on his way. He had learned what Stiger had wanted him to know about Aetius.

"Shouldn't you be checking the guard," Stiger asked, "or making sure the building is secure…something like that?"

"Yes, sir," Ruga said, taking the hint. The centurion drew himself up to attention, saluted, and made his way to the door, stepping out into the corridor. His footsteps could be heard thunking on the wood planking as he moved down the hall toward the front door.

"He's impudent," Aetius said, "and disrespectful."

"Ruga's a fine officer." Stiger shifted on his stool to get more comfortable. "He's loyal, relatively honest, and a good combat leader. His men are some of the best I've ever seen. And more important, I've been through a great deal with them."

"That's high praise coming from you." Aetius glanced to the doorway as he expelled a breath. "He is also quite correct in his assessment of what will need to be done."

"It's why he's commanding my personal guard." Stiger rubbed his jaw as he considered Aetius. "He's smart and I trust him with my life."

"I see," Aetius said. "So, I should trust him with mine as well?"

"We both know you trust almost no one," Stiger said. "But in answer to your question…yes."

Aetius inclined his head slightly.

"What would you have me do," Stiger asked, "with the nobility and the senate? I would hear your thoughts on the subject."

"About the curule chair?" Aetius asked.

"Yes," Stiger said, "for I do not think it will be given up easily."

"No, it will not be given up easily. First let me say, you have my support and General Treim's."

"Which means," Stiger said, "as the elders for your houses, I have your families' support as well."

"That is correct," Aetius said. "Our allies and our clients will fall in line and back your claim. But, there are those in the senate who will oppose you, likely a good number."

"No doubt," Stiger said. "Most of my family's supporters were purged after the civil war."

"True. You will want to speak to Treim to seek his advice too. However, I would send news to the capital as soon as you can... immediately if possible. Let the senate and the masses know that you are emperor. The mob has more power than the average senator would like to admit. As I said, the news has not been the best of late. Hearing of your victory over the enemy should reinforce your support and claim on the curule chair, especially amongst the people. It will make the job of usurping your claim more difficult for those who oppose you. In a manner of speaking, you will be going on the offensive before they even know an attack has been launched. It also helps that you are descended from Karus. We should play that up too."

Stiger looked up at the ceiling for a moment as he thought, then returned his gaze to the colonel. "I am thinking it would be better were I there than here. That way, it will be hard for the senate to ignore me. My presence would force them to take some action, sides even. It will get friend and foe squarely out in the open."

"Not all of them," Aetius said. "Some will still remain in the shadows and work against you, but for the most part, what you say is true. The direct and immediate threats will reveal themselves." Aetius paused. "If you send word tonight, it will reach the capital within two and a half to three days."

"How?" Stiger asked. Though he knew the dragons could get there quicker, he suspected Aetius had another means, even though the capital was hundreds of miles away. "Three days ... how is that possible?"

"You have not been gone from the empire for that long," Aetius said.

"Longer than you might think," Stiger said, recalling the five years he had spent in the past. Aetius did not know that yet. He would be told soon enough.

"The courier stations," Aetius explained. "The enemy marched east to the coast, not west or north. They never fully cut communication with the capital. We were only isolated when the city was besieged. Once the enemy marched off, communication with the capital was restored."

"I'd forgotten about them." Stiger rubbed his jaw as he considered Aetius. "I never really gave the stations much thought as we rode south. Our messengers will be able to change horses at each station. Two and a half to three days you say? That's all?"

"Correct."

"I'd hate to make that ride," Stiger said. "So, the senate already knows of our victory?"

"No," Aetius said. "They do not. General Treim and the emperor only informed them that the siege had been lifted and the enemy marched off. Nothing more was sent. No mention of you was included in the dispatch and we made sure our messenger will say nothing. He is a reliable man and has been in my service for years. There has not yet been time for a reply from the senate."

"But why did he ... say ... nothing ...?" Stiger trailed off. He snapped his fingers. "That sneaky bastard. All along, the general knew the emperor's plans to elevate me to his own bloody chair."

"He did," Aetius admitted. "I hope you will forgive our lack of candor when we took you to see him. In the emperor's eyes, it was necessary, and we were duty bound to carry out his orders. Besides, after the letter you sent us and your victory over the confederacy's army...well...we both agreed with Tioclesion. It also helps that you are the High Father's Champion. That sort of swayed Father Restus, and he is a difficult man to ignore."

"No doubt." Stiger tapped his thigh lightly with his fingers as he regarded the colonel for a prolonged moment. Their actions meant Treim did not want the chair for himself and was content to let Stiger have it. He was not so blind that he did not see what was obvious. Treim and Aetius would expect influence and other favors in return for their support. They would be power brokers in their own right, standing out in the open and right behind the curule chair. "Continue."

"Just as they carried you here, I imagine, if need be, your dragons can get you to the capital as well," Aetius said. "Probably much quicker than the couriers can travel by horseback."

"They can," Stiger confirmed. "Are you suggesting I leave now? I thought you wanted me to send word first?"

"You cannot leave Lorium until after the emperor's funeral. To do so would be a black mark in the people's eyes. You must be seen paying homage and proper respect to the man who elevated you to his throne. It is more symbolic than anything else and something the masses will expect. Word of what happens here will filter back to the capital."

"That quickly?"

"I imagine that once we allow the gates open," Aetius said, "the populace will flee northward. There is nothing left in this city but ruin. It will take years to rebuild."

"I assume food will be a problem as well for those who remain," Stiger said. "We will need to address that, figure out some long-term solution."

Aetius gave Stiger a slight nod of agreement.

"Even though I need to be there, I really don't want to go to the capital," Stiger said, thinking of Taha'Leeth. By all rights, he should be at her bedside, looking after her. His slave, Venthus, was there in his stead. "Not yet, anyway."

"You need to go," Aetius said firmly, "as soon as the funeral is over. To delay would be dangerous. Doing so might throw everything away."

Stiger knew the colonel was right … His personal desires did not matter. He had to go, and the sooner the better. He just wished he could delay for a few days, until Taha'Leeth had awoken. He wanted to see her out of danger and on the road to recovery. Then, when he did go … bring his army with him. But … he understood he could not afford to delay, and the army would have to go the old-fashioned way, by foot. That would take time, weeks of hard marching.

"As I said, I would send word first," Aetius said. "It is not wise to delay on this important news. We might as well dispatch word to all corners of the empire while we are at it. When the news spreads in the capital, it will build excitement amongst the mob, hope even, at what has occurred here in Lorium and your victory over the enemy. Once you arrive … nearly everyone will want to see and cheer you. The entire city will turn out." He gestured with a hand toward a window. "Just like those people outside, who rightly view you as their savior. Your entrance into the capital will effectively be an unsanctioned triumph, something the people have not seen in at least a hundred years. It will be hard, if not impossible, for the senate to ignore and act against you. Doing so would test the will of the mob, and that always is dangerous, for the mob loves victorious generals."

Stiger considered Aetius for a long moment. What the colonel said made sense.

"Excuse me, sir." Ruga poked his head back into the room. "I am sorry to bother you. There's someone here to see you. I believe he is a messenger. He says he's from General Treim's headquarters."

"Send him in," Stiger said.

"Yes, sir."

Stiger turned back to Aetius. "As you have suggested, I would meet with the general and Father Restus to discuss this further. I am thinking a letter from Restus, as the head of his order, to the senate will add weight to my claim."

"I agree," Aetius said. "That is a smart move. I think we should also sit down and come up with a list of those families we can count on, ones that will support your claim and position. Writing them will help move matters along. We need to lay the groundwork for your grand entrance into the city."

"And those who can be cowed and counted to fall in line," Stiger said. "We will want to make a list of them as well. There is too much at stake not to use every tool at our disposal."

Aetius inclined his head in agreement. "There are agents we can hire in the capital to help lean on those that are pliable. There are others we can outright bribe for their support."

"To do that," Stiger said, "we need money."

"It is a lucky thing General Treim is a wealthy man," Aetius said. "I am certain he would be pleased to loan you the money. I may even loan you some myself. I am sure, as emperor, you will be good for it."

"With interest?" To call the general wealthy was an understatement. Treim was one of the richest men in the empire. And Aetius was not exactly destitute either.

"Of course," Aetius replied without any shame or hesitation.

Stiger was about to reply when someone stepped into the doorway. He froze, then broke out into a grin, genuinely pleased.

"Tiro!" Stiger stood.

"It's good to see you too, sir." Tiro stepped into the room, looking between Aetius and Stiger, a little guiltily, as if he had interrupted. "I can wait until you are done, sir."

Tiro turned to go.

"Not so fast, Sergeant. Remain, if you would." Aetius turned back to Stiger. "As soon as they have concluded their responsibilities to the late emperor, I will return with General Treim and Father Restus. With your permission, that is, Imperator, I will withdraw?"

"Thank you, Colonel," Stiger said and stood. "We will continue this conversation then."

The colonel saluted, which, for a moment, surprised Stiger. Aetius had always been his senior. He'd have to get used to that sort of thing. Barring the High Father, no one was now in a position higher than himself. Stiger returned the salute, and with that, Aetius backed up two paces, turned smartly on his heel, and left.

Tiro suddenly remembered himself, snapped to attention, and saluted.

"We're alone," Stiger said and approached. He clapped his old sergeant warmly on the shoulder. "No need for that. You taught and gave me more than I can ever repay. Understand me?"

"Ah, yes, sir." Tiro suddenly looked uncomfortable. "Do I call you sir, Imperator, or Your Majesty?"

"I suppose all are correct forms of address," Stiger said. "Over the years, we've chewed a lot of ground together. How about you choose? I believe you've earned that right."

"Then," Tiro said, "I will continue sir-ing you. After all those years it seems unnatural to do otherwise."

"That works for me." Stiger eyed the old veteran, who had aged greatly since they had first met all those years ago. Tiro was a year or two from a well-earned mandatory retirement and was old to Stiger's eyes, though he appeared tough as a nail. Despite his advanced years, it was quite possible Tiro could still kick his ass in hand-to-hand combat. Stiger wondered what Tiro would think of Therik or the dwarves, not to mention the Vass.

"Is the Seventh here?"

"No, sir," Tiro said. "When we passed through the capital on our way south, the general left them there, along with two other companies from Third Legion, the Tenth included. With the Praetorian Guard gone, there was some civil agitation. The High Command asked that the general leave some men to help keep order on the streets. General Treim left some of his best, sir. I would have stayed too, but I was on detached duty and assigned to headquarters. The general's been kind to me, sir ... doing his best to make sure I get to retire, if you know what I mean, sir."

Stiger gave a nod of understanding. But he was still disappointed. He would have liked to have seen his old company, spend some time with the men and Lepidus too from the Tenth. Next to Eli and Menos, Lepidus was one of his few true friends, along with Hollux, Stiger's former executive officer from Seventh Company. It was good they had not marched south. Had they done so, they might have been butchered with much of the rest of the emperor's army.

"Who is the new commanding officer of the Seventh?"

"Captain Ikuus," Tiro said.

"I know of his family," Stiger said, "but I don't know him."

"He was a recent replacement, sir," Tiro said, "transferred over from Eighth Legion. He came highly recommended."

The sterile and passionless way he spoke about Ikuus told Stiger that Tiro did not approve of the man. There was no warmth there, no love lost. Treim had likely realized that Ikuus was a potential problem and had arranged for Tiro's transfer to headquarters.

"Is he as bad as Cethegus?" Stiger asked, suddenly concerned for his old company.

"I would not know, sir," Tiro said. "I've not seen him in action yet." Tiro paused a moment. "I wish Varus would have been here to see this, sir."

"Me being emperor?" Stiger decided he would have to look into Ikuus. The Seventh deserved a competent commanding officer. It was the least he owed his men for their hard service and dedication over the years. And in a few days, Stiger was certain he would be in the capital and potentially in a position to do that.

Tiro gave a nod. "Varus would have loved it, sir."

Both men fell silent, each suddenly lost in their thoughts. Though it had been more than ten years, fifteen really with his time in the past, Stiger still found Varus's death painful. So too, he knew, did Tiro. Varus had been Stiger's first corporal and a damn fine legionary. He had learned much from the man.

"If you don't mind me saying, sir." Tiro's brows drew together. "You look older."

"Isn't that a bit like calling the kettle black?" Stiger said with a sudden grin.

"There's no doubt I'm feeling my age, sir," Tiro said, eying Stiger closely. "It's only been a few months since we last saw one another … though … you've aged. I mean really aged, and I don't think command did that to you. What happened?"

"It's a long story," Stiger said, and then glanced around and spotted another stool. He pointed at it. "Pull up a stool. If anyone deserves to hear it, and I mean everything... that's you."

CHAPTER TWO

"They're on their way, Imperator," General Treim announced as he stepped into the room, with Colonel Aetius following a few paces behind. As was customary for serving officers, both men wore their legionary armor and were armed.

Stiger was sitting on the stool in the center of the room. He and Eli had been speaking with Father Restus, who was before him. Eli stood to Stiger's right, a mug of wine in his hand. Stiger's empty cup sat on the floor off to his side. Restus had declined the offer of wine.

It had been a long day and would likely end up being much longer, with meetings stretching far into the night. He understood from Ruga that the city elders were waiting and wished to meet with him next. After that, the city's priests were looking to pray with him. A group of local merchants were cooling their heels too. Ruga had explained that a veritable line of supplicants had formed after that, all wanting a moment with the new emperor.

Stiger shifted on his stool as the general stepped up before him and saluted. General Treim was ten years Stiger's senior. He was fit, with a rugged, confident air about him. Though his armor had been well-maintained, there was a used, almost comfortable look about it that marked him as an officer who had spent years leading men in the field.

Like Stiger, he wore the blue-colored cloak of command. Also like Stiger, he had earned the right to it the hard way.

Exhaustion and weariness lined the general's face. He had spent the last ten years spearheading the effort against the Rivan, only to be ordered south to lead the emperor's ill-fated army against the confederacy. Especially after having weathered the siege of Lorium, Treim clearly needed a well-deserved rest—only, Stiger knew he could not give him one. Stiger desperately needed Treim's services as an extremely capable commander and would only ask more from him this day and surely in the days to come.

"Our man has an escort of six," Treim continued. "He and they will die first before giving up the letters."

Stiger glanced to the window as he considered the general's words. It was late afternoon and, inside, the room had grown dim. Outside, the ruined streets of the city were surely heavily shadowed. Another lantern had been brought in to combat the growing darkness within the building, but that had not helped much. The crowd of civilians that surrounded the building was still there. They had been singing hymns and praying all day long.

"No one knows they are coming, or what they carry," Aetius added. "So they should not be troubled. There is no good reason for anyone to hinder their progress."

All seven men were risking their lives on Stiger's behalf and he had never even met them. The hopes of an empire rode with them. Stiger blew out an unhappy breath, then gestured over to a small table that held two jars of heated wine and several mugs. After he had left, Tiro had arranged for it to be sent over from headquarters, along with some food. The uneaten salt pork lay on a clay plate next to the jars.

"Wine, gentlemen?" Stiger asked.

"Thank you." Treim stepped over. He poured himself and Aetius a mug before handing it to the colonel. "They are some of my best," Treim said, after a sip, "from Sixth Company. Lieutenant Kerrog is leading them. I believe you know him."

"I do," Stiger said. Though he had never been overly friendly toward Stiger, Kerrog was a good man, and loyal to Treim. He was also a good officer. "If I recall, he is your nephew."

"Yes, that is right," Treim confirmed as he took another pull from his wine. "I saw them to the gate myself."

"Barring any unforeseen difficulty, they will be in the capital three days from now," Aetius said.

"The day after the funeral," Stiger said, knowing that the time for him to leave was fast approaching. In a way, by going, he felt like he was abandoning his wife. It was a very unsatisfactory feeling. Who knew how long it would be before he would see Taha'Leeth again? If she survived... That thought alone tore at him, but there was just too much at stake for him to remain or delay. To do so would be incredibly selfish. Not only was the fate of the empire resting in his hands, but as strange and outlandish as it sounded, so too was the world.

"Perhaps when you go, you might consider carrying Tioclesion's ashes with you," Aetius said. "Hand delivering the remains to his family will be a powerful display of respect. It will only play to our advantage with the mob."

Stiger did not enjoy the idea of such overtly symbolic games, but he understood the necessity of them. He thought again on the letters that had been written. So much rode on them being delivered to the right people.

Would the people... the mob, rejoice as Aetius and Treim thought they might? If things were as bad as the two men believed, Stiger considered he might very well be received as the people's savior, just like those in Lorium had done. Would it be enough to force the senate to do the right thing? He was not so certain about that and had a sneaking suspicion things would be far from easy.

"Our messenger will go directly to Senator Navaro," Treim said. "As we've told you, he is our man in the capital and can be relied upon. He will see the letters are distributed and forwarded before he personally breaks the good news to the senate."

"Will he read them?" Stiger asked, for he had never met Navaro. He only knew the man by reputation. The Navaro family was not an outright enemy, but they weren't friends of the Stigers either.

"It is expected," Aetius said. "Navaro is no less a player of the game than we are. He will, of course, want something in return for his support."

Stiger glanced over to the wine. He considered for a heartbeat getting some more, then turned his attention back to Aetius. "And what will that be?"

Aetius gave a sort of shrug.

"Navaro is wealthy," Treim said. "He will desire something else beyond just money as a reward for his service. Whatever that is, it will be for you and him to negotiate at the proper time. The important thing to know is that Navaro will prove a loyal and steady ally. Once on board, he will not betray us, nor will he ask for more than you both agreed to. His honor is strong and unassailable. You can trust him, as you do me."

Stiger gave a nod of understanding. Navaro might want a reasonable reward, but others would crave more ... demand more. It pained him that many would not be motivated to do what was right for the empire, but what was right for themselves alone.

"Once the letters have gone out, our agents will then go to work," Aetius continued, "stirring up the mob and spreading the wondrous news of Lorium's deliverance by the new emperor, who is Champion of the faith and blessed of the High Father. With the confederacy bearing down on the capital, word should spread like wildfire. It will be difficult for the senate to conceal what has happened here, not to mention the miraculous return of the lost Thirteenth Legion. Couple that with your victory over the enemy...not once but twice...and excitement will grow to a fever pitch as desperate people begin to believe in you. That will be a power unto itself."

Stiger rubbed at his jaw as he thought about all that was being set into motion. For much of the day, the four of them had planned carefully. All of the letters had been written directly by Aetius, Restus, and Treim. Stiger had only written one himself. That was to his father. It had been one of the most difficult things he'd ever done, and he had no idea how it would be received.

"They will not be able to ignore you," Aetius said. "That is for certain."

"Impossible is more like it," Treim said. "After the funeral, and as soon as practical, you go directly to the capital. Doing so will deny the senate sufficient time to react to the news of Tioclesion naming you his heir. The men in that chamber love to talk and debate before taking any action. It is a painful and tedious process. With any luck, that will work to our advantage."

"The more they debate, the more time we have," Aetius said.

"The dragon you arrive upon"—Treim paused and glanced at Father Restus—"not to mention being the High Father's Champion, should only add and strengthen your claim to the emperor's chair."

Stiger shifted his gaze between the two men. Much of what they were now discussing had already been exhaustively covered. It was almost like they were reviewing a plan of battle, making sure they'd not missed anything. Only this wasn't battle, it was politics. Like war, there were no rules. Going forward, politics would forever be part of his life, no less important than breathing. There was nothing to be done but to embrace it, which he was beginning to do. Still, he felt like he was being dropped naked into a pit of vipers.

After he arrived in the capital, the army would be hundreds of miles away and unable to help should he have need of its power in securing the throne. The dragons would only be able to deliver a handful of men for his protection. Bringing the massive creatures into the city was not an option either. Fire would raze Mal'Zeel, just as surely as the enemy army sacking the great city. He could not have that.

He wished there was some other way to see it all done, but knew there was not. If he was to be made emperor, and accepted by the senate...without undue delay, he must go and put himself before the treacherous knives of the senators. Stiger rubbed his jaw, feeling not only budding stubble, but the frustration of his current predicament. For all intents and purposes, he would be nearly on his own. But that did not mean he would be defenseless. He was the High Father's Champion and weapon. But still, despite all that he had been given by the great god, he needed to be cautious, for a dagger in the back could kill just as surely as a sword thrust to his front.

"There are people we can count upon to help guarantee your security," Aetius said, guessing correctly on his concern. "They will begin mobilizing once they get word from our agents."

Stiger looked up at that.

"How many?" he asked. "How many can I count on?"

Aetius and Treim shared a brief look before the general answered. "About two hundred, all retired veterans, who have since become clients of ours."

"They have been positioned," Aetius said carefully, "in the event either of us ever needed armed support. We pay for their lodging and food. In return, they are our muscle should we have need."

Stiger considered that for a long moment. Coming from prestigious families, both men were not only military officers but also senators. They, like Stiger's family, had enemies. How many other senators had made similar contingencies? Hidden in plain view, how many others had their own private armies? Did his father have similar muscle? Stiger suspected he had. In a way, he could almost imagine the capital being an armed camp. The more he thought on it, the more it made sense.

"And the senate has an army at their disposal." Stiger's thoughts had swung back to his father.

"Twelve legions," Aetius said. "Four of which are veteran formations pulled from the eastern frontier. The rest are fresh conscripts and are likely still undergoing their initial training. The important thing to remember is that your father commands them all."

"Three hundred or so years back," Eli said to Treim and Aetius, "I spent some years in your capital as a representative for my people. I got to know the inner workings of the empire quite well, especially the senate. I cannot imagine it has changed much since then, beyond the people wielding power."

Stiger looked over at his friend, wondering on not only where he was going, but also what else he might reveal. Eli was treading on the edge of dangerous ground.

"What is your point?" Aetius asked.

"Once they learn of Ben's ascension," Eli said, "the senate might choose to replace Marcus Stiger and put someone in command who will do as they desire. Or really might prove more malleable and compliant. There are always senators longing to distinguish themselves through battle, like you both have done. They seek prestige and the power that comes with it."

"True," Treim said, "but I do not think that likely. The senate needs a general who has proven he can fight and win. Marcus Stiger is it. During the entirety of the civil war, he did not lose a single battle where he was in command. They cannot afford to alienate him and will not relieve him." Treim gestured toward Stiger. "Like him, Marcus inspires loyalty in those who serve under his command. Attempting to replace Marcus may prove risky for the senate, for the legions themselves may not accept his replacement."

"That is true," Aetius said. "The senate, if they chose to oppose your elevation to emperor, will be in a difficult position. Whether your father is to meet the Cyphan on a field of battle or at Mal'Zeel's walls, the senate needs a soldier's soldier to keep them safe. In a way, it makes denying the son's claim that much more difficult."

"Choosing someone else as emperor requires the church's blessing," Father Restus said. "I do not see the High Priest sanctioning such a thing, especially after my letter to him."

"High Priest Melevan has always been a political animal," Aetius said.

"True," Restus said, "but I do not see him going against me. Melevan has more sense than that. At least, he should."

"Let's assume the worst … the senate chooses someone else. What then? What if my father does not support me?" Stiger asked. "You two know my father. His word is his bond. What if he chooses to back the senate? What then?"

Neither man said anything to that. Stiger could tell the thought had occurred to them both. It was something to be concerned with. The singing outside by the crowd filled the silence in the room that seemed to stretch uncomfortably.

"I will just have to cross that bridge when I come to it," Stiger said finally. "Is that it?"

"Like you do with most everything else," Eli said. "I am sure that will likely involve some excitement. Though this time, do me a favor, Ben—for my benefit—don't try so hard."

Stiger looked over at the elf and saw a mischievous gleam in his eye. He was feeling a headache coming on and was in no mood for games. Eli likely knew it as well. He was always one to poke the bear.

"Then again," Eli said, "the senate might surprise us all and do the right thing."

"That would be nice," Restus said.

"Excuse me, sir," Ruga said, stepping into the room. He marched up to Stiger and held out a dispatch. "This just came in for you, by rider, from the Thirteenth."

"Thank you," Stiger said. "See that the messenger has a place to get some rest."

"Aye, sir." Ruga saluted and left as Stiger opened the dispatch. It was from Salt and in the camp prefect's own hand, no less. Stiger recognized the neat scrawl.

"Taha'Leeth still has not awoken," Stiger told Eli, once again feeling dreadful that he was not by her side. It was almost a physical pain as he voiced the next words. "Her condition is unchanged."

"I am sorry, Ben." Eli placed a hand upon Stiger's shoulder armor. "She is strong-willed. With some good fortune, she will get better and once again be standing by your side."

"Who is this Taha'Leeth?" Treim asked, looking between them curiously.

"My wife," Stiger said.

"Your wife?" Treim said. "I sent you south with Eli, just a few months back. You found a wife in so short a time?"

Stiger gave a nod. Since he had ridden south, it felt like an eternity had passed, and in a manner of speaking, one had.

"Not only do you come back with the lost legion, the Thirteenth ... but allies and a wife to boot." Treim seemed amused by this, then sobered. "She is from a good family? If she is not, it could complicate things with the senate and succession."

"She is from the best of families," Eli said. "It does not get more pure than the blood that flows through her veins."

"What happened to her?" Aetius asked.

"She and I were the target of an assassination," Stiger said. "The attempt occurred just prior to the battle we fought against the confederacy. She was seriously injured."

The room was filled with a long moment of silence before the general broke it.

"I am sorry to hear that." Treim paused a moment. "What family does she hail from?"

"She is not from any family you would know," Stiger said.

"Eli just said she was from the best," Treim said. "I don't understand."

"She is an elf." Stiger was mindful of the advice Eli had given him weeks ago about not only some of his people, but Stiger's own being unwilling to accept their union.

Treim's eyes widened a tad and he straightened slightly before returning his wine mug to the table. Marriages between elves and humans just did not occur, ever. Aetius took a slow sip from his wine as he contemplated his new emperor. Stiger knew both men were thinking how this complication might hinder or help his claim on the curule chair. Politics again.

"A belated congratulations," Restus said, sounding genuine, as Stiger looked to him. "I suspect the High Father's hand is in this unique union between peoples."

"The gods most assuredly have meddled," Eli said.

"And, before you ask," Father Restus said to Stiger, "I am beyond the age of healing. The High Father has prohibited me from even making the attempt."

Stiger had been just about to ask. But now that the paladin had said what he had, the words seemed truthful and right to Stiger. He suddenly felt guilty for wanting to make the request. The price paladins paid for each healing was some of their own life in exchange. And Restus had little life left to give. Stiger could also sense, through his own connection to his god, the High Father had another path for the paladin to walk.

"As you are undoubtedly aware, we paladins of the High Father are few in number," Restus continued. "However, there may be another in Mal'Zeel who might, just might, be able to render assistance."

Stiger glanced downward a moment at the floor and ran a boot across the floorboards. He looked back up, knowing he could not get his hopes up.

"My wife follows the teachings of Tanithe," Stiger said, "not our god."

"Tanithe sits in the High Father's alignment," Restus said. "I do not believe it hurts to try. The worst that can happen is the High Father denies his blessing. Perhaps, if one of my order is available and he feels so called, he might return to aid your wife."

"Very well," Stiger said, still daring not to hope.

"I think it wise," Aetius said cautiously, "to withhold information on your wife from not only the mob, but also the senate. At least, until the succession is resolved. Then we can find a way to share the good news in a manner that helps us."

"Taha'Leeth," Eli said, "is what you might consider High Born royalty."

"We can work with that," Aetius said, "but still, there is no need to complicate matters, not now. The focus is getting the emperor control of his empire."

Stiger looked over at Aetius for a moment before returning his attention back to the dispatch. He continued reading. When he finished, he folded it back up and taped the parchment with a finger, then looked back up at Treim. "The vanguard of the army should start arriving by midday tomorrow. We will likely see the cavalry sometime in the morning. It will take two entire days for the whole of the army to come up."

"That's good news," Treim said.

"Maybe after two or three days of rest, the march to the capital can begin. It was a long and hard march just to get north. The battle for the legion was a real bitch. The men need a break before pushing onward." Stiger paused. "The question I have ... is how soon until your men can be made ready for an extended movement?"

"All the way to the capital?" Treim asked.

Stiger gave a nod.

"Will you be leaving a garrison in Lorium?" Treim asked.

"No," Stiger said. "Let's face it. Lorium is expendable, especially since the city has been basically razed. Mal'Zeel is not, and that is where the confederacy is headed. You've told me you have around seven thousand trained men capable of bearing arms. Do I have that right?"

"Your understanding is correct," Treim said. "Most are from the Third; the rest are remnants from several legions and a mix of auxiliary cohorts."

"They will all need to be reformed," Stiger said.

"Since the Third is mostly intact," Treim said, "we could easily consolidate the remnants from the other legions. Rolling them into the Third would make her an over-strength legion, with more than ten cohorts, maybe fourteen at most. The auxiliaries could also be consolidated to form a new allied cohort."

"I like that," Stiger said. "Who is the general of the Third?"

"General Selvarin died in the fighting," Aetius said.

"Did any other general survive?" Stiger asked.

"Tegea," Treim said. "Though he was badly wounded. He will not be returning to service anytime soon."

Stiger did not know the man. But he was well acquainted with the family. There was bad blood between theirs and his... had been for years, ever since the civil war when Marcus Stiger had defeated Tegea's father in battle. It was likely a good thing the man was wounded, for Stiger would have likely been forced to replace him. That would only have hardened feelings further.

"Do you have any good candidates in mind?" Stiger asked, for Third Legion would need a commander, and Stiger had other plans for Treim.

"What about Ikely?" Eli suggested, before Treim could speak. "Or Salt?"

"No," Stiger said. "Ikely has serious potential, but he still has much to learn about fighting a legion and will remain the Thirteenth's senior tribune. Salt, though I am sure he will hate it, will take my place as legate. He has much more combat experience and can work toward furthering Ikely's education."

"Salt?" Treim said. "I take it he's a tough old salt?"

"Camp Prefect Oney of the Thirteenth Legion," Stiger said. "You will like him. And he's one of the toughest men I know, experienced too."

"I look forward to meeting him, especially if he is from the Lost Legion. I may have someone who could command the Third," Treim said.

"Who?"

"Tribune Theego," Treim said. "He was senior tribune to the Twenty-Ninth. He has a good head on his shoulders and is also experienced. I know for a fact he was being groomed for legion command."

"More important," Aetius said, "his family survived the purge after the civil war. He served under your father, and by appointing him command of the Third you are assuring the family's wholehearted support."

"I want to meet him," Stiger said. "Can we do that tonight?"

"Yes," Treim said. "I will arrange it."

"Good."

"Once the Third is reformed, I take it, your intention is to march them north," Aetius said.

"I am certainly not going to leave them here in this ruin of a city," Stiger said. "We're going to need every available sword before this war with the Cyphan is over. The fighting is going to be hard and brutal." He looked over to Treim. "Back to my original question. How soon can they march?"

"They're half-starved and worn down by the siege," Treim said. "With proper rations and rest, I believe they will be ready in three weeks, maybe four at the worst."

That was longer than he'd hoped, but Treim was an expert in such matters. If the general said it would take three to four weeks, then it would. Besides, Stiger wanted the Third in good shape after its long march to the capital. They needed to be in fighting trim.

"With the capture of the enemy's supply train," Stiger said, "we have plenty of food, at least for a time. The dwarven nations are providing additional stores, which will be shipped north from Vrell. As long as the enemy does not cut our supply, we will have an indefinite source of food. That said, the confederacy landed a small army to the south. We have no idea what their intentions are yet, but our supply from Vrell could be put at risk."

"If they march north, it could prove a problem then," Treim said.

"Yes," Stiger said, "but as of now, we have several weeks of food on hand. Plenty to get the army to Mal'Zeel." Stiger paused and gathered his thoughts. "How many able-bodied men do you think are available in Lorium?"

"To be pressed into service?" Treim asked.

"Yes," Stiger said.

"Right now, we've got about fifteen hundred civilians under arms," Aetius said. "They are poorly equipped, and their training is even worse. About twenty percent are old men and boys, not fit to march a good distance. They are more of a danger to themselves than the enemy at this point."

"Besides the age issue, the only real problem is equipment," Treim said. "We're light on weapons and armor."

"We can put the blacksmiths in the city to work," Aetius said, "fashioning arms and equipment. But that will take some time to fully kit them all out."

"We seized a good deal of loot in the battle before Vrell," Eli said. "I would think we have enough to equip them to some degree."

"You're right," Stiger said. "Ikely can get much of it here in six to eight weeks, maybe sooner if we push the transport." Stiger turned back to Treim. "Cut the old and young loose. Of the rest, I want them formed into two light auxiliary cohorts. You will need to leave a training cadre behind to see to their training."

"It will be done," Treim said. "When they are ready, they can march north and join us."

"You will need good men to command them," Stiger said.

"I believe I can find some solid men," Treim said.

Stiger was pleased with the response. He thought on all that needed doing before he could depart for Mal'Zeel. It was overwhelming, almost too much. At some point, he needed to begin putting together an administrative staff to help him manage things.

"I want you to meet all of my officers from the Thirteenth," Stiger said, "particularly my key men, Salt, and Tribunes Ikely and Severus."

"It will be my pleasure, Imperator," Treim said.

"Then there is Braddock," Stiger said. "Dealing with dwarves can be tricky."

"I've never met a dwarf," Treim said, seeming surprised. "You expect me to work directly with them?"

"Yes, I do," Stiger said. "You will need to directly coordinate with our allies because in my absence you will be commanding my legion, the Third, and all of the auxiliaries. You will have responsibility for our army."

"I am honored, Imperator," Treim said with a slight bow of his head. Stiger understood Treim had anticipated this move. It was the logical step. "I will strive to live up to your expectations."

"I believe you already know Tenya'Far," Stiger said.

"I do," Treim confirmed.

"He doesn't know Cragg yet," Eli said and chuckled softly. "Or Therik."

Stiger let out a heavy breath. "Our gnome allies are not the easiest to work with. They are problematic during the best of times."

"Gnomes?" Treim shared a look with Aetius. "What are they?"

"A troublesome people," Stiger said, "allied with the dwarves. They will prove to be a pain in your ass, but are worth their tiny weight in gold, especially in a fight. Braddock will help guide you in managing them."

"That is, if they can be managed," Eli said.

"Sorry to bother you, sir," Ruga said, entering once again.

Stiger thought the centurion looked irritated, almost flustered. That was un-Ruga-like, for Stiger had seen him in battle. Very little ruffled the centurion's feathers.

"What is it?"

"A Prefect Nouma is here, sir," Ruga said. "He is insisting to see you and wants to move to the head of the line. He is very demanding, sir, and rude. He brought some of his men and seems bent on replacing mine as guard, sir. Can you believe that bullshit?"

"Who is Nouma?" Stiger asked, looking to Aetius and Treim, wondering what the man was thinking.

"The Praetorian Guard's commander," Treim explained. "He can be a bit insufferable and has airs of importance

above his station. Our late emperor relied heavily upon his advice and that of Tribune Handi as well. You met the tribune in the crypt."

"Since the siege began," Aetius said, "both have been inseparable."

"I know Handi," Stiger said unhappily. "I've had dealings with him in the past. He was General Kromen's chief aide."

"We've had to put up with them both," Aetius said. "Nouma commands what's left of the Guard, around three hundred men in total."

"Once the siege began, he should have been removed," Treim said. "However, we needed him and his men to help hold the walls. I had no idea how the Guard would react to his replacement. And since he had the emperor's ear and trust... removal was not a viable option either."

Stiger felt his irritation mount again. As a legionary, he had a ready dislike for the praetorians, who were not considered true legionaries by the regulars. "Then he is no longer important."

"The term importance varies," Aetius said. "I am certain he sees things differently."

"He's going to have to see it my way," Stiger said. "I already have a guard, one I know I can rely upon and that has been battle-tested." Stiger looked to Ruga. "You're not getting off that easy, Centurion."

"Thank you, sir," Ruga said, with evident relief.

"What with the siege, it could be said the praetorians have been battle-tested as well," Aetius said.

"How did they perform?" Stiger asked.

"They fought," Treim said simply.

"Right then." Stiger looked to Ruga. He would deal with one headache at a time, and he still had business to finish that was much more important than assuaging a praetorian's puffed-up sense of self-importance. "Tell him to wait. I will see the prefect when I am done here, not before."

"Yes, sir." Ruga saluted and left.

Stiger turned back to the three men and considered them for several heartbeats. It seemed so unnatural to be giving orders to General Treim and Colonel Aetius. For more than a decade, he had been the junior officer and had looked up to both men. They had been his role models and Treim his unofficial patron.

Since that time, Stiger had learned much, seen even more, become seasoned and hardened. He had dealt with exotic and alien races, with princes, princesses, kings, thanes, a troublesome kluge, a wizard, and more. He had even named an orc a friend. He'd fought multiple battles, all desperate fights, and each time managed somehow to come out on top.

The young man who had joined Seventh Company and marched north to fight the Rivan was wholly different than the one who'd been transferred to the southern legions, restored the Compact with the dwarves, retrieved the dread sword Rarokan, traveled into the past, and returned as the High Father's Champion with the entirety of the Lost Thirteenth Legion at his back.

Cut off from command, Stiger had long since become accustomed to being the highest man on the ladder, making the hard decisions that needed to be made. And now that he had returned to the empire, nothing had changed. Unexpectedly, he was in command, still calling the shots. It felt both odd and at the same time right.

"I would appreciate you accompanying me to the capital," Stiger said to Restus. "Having you along and in support will help bolster my case before the senate, more than a simple letter ever could."

"I figured you would ask," Restus said. "And if you had not, I would have insisted on going with you. I feel called to do so. Though I must admit to some trepidation about how we will be getting there." The paladin gave a raspy laugh. "Flying seems so strange. At seventy-two years of age, it will be a new experience for me."

"It is quite exhilarating," Eli said. "You will love it."

"I am not so sure about that," Restus said to the elf, "but I promise to keep an open mind."

Stiger eyed the old man for a long moment. Any time a paladin had ever felt called to go with him... there had been trouble waiting for them both, some evil to wipe from the world. He could not imagine worse trouble than he had already faced himself.

But in truth, Stiger knew he should not fear what might be. Restus was on his side, and Stiger understood he needed the man. The High Father would not be sending the paladin a call to action unless there was good cause. In the end, Stiger decided it did not matter. They both had a job to do and would do it to their last breaths. If the paladin felt drawn to go with him, that was the end of it. He was going and they would both face whatever was waiting for them.

"Father Thomas is gone." Restus was the head of order. He deserved the truth, and Stiger owed Father Thomas. "He gave his life saving mine."

"I know," Restus said.

"You do?" Stiger asked, surprised.

"Whenever one of my paladins passes from this world, the High Father sees to it that I know. I saw it happen, Father Thomas's death, what you faced, the minion of Castor, the terrible wound you took, that despite my paladin's best efforts has yet to fully heal and troubles you to this day."

Stiger almost placed a hand to his side. Almost.

"I was shown it all, in a vision. I was able to witness the rising of the High Father's Champion, you, as you rightly embraced your destiny. For that vision, I shall always be grateful. It was a tremendous blessing in and of itself and has only reaffirmed my faith and my life's work."

Aetius and Treim shifted their stances, as if suddenly uncomfortable by the paladin's words. Stiger had not expected the revelation. He did not know what to say, so he remained silent.

"It was I, along with another," Restus continued, "who passed on the vision to Emperor Tioclesion and shared the prophecy with him. I helped set the stage for your coming, as did my predecessors before me with Emperor Atticus."

"I see," Stiger said, another huge piece of the puzzle falling into place.

"As to Father Thomas, though a fine man, a faithful servant to our lord, and a personal friend," Restus continued, "I grieve for his loss. At the same time, I am comforted in the knowledge that he fulfilled his destiny and in death is held close to the High Father in everlasting love. Also, another of the faithful will rise to take his place within my order. One always does."

"Arnold," Stiger said.

"Is that his name?" Restus turned and gestured at the wall to Stiger's left. "I sense his presence somewhere to the south. I have felt him for several months now as he's grown in power and passed his tests."

Heated voices bordering on outright shouting drew their attention back toward the doorway. Aetius moved over to the table and set his mug down.

"I will not be held off like a common supplicant," an outraged voice came from the hallway. "I am a praetorian officer. My place is with the emperor."

"Prefect Nouma," Ruga could be heard. "If you'd just wait...bloody hell."

A man in the armor of a praetorian officer appeared, with Ruga in tow. He was wearing the purple cape, the emperor's own color. Two of Ruga's legionaries, shields in hand and swords drawn, followed them into the room.

"I am sorry, sir." Ruga's face was beet red. He looked about ready to throttle the praetorian. "They wouldn't just take no for an answer. Were he not an officer, I would have cut him down to size. Give the order and I will show him some manners."

"How dare you?" Nouma turned to Ruga. "I am a praetorian, and a prefect of the first order. I do not answer to you."

Behind Ruga and the two legionaries appeared Handi, the former aide to General Kromen and tribune to the late emperor. Handi pushed his way by Ruga's legionaries and joined Nouma. The tribune's armor was expensive, well maintained, and as perfectly perfect as could be. Even the blue ribbon signifying his rank tied around his chest was a model of perfection. Stiger felt an intense wave of disgust overcome him. He found his irritation rising to new levels at the interruption. It had been made worse by the tribune's presence.

Oddly, Stiger found Rarokan's attention fixated on Handi. He could feel a mounting hunger for the tribune's soul that was akin to a man dying of thirst. He'd not felt such interest, or really effort, on the sword's part for some time. With not a little effort, Stiger turned his gaze back to the praetorian officer, who snapped crisply to attention and, fist to chest, gave a perfect salute.

"I assume you are Prefect Nouma," Stiger said.

"I am, Imperator," Nouma said.

"Well then, you answer to me," Stiger said in a quiet tone, "your emperor. Isn't that right?"

Nouma gazed at Stiger for a long moment. The man's eyes narrowed ever so slightly. The prefect was not an attractive man, nor was he very tall. He stood a little over five feet. The pox had marked his face, badly scarring him. Along with a heavy brow, it gave him a brutish appearance. Where so many people were underfed and outright starving in Lorium, Stiger found it incredible that Nouma appeared well-fed, almost pudgy.

By comparison, Treim and Aetius's cheeks looked sunken and hollow. Both men had lost some bodyweight during the siege. Stiger was beginning to take a dislike to the praetorian. With so many headaches, Stiger did not need one more, not when he was so overwhelmed by all that needed to be accomplished. And this was a very minor headache at that, at least in Stiger's estimation. By all rights, Nouma should have had the common sense to wait.

"I asked you a question," Stiger said, as he realized the tribune, who stood at attention next to Nouma, had not bothered saluting. Stiger suspected that was calculated, but not as an insult. He had a suspicion that Handi felt he had something to bargain with or trade for access to power. Whatever he had, Stiger did not care. Handi had miscalculated badly. Stiger wanted nothing from him. He felt only disgust for the man and well recalled him playing petty games of camp politics in the south. "Well?" Stiger asked the praetorian before Nouma could speak. "You and your boys answer to me. Isn't that correct, Prefect?"

"Yes, Imperator," Nouma said. "The praetorians answer to you and you alone."

Ruga motioned for his men to remain by the door. Both took up a position on either side of the doorway and sheathed their swords.

"Should I throw him out on his ass, sir?" Ruga asked as he stepped to the side, staring with hard eyes at Nouma.

"I beg your pardon," Nouma said, in a tone that was an octave too high. Even the man's voice was beginning to grate on Stiger's nerves.

Stiger waited a long moment as he considered the praetorian's armor, which, just like Handi's, was in pristine shape. There wasn't even a scratch in evidence, let alone any rust, a legionary's toughest foe.

"Has the enemy been spotted?" Stiger asked.

"The enemy?" Nouma looked confused.

"I am wondering what is so important that you would choose to interrupt your emperor," Stiger said. "I believe I specifically gave orders that I would meet with you after I concluded my business with General Treim, Colonel Aetius, and Father Restus. You are interrupting important matters, sir. I would like an explanation."

"We are your guard, Imperator," Nouma said. "It is our sworn and sacred duty. I could not in good conscience stand by while you lack proper protection."

"In good conscience?" Stiger asked.

"That's right, Imperator," Nouma said.

"I have a guard," Stiger countered and gestured toward Ruga. "Why do I need another?"

"Him and his boys?" Nouma asked. "They are common legionaries, with no understanding of proper etiquette. We are the praetorians, Imperator. We stand apart from the riffraff."

Ruga stiffened.

"He is an officer." Stiger hardened his tone to a sharp edge. "Due not only common courtesy, but your respect."

"If you say so, sir," Nouma said.

Stiger's dislike for the man reached new levels. Nouma reminded him suddenly of Cethegus, his first commanding officer. Stiger had been on the receiving end of such arrogant bastards for much of his service in the legions. In his experience, men like Nouma and Cethegus were bullies, weak on character and more often than not, when push came to shove, proved cowardly. They pointed out the flaws in others to conceal their own.

Outside, the sound of yet another hymn could be heard on the air. Though Stiger had not yet made an appearance, he had been told by Ruga the crowd had only grown in size as the day had progressed. Their singing, in a way, soothed him and kept him from striking the obnoxious man who stood before him. He glanced toward the window and took a deep breath, slowly letting it out. That they had been there all day amazed and worried him at the same time. He had no experience leading civilians. He knew he would have to learn to deal with them, for they were now his subjects and his responsibility, just as surely as his legionaries.

"What Prefect Nouma is trying to say," Handi said smoothly, "is that, by custom and right, the Praetorian Guard should be protecting your person, Imperator, keeping you safe." He glanced over at the prefect. "There is no one better suited and prepared to handle this task than Nouma and his men, a detachment of which are waiting just outside."

"Exactly," Nouma said. "We are here to help, Imperator, not hinder."

"So," Stiger said, "you would guard my person?"

"We would," Nouma said. "By custom and right, it is our duty. There is also the matter of the donative. But that can wait for a later, more appropriate time."

"Donative?" Stiger felt himself scowl. He rubbed his jaw, not liking the sound of that.

General Treim shifted his stance and crossed his arms. Aetius stepped over to the nearest window and glanced out at the crowd beyond, who were singing so loud the words of their latest hymn could clearly be heard through the thick walls of the building.

"It must be negotiated." Nouma shot General Treim a disdainful look. "This is done between the emperor and the guard. It does not involve you." Nouma turned his gaze back to Stiger. "It would be better handled in private, Imperator."

"I see," Stiger said and looked to Handi. "And why are you here?"

"I am the emperor's tribune," Handi said importantly, as if that explained everything. When Stiger did not immediately reply, he continued. "I belong at the imperator's side, as your aide, helping to guide you through the more difficult matters that arise. I offer my counsel, experience, and connections."

"Your counsel?" Stiger slowly stood and then stepped closer to the man. He examined Handi's perfectly made and fitted armor. It was exquisite work. The smith who had made the armor was truly a master at his craft. It had likely cost the tribune a fortune. Handi's armor was as unlike Stiger's as could be, which, though well maintained, was scratched, pitted, and dented from battle. It had belonged to his ancestor, Legate Delvaris.

Stiger had taken the armor, along with Rarokan, from the great man's tomb. Though it was old and looked slightly archaic when compared to modern armor, Stiger had become quite fond of it, attached even. His armor had become like an old friend. He supposed, with his ripped and tattered blue cloak, he looked shabby in comparison to the tribune.

Oddly, Rarokan's attention was still fixated on Handi. That in and of itself was worrying. Why?

Kill him now, Rarokan hissed. *To allow him to live is dangerous. He is an enemy. A strong will has been used around him. He is dangerous. Kill him.*

No, Stiger thought back, wondering what game the sword was playing at. *Not without good cause.*

Mark my words, you will regret this...

"What happened?" Stiger asked Handi abruptly, ignoring the sword. "I'm curious. Do tell."

"I am afraid I do not understand, Imperator," Handi said.

"Sure you do." Stiger's anger had been kindled to a burning fire. All it would take was a spark to fully ignite into an inferno. He could feel the sword trying to feed and stoke the rage, encouraging him to draw and attack. Rarokan wanted Handi dead, and badly too. He felt his fingers begin to twitch toward the hilt of his sword. The urge to draw it became almost overpowering. Stiger pushed back, shoving the mad wizard's mind down into its prison and closing the door, locking it away... at least for a time. Surprisingly, it took some effort and some of the *will* the High Father had lent him.

"When the southern legions marched north," Stiger said, "why was word not sent to me at Vrell? Why was I abandoned? Why was I left to die?"

"I'd like to know the answer to that as well," Treim said.

"I don't understand." Handi licked his lips. "I dispatched a messenger to you just as soon General Mammot made the decision to pull out, which was a hasty one at that. You see, the enemy had surprised us, stealing a march and flanking the encampment. Their movement threatened to cut us off from our supply."

"Oh really?" Stiger said.

"Something must have happened to the messenger. We would not ever willingly abandon our own." Handi took a breath that almost shuddered as he let it out. "Personally, I am shocked that you think we would have done such a thing."

Stiger could see the lie in the man's eyes, as if it were plain as day. He felt the comforting tingle race from his palm up to his arm as he touched the hilt of his sword. The door to the prison had inched open again and Rarokan's influence crept out. He itched to draw the blade, to end the life of this insufferable bastard. Despite being partially locked in his prison, Rarokan was still working to feed Stiger's anger to goad him into action. Stiger resisted, for he'd long since learned it never ended well when he gave into the sword.

"Let me tell you what I think happened." Stiger stepped back toward the stool he had been using all day. He stopped and turned back to face Handi. "You, Mammot, and Kromen, if he still lived at the time, decided to abandon me."

Handi made to reply.

Stiger raised a finger, forestalling him. "I know your type only too well. You, sir, are a player of camp politics, using and abusing your position for personal gain, making others suffer for your own edification. I do not know how you managed to attach yourself to Tioclesion, but you won't find a ready host in me. You are a parasite, a leech, and utterly untrustworthy."

"But, on my honor," Handi said in a strangled tone, "I ..."

"People like you have no honor," Stiger growled. "You disgust me. You have no place at my side."

"But," Handi said, "I never..."

"Silence," Stiger barked, using the voice of command he'd developed over years of leading men into battle. The tribune paled at the verbal onslaught. "Should you wish to redeem yourself," Stiger continued, "I am sure General Treim can find an open vacancy for an officer of your caliber. After the recent fighting, he is certain to have need. Perhaps by leading men in the field, you might one day prove your worth, sir." Stiger turned to Treim, struggling to contain his anger. "General, do you have a vacancy for a lieutenant? Preferably under a good officer that might make something of this man?"

"I do, Imperator," Treim said. "I have the perfect captain for it, Haxus."

"He'll do," Stiger said, remembering the cantankerous captain of Eighth Company from Third Legion. The man had been a friend of Corus, another captain in his old legion. But he'd not been an outright enemy, not like Corus.

For a moment, Stiger wondered if Corus had died in the fighting or was somewhere in the city. He forced such thoughts aside. Corus was no longer important, not anymore.

The general turned to Handi. "Stop by headquarters and an assignment will be given to you before the end of the day."

"But," Handi said, looking toward Stiger, "I am useful. I have connections in the senate, influence...I...surely...you need me."

"I do not need your services," Stiger said, taking a step nearer. "Now, leave...before I lose my temper and things become ugly."

Handi's eyes had gone wild, looking everywhere but Stiger's gaze. He turned finally to Nouma. "Are you going to let him talk to me that way? You said you could control him."

Nouma shot Handi a nervous glance but held his tongue. It was clear he had no intention of intervening. After an uncomfortable moment, it started to become apparent to Handi too.

"I have known the emperor for many years," Aetius said as the crowd outside continued to sing, so loud it required the colonel to raise his voice slightly. "You should consider yourself fortunate. You are being given a second chance. Now, I'd leave, son, while you still can. He is not the most forgiving of men, especially when he believes he's been wronged."

Handi had gone thoroughly white in the face and his hands had begun shaking, whether from rage or fear, Stiger did not know. His shoulders slumped and he suddenly looked broken as he took another step back. He turned and fairly fled from the room, pausing at the doorway to shoot Stiger one last look that promised blood.

Stiger, in his anger, had not realized he had taken a couple more steps toward Handi. He moved back to his stool and sat down before looking back up on Nouma.

"I believe we were speaking of your duties and a donative?" Stiger asked.

"Yes, Imperator, we were." Nouma's tone was a little less sure.

"You would protect me," Stiger said, "like you did with my predecessor, Tioclesion?"

"It would be my honor," Nouma said. "We would guard you with our lives, Imperator."

Stiger wanted to ask the man why he still lived when his former charge had fallen in battle, for surely he had not done his job. Stiger doubted Nouma could even stand in the press of the line with common legionaries.

"I see." Stiger shifted on the stool, settling into a more comfortable position. "And a donative would be a requirement for that service?"

Nouma glanced toward the others, suddenly appearing uncomfortable. "We can negotiate the donative any time you desire and in private, Imperator. It binds the Guard to your person."

"I do not bribe those who work for me," Stiger said, his gaze going to Ruga meaningfully. "Though there may occasionally be a reward for services rendered, I choose to trust them instead."

Nouma's expression became rock-hard. Color rushed to his cheeks. "Trust?"

"Yes," Stiger said, "trust. It is a simple concept. They trust me to look after them and I trust them with my life."

After a moment's hesitation, Nouma spoke. "You can trust us, Imperator."

"As for my guard," Stiger said, "like I told you, I already have Ruga and his men. I have no need to rely upon the Praetorian Guard."

"But, sir," Nouma said, "I believe there has been a misunderstanding."

"There has been no misunderstanding." Stiger's anger was beginning to get the better of him. The sword still wanted blood, and even with Menos's training, it was an effort to keep the floodgates closed. "I am well aware of the praetorians' history and treacherous reputation."

"I must protest." Nouma's voice suddenly sounded weak. He likely was not accustomed to people standing up to him, even the emperor. Stiger wondered how much power the man had wielded over Tioclesion and his court. How much fear had Nouma held over others? How much injustice had been done at his hands and in the name of the emperor, whether commanded to do so or not?

"There is no need to protest. The past deeds of the Guard are well known. You don't like an emperor, or he does not pay enough to the Guard...you murder him," Stiger said. "Perhaps his successor will learn a lesson? Be cowed by the Guard? Isn't that the thinking?"

"Again, I feel I must protest, Imperator," Nouma spluttered. "That is quite unfair."

"Is it? I think not." Stiger paused, looking over at Treim. "General Treim?"

"Imperator?" Treim stepped forward.

"Have the prefect's men reassigned and their officers given commands suited to their ability levels," Stiger said. "Roll them into one of your cohorts that is understrength."

"With pleasure, sir," Treim said.

"You can't do this," Nouma exclaimed.

"I am emperor. And you just said you are answerable to me. I can do what I like."

"The senate will not stand for this," Nouma said.

"They are not here," Stiger said, feeling utter contempt for the man, almost as much as he'd felt for Handi. "Are they?"

The prefect did not respond.

"Prefect Nouma, you are dismissed."

There was a long silence before Nouma, trembling with visible rage, turned and stalked from the room.

"That," Aetius said, once the prefect's boots could no longer be heard out in the corridor, "may have not been the wisest of moves."

"You think I should have bargained with him?" Stiger asked. "Sold my throne and safety by buying the man with some spare silver? Colonel, you of all people should know, a bought man, especially one like that"—Stiger gestured toward the doorway—"doesn't always stay bought for long. He has no honor and neither does the Guard. You need to keep paying them, repeatedly to purchase their loyalty... only they don't have any, but to their own purse. My father learned that lesson the hard way during the civil war. It nearly cost my family everything. Come now, would you have people around me who did not have my best interests to heart?"

"Of course not, Imperator," Aetius said, his voice calm and steady. "But you might have handled it differently. There are over three hundred praetorians in the city. You could have heard him out and told him you would consider his words. Then, we would have had time to organize and send in sufficient men to disarm them before disbanding the Guard. Try it now and there will surely be trouble, maybe even bloodshed."

"He has a point," Eli said, looking over at Stiger. "Sometimes you let your anger get the better of you. I think this is one of those moments."

Stiger felt himself scowl as he looked over at Eli. His anger had fully drained away. It was replaced with an intense frustration, a sense that he had just made a mistake.

He gritted his teeth. Aetius was right. He should not have let his anger get the better of him. It was a lesson for the future. "I could have handled that better."

Aetius inclined his head slightly in acknowledgement.

"Ruga," Eli asked, "how many men did Nouma bring?"

Stiger looked up sharply, with a sinking feeling in the pit of his stomach.

"About forty," Ruga said. "All polished up, they looked quite pretty... not at all like men who've stood in a line of battle against a determined enemy."

Without a doubt, Stiger realized he had just acted foolishly, terribly so. Ruga had only twenty men, thirty if you counted those Aetius had assigned, and half of his men were stood down upstairs. In the sudden silence, the sound of those singing outside filled the room. The centurion's eyes widened as he turned his gaze and met Stiger's. It was clear they were thinking the same thing.

"Get your men rousted," Stiger ordered, standing and kicking the stool away. "Anyone who is outside on guard, get them inside right now. Send a man to the general's headquarters for reinforcement. Hurry."

"Yes, sir." Ruga turned and started for the door. Before he could reach it, there came shouts of alarm, followed by the ring of steel on steel.

You should have killed them both, the sword hissed and Stiger knew without a doubt Rarokan was correct.

CHAPTER THREE

S tiger watched as Ruga moved up to the doorway and looked out, down the hallway, toward the building's entrance. The centurion's two men were close behind him. Grim-faced, they had drawn their swords and were holding their shields ready. A quick look was all it took. Ruga hastily backed up, drawing his sword as well.

"Quickly…block the doorway," Ruga ordered as he stepped aside so his men could move forward. "No one gets through. Protect the emperor with your lives. Understand?"

"Yes, sir," both men said together as shouts, cries, and the harsh ring of steel could be heard out in the hallway. The guards who had stood on duty at the building's entrance were clearly battling for their lives and, Stiger knew, being overwhelmed. There was no helping them. He felt wretched about that.

Both took up a position just inside the doorway. Swords held at the ready, they locked their shields together with a solid *thunking* sound. Treim and Aetius drew their weapons, as did Eli, who pulled out a pair of long daggers that could nearly be called short swords in their own right. One of the blades was bent and angled, giving it a vicious look. To say Eli was proficient with the weapons was an understatement. He was deadly with them.

Grinding his teeth in frustration, Stiger wrapped his hand around Rarokan's hilt and pulled the dread weapon from its sheath. He had let his anger get the better of him and now there was a price to pay, a steep one, not just for him, but for those who served him. That pissed him off.

Free of the scabbard and under the dim lamplight, the sword, feeding upon his anger, began to burn with blue fire. The fire was sullen at first, then grew with intensity until it began to outshine the lamps. The brightness seemed to match his anger. Stiger noticed Aetius's and Treim's eyes upon the blade in clear startlement. Stiger shifted his attention back to the doorway as a clipped scream sounded just beyond. It was followed by a thudding sound as a body hit the floorboards.

A praetorian with a shield and bloodied sword appeared in the doorway a heartbeat later. The man was big and muscular, almost impossibly so, and stood over six feet. He had to hunch slightly to keep his head from bumping the low-hanging ceiling.

Shield held before him, the praetorian immediately pushed his way forward at Ruga's men, who were blocking entrance to the room. They met him with their own shields. Both sides battered at each other violently. Another praetorian joined the fight. This one carried a javelin. The limited space and the sheer bulk of his compatriot caused him to jab rather clumsily and ineffectually over and around the big praetorian.

Shouts, curses, oaths, and the harsh clash of steel on steel could be heard in other parts of the building as the fighting spread. Stiger imagined that the praetorians were attempting to force their way up the stairs by the entrance to the second floor. He glanced at the windows. They were too small to make an egress.

Stiger moved over to a window and looked out. The praetorians had formed a thin ring around the building, clearly with the intention of cutting off any escape. The crowd was still there but had backed up and away from the guardsmen. They were no longer singing but were looking on with what Stiger thought was apparent confusion. The guardsmen faced the crowd and were armed with shields and javelins, almost as if they feared the civilians might intervene.

Once again, Stiger cursed himself. Before acting, he should have considered the consequences. He had been a fool. Worse, he did not even know the layout of the rest of the building. That was an unforgivable lapse. Stiger had long since learned the importance of knowing the lay of the land before setting up shop.

"Ruga," Stiger called, looking away from the window. He knew he had to ask to be sure. "Is there another exit?"

Ruga looked around from the fight and, biting his lip, shook his head. "Even the windows upstairs are too small to fit through, sir. This place is built like a bloody fortress... which, given the circumstances, gives me some comfort."

"I wish Therik were here," Eli said, "along with a few dozen more men. I think, when it comes to a fight, you can never have too many on your side."

"Wishes are like daydreams," Stiger said. But he too wished Therik was with them. He glanced around the room. There was nothing they could use to block the doorway, no large pieces of furniture. It had all been removed. The thin cots in the bedrooms were useless to them. They were simply too flimsy. Even the door itself was missing. Like the shutters, the door had likely been broken up and gone to a fire for warmth or cooking.

The fighting in the rest of the building seemed to intensify. It was clear Ruga's men were putting up a serious fight. He had expected nothing different, for the centurion's men were fighters.

"There's only the other staircase … the one at the front of the building, right?" Stiger asked.

"Yes, sir." Ruga pointed to the stairs. "It leads to the second floor, just like that one there."

"General." Stiger turned to Treim. "We need to hold this position and, at all costs, the other stairway. Would you and the colonel kindly get to the second floor and see what good you can do there?"

"We've got it." Treim slapped Aetius on the shoulder. "Come on."

Aetius looked hesitant to leave but followed after the general. The two senior officers literally ran up the stairs, taking them two at a time.

Stiger turned his attention back to the fighting. As he did, the big praetorian was jabbed deeply in the thigh with a short sword by one of Ruga's men. Groaning, he collapsed to a knee, dropping his shield and weapon. He grasped the wound with both hands as it fountained blood. A heartbeat later, a legionary shield hammered into his face, knocking him violently to the floor, where he lay still and unmoving.

The praetorian with the javelin stepped over the body of his comrade and swung the javelin down from above like a club. Shouting incoherently, he slammed it into the helmet of the legionary who had just taken down his comrade. The legionary stumbled backward, himself falling to a knee, clearly dazed.

Without missing a beat, Ruga lunged forward and stabbed, punching his sword into the praetorian's extended arm and cutting a chunk of flesh free. The man screamed, this time with agony.

Dropping the javelin, he attempted to fall back but was shoved roughly forward from behind by another praetorian, who was trying to come up the narrow hallway and enter the room. Ruga jabbed again, this time just above the man's armor, stabbing him through the collar. The guardsman shrieked, like a pig being slaughtered, before collapsing onto both knees, almost held in place by the centurion's sword stuck in his collar. Ruga gave the sword a savage twist, eliciting yet another scream, this one weaker. The centurion placed his foot on the man's chest and pushed with his leg, while also pulling the sword back. Blood, bone chips, and cartilage came with it. His finished opponent fell backward onto the floorboards and expired, spilling his blood out in a gush.

To Ruga's immediate left, the other legionary was roughly pushed back by a newcomer who charged forward past his dying comrade. This one was using his shield as a battering ram. The legionary fell back from the doorway as two more of the Guard followed the first and, using their shields, shoved their way forward, knocking Ruga back as well.

Stiger felt his anger flash hot. He opened the door to the prison and allowed a measure of Rarokan's power to flow into him. He welcomed it. Time seemed to slow. The room grew brighter as the power infused his being, coursing through him in a flood.

With an abrupt surge, time snapped back to normal speed, and as it did, Stiger moved forward and attacked. He brought with him death as he stepped past the dazed legionary and jabbed his weapon at the nearest praetorian, who hastily threw up his sword to block the attack. It was a slow, clumsy, and poorly executed attempt to check him.

Dropping his sword by just a hair, Stiger allowed his opponent's blade to sail over his and easily avoided the block. His opponent's blade only found empty air. The guardsman had overextended himself, and recognition of that fact registered in his eyes as Stiger lunged forward and stabbed hard. The tip of his blade punched into the chest armor of his opponent, sliding easily through. The hilt grew warm in his hand as Rarokan took the man's life force. The praetorian's eyes rolled back in his head. He dropped limply to the floorboards. The steel of Stiger's blade as it emerged from his chest hissed almost savagely. The man's blood, like so many others had, boiled away on the air.

A breath later, Eli was by his side. Movements graceful, elegant even, Eli's daggers were a veritable blur as he attacked a praetorian. With ease, he countered a strike with one dagger, then spun completely around and with the angled blade reached out over the shield and neatly slit the throat of his opponent, cutting in one motion straight through to the spine. The man, gushing blood into the air, was dead before he even hit the floor. Eli had already moved on and was engaging the next praetorian.

A spray of blood splattered Stiger's right cheek as Ruga took down a praetorian. He ignored it and instead focused on advancing toward the door, where two more praetorians had entered and were about to join the fight. If they could retake that chokepoint, they could hold off the enemy. That was all that mattered.

One of the newcomers moved to meet him, while the other hesitated, his eyes upon the burning sword. The first lunged, jabbing out. Stiger dodged to the side, while blocking and shoving the sword roughly away and to the side. At the same time, he took another rapid step forward, surprising his opponent, and hammered a fist square into the praetorian's face. The blow was powerfully delivered. Stiger felt the man's teeth give way. At the same time, pain exploded in his hand, for the praetorian's jaw was solid. Despite the pain, the punch had the desired effect. The man's head snapped back, and he crashed backward to the floor, landing atop the body of another.

Only too aware that momentum was the key to regaining the initiative, Stiger continued forward, attacking the man who had hesitated. The praetorian threw up his sword and blocked Stiger's first strike. Their swords met, sparks flying through the air and the steel ringing loudly with the contact. Lightning fast, Stiger shifted the momentum of his attack and, using the end of the hilt as a weapon, hammered it into the side of the man's helmet.

The praetorian staggered under the unexpected blow, hitting the wall with the other side of his head, which Stiger knew had hurt. Understanding that his opponent was dazed and not wanting to give him even a moment to recover, Stiger leapt forward and brought his blade around and drove the tip of his burning sword up under the man's chin. With little resistance, the point went in deep and drove up into the brain, killing him instantly. Hot blood cascaded down Stiger's arm and across his face and chest.

With his free hand, he threw the body of the man aside and turned to confront the next attacker. Instead, he found himself at the doorway. There were no more opponents in the room itself and none to his front. Ruga and one of his legionaries were suddenly to either side. Eli was just behind him. Stiger peeked out into the hallway. He saw two praetorians coming down it from the entrance. A body lay by the door and was, by the red cape, one of Ruga's men. The sight of one of his legionaries dead only served to fuel Stiger's anger.

Beyond, he could see more of the Guard out on the street as they moved to enter the building, along with Nouma and Handi. The two were clearly directing the show.

Stiger's rage increased. He nearly took a step out into the hallway, then reason returned in a rush and the terrible anger that he had almost allowed to consume him dimmed. To go outside where the enemy had numerical superiority was stupid and foolish. He ducked back inside. The fighting was still raging on the other side of the building.

"We need to hold," Stiger said to Ruga. "We need to hold this room."

"You two," Ruga said to the two legionaries. The one who had been knocked down was back on his feet. His lip was split and he was bleeding profusely down his chest, but he looked as if he had his wits about him. He also appeared ready to fight. "Bloody hold the door this time or you'll be on a charge."

"Yes, sir," the bleeding man said as he spat a glob of blood onto the floor. "We'll hold them."

Satisfied, Stiger took a step back. As he did, the two legionaries resumed their place blocking the doorway, shields held to their front, swords at the ready. Stiger was concerned about how the fighting in the rest of the building was going. He could hear Treim calling out orders and encouragements, men cursing and shouting at one another, sword ringing against sword.

He looked around and saw the paladin. Restus had stood back from the action. He had not even pulled his sword out, which was a common legionary short sword by the looks of it. Restus was so old, Stiger very much doubted he could wield it effectively. But he knew that when it came to paladins, looks could be deceiving.

"Can you find out how they're holding?" Stiger asked Restus and jutted his chin toward the stairs.

"I can," the paladin said and started up the back stairs, moving surprisingly quickly for his age.

"Get them," a praetorian shouted from the hallway.

The shout snapped Stiger's head back around. Two more guardsmen had appeared. Shields held out before them, they met the two waiting legionaries. Stiger watched as the praetorians struggled against his determined legionaries and was pleased by what he saw.

"They're holding the back stairs just fine," Restus shouted back down the stairs. "Nothing to worry about at the moment."

"Well that is something at least," Ruga said, then looked back on Stiger. "Do you think help is coming, sir? From the general's boys?"

"Eventually someone will notice something's not right," Stiger said, doing his best to sound convincing, for he knew Ruga's men could hear every word. He needed them to believe that relief would come. And yet, he honestly had no idea how long that would take, if it happened at all. "My old sergeant, Tiro, is at headquarters. He will see that help is sent. We just need to hold long enough for that to happen."

"Then that's what we will do, sir," Ruga said. "You heard him, boys. We hold."

"Ahhhh!" one of the praetorians yelled, his sword clattering to the floor. The man's arm had been opened with a viciously deep cut. He fell back from the doorway, holding his shield before him defensively. Both of Ruga's men shoved forward with their shields, hammering at the guardsman's shield and knocking him and his companion backward through the doorway. They jabbed out with their swords but were unable to score either a disabling or killing strike.

"Hold," a voice shouted out in the hallway. Stiger recognized it as Nouma's. "I said hold. Stop fighting. I said stop fighting!"

The sounds of battle on the other side of the building petered off. The injured man in the doorway, along with his comrade, backed away. They rapidly moved down the hallway and out of view.

"Let him go," Ruga snapped. "Do not follow. Maintain your position."

"Stiger?" Nouma shouted down the hallway. "Can you hear me?"

Stiger shared a look with Eli.

"What do you believe he wants?" Eli asked with a sudden grin.

"I don't think he's gonna invite us to have tea," Stiger said, "if that's what you are thinking."

Eli's grin grew wider.

One of the praetorians on the floor moaned and stirred. It was the one Stiger had punched in the face. He started to pull himself to all fours. Ruga stepped over and, without hesitation, kicked the injured man in the face. The praetorian's head snapped back with a crack and he once again went limp. Outside, cries of alarm and a few angry, outraged shouts could be heard from the crowd. Stiger could only imagine how confused they were about what was happening.

"Stiger," Nouma shouted again, "can you hear me?"

Ruga moved by his men and carefully peeked around the doorway. He looked back. "He's just inside the building, sir," Ruga said. "Along with that slimy tribune. There are three men between us and them. I can see additional guardsmen behind and out on the street. More than initially came with them." Ruga heaved a heavy sigh. "I don't believe we can easily get to him and murder the bastard. If we try, he'll just step out on the street where all his boys are. It wouldn't end good for us, that's for certain."

Stiger gave a nod. He had figured as much.

"Well?" Nouma called.

"I can hear you," Stiger hollered back from where he was.

"You should have taken me up on my offer," Nouma said. "There was no need for such unpleasantness. We could have worked things out between us like men, come to a mutually beneficial solution."

"We can still make a deal," Handi called. "You just need to be reasonable, is all."

"Reasonable...like that's going to happen," Eli said in a low tone of voice. When Stiger looked over at the elf in question, Eli added. "The reasonable part, I mean. You can be...I think the word is obstinate, when you want."

Stiger just shook his head.

"Why would I want to do that, Nouma?" Stiger yelled back. "You can't get in. Eventually help will arrive. There are over seven thousand legionaries in the city. Many more than your praetorians."

"That may be true," Nouma said, "but they won't get here before the rest of my praetorians get to you."

"Do you really think the legion will let you kill me and just walk away?" Stiger asked. The thought of it was so preposterous, he almost laughed.

"We're not gonna kill you," Handi said, "just everyone else with you. No, when this is all said and done, you will be our charge...just like it should have been from the beginning."

"You mean your hostage," Stiger said.

"Call it what you will," Handi said, "it does not matter. We will own you, like we did Tioclesion. That will be the end of it."

"Our story will be that the general and colonel had taken you hostage," Nouma said. "We gallantly rescued you and in doing so had to storm the building. When we have you … well, let's just say you will see things our way and sing our tune. I think you will want to at that point."

"It's as good a plan as any," Eli said to Stiger. "It may just work."

"You will fail," Stiger called.

"Maybe," Handi said, "maybe not. We'll see. I'd surrender were I you. It will be harder on you if you don't."

"It's not gonna happen," Stiger called back, feeling his rage spike. "I will see you both dead first."

"All right," Handi said with an overdramatic sigh an actor would have been proud of. "We will do this the hard way, then."

"He's right," Eli said, sounding amused, "you like doing things the hard way."

"That's not helpful," Stiger said, though he could not help but grin slightly at the stupid humor.

Ruga looked back toward the stairs. "Sir, while it's quiet, if you don't mind, I'd like to go check my boys and eyeball how things are over on the other side of the building."

"Go ahead. I've got this," Stiger said.

"I'll be back shortly." Ruga moved off, climbing the stairs.

There were indistinct shouts from Nouma outside that sounded like orders. Stiger could hear praetorians moving into the building again, preparing for the next assault.

"Stand ready," Stiger said to the two men by the door. With grim expressions, they raised their shields up into the air and held their swords ready.

"Wait a moment," Eli said, his grin abruptly returning. He chuckled softly. "I think I've had an absolutely fabulous idea."

"What?" Stiger looked over. "What do you mean?"

Sheathing both daggers, Eli ignored him and went over to one of the tiny windows. He looked out for a moment, seeming to hesitate. Then he cupped his lips with his hands.

"They're trying to kill Emperor Stiger," Eli shouted out through the window. "The praetorians want to kill the man who saved you from the confederacy. They want to kill the High Father's Champion. He needs your help. Your emperor needs you. He's calling you. Will you stand idly by and let such a foul deed be done? Or will you step up to defend him and the empire?"

Silence followed. Stiger glanced over at Eli, surprised. He wondered if the elf's effort to stir up the mob might work. The silence seemed to stretch for several heartbeats.

"Foul deed?" Stiger asked Eli.

"What would you call it?" Eli asked, looking back on Stiger. "Do you think they're doing us a good deed?"

"Fair point," Stiger said.

Eli gazed back out the window.

"You know," the elf said, "you keep concerning yourself with the mob. I wanted to see if this mob had any real power." He breathed out a heavy breath. "They are not doing anything, and I mean anything. They're just standing there and watching like before. I must say I am truly disappointed. I wanted to see your mob in action. Well … shit … I guess it was worth a try." He turned back toward the door, drew his daggers, and spun both around in his hands. "Now we must really do it the Stiger way...the hard way."

It had been a worthy attempt on Eli's part and good thinking too. However, he'd be surprised if the civilians, half-starved and having just endured a brutal siege, had the strength left to put up any type of resistance. They likely could not be motivated to do much beyond what they had been doing at the priests' behest...singing religious hymns and waiting for their emperor to show himself.

"All right," Stiger said to the two legionaries. "When they come again, let's murder the pretty-looking bastards. We'll show them how real legionaries fight."

"Yes, sir," both men said in unison.

Stiger turned back to the doorway, knowing the praetorians would soon begin their attack, likely a final assault that would continue until they thoroughly broke the defenders. If they had enough men, he understood, they would be able to do it. But...he'd see they paid with blood for their effort. As sure as the sun would rise in the morning and set in the evening, that was a certainty.

From outside, there came an abrupt, muffled shout that sounded intensely outraged. This was followed by what could only be described as a massed growl of deep-seated anger. Then followed much enraged shouting that was more a communal roar than anything else. It was so loud that the building itself seemed to vibrate and dust drifted down from the ceiling. Incredibly, it had clearly come from the gathered crowd outside. It sounded like they were working themselves up to action.

Eli returned to the window and glanced out before looking back at Stiger. There was a strange look on the elf's face.

"Well?" Stiger asked.

"It worked." The elf seemed genuinely surprised, almost as if he did not believe his own eyes. "The crowd is rushing the Guard and the building."

Out in the hallway, Stiger could hear shouts of alarm and panic from amongst the praetorians, who moments before had been preparing to attack. Outside, the screaming began.

Moving over to a window, Stiger looked out. What he saw was incredible, awesome to behold. Like a wave of pure rage, the crowd of civilians had pushed forward and was rolling over the praetorians. They used their hands, rocks, daggers, the occasional sword, or whatever weapon they could find easily at hand. The guardsmen were literally torn apart. Even the women were part of the action. He saw several gathered around a praetorian, beating him senseless with large stones and bricks.

When the killing was done, the dismembering and mutilation continued. It was horrific. He had never seen anything like it and knew he would carry this scene in his memory to the end of his days.

Stiger understood that Eli's call to action had been like a damn bursting. The floodgates had broken and the pent-up frustration and rage built up by the siege had been given release, explosively. The civilians of the city were venting everything upon the hated praetorians.

Within mere moments, the only thing in view was the mass of the crowd. The guardsmen had disappeared, as if they had never been there to begin with. An institution that the first emperor, Karus, had begun near two thousand years before had ended. It had been destroyed, broken and shattered. And Stiger knew he had no desire to rebuild the Guard, for they had become corrupt, a cancer within the heart of the empire itself.

The building was stormed next by the crowd. More screams followed. Ruga rushed down the stairs and up behind his two men.

"Gods," Ruga said, "they've gone mad."

Three civilians appeared in the doorway. They saw the red-caped, grim-faced legionaries, shields locked, swords held at the ready. All three hesitated, as if unsure what to do next.

"Hold," Ruga shouted, stepping up next to his men. "We're legionaries. We're not guardsmen. We're protecting the emperor."

First one and then the other backed away, going back the way they had come. A struggle could be heard coming from inside the building. The howls of the crowd as they dragged the last praetorians screaming and pleading for mercy from the building were awful to behold. It continued for a time as the mob took out the anger and rage upon those unfortunates. Then, oddly, everything went silent.

"Emperor Stiger," a lone voice called. "We have answered your call. Will you come out and see your people, bless them with your presence?"

Stiger stepped to the doorway, where the two legionaries still stood, their shields up and held at the ready. They looked at him nervously, unsure.

"Sir," Ruga said. "Were I you, I'd not go out there."

"Stand aside," Stiger said to the two men, then looked back over at the centurion. "I'll be fine."

The legionaries stepped aside, setting the bottoms of their shields down on the floor. Stiger moved out into the hallway. It was drenched in blood. Several bodies lay on the floor, including civilians and one of Ruga's men, the one he had seen earlier.

Two civilians wearing brown tunics stood by the entrance to the building, as did a priest. They looked ragged, half-starved. Their clothing was threadbare and dirty. Both carried short swords that had been bloodied up to their hilts. They eyed Stiger with deadened, exhausted gazes, which shifted from him to Rarokan.

Stiger realized he still had his sword out. It was glowing brilliantly, lighting the hallway around him. In a silent fury, tongues of blue flame licked at the air. He hesitated a moment, then started down the hallway toward the two men. They stepped backward and out onto the street.

"Are you he?" the priest asked as Stiger neared the doorway. "Are you Emperor Stiger?"

"I am."

"Gods blessed." The priest made the sign of the High Father.

Their expressions instantly changed. The deadened looks vanished. In their gazes, Stiger saw hope and something more. Was it faith? Love? Or was it a mixture of both? The beginning of zealotry? He had a sudden memory of Therik telling him such things were fleeting ... that it could all be snatched away in a heartbeat.

"Remember," Stiger breathed to himself, "you are mortal."

"Praised be the High Father." One of the men pointed his sword down into the ground and knelt, head bowed. The other followed a heartbeat later, assuming the same position of respect.

Just before stepping out onto the street, Stiger hesitated. He looked left, toward the other staircase. He saw several of Ruga's legionaries on the stairs and Treim behind them. A number of bodies, all praetorians, lay in a heap on the landing, clearly their work. Stiger gave the general a slow nod and, with that, stepped outside. Bowing respectfully, the priest moved aside for him.

"I stand ready to serve, Champion," the priest said.

Stiger gave a nod and gazed around. In the rapidly dimming light of the day, there were thousands of people gathered on the street. They had grown thoroughly silent as he appeared. There was not a whisper on the air. It was as if all were collectively holding their breath. Every eye, it seemed, was on him.

Parts of praetorians littered the ground...an arm ripped from a socket, a head, a mutilated body next it. The purple cloak had been torn away and discarded. Blood was all over the street before him. Nowhere did he see Nouma or Handi. Their bodies were likely somewhere amongst the tightly packed throng of civilians. Both would have to be found sooner than later, to confirm they had been killed.

Stiger's sword still burned with an ethereal fire, long blue tongues of flame licking at the air, even more violently than before. Behind him came Eli, then Ruga. Treim and Father Restus followed a few heartbeats later.

Almost as one, the crowd went to a knee, bowing their heads as respectfully as the first two men he had encountered. Stiger rubbed his jaw as he considered them. Imperials knelt to no one, only their god. He suddenly had no idea what to do or how to respond. He could deal with soldiers, but civilians?

"I believe," Eli said in a low voice that only the two of them could hear, "they deserve a thank you and a few kind words. Don't you think?"

Stiger glanced back at his friend. Eli was right...more than right. These people deserved a thank you and then some. Ragged and desperate as they were, they had risked all they had left, their lives against the swords and javelins of the

Praetorian Guard, to save him. They deserved more … they deserved to hope again … to believe, something to work toward, an ultimate goal. That was what he would give them. He returned his attention to the crowd and gathered his thoughts.

"I came here, to Lorium, to save you," Stiger shouted, using his parade ground voice so as many as possible could hear him. He well understood that word of what happened here would spread and grow in the telling, likely for years to come. If he was successful, it might even become something akin to legend, something that would motivate people in the hard months ahead. "I came to save the empire. As his Champion, the High Father has charged me with this solemn duty, a burden I willingly bear, but an honor no less. I have been greatly blessed, as has the empire, for the High Father is most assuredly on our side."

Stiger paused, running his gaze around the crowd. The heads had come up and all eyes were once again upon him, though everyone still knelt. It seemed as if the crowd hung on his every word.

"As I said, I came to save you. Instead, you saved me and in doing so saved the empire we all love. For that, you have my heartfelt thanks and gratitude." He paused briefly to allow that to sink in. "I promise to repay that debt. I swear I will do everything within my power to return your kindness. To my dying breath, I will defend the empire, defend you, and defeat the Cyphan Confederacy. You live on the edge of the empire, but each of you is the empire." Stiger sucked in a breath. "Your anger, my anger"—he thumped his chest with a fist—"*our* anger has been well earned. Yet, I cannot do this alone, not by myself. Today, you have shown me that. This is something that all of us will do together. Each of us will have a hand in defeating the confederacy. Whether you are a soldier or civilian…each of us has an important part to play. And when it is said and done, the empire will be stronger, and our enemy…will rue the day they came against us, for it shall have proven to be the day of their undoing."

Stiger paused as he gathered his thoughts once again for the next part. He thought suddenly on what had been done to the civilians in Aeda by the enemy, the mass slaughter, the crucifixions along the road. The Cyphan followed a dark god and had more than earned what was coming. His anger flared, and with it, the sword burned brighter.

"With the High Father's help," Stiger continued, "we will stamp out their evil. Our vengeance will be terrible and unforgiving. It will be delivered without mercy and quarter. We will set an example with the confederacy that will be remembered for an age. By the High Father…I swear to see it done, and with your help, it will be done. I just ask that you help me see it through to the end. Join with me in getting it done."

There was a long moment of silence. For a heartbeat or two, Stiger wondered if he had misjudged, for no one moved or reacted. The moment seemed to stretch for an eternity, then the crowd, as if of one mind, abruptly sprang to their feet and began madly cheering. No, he had not misjudged them. He had succeeded. He had given them hope, something to believe in, something to work toward, a cause. His coming and saving the city had restored their faith, in not only the empire, but more importantly, the High Father. He could see it, feel their faith…faith in their lord and in him.

Stiger held Rarokan up in the air above his head. Seeming to feed upon the energy of the crowd, the sword blazed anew with fiery light, casting those assembled directly before him in a bath of the purest blue. The crowd cheered louder, more exuberantly. A chant began to form, with just a few at first. More took it up. In moments, all were shouting the same thing. The air thundered with it, hammering at the ears, much louder than any battle he had ever heard.

"STIGER...STIGER...STIGER." The crowd continued to chant. On and on it went. "STIGER...STIGER...STIGE R...STIGER!"

He turned to Eli and leaned over so he could be heard over the chant of his name.

"This is the power of the mob," Stiger said to the elf. "It is never to be underestimated. That is why the senate and the rest of the nobility rightly fear the people...for though they don't realize it themselves, true power lies within their hands."

Eli gave a simple nod, and with that, Stiger straightened. He sheathed Rarokan before stepping forward and moving into the crowd. They stepped aside for him and drew slightly away. Almost tentatively, like children, many, with tears in their eyes, closed back in upon him and began to reach out. All they wanted was a simple touch...his shoulder, his arm, side, or back. They wanted a personal connection, no matter how brief, with the man, their emperor, the Champion of their faith and, by extension, their divine god, the High Father.

Women kissed him on the cheek or his hand. Stiger denied them nothing, for through their actions, they had given him a path for the future. They had also saved the empire.

A child, a boy no more than six, patted his leg, drawing his attention. Just skin and bones, the child was clearly starved. His clothes were tattered, and he was filthy, likely vermin-ridden. He looked like he had recently lost one of his front teeth. The sight of the child tore at Stiger's heart. This boy deserved better. Stiger resolved to see that he got it.

He was about to move on when the boy gave him a huge gap-toothed smile that was infectious. The child's spirit seemed irrepressible. Stiger returned the boy's smile, and reaching down, he tousled his hair before continuing on, moving amongst his people. Like the legion, they were his and he was theirs.

As you are mine, Rarokan hissed in his mind. *Together, we are one.*

CHAPTER FOUR

Conscious that thousands upon thousands of eyes were upon him, Stiger stood straight as he could. He had personally polished and cleaned his armor to the point where, under the late-day sun, it gleamed. His kit had been badly in need of a thorough, deep cleaning. The job had taken hours of work, but at the same time, the tedium had been calming to the mind. He had always enjoyed that. It gave him time to think.

A light wind gusted around him, stirring his tattered blue cape and wrapping it around his left leg. With a hand, Stiger pushed it behind him. He had yet to adopt the imperial purple. That would come soon enough.

Just behind him, formed up, were both the Third and Thirteenth Legions. Third Legion spread outward to his left and on his right was the Thirteenth, along with her auxiliary cohorts. Century and cohort standards rose above the neat block-like ranks. Two imperial Eagles were out too, their bearers positioned before each legion. The gold paint on each Eagle glinted brilliantly with flashes of reflected sunlight.

To their front, a massive funeral bier had been constructed. On it, draped in rich purple robes, lay the late emperor's body. The bier had been completed the day before. Tioclesion had been moved from the city and placed there around noon. The process had turned into a veritable parade, for much of the city had turned out to watch the body pass.

Once the body was installed on the funeral bier, seven priests of the High Father, under the close supervision of Father Restus, had gone to work. They held an open service, where any who wanted could attend. After that, for two hours, civilians from the town had been permitted to come by and pay their respects. Many openly wept as they laid flowers or tossed coin onto the funeral bier. The coin was payment for the ferryman's services. The flowers represented their regard for the late emperor. Then, the rituals, songs, and chants had begun as the priests worked to help prepare the way into the next life for Tioclesion's spirit.

All throughout it, the two legions, along with Stiger, had stood by and watched. And like the sides of a great box, the bier was now ringed on the left by the combined dwarven and gnome armies. On the right side of the box were the elves and the two new auxiliary cohorts General Treim had formed from the men of fighting age the city had to offer. Opposite the two legions, on the far side of the box, stood masses of civilians from the city. For many from the city, the sight of the dwarves, gnomes, and elves had proven intense and fascinating curiosities.

The Vass were not present. Jeskix and Arol had left earlier in the morning, taking most of their dragons to the south to link up with their army marching north. They had left the legion four dragons for protection against the enemy's wyrms. Two of those dragons would carry Stiger and a handful to Mal'Zeel, before returning to the army.

Jeskix had told him if the opportunity presented itself, the Vass might deal with the small enemy army that had crossed the Narrow Sea far to the south. If not, then they would march northward and join him. If they could manage to deal with the Cyphan, it would be one less headache for him. If not... well, then Stiger would just have to focus on that enemy army when they became a problem.

Menos and Ogg had left as well. The two had not even told him they were leaving. That had been surprising. Both had just gone. To his incredible frustration, Stiger had only found that out this morning from Braddock. The thane had no idea where they'd gone or what they were up to. He was just as perplexed and irritated as Stiger.

When he had gone to ask Menos's mate, Currose had informed him she was remaining with the army for the foreseeable future. Having a noctalum with them, even if she was still recovering from her wounds, was a serious advantage. That was a bonus at least.

Still, as if to frustrate him further, she would not tell him why both her mate and the wizard had gone. Stiger thought he detected worry in the noctalum. Whatever the reason, they were likely doing something dangerous.

Sensing movement, Stiger glanced down as Dog padded up. The shaggy-looking animal sat by his side, so close he brushed against Stiger's leg.

"And where have you been?" Stiger asked. When the army had arrived, Dog had not been with it.

Dog looked up at him with sad brown eyes and gave a soft whine. The animal tilted his head to the right in question, as if he had not understood. Only Stiger well knew Dog followed and understood every word, for he was a naverum, one of the mystical guardians of Olimbus, the home of the gods. At one time, Stiger had had his doubts about Dog, but no longer. He still did not know which god had sent him, but one surely had.

"Right, keep your secrets," Stiger said and reached over, giving the shaggy creature a friendly scratch on the head. Dog leaned into the scratch and closed his eyes, clearly enjoying the moment. In a manner of speaking, next to Eli, Dog was his oldest companion and friend. To say Stiger had become quite fond of the animal was an understatement.

"That is by far the largest dog I've ever seen," Treim said. "It should be sent on its way. Dogs do not belong here, not now, not during this august moment."

Stiger glanced over at the general, who stood off to his right. Like his own armor, the general's had been cleaned and polished until it shone brilliantly under the rapidly fading sunlight of the day. Just behind the general stood Salt, Ikely, and Severus. Eli was off to Stiger's left, Therik too. The orc looked bored and impatient for things to move along. Ruga and a strong cordon of guards had been arranged around Stiger and the senior officers. They looked like they meant business.

Upon his arrival with the army and once he'd learned of the praetorians' attempt, Salt had seen that Ruga was reinforced to an overstrength century, numbering one hundred men. Those men had been pulled from across the entirety of the Thirteenth. They were the best the legion had to offer, some of the most efficient killers that the empire had ever trained. All were long-service veterans.

"I'd like to see you try to remove that animal," Therik said with a nasty chuckle.

The general glanced over at the orc, clearly uncomfortable. Though it was rare to find an orc within the empire's borders, they were looked down upon by humans as mere beasts. Stiger had once thought that too, but no longer. That Stiger considered Therik a friend and relied upon his advice had clearly taken Treim by surprise, Aetius too.

Orc and general had met hours before. Their initial meeting had not gone well. When Therik had heard about the praetorians' attempt, he had become incensed and had placed the blame squarely on the general for not better seeing to Stiger's safety. The orc was even more irate that Stiger had not taken him along in the first place to Lorium. He had made that plain. Stiger had listened and let the orc vent his anger.

When he traveled to the capital, Stiger had hoped to leave Therik behind with the army. He let out an unhappy breath, for he understood that would no longer be possible. He was stuck with the former king of the orcs and was certain having him in tow would bring its own complications. Then again, Therik was good in a scrap. Having him along also might prove advantageous.

"What do you mean?" Treim asked Therik.

"He is not some random stray looking for a meal," Eli said to the general and then nodded toward Stiger. "Dog is his companion and has been for a very long time."

"Do not be fooled," Therik added as the priests, just a few yards away, continued to pray and sing over the emperor's body. "He is no pet, but a vicious and merciless killer." Therik turned his gaze knowingly to Stiger. "Just like his master."

Eyes on the orc, Dog gave a low whine of protest, clearly objecting.

"Do not even bother trying to deny it," Therik said to Dog. "You know what you are."

Dog gave another whine, this one almost a whimper.

"I am not his master." Stiger heaved a heavy breath and then decided to explain a bit for Treim's benefit. "He showed up one day at the farm and ... well, just sort of never left. He's been with me ever since. But ... he is free to come and go as he pleases, and he does."

"The farm?" Treim asked, clearly confused. "What farm?"

"It is a long story." Therik's tone became softer, guarded. "One best not brought up today."

Treim did not look satisfied by that.

"I will explain more later…in private," Stiger said. "But…in short, I traveled into the past. I spent several years there. At one point, I thought I wasn't coming back. It's where I picked up this big green bastard."

Therik gave a snort.

Stiger gestured at Salt. "It's also where I found the camp prefect and the majority of the Thirteenth."

"Your letter only mentioned the Thirteenth was in a magical stasis." Treim shook his head in dismay. Though Stiger thought he read disbelief in the other's eyes. "You went back in time yourself? That is incredible. Truly?"

"With the help of a wizard and the World Gate, it's true."

The general turned to look at Salt, who gave a curt nod.

"He most certainly did," Salt rasped. "We fought one heck of a battle there too." Salt paused, then pointed back at Stiger. "He took down a dragon by himself also. I've never seen anything like it."

"A dragon?" Treim asked, incredulous.

"Don't forget the mountain troll," Therik added. "It is very difficult to kill them, and he only had a knife when he brought that monster down."

Stiger shot both Salt and Therik an unhappy look. Recalling the past brought on memories of the farm and a sudden feeling of loss, the sting of pain. He still missed Sarai. He knew he always would. She had been a good woman, one he had planned on spending the rest of his life with. Only, She had been killed when the Vrell Valley had been raided by the Horde. Stiger had been away at the time and would never forgive himself for not being there when it mattered. He had a sudden flash of burying her burned and charred body with Theo, another friend, lost to the mists of time.

Since then, he had gained much with Taha'Leeth. She had filled the hole that had been ripped out of his heart and then some. But at the same time, he felt a terrible dread that she might not survive her wound. He did not think he could withstand losing her, not after what he'd gone through with Sarai's death ... not again. Who could?

A legionary messenger approached Treim, forestalling further conversation, for which Stiger was immensely grateful. The messenger saluted and handed the general a dispatch. The general opened it, read the contents, then said something to the messenger, who gave another salute. The legionary turned on his heel and left. There was a long moment of silence before the general stepped nearer and spoke. Something about Treim's manner told Stiger the news was bad.

"I am afraid Colonel Aetius reports that we've still not found him," Treim said. "Though we've turned the city upside down, he expects our man is no longer in it."

Stiger felt his anger spark. That was not good news, not by a mile.

"A horse is missing," Treim added.

Stiger turned to fully face the general.

"We're just learning this now?" Stiger asked. "It's been two days. Why not sooner?"

"The mounts we had," Treim explained, "were not assigned to a cavalry unit, but were an officer's personal property. There was no daily roll call and count taken, which would then have been forwarded to headquarters."

"So," Stiger said, thinking it through, "someone's personal horse has been stolen, then? Is that it?"

"Yes," Treim said, "and that's not the worst."

"Of course not," Stiger said, for he now well understood the general was intentionally cushioning the news, dolling it out slowly so that the awful blow did not come all at once. "Tell me, as bluntly as possible, if you please."

"The officer in question, a Captain Sectanus, Imperator," Treim said, "his body was found a short while ago. His armor was missing, and in its place, we found the tribune's. After checking the logs, it seems Captain Sectanus signed out of the city for a ride. This occurred shortly after the Praetorian Guard made their attempt to take you."

"He could be anywhere now." Stiger slapped his thigh. Handi had escaped. "How could this happen? We control the city, both access in and out."

"He was in officer's armor," Treim said, "and not a civilian. The guard at the gate would have let him pass, and with few questions at that."

"Bloody gods," Stiger growled. "I can't believe he survived the mob's wrath, and then managed to escape the city."

"Sectanus was a good officer," Treim said. "His father just reached senatorial rank too."

"Which means," Stiger said, "that once he learns of his son's murder, while under my command, he may blame me. He may even believe I was responsible and that the murder was intentional."

Closing his eyes for a long moment, Stiger brought his anger under control. It was threatening to slip the leash. He had to watch that, especially now.

"Technically, he was under my command," General Treim said. "But you are correct. Due to Handi, we may have turned a potential ally into an enemy."

"You mean I may have," Stiger said and then held up a hand when Treim started to protest. "This is my mess. I started it and now I have to live with the consequences of my own actions."

The sword had been right. Bloody gods.

"Nouma's dead," Eli added. "What can Handi do by himself?"

"I don't like the idea of him out there on the loose," Stiger said.

"He's just one man," Treim said.

"He's an enemy." Therik's tone was hard and unforgiving. "It is best to kill enemies, before they create new problems or come after you again. We should find him and kill him, end it now. Then you don't have to worry."

Stiger spared the orc a look. Therik was right.

"We can send a party after him," Treim suggested. "Though I feel compelled to point out that if he has any sense, the tribune's long gone, which likely means our search party will have a difficult time locating him. Handi may be a vile and detestable person, but he did not strike me as stupid."

"I bet Hux could find him," Salt said, having stepped forward and joined the conversation. "Our cavalry prefect can be very determined, when he puts his mind to it. Give the word and Hux will run him down."

Stiger was tempted to take Salt up on his suggestion. Only he knew he could not do that. His cavalry commander's attention must be focused on screening the army as it marched northward toward Mal'Zeel, not hunting a lone fugitive who had had his power and influence stripped from him. The cavalry could not be spared for such an undertaking, for they would be General Treim's and Braddock's eyes and ears, providing security against a surprise move by the confederacy. The elves would help with that too, but the cavalry would be able to range farther afield.

"Don't waste the effort," Stiger said, shaking his head slightly. "The security of the army is more important."

"An enemy is an enemy," Therik said, clearly wanting to get the last word in.

"No doubt," Stiger said, "and I've got plenty to go around. If we can run him to ground at a later time, then we will. If not, maybe we will never see or hear from him again. I'd settle for the latter."

Therik gave a disbelieving grunt to that.

"When we're done here," Stiger said, "tell Colonel Aetius to stand down. He is to stop hunting for the traitor."

"Yes, Imperator," General Treim said.

Turning his attention back to the priests, who were still singing and chanting, Stiger tapped a finger on his thigh. It never got any easier. There were always complications, headaches, and problems to be overcome. Handi was just one more enemy on a list that was sure to grow in the coming days, months, and years.

No matter how benevolent a ruler Stiger was, there would always be enemies just around the corner, waiting to pounce. What had happened with Nouma and the praetorians was not only a warning, but also a lesson to be learned. Moving forward, he had to be two steps ahead of such people. In short, he had to be more careful.

His gaze sought out Braddock, who was standing stoically before his army a few hundred yards away. Though he could easily have kept his dwarves in their encampment just outside the city, the thane had paraded his warriors in full kit and was honoring the late emperor, showing proper respect for an ally. So too was Tenya'Far with his elves. Stiger appreciated that.

When it came to the gnomes, he was not so sure on their motivation. Had Braddock forced them to attend? Or did Cragg see it as his duty to honor the late emperor, as an ally? More likely, the conniving little troublemaker thought there was some advantage to be gained by making a show of respect.

Cragg was standing before his assembled warriors. Though many of the gnomes wore multicolored armor, Cragg's was jet-black. So too was his standard. It had something to do with him being the kluge. Stiger wished he understood gnome culture better. He had gotten to know them to some degree, but for the most part, the little bastards were as much a mystery to him as they were to the dwarves.

"I believe they're ready for you, Imperator," Treim said.

Stiger looked over to see a priest approaching with Father Restus at his side. He had not noticed the singing and chanting had concluded. Both the priest and Restus stopped five feet from him and bowed respectfully.

Restus wore a cloak around his armor that was as white as the freshest snow. It had the High Father's lightning bolt emblazoned on it in gold. The priest wore white priestly robes. Beyond them, toward the funeral bier, a small fire had been started. It burned rather sullenly, smoke drifting lazily up into a clear sky. A priest, standing next to the fire, held an unlit torch. He was waiting expectantly, his eyes fixed upon Stiger.

"Father Hone," Stiger greeted, turning his attention back to the priest with Restus. He had met with the priests of the city the night before last. Though he was the most senior priest in the city and prematurely balding, Hone was only middle-aged. "I thank you for your service. Though it had been many years since I'd seen him, Tioclesion was one of my few friends in this world. I truly grieve for his loss and I appreciate all of your efforts."

"That is most kind of you, Imperator." The priest gave a bow again.

Stiger's eyes tracked back toward the funeral bier.

"It is time for you to pay your respects, Imperator," Hone said in a gentle tone, "and perform your duty as successor."

"Right then." Stiger was not looking forward to what was coming. Final goodbyes were always the most difficult and painful. "Let's get to it, then, shall we?"

"As you wish, Imperator," Hone said and stood aside to make way.

Father Restus had coached Stiger earlier in what would be expected of him. Stiger started across the field toward the funeral bier. He made sure his pace was steady and measured, knowing that all eyes would be upon him. Restus and Hone followed a few steps behind him. Everyone else remained behind, even Ruga and his men. This was something only Stiger could do.

As he approached, the priests, who had been offering prayers, drew back and formed a line behind the fire and the priest holding the torch. Stiger ignored them and stepped up to the bier. It was over ten feet tall and made of freshly cut logs. Straw had been stuffed between the logs. The smell of oil was strong, almost overpowering. It seemed the priests had doused everything with it.

Looking up, Stiger could see Tioclesion lying atop the bier. Face pale and eyes shut, he almost looked like he was asleep. His one-time childhood friend was gone. All that remained was what the elves called a shell. Stiger felt a wave of regret flow over him. The civil war that had seen his childhood friend come to power had cost Stiger so very much. He still felt pain at all that had happened so many years before. Sometimes it seemed his entire life had been filled with pain, sacrifice, and sadness, with only a few pleasant moments mixed in between.

The priests taught that the High Father challenged his followers through pain and suffering. The truth behind that was Stiger himself. He understood that. He really did. His struggles had forged him into the honed weapon he was now. Pain and suffering had made him the man he was today, a leader of men, the High Father's Champion, and the hope for the empire, the future.

Though in Lorium he was considered the emperor, Stiger knew without a doubt, no matter what Treim and Aetius thought, a faction in the senate would not see a Stiger sit on the curule chair and adorned with the crown of wreaths, ever. Blood would need to be shed before it was all said and done. And Stiger was prepared for that. The only question was … how much blood would be required to settle things?

Thoughts of the curule chair caused Stiger to recall a memory of playing hide and seek in the vast palace with Tioclesion. He remembered hiding behind the chair's marble legs, the gleam of the floor, the cold feel of it all to his hands and knees. Those days had been so simple, and without worry or adult concerns. Now, things were different. He had plenty of worries and concerns, an entire empire's worth.

As if a cloud had slipped across the sun, his thoughts darkened once again. As a boy, he had thought the world a wonderful place. Only now he knew better. It was anything but. The world he lived in was a hard one, at times callous and cold, like the marble of the palace. Some preferred to believe it was not so, turned blind eyes to the reality all around, but Stiger understood the truth. In a way, he was fighting to make this world a better place. If he won, achieved all that needed doing...could he change it? He hoped so.

Stiger's thoughts returned to Tioclesion. What had his friend fought for? He rubbed his jaw as he considered the body that would shortly be turned to ash. How much power had the man actually wielded? Handi said he and Nouma had controlled Tioclesion. How far had that control extended? Who else and what else had they power over? It was an interesting thought and one he had to be concerned over...for he could never allow anyone to gain such control or influence over him...ever. He needed to be his own man, and others would hate him for that.

He sucked in a breath, then let it out through his teeth. Stiger bowed his head respectfully. Clearing his mind, he took a moment to offer up a prayer, commending Tioclesion's soul and spirit into the High Father's loving embrace. He asked that his one-time friend have an easy crossing of the great river and a peaceful, undisturbed slumber in the next life.

"Rest well, my friend."

He looked back up and regarded the body a moment more before turning to the priest with the unlit torch. Stiger held out his hand expectantly. The priest dunked the torch into the low-burning flames. It instantly caught, hissing and spitting angrily, like an unhappy serpent pulled from its hole. The smoke that issued forth was dark and black.

He took the torch from the priest and turned back to the bier. Stiger hesitated for a long moment. He could feel the heat from the hissing flames against his cheek. He took a step closer, within arm's reach.

"Is this how I will end my days on this world?" Stiger asked himself quietly so that the priests could not hear.

"Burned by the next emperor? What will people think of me when I am gone? Will they remember me as a butcher of my own people? A heartless killer? Just another vile Stiger who seized power? Or will I be viewed as a savior?"

The mad wizard imprisoned within his sword laughed darkly. It was malevolent and sinister. Instantly, Stiger felt a wave of cold slither down his spine.

I have seen your end.

Stiger froze. Though the sword had recently begun speaking to him again, he no longer feared its power, not completely. Menos had taught him how to master his mind and gain control over the mad wizard within.

And? Stiger asked, for the imprisoned wizard had once been a master of time and space, at least that's what Thoggle, Ogg, and Menos had told him. Rarokan had once shown Stiger a vision of himself in the past, one Stiger had thought was of his ancestor, Delvaris. But it had not been. The sword had shown him the future, only, as confusing as it sounded, the vision had been his future in the past.

Are you going to tell me of my death? Torment me with it? Attempt to use it as a tool to gain some advantage? If so, you will fail.

No, I will not show you your death, Imperator.

Then why bother me, now? In this moment?

When compared to your end, Tioclesion got off easy. You will suffer greatly before you know peace.

Stiger was in no mood for games. With his mind, he shoved Rarokan back down into his prison and then slammed the door shut. He could almost sense the sword darkly laughing at him, mocking him. He thrust such counterproductive thoughts from his mind and stepped forward. Stiger touched the torch to some of the straw. So doused was it with flammable oil that flames shot outward and spread rapidly toward the body at the top. The heat increased, and with it, Stiger took an unconscious step backward. Almost casually, he tossed the torch onto the growing blaze.

"Good bye, old friend," Stiger said, "and thank you."

A man in the ranks began hammering his sword against the backside of his shield. In moments, more picked up the beat, and then all of the legionaries were doing the same. The sound of it hammered at the air, in a steady thunking rhythm. This was their way of saying goodbye to the emperor. Stiger turned around to look on his two legions. Until recently, he had been one of them, an officer.

Now, he was emperor.

"I must never forget who I am," Stiger said to himself. "I will always be an imperial legionary officer at heart... always."

He took another step back as the heat from the blaze began to grow, radiating outward. The priests started chanting in the old tongue. As the fire blazed, reaching the body atop the pyre, the chant continued. Stiger stood there, watching the fire burn. In the flames, he saw those he had left behind: Varus, Sarai, his mother... the list went on.

"All men die," Restus said, having stepped up next to him. "Death will one day... come for us all. That is assured."

"I have just been reminded of that," Stiger said, thinking on the mad wizard trapped within his blade. "Despite being the High Father's Champion and emperor, I am mortal. It is as you say, my days will eventually come to an end, much like any other."

Stiger was different now. Mortal... yet, like an elf, longer lived. That assumed the enemy did not kill him first.

"Life is a journey and death just another destination," Restus rasped. "Each soul's spark eventually fades, detaches, and returns to the High Father. We are only loaned that which makes us unique in this world…a portion of the divine. When we die, we go with it, crossing over the great river. That is what we, on this plane, call death."

Stiger thought on his sword, which over the years had taken that very spark from so many. He glanced down at it. "My sword has the ability to take what the High Father wants back."

"I know," Father Restus said, sounding saddened. "Even that which Rarokan takes and burns to manipulate events in this world…that too eventually returns to the High Father…just in a different form."

Stiger had not known that. He fell silent and turned his gaze back to the funeral pyre.

"You carry a dread weapon," Restus continued after several moments, "but it was the High Father who commanded that it be forged. It was our lord who set limits upon the wizard, an individual who thought he had none. We must have faith the High Father knew what he was doing when he had that weapon forged and the wizard locked within."

"So, I should let him take the full measure of the souls it kills? Hold nothing back from its dreadful thirst?" Stiger asked. "Let the wizard grow powerful? I think that would be dangerous, don't you?"

"I did not say that," Restus said. "I only understand the sword to be a dangerous tool, a weapon to be used when needed. Only you and you alone have the ability to control and contain Rarokan's ambitions. When it comes to the Soul Breaker, you must use your own judgment and be guided by the High Father. Just as I am guided to do what I deem necessary."

Stiger looked over at the elderly paladin and their gazes met. He wondered for a moment if the paladin understood what it meant to be the High Father's Champion.

"I am a Stiger," he said. "I too am a weapon, and where I go, death follows. I have come to accept that."

"You are the High Father's weapon on this mundane world," Restus said. "You have the ability to shape events like none other since Karus himself."

Though he understood the truth in Restus's words, he still felt a wave of unease at hearing it put so plainly. So much rested on his shoulders.

"When I go to Mal'Zeel," Stiger said, "we both know death will follow after me. With what needs to be done, I must be ruthless, uncompromising. Only the end goal matters at this point, for we are mere months away from the planes and planets aligning. When they do, the World Gate can be opened again. We cannot afford to lose, for if we do, a darkness will fall over this world. That is why I must hold nothing back and do what needs doing, no matter how distasteful. That is why I will fight to make certain it is our side, our alignment, that has the choice as to whether or not *we* open the Gate."

"And that, my son," Restus said, "is why you are his Champion, his choice for the future of us all. You will hold nothing back when it matters."

The fire gave a gushing roar as it fully consumed the funeral pyre, drawing their attention. The waves of heat rolling off the fire were intense; so too was the smoke. Both men took several steps back, then stood and watched. Stiger found himself lost in the flames. He felt the High Father's presence here this day. It seemed to be all around them, on the air itself, like a great warm blanket wrapped around one on a winter's day. Stiger found it comforting and knew the great god was watching in approval.

"It is time for you to cement the loyalty of the legions," Restus said. "That which was promised so long ago ... empire without end ... begins here, this day."

The paladin's words broke the spell. Stiger blinked. Tioclesion's body could no longer be seen within the flames. He wondered how long he had stood there. Had it been just moments or longer?

He looked over and saw General Treim standing with both Eagle-bearers. The general held two thick pieces of rounded wood that had been painted white. They were legate batons. Each had been carved from an oak, shaped, smoothed, and polished before being painted white.

Standing just behind Treim were Legates Oney and Theego. It had not been a pretty moment when Salt had learned that he was to be promoted. The man had been deeply unhappy by the move. But, in the end, he had accepted it. Salt had understood the necessity of having a highly experienced professional officer in command of the legion.

Stiger shared one last look with Restus. "An empire without end."

The paladin gave him a nod, and with that, Stiger started over toward them, leaving the burning funeral pyre behind, along with Father Restus. He stopped before the general.

"The legions present you their honor," Treim said loudly.

Those in the nearest ranks could hear him. Those unfortunates farther away would only be able to see what was happening. And yet, they also would know what was transpiring. What was about to be performed was a ritual as old at the empire itself. Perhaps even more ancient, Stiger considered, now that he knew the Roman Empire had been real and was not just legend. Karus had been from Rome, a true Roman. Which meant, he, as a descendent of the great man, had Roman blood running through his veins.

"I stand by to receive their honor and return it," Stiger said. "The legates may approach."

Salt and Theego stepped forward and up to Stiger. Theego was a hard-looking man, muscular and compact. His forearms bore the telltale marks of years of arms training. He was a fighter, Stiger was sure of it. From the man's eyes, Stiger could tell he'd seen his fair share of hard fighting. They had met the day before and Stiger had been impressed with Theego.

Both legates were at attention. They saluted.

"I present Third Legion," Theego said first. "I swear my loyalty and that of my men to you, Imperator. We will defend the empire with our lives. In the High Father's name, I swear it so."

"I present Thirteenth Legion," Salt said. "I swear my loyalty and that of my men to you, Imperator. We will fight for you and defend the empire. In the High Father's name, I swear it so."

"I have no doubt." Stiger turned to Treim and gave a nod. Treim stepped forward and handed over the two batons, then stepped back a pace. Stiger glanced down at the two white batons in his hands. The wood had been polished completely smooth. The High Father's Eagle had been carved onto both, as had the god's lightning bolt. The work done was exquisite. One baton had *XIII* fashioned into it on the bottom and the other *III*. On Stiger's orders, both had been made by a master carpenter in the city. The man had done excellent work.

"With these batons, I grant you both a measure of my imperium." Stiger turned his attention to the two legates. "With imperium comes the power to do your duty for the empire. Do you understand this?"

"I do, Imperator," Theego said.

"Understood, sir," Salt said.

"Do not ever hesitate," Stiger said, "to do what you feel is right and in service of the empire."

Stiger held out the Third's baton to Theego, who, without hesitation, took it. The man's hard look grew sterner. By accepting the honor, Theego was tying himself inextricably to Stiger. There would be no turning back, no returning the baton. If he broke his word, forever after, his honor would be tarnished, as would that of his family's name. He might be tolerated in polite society, but people would always have their doubts, and the whispers behind his back would forever be there. Stiger knew what that was like. It was clear Theego understood as well.

Salt took the baton when Stiger offered the Thirteenth's to him. Salt studied it, turning it over slowly in his hand. Then, he looked up. Stiger was surprised to see tears in the old veteran's eyes.

"You've gone and done it," Salt said. "You've made me a gentleman, sir…you know I was born in the slums. A gentleman? A noble?"

"Aye, that I have," Stiger said, amused and enjoying the moment. Salt was a good man, the embodiment of what a legionary should be, and finally a friend. "I don't care where you were born. It is the man you are that I care about. The service you have rendered the empire is beyond compare, as is the sacrifice you made by choosing to go into stasis and giving up all that you had known. Salt, you have earned this. There is no doubt in my mind. Bear this imperium with pride."

"Thank you, sir," Salt said. "I love the Thirteenth and the empire. I will not let you down. You have my word on that."

"I know," Stiger said. "Take care of the boys for me, for I love them too."

Salt cleared his throat before answering. "I will, sir."

Stiger gave a nod to the Eagle-bearers. "Bring forth your Eagles."

Salt and Theego turned to look back on the two Eagle-bearers and stepped aside. Both men moved forward and lowered their Eagles before their emperor.

The sight of an Eagle always moved Stiger. Before him were two Eagles under which he had personally fought. He reached forward and rested his palm upon the Third's Eagle. He missed the Third, just as he missed Seventh Company.

"I give you Third Legion's honor and that of the empire, Imperator," the Third's bearer said. Stiger recognized him, but he did not know the man's name.

Stiger took the standard into his hands. He was about to speak but was suddenly overcome with emotion. How many had served under this Eagle? How many had died for what it represented? Varus and others of Seventh Company had lost their lives under his command, all while he'd been attached to Third Legion.

In a manner of speaking, those who had given their lives *were* the Eagle. So too were the men who currently served. They would continue to fight under this standard. It was made of wood, the top of which had been shaped into a fierce-looking bird of prey and then painted over in gold. Each imperial Eagle was slightly different. This one clutched a fish in one of its claws and its mouth was open in an exultant scream. The implication was clear...the hunt had been successful.

Under this Eagle, the men of Third Legion would fight for the empire, the High Father, and most importantly, he understood, they would fight for each other...for that was what comrades did when things truly got ugly. And they would do it all in the name of the empire.

Stiger felt a tear run down his cheek. He cleared his throat and raised the Eagle high up into the air, studying it under the fading light of the day. He turned his gaze to the bearer.

"What is your name?"

"Santuus," the legionary said.

"I give you back Third Legion's honor, my honor, and that of the empire," Stiger said. "The High Father's honor goes with it. Protect and guard this standard with your life."

"I will protect and guard this Eagle with my life, Imperator," Santuus said.

Stiger handed the Eagle back to Santuus.

"Beck," Stiger said, turning to the Thirteenth's bearer. The man had been part of Stiger's company and had been with him the day they'd found the standard in Delvaris's tomb.

"Sir," Beck said.

"I bet you never thought to see yourself here, eh?"

"No, sir," Beck said. "And I bet you did not see yourself here either, sir."

Stiger gave a chuckle, then sobered. Beck got the hint.

"I give you the Thirteenth Legion's honor and that of the empire, Imperator," Beck said, offering it up.

Stiger took the standard into his hands. Again, he found himself overcome with emotion.

"I give you back the Thirteenth's honor, my honor, and that of the empire," Stiger said. "The High Father's honor goes with it. Protect and guard this standard with your life."

"I will protect and guard this Eagle with my life, Imperator," Beck said.

Stiger handed the Eagle back to Beck.

With that, both legions erupted into a thunderous cheer. The legions were now formally his. They were sworn to serve him and the empire. Behind him, Tioclesion's funeral pyre continued to burn furiously.

"And now comes the hard part," Stiger breathed to himself as he turned his gaze northward, "the taking of my empire."

CHAPTER FIVE

Placing a hand on the side of the sick tent, Stiger stopped, hesitating to enter. The fabric under his hand was coarse and rough. He dreaded facing what he knew waited just inside. This was one battle he could not fight, one to which he was only a helpless bystander. That was an uncomfortable feeling, one he did not like.

Dog nosed his leg. Stiger glanced down at the animal, who looked right back up at him with sad brown eyes that carried so much expression. He held the naverum's gaze for a long moment. An order snapped somewhere off in the distance caused him to look behind them both.

The sun was just coming up and the sky had lightened considerably. Stiger was in the heart of the fortified legionary encampment that had been constructed a half mile from Lorium. The encampment spread out in all directions, tents by the thousands. He never ceased being amazed at all that was fit, or really crammed, within the turf walls: the orderly streets, training grounds, mess areas, latrines, supply depots, leather maker tents, numerous smithies, depots, animal pens ... the list went on and on. It took an incredible amount of effort and support to keep a legion operational, so much so that each encampment became the equivalent of a small city.

Though there was plenty of noise on the air, it was still relatively quiet. Even when the legion slept, no encampment was ever truly devoid of noise. There was always someone calling to another, a challenge shouted, the clattering of armor or a hammer at work.

Legionaries learned to sleep amidst such continual noise. Stiger himself had long since mastered the ability to nap whenever the opportunity presented itself. He had once managed a few hours' rest while his company was stood down during an active assault on his encampment's walls. Sleep in the army was always a precious commodity. You took it when and where you could get it.

On a normal day, the morning horn would have already been sounded. This, however, was not a normal day. After everything the men had gone through to get to Lorium, and the latest battle against the confederacy, they were being allowed the rare privilege of sleeping in, given a well-earned extra two hours of sleep. That did not sound like much, but for the average legionary it was more than enough.

Once they were up, rousted from their bedrolls, the day would begin for the thousands of legionaries and auxiliaries that occupied this fortified encampment. Things would go from being relatively peaceful to a bustling hive of regimented and closely supervised activity.

First the men would parade. Roll call by century would be taken. The count of those present, in the sick tents, or absent for whatever reason, would be reported on up to the cohort commander and then forwarded to headquarters. The men would be set to maintaining and cleaning their equipment. They would parade once again and an inspection would follow, not only of their person, but the legionaries' communal tents. For those who did not measure up to the legion's exacting standards, a punishment charge would be issued. They would also be sent back to correct the deficiency. Something no veteran legionary wanted to do.

Only after the cohort and century areas were policed and straightened up would the men be fed. The morning meal for the day was mush, a standard porridge of millet and chopped fruit that had been dried. Stiger had always found it quite tasteless. He hated the stuff, almost as much as he despised salt pork. Yet it kept the men marching.

Once fed, the men would be put to work, for idle soldiers were trouble waiting to happen. And the officers would see that their men were far from idle. Headquarters would assign each cohort work for the day, whether that was arms or formation drilling, enhancing the encampment's fortifications, standing watch on the walls or performing sentry duty, distributing the supplies of captured food stores to the hungry citizens of Lorium, or patrolling the city or the surrounding region. In the army, there was always something that needed doing and plenty of men to see that it got done right.

The wind gusted, rustling the fabric of the tent. The air was cool, crisp, cold even. Sourly, Stiger glanced up at the sky. Overhead, it had clouded over, as if in promise of a coming rain, perhaps even a storm. Though he did not think it felt or smelled like one was coming on.

Despite that, he was warm, primarily because he wore his bearskin cloak. It was something he was incredibly fond of. Even in the harshest of weather it kept him warm and comfortable.

Though they were still in the south, winter had arrived. The incessant and continual rains that plagued the region had, for the most part, ended. The ground had dried out and hardened, allowing large-scale combat operations. Still, it was not quite cold, and where he was, it likely would not become so. Lorium was just too far south.

The winters were fairly temperate. Farther north, toward the capital, there would be snow, and that was where Stiger would be heading this day. He would be leaving behind his army. It was why he had on his heavy cloak. The time was fast approaching when he would climb onto a dragon and depart, soaring up into the clouds.

Having served in the far north against the Rivan, he had seen more snow than he ever cared to admit. Northern winters were just plain brutal. There was just no other way to describe it but as a miserable experience. It wasn't just the snow the men had to struggle against, which frequently fell feet at a time, but the bitter cold, which stung and froze exposed skin.

The pervasive cold seemed to sap the energy from even the strongest of men. Doing anything took more effort, more energy. There had been times during the darkest months of winter when the temperature had dropped to the point where it seemed to steal breath from the lungs. When they weren't huddled around meager fires, or standing watch, the men amused themselves by spitting into the air. The spit had frozen solid before it hit the ground. It had been so bitterly cold, any who were not careful were at serious risk for freezing.

Stiger had known men who had frozen to death or lost fingers and toes to the cold. The north was a harsh and unforgiving land, a place where only the hardiest of people could manage to survive. The Rivan, once the most dangerous enemy he had ever faced, had not only survived but thrived in such weather.

The legions, when they pushed north, despite early success, had been ill prepared when the cold and snows had come. The men suffered terribly as a result. Thousands were lost to the cold alone, and even more to enemy action. Worse, the imperial army had almost faced complete destruction at the hands of the enemy, with two entire legions shattered.

Stiger himself had almost died, not once, but several times. He had come perilously close to closing the book on his own personal story.

It had taken several years, but eventually the legions had been able to adapt to the brutal winter conditions. That was the real strength of the empire. When the going got tough, the legion never quit. And if there was a defeat, the empire always came back, with more legions filled with hard men spoiling for a fight.

Dog nudged at him again, more insistent. He looked back down at the animal and felt himself scowl. Dog snapped his jaws and gave a low growl that caused Stiger's escort of four, who had taken up position a few feet away, to look around.

The animal gave a bark and then snapped his jaws with a clicking sound. Dog seemed quite insistent, impatient.

"Alright, I'll stop dragging my feet." Stiger let out a long breath. He'd been dreading going in. He pulled the tent flap aside. Ducking, he stepped through into the tent. The light was dim, for only a single lamp hung from the ceiling.

The tent was warmer than the outside and smelled strongly of herbs that burned in a brazier along the back wall. Unlike the other sick tents in the medical compound, only one patient was present, his wife.

Venthus had been seated on a stool. Next to him was a cot, upon which lay Taha'Leeth. She had been wrapped up in a heavy blanket. Only her head, neck, and arms were exposed. The terrible wound she had received was concealed by the blanket. Stiger could see the small bulge along her side where she had been heavily bandaged.

A small table lay within arm's reach of Stiger's slave. It held a bowl filled with water. Several cloths had been laid upon it, as was a pitcher and a clay mug. A bucket underneath held soiled bandages, thick with dried blood.

"Master." Stiger's slave rose stiffly to his feet, more through age than anything else. He bowed with his usual show of respect.

Stiger did not hear Venthus greet him. Despite the warmth of the cloak, ice abruptly coursed through his veins, seeming to freeze him in place by the entrance flap. His breath caught in his throat. Though he had spent several hours with her the evening before, seeing his wife this way was incredibly painful. He did not like it one bit. She looked so still and pale, he thought she might have expired during the night. Then he spotted the telltale steady rise and fall of her chest.

Relief flooded through his heart and suddenly he was able to move once again. The paralysis was gone. He took two wooden steps forward. She was so very pale and frail-looking, it tore at him. Stiger had become accustomed to seeing her strong, confident, and full of life that it was still a shock to see her on death's doorstep. He longed to hear her voice, feel the touch of her fingers against his skin, the warmth of her naked body pressed close against his, her soft lips…

"How is she?" Stiger asked in a near strangled whisper, pulling his eyes away from his wife. "Has she shown any improvement?"

Venthus clasped both hands before him. "I am sorry, but no. Since last evening, her condition remains unaltered, master."

As he turned his gaze back to Taha'Leeth, Stiger did not immediately respond. Ignoring Venthus, Dog moved around Stiger and padded up to her. He laid his big, shaggy head upon the side of her cot and against her arm. He licked her hand, then whined softly. It was a pathetic sound and made Stiger feel even worse.

"The wound she took would have killed anyone else," Venthus said in a tired and weary tone. The old slave blew out an almost ragged breath before continuing. "She is strong-willed. I believe, given time to heal, she will recover. I have no idea on whether it will be a full recovery or…"

Venthus gave a shrug of his shoulders as Stiger looked back over at him.

"Or there will be complications," Stiger finished.

"That is certainly one way to put it," Venthus said. "The blade went in deep and she lost a lot of blood. There is no telling what, if any, long-term damage was caused."

"And the baby?" Stiger asked.

Venthus said nothing.

Sucking in a deep breath, Stiger considered Venthus. The man was more than his slave. He followed a god that was not in the High Father's alignment or the enemy's. His god was involved in the Last War somehow, but he stood apart. At least that was how Venthus had explained it. From Delvaris, Stiger had inherited not only Venthus, but the relationship as well. And it was a complicated one.

At times, it had proven a mixed blessing and, truth be told, Stiger was not wholly comfortable with it. But Venthus had proven to be a man of his word and, once pledged, had shown himself to be incredibly loyal. More than once, he had demonstrated his loyalty in a manner which could not be mistaken. And he was doing it yet again, by caring selflessly for Taha'Leeth. Stiger doubted Venthus had left her side since he'd been away. The loyalty, in the end, was all that mattered to Stiger…well, that and the arrangement, for the two of them could never be friends. But they could respect one another and fulfill their mutual obligations to one another's cause.

"Tenya'Far mentioned he would be sending over one of his surgeons," Stiger said.

"He came," Venthus said, "and examined her wound. He also changed out her bandages and put a poultice on. He claims it will guard against infection. Beyond that, there was little he could do for her. He said as much. I expect him to return around midday. If they had a paladin of Tanithe..." Venthus rubbed at his eyes. "Or if the warden were here... well, that would be a different matter and make things easy on us both."

"The what-ifs again," Stiger said to himself.

"The surgeon explained that when elves become gravely injured, they go into a state of deep sleep, almost like how some animals hibernate. It is supposed to help speed the body's healing process." Venthus glanced over at Taha'Leeth. "He confirmed she was in such a state. He said he could feel her soul working at repairing the damage."

Stiger felt a stab of worry, for he knew this from his time living with the elves. "Sometimes the damage is too great to fix and they do not come out of it and simply die."

"I am no doctor," Venthus said. "You know that, and yet I am not without medical knowledge. I feel she will recover. And no... my god is not telling me that."

"I pray you are right," Stiger said.

"I pray as well," Venthus said, "for I have bet everything upon you. And you know my master is an unforgiving one."

Stiger understood Venthus was not referring to him, but his god. The man had only one true master and Stiger was most assuredly not it.

"We will not fail," Stiger said. "We cannot. For if we do... we all lose."

"Truth."

A strange expression overcame the slave. His gaze went to the tent wall and became strangely unfocused. A moment later, he looked back at Stiger with distaste and his expression twisted slightly. "There is a paladin of the High Father in the camp. He came with you."

It was not a question, but a statement of fact.

"Yes," Stiger said. "Father Restus. He is traveling with me to the capital. We will be departing just as soon as I am done here."

"He is strong with *will* and faith. So much so, I can taste it."

"As head of his order," Stiger said, "I would think he would have to be, or at least should be. Don't you?"

Stiger suddenly realized he knew little about the order of the High Father that the paladins served. He scowled slightly with the thought. Though he had known several paladins, they were still, in a way, a mystery. Yes, they served the High Father and were the guardians of long-forgotten knowledge, but beyond that, he knew very little about them.

So far, their purposes had aligned with his. He had relied upon them and taken their cooperation for granted. In fact, as Champion, he now expected it. Stiger realized that was dangerous. What if they ever disagreed or Restus felt he was making the wrong decision and refused to support him? What then? Stiger's mind raced. What about the rest of the church? The High Priest and everyone else who wore the holy cloth? Would they give him their unconditional support? Or would there be limits? Those questions concerned him greatly. What if some refused to accept him as the emperor and High Father's Champion?

"Though Father Thomas honored it," Venthus said, "my arrangement might not extend to Father Restus."

"I don't think you have anything to fear there," Stiger said. "Restus seems to know nearly everything that occurred in the past. It would not surprise me if he was well aware of your bargain."

Venthus regarded him for several long moments before giving a slow nod. Under the dim lamplight, the slave's eyes glittered darkly. "I have no wish to fight him. You know the truth of my words. He may not."

"I will see that it does not come to that."

The slave gave another nod. "That would be much appreciated, for I would be forced to kill him. And I would do so without hesitation."

Stiger felt himself scowl at Venthus.

"You will watch over her while I am gone?" Stiger asked, though he knew he need not have done so. It just felt better asking, making certain. Stiger wanted reassurance, for he felt wretched about leaving her.

"My word is my bond," Venthus said simply. "As such, you know I will lay down my life for hers. Though I suspect we both know I likely will not have to make such a sacrifice. If more assassins come, whether they be elvenkind or not"—Venthus gave a dark chuckle—"they will find a nasty surprise waiting, several nasty surprises."

"You have summoned your pets?" Stiger asked. He had not explicitly forbidden Venthus from doing so. It had, in a way, been an unspoken understanding between them that he would not.

Venthus gave a nod and smiled. It was a smile without warmth, one filled with a terrible hunger that Stiger found not just uncomfortable, but unsettling.

Glancing around the tent, he saw nothing, but Stiger knew they were there, hiding and concealed in the shadows...watching. He closed his eyes, cleared his mind, and reached out to touch the High Father's power that burned within him.

His connection with the High Father was a shining, fiery, white sun in the darkness. Over the last few months, the fire had grown in intensity, and with it, Stiger's strength of *will* had also increased. With each passing day, he felt himself growing in power and mastery of what the High Father had given him.

As he touched it, he felt his god's power, the warmth, the love. A sense of serene calm settled over him. It was akin to a loving embrace from a parent to a child. All sense of regret and pain at leaving washed away. He felt content, happy, loved. There was no other way to describe the feeling of being so close to his god ... it was pure and utter bliss.

And now, without opening his eyes, Stiger could feel the presence of Venthus's pets close at hand. They were a disturbance to the peaceful bliss. There were four of them and they were dark, vile things. They seemed to squirm under the gaze of his mind's eye and the High Father's power, edging away, attempting to shift back out of phase, to flee this realm. Only Venthus's *will* kept them on this plane of existence, holding them firmly in place. Stiger could even see Venthus himself, a dark stain upon the world, nearly as vile and black as his pets.

Oddly, Stiger felt no urge from the High Father to deal with the pets ... to send them on their way. Nor was there any push to confront Venthus. The message was clear. The pets were being tolerated, as was Venthus ... accepted even.

Some sort of an accord had been made between their respective gods. Of that much he was certain. With effort, Stiger released his hold on the High Father's power and opened his eyes, breathing in deeply as he did so.

The feeling of having lost something dear struck deeply at his heart as the connection was broken and wrenched away. Stiger almost sobbed as he blinked, looking around. The lamplight inside the tent suddenly seemed incredibly bright.

"I wish you would not do that." Venthus's voice was strained, as if he were lifting something that took effort. "It is taking considerable *will* to hold them here. Accessing your *power* like that makes my pets uncomfortable and nervous, more difficult to contain. I think we can both agree it would be better if I did not lose my control over them."

"You are right. My apologies," Stiger said.

With Venthus and his pets about, Taha'Leeth was better guarded than if an entire cohort had stood guard on the tent, rather than the century that had been assigned. If another attempt was made, and assassins got by the guard, Venthus's pets would tear the attackers apart, literally, and then likely set about eating the bodies. He had witnessed that happen and had no wish to see it again, ever.

"I should be going with you," Venthus said plainly. "My talents will be of use to you in Mal'Zeel." The slave jerked a thumb across his throat. "I could easily handle some of your enemies, make things somewhat easier for you in taking your throne. No one would know it was murder. It could be arranged as an accident, or a death by natural causes. I could help ease you onto the throne."

"No doubt," Stiger said, "but I dare not take you, not yet. Our success is not just tied to me, but to her as well. You well know that. I need you here, watching my wife, seeing her safe from threat."

Venthus let out a breath full of regret and disappointment. His eyes went to Taha'Leeth and the cot. "You should have let me summon my pets sooner. It might have made a difference."

"I appreciate your efforts." Stiger decided not to take the bait that had been dangled. Summoning the pets was always a risk. Stiger also had his doubts whether Venthus could manage to sustain them in this world for an extended period. The man appeared worn, haggard, and run down. Stiger well understood, it was not just lack of sleep, but the effort of maintaining his pets on this plane ... forcing them to remain in a place they wanted nothing to do with. Should he lose control, the pets would vent their rage on those nearest for a time, before returning home.

"The noctalum and I are doing everything we can to make her comfortable. It is up to Taha'Leeth now. Her body needs time to heal."

"You speak of Currose?" Stiger asked.

"She checks in on your wife several times a day," Venthus said. "Even though she herself is still healing from the wounds inflicted by Castor's minion, Currose loans some of her *will*. It seems to help." Venthus paused, suddenly becoming animated. The haggard look faded slightly. "I never thought such a thing possible. Not once in a thousand years did I consider it. Noctalum are truly masters of *will*, beyond anything I ever imagined. This is something I will have to research, study. I might even be able to replicate it, given sufficient time. The possibilities are endless ..."

Stiger's gaze traveled back to the cot. Dog was still there, his head resting on the cot. The sight of his wife brought on a wave of such terrible anguish that it almost physically hurt.

"I will give you some privacy." Venthus seemed to sense the change in mood and his excitement faded. "Before I go ... I want you to take this."

Stiger looked over. In the palm of his hand, Venthus held a small clay vial with no apparent opening where one would normally be.

"What is it?"

"A pet," Venthus said, "or more correctly what is called a wraith. Think of it as a more dangerous pet, one I would not normally attempt to summon."

Stiger did not reach out to take the vial. He felt uncomfortable doing so, for he sensed a malevolent darkness residing in the vial.

"Since I can't go with you," Venthus said, "I am giving you something that might help...in a time of need, a desperate moment."

"Oh?" Stiger was still hesitant. He was not quite sure what a wraith was...heck, he wasn't even sure what the pets were...only that they were evil things.

"When you have need," Venthus said, "crush it in your right hand...only your right hand. Once you do, you free the creature from imprisonment. The wraith will be yours to command and will attack whoever or whatever you wish. It will only remain on this plane for a short span of heartbeats...then it shall return home, to the Third Level. Its appearance might shock, but be quick on sending it to attack. Just point or tell it what you want it to go after and it will. The point is not to hesitate too long, or you will have wasted your chance, understand?"

"How many heartbeats?" Stiger asked. "How long will it remain on this plane?"

"A count of thirty at most, maybe less," Venthus said, his palm still out. "That is more than enough for it to kill several of your kind, maybe even take on a dragon. Who knows? Only use it if the need is dire. Now take it, before I change my mind...for I went to a lot of trouble to obtain it."

Stiger reached out and took the vial. The clay was warm to the touch, radiating heat from within. He looked back up. "The wraith is inside?"

"Yes," Venthus said. "Remember … right hand only."

"And if I use my left?"

"Then it will finish you," Venthus said. "You would be committing instant suicide. I would not recommend that."

"And if the vial breaks another way?" Stiger asked. "Say I drop it by accident or fall on it?"

"It will not break," Venthus said. "At least it shouldn't. The vial has been crafted magically to shatter the seal only in one's hand. I doubt there are any others like it left. The wraith has been trapped within since the Age of Miracles. When it comes out, I expect it will be very irritated at having been locked away in a cage for so long." Venthus paused, eyeing the vial in Stiger's hand for a long moment. "I only had one other like it and when I used it … let us just say it was something to see, a sight I shall never forget."

With that, Venthus moved toward the tent flap. He looked back. "Use it only if you need to. It is an artifact not to be expended lightly."

"Thank you," Stiger said, looking over. He slipped the vial into a pocket in his cloak. "Thank you for everything you've done."

"Can I get you anything, master?" Venthus asked, raising his voice and slipping back into the role of his slave. He held open the flap to the tent, prepared to exit. "Some wine, perhaps? Food before your long journey?"

"No," Stiger said. "You have done more than enough. I will be only a few moments. You can return to your duties once I've gone."

"Very well, master." With that, Venthus bowed and ducked out of the tent, letting the flap fall back into place and leaving Stiger alone with Taha'Leeth, Dog, and the pets.

He moved toward the cot. As he knelt, Dog shifted aside for him. He reached out and took her hand in his. It was cold to the touch, clammy. Before, she had radiated heat, now...

"Gods."

Despite what Venthus felt, he knew she could still die. That frightened him more than anything ever had. He suspected that without Currose's assistance and intervention, Taha'Leeth would have expired and passed from this world. He owed the noctalum a debt he could never repay. Still, it might not have been enough.

With his newfound longevity, he could potentially live centuries alone, without her. That in and of itself was a painful thought, a torment beyond imagining. He did not even want to consider it, knew he could not. She was truly his soulmate; he felt that with all his heart. They were meant to be together. She had to live... for without her, he could not.

As if reading his thoughts, Dog gave a low whine and placed his shaggy head upon both of their hands.

"I know, boy." Stiger reached up with his free hand and rubbed the dog's head. "Don't I know it."

His gaze traveled back to Taha'Leeth's face. Though exceedingly pale, he found her so beautiful his heart ached. Her red hair had been brushed straight and laid over her right shoulder. He wondered who had done it. Venthus? Currose? In the end, it did not matter. She was being looked after, cared for. Taha'Leeth was in good hands. When he left, he would take comfort in that. He had to.

"I have to leave." Stiger's throat caught with the admission. He did not know if she could hear him, but he felt the need to explain anyway. "Gods, I don't want to go, but

I must. As incredible as it sounds, I am the emperor. I must go to secure my throne. Without the might of the empire, we will be unable to stop the confederacy and ultimately do what needs to be done. I also need to go to find the World Gate Key...wherever it is." Stiger paused and, with some effort, cleared his throat. He felt the stinging prick of tears not yet fully formed. "While I am gone, Venthus and Currose will watch over you. They will care for you, help you get better."

He fell silent for several heartbeats, feeling intense frustration born of feeling helpless. It was in her hands now, not his...

"By the High Father and Tanithe, live. Fight." He gripped her hand in his, squeezing. "Don't you dare think of crossing over the great river without me. Do you hear me, Taha'Leeth? Fight to live, damn you. Come back to me."

She did not respond or stir. There wasn't even a flicker of her eyelids. Stiger's heart almost broke at the lack of reaction. He bowed his head and offered up a silent prayer to the High Father, asking...begging for her speedy recovery. He felt a warming of his connection with his god, but not much more. That only added to his frustration, but he knew he had to have faith. He had to have faith in his god and hers.

"Surely there must be a plan," Stiger said aloud. He kept telling himself that. But...had the enemy ruined or damaged the plan? Stiger just did not know. That was the most frustrating part...not knowing. It was maddening.

The tent flap was pulled aside. Stiger looked over as Eli entered. His friend let the flap fall back into place, and with it, once again the light inside the tent dimmed. Eli moved over to him. The elf's expression, as he took in Taha'Leeth, was one of intense sadness and feeling. He placed a hand on Stiger's shoulder.

He and Eli had been through so much together, just having him here was a comfort. Stiger appreciated his presence. Eli was his best friend, someone he knew he could always count upon, who would be there for him when he needed it, just as Stiger would be there for him. Over the years they had supported each other and forged a strong bond between them, one that was unshakable.

After a time, Eli broke the silence.

"I know you do not wish to leave," the elf said. "Were she my mate, I would not want to either. But, my friend, it is time. No matter how painful, we must both take our leave."

He was correct. Stiger did not want to go. Doing so felt like a betrayal. And yet, duty compelled him to depart. His duty to the empire and his god was a higher calling. With effort, Stiger separated his hand from hers and stood. He regarded Taha'Leeth for a prolonged moment before leaning forward and placing a kiss upon her forehead. Again, there was no response, no flicker of recognition.

"Bloody gods." His anger sparked, igniting its way toward a vengeful fury. Stiger clenched a fist. He felt like hitting something. Turning, he moved toward the tent flap, with Dog and Eli following. As he pulled the flap aside, he glanced back at his wife ... one last time, soaking her in. His anger became terrible, almost a living thing.

Rarokan had no part in feeding his rage, for that mad wizard was still locked within his prison and Stiger was unwilling to let him out. This rage was all Stiger, and with it, the High Father's power within him surged slightly, the white fire burning bright. Without needing to search, he knew Venthus's pets were stirring, edging away again. Stiger swore a silent oath to make the Cyphan pay for what they had done, Veers especially. That dark paladin would die by Stiger's hand.

With that last thought, he stepped out into the morning sunlight. His guard waited, as did Venthus. The slave had a strained look on his face. Stiger nodded once to Venthus, more an apology than anything else for upsetting the pets again, and then started down the street with a purpose. Eli and Dog followed. His guard trailed a few feet behind.

Men who were up and about for whatever reason stepped aside, snapped to attention, and saluted as he passed. Stiger hardly noticed them. His mind was focused on what lay ahead. The empire came first, then the confederacy. He moved from one street to the next, until he came to a large, open field of trampled grass that had been set aside for drill.

Two of the dragons that had come with the Vass waited. Both were lying down. They were massive creatures, but not as large as a noctalum. Still, Stiger found himself deeply impressed with their size. They were ferocious in their own right and at the same time fearsomely beautiful.

Men were secured to their backs or were busy tying themselves and supplies down in preparation for flight. All wore heavy cloaks, for the dragons had told them it would soon become cold, frigid even, as they traveled northward, much faster than a horse ever could.

Ruga's entire century would be going with him. Stiger spotted Restus, Tiro, and Ruga amongst them, as well as Therik, who looked mightily uncomfortable. The orc was already strapped down. The centurion and sergeant were walking along the back of one of the dragons, checking each man to make sure they were secure.

Stiger stopped and looked back at his personal guard. "Go see your centurion and find your places. Get yourselves situated."

"Yes, sir," one of the men said. He offered Stiger a crisp salute. "Come on, boys, let's get moving."

We are waiting on you, human. I hope you are ready.

Stiger turned to look. It was Inex who had spoken in his mind, the dragon he would be riding. He started forward again. As he approached with Dog and Eli, the dragon's great head lifted off the ground and swung around to look at him. There had been no accusation in the tone, just a statement of fact.

"I had business to attend to," Stiger said.

I understand, human, the dragon said with sudden feeling...sympathy even. It caught Stiger off guard and took him a moment to recover from the sudden rush of emotion the creature had sent his way. *We all wish your mate a swift recovery. Many of our kind have lost loved ones, mates, children... in this long war. We understand what you are going through.*

"Thank you," Stiger said as he came closer. "I appreciate your sentiment."

We suffer so that some future generation does not have to.

Stiger thought that a fine way of looking at their struggle. He liked it.

"To make the world a better place," Stiger said.

Yes, you understand correctly.

Salt was waiting by the dragon's massive side. The legate saluted him as he came up. Stiger returned the salute.

"Your pack is secured above, sir."

"I will see you in a few weeks," Stiger said. "Do you have any questions on your orders?"

"No, sir," Salt said. "The orders are clear and straightforward. Two days' rest, then a hard march for Mal'Zeel. I am to follow General Treim's orders as if they were your own."

"That sounds about right," Stiger said. "If it comes to trouble or a fight, you can trust the general. I would ask that you put your faith in him. He is a superb tactician and leader. As difficult as it is to imagine, he has commanded more fights and battles than you and I combined. He's a professional and knows what he's about."

"Yes, sir," Salt said. "I understand. No worries. He is in command. I am sure we will get on just fine, sir. We will be right as rain."

Pleased, Stiger gave a nod. "I expected no less. Look after Ikely and Severus for me and my wife."

"I will, sir."

"Thank you."

"Good luck, sir. I will see you when we get to Mal'Zeel."

"You too." Stiger gripped an armored scale. He began to pull himself up. Dog gave what sounded like a frustrated bark. He looked back and stopped in mid-climb. Stiger considered the animal for a long moment.

"You want to come with me?" Stiger asked.

Tail wagging, the big dog gave an enthusiastic bark.

"Right then," Stiger said. "Salt, get some men and rope, straps, whatever." Stiger pointed toward Dog. "He will need to be lifted up and secured. See that he also has a blanket for added warmth."

Dog's tail began wagging furiously, so much so, it shook his entire body. He gave a clipped bark.

"Yes, sir." Salt moved off, shouting at several men who were standing nearby, clearly waiting should assistance be required. Close on his heels, Dog followed after the legate. Stiger watched them as they crossed the field toward the men.

In a way, leaving felt like he was closing the door on a chapter in his life. A new path lay ahead for him, almost a new beginning. Only Stiger did not know if he was ready for it. Yet he was prepared and resolved to boldly travel down that path. As he had always done, he would do whatever was required to see the job done and duty satisfied. There was no question in his mind about that.

"Do you think the senate will be more impressed with your dog?" Eli asked with a smirk. He then gestured at Therik, who was mounted on the other dragon, a male named Tyven. "Or the orc?"

That is no simple dog, Inex said, *and I am already impressed.*

"They better be impressed with me," Stiger growled. "For if they aren't, by the time I am done, they will be."

With that, he continued pulling himself up the side of the dragon.

CHAPTER SIX

Leaning over slightly, Stiger gazed out past the dragon's extended left wing at the snow-blanketed land far below. The air was bitingly cold. It whistled and rushed around him, making his eyes water, blurring his vision slightly. With a gloved hand, he tugged his bearskin cloak tighter about his person and then made sure the scarf covering his face and ears was secure. He did not want it to come loose and fly off.

The morning sky for the most part was clear. There were only a handful of clouds in view. These were brilliantly lit in hues of red and pink from the sun that had just peaked over the horizon to the east.

Everything below seemed to be made in miniature. Farms and isolated buildings moved slowly by, almost as if he and the others he traveled with were on a ship and some strange and distant coast was sliding past. Only he was not on a ship, but mounted on a dragon, soaring high over the land.

Wings also outstretched and riding on an invisible current of air to his right, Tyven flew several dozen yards away from Inex. All of Ruga's men, as well as Tiro, Therik, and Restus, were bundled up against the cold. He figured they were just as cold and miserable as everyone else.

Turning his gaze away from Tyven, Stiger looked down once again. The view was not only commanding, but breathtaking. He could see towns and villages off in the distance, along with roads crisscrossing the land. Some were small, meandering local roads, while others were wide, arrow-straight arteries, clearly imperial highways. Looking like ants, people moved along these snow-covered roadways afoot, in carts, on wagons, and even by horseback.

It did not surprise Stiger that at such an early hour, the roads of the empire were busy with commerce for the coming day. Living miles from the nearest village, town, or city, many would start out from their farms well before dawn to make it to the markets to sell their goods. They would likely return home well after dark. Farming was a difficult life. Stiger had learned that.

The extensive road network, which spread to the far corners of the empire, had been primarily constructed with the military in mind, for the rapid deployment and movement of the legions. The roads also served a secondary purpose, encouraging and allowing both trade and commerce to flow from city to city throughout the empire and back to the capital. Both the military and subsequent trade generated by imperial peace had made the empire wealthy.

He turned his attention ahead. There was something off into the distance. Stiger squinted as he stared at the sight that seemed to slowly materialize and spread across what looked like the entire horizon. At first, he did not quite understand what he was seeing. It was just a smudge of gray and white, unlike any terrain he had seen so far on their journey. With every passing heartbeat, the dragons brought them closer and it only seemed to grow larger, more expansive.

Realization abruptly dawned, and with it, Stiger found himself awed, just awed. He was gazing upon Mal'Zeel, a home he had not seen in years. And he was seeing it in a way he never thought he would, from the air.

Slightly off to the dragon's left, the city stretched out ahead of them. The great city was truly a testament to the will and vision of a people, his people. There, Karus, the first emperor, had planted the seeds for an empire. From fertile ground, the empire had sprouted and had grown into the behemoth and dominating land power it was today, with many major cities, hundreds of towns, and thousands of villages. The empire spanned an almost unimaginably huge area, covering thousands of square miles, with millions of civilians.

Mal'Zeel was the crown jewel, the beating heart of the empire. Each of the Seven Hills, over which the city had been built, were now plainly visible. So too were the banks of the River Dio, which flowed from the Inland Sea, by and around the capital, before taking a meandering path to the Eastern Ocean. Boats, some large and others quite small, some with sails but most powered by oars, moved serenely along the river.

Just over the city itself hung a sort of smudge on the air, an ugly gray pall of a cloud. This was an ever-present sign of civilization for cities, a byproduct. Smoke from an unknowable number of hearths and fires caused it. Despite the cloud hanging ominously over the city, Stiger was deeply impressed by all that he saw.

The sight of the city touched him to his core. Stiger had struggled over the years to prove himself worthy to serve, to redeem his family name, to undo the damage his father had done, and to honor the empire. In a manner of speaking, Mal'Zeel represented all he had labored for over the years. And now, as impossible as it all seemed, like one of the great epics, he was returning home as the emperor.

Him, Stiger…an outcast from polite society, a veritable pariah…emperor. In his hands he now wielded the ultimate power in the empire, imperium.

The sun had not yet risen high enough to bathe its warming rays over the entirety of the land. Much of the city was still shrouded in shadow and the gloom of early morning darkness. But what he could see was impressive, including the Great Colosseum, where the gladiatorial games were played. It towered over everything around it.

Stiger's tutors had told him more than a million people called the city home, perhaps even as many as two million. No one knew for certain. Though it had been talked about and debated for years in the senate, a complete census had never been taken. Seeing it all from a bird's-eye view on the dragon's back, he could readily believe that close to two million people called the capital home.

So transfixed was he by the sight of the capital, Stiger's worries about what waited for him faded slightly. Under the early morning light and partially hidden in shadow, he found the heart of the empire beautiful, a sight for sore eyes. He had not expected to be so touched and moved, yet he had been.

Even as he continued to stare, Stiger offered up a silent prayer of thanks to his god. He thanked the High Father for his many blessings and those he had bestowed upon the empire. He asked for the great god's guidance and support in not only the hours to come, but also the days ahead. For he suspected they would be challenging in the extreme.

The city appeared disorganized and built without any thought to preplanning. Buildings by the tens of thousands were jumbled almost impossibly close together. Streets zigzagged their way madly throughout, as did dozens of major aqueducts. The latter, which brought in the city's lifeblood, water, ran off into the far distance toward whatever water source they drew upon like the spokes of a wheel.

Without fresh water for drinking and bathing, and the sewers that carried waste out of the city, sustaining so many in one place would have been impossible. His tutors had explained how it all worked and the critical significance of such infrastructure.

Civilization set the empire apart from the barbarians. Aqueducts were just one vital component. Education was another. The majority of the people in the city, no matter how mean their circumstances, would be able to read and write, at least on a basic level. The empire saw to that.

Wherever the empire went, whatever lands it gobbled hungrily up, it brought with it trained engineers, educated people, and in the end…civilization. That and imperial peace, which was an opportunity for newly acquired provinces to thrive.

From the air, everything looked in miniature. It was as if he were a giant and an incredibly detailed scale model of the city had been made just for him. The closer they came, the more Stiger was utterly transfixed by what he took in, his city, his empire…his home.

He was beginning to feel the terrible responsibility of all that now rested upon his shoulders. It was not just the men of the legions he commanded who depended upon him, but now, every single citizen and slave within the empire's borders. Even those who were not citizens, but lived within imperial territory, freedmen, were his responsibility now. So much was riding on what would occur in the conflict between the empire and the confederacy, it was almost impossible to fathom. Stiger just shook his head as he continued to stare at the city.

Surrounding it all, like a great boundary holding everything in, were the white, plastered walls of Mal'Zeel. They had never, in the empire's entire history, been overcome by an enemy. As a youth, Stiger had been impressed by them. He had even had the privilege to walk and study the walls. It had been part of his education on fortifications. Stiger's father had paid an engineer who supervised the maintenance of the walls to give the young Stiger a detailed tour.

The walls themselves were constructed of brick-faced concrete that had been reinforced and then plastered over. From one side of the city to the other, the walls traveled a distance of just under fourteen miles and stood over thirty feet in height. They were also twelve thick. Every hundred feet along its length, a square defensive tower had been erected, with an arched, tiled roof. Next to Castle Vrell, Mal'Zeel's defenses were some of the most impressive defensive walls he had ever seen.

Stiger shifted his gaze to the central hill that dominated the city. It was called Palatheum Hill and it towered above all others by more than a hundred yards. Upon its perch lay the emperor's palace, Stiger's palace now. The entire hill, including the slopes and extensive gardens, was the emperor's personal domain, a refuge.

Just below it, the next hill over, was the temple district. The temples were massive marble constructions, built not only to honor the spirit of the gods, but also to impress the populace. These were some of the most important buildings in the empire, with many personal, state, and religious activities revolving around them. As such, special care had been given to their construction, decoration, and upkeep. By comparison, the temples made most other buildings look shabby and poor.

To the left of the temple district was yet another hill, the Aetiriana. On its crest was the senate building, a large square brick construction. Stiger had always found it plain and ugly, a structure without much imagination. That was really the idea. The people's business was a serious affair and the building reflected that idea.

The forum lay before the senate, an open square area for people to assemble, approved news to be read, and important announcements to be made. It was bordered by several administrative buildings of government and trade that kept the empire functioning.

Almost all the buildings on or near the crests of the four other hills were large marble-faced structures of the homes of the wealthy, representing the patrician and equites classes. Under the first rays of sunlight, these marble-faced homes gleamed with reflected light, almost blinding.

Many of these buildings were veritable compounds, grand palaces in their own right, furnished with all the comforts that vast sums of money could purchase. Below, and shrouded in shadow, much of the city still slumbered, the plebeians and the rest of the masses. For those with little means, life in the capital was not an easy one.

Stiger located the Teritine Hill, where his family home was located. He searched amongst the many compounds. At this distance, he could not pick it out from the sheer number of buildings that crowded closely in upon each other. It might be hidden from view on the side of the hill, which was still mostly hidden in shadow. They were simply approaching the city from the wrong direction to get a good enough view of his home to pick it out.

"Look there," Eli shouted. The elf was seated just ahead of Stiger. He was pointing off to the right, away from the city. Stiger looked and saw a series of massive military encampments, clearly the temporary homes of several legions, his father's army.

By long-standing custom and law, the legions were not permitted to approach the city, unless invited to do so by the senate. Nor could they cross the Dio. That was clearly why the encampments had been set up outside the city and along one of the imperial highways, the Perminuam Way, that bridged the great river. It had long since been clear neither the senate nor the emperor trusted their own legions, and for good reason, too. Several times in imperial history, the legions had turned on their masters. Stiger resolved to be different, to make sure that such a thing did not happen.

"If I am not mistaken," Eli shouted over the wind, "that is your father's army and they are on the march."

Stiger had seen it as well. A long, thick column was marching along the road, away from the camps and the capital. The column of men, along with wagons, horses, and mules, stretched off into the distance, for as far as the eye could see. They were clearly marching away to the east.

But why?

Were they off to meet the enemy somewhere along the coast? The enemy had to be hundreds of miles away and the roads along the coast were narrow and not the best. They would hinder a rapid march north. So ... why leave the defensible walls of the city?

His father surely had to know he stood no chance against dragons out in the open. There had to be a good reason, he knew, one he was not yet aware of. Did that mean his father was not in the city? Was he at the head of the army, miles away? Were the enemy closer than he thought? Stiger had so many questions.

Inex broke into Stiger's thoughts. *We will put you down about a half mile from the city walls, by one of the main gates. That reduces our risk of being attacked by your people.*

"It works," Stiger said, for he understood bolt throwers may have been mounted on the city walls. It was possible larger ones to tackle a dragon had been constructed too. If the dwarves and the defenders of Lorium could build them, why couldn't the engineers of his father's army? And the capital had a vast pool of labor to tap to make such an enterprise a reality.

After the reports of what had happened to Tioclesion's army reached the capital, it only made sense that they would have taken such precautions. At least, Stiger would have done so. He suspected his father would have too.

Unexpectedly, the dragon banked, turning almost sideways, so that Stiger was looking nearly straight down. As the wind picked up, blasting at him with more force, his stomach gave a flip. Inex seemed to slide downward toward the snow-covered ground. The wind whistled past, almost screaming through his helmet. He held the scarf around his face to keep it from coming free and closed his eyes against the stinging wind.

One of the legionaries mounted somewhere behind him gave an unnerved scream. Eli laughed, thoroughly enjoying himself. Despite the cold, Stiger was enjoying the flight too, though not as much as Eli seemed to be.

After several moments of what felt like freefall, Inex leveled off. The dragon started into what could only be described as a lazy spiral downward. Stiger opened his eyes as the blast of wind diminished. He watched in fascination as the snow-covered ground moved rapidly up to meet them.

As Inex continued the descent toward the ground, Stiger had a flash of people, wagons, and carts along a road just below. The appearance of the dragons had caused quite a stir, for people were running for their lives, with horses and wagons thundering along the road toward the city. Those unfortunates on foot were fleeing off into the fields or attempting a desperate dash for the safety of the city walls.

The dragon extended his wings fully again and began flapping mightily to slow his rate of descent. Stiger could feel the powerful muscles of the creature under him working mightily.

The fleeing people were abruptly lost from view as the spiral continued. The ground was now impossibly close as the dragon's flapping became more intense. A heartbeat later, the dragon's claws touched down. Stiger was thrown forward as the creature's momentum was suddenly arrested. He was barely able to catch himself on the spike before him. The dragon took several steps, causing Stiger and everyone else to rock backward. Then the dragon stopped and folded his leathery wings against his body before settling his bulk to the ground.

There are no immediate threats about us, Inex said. *No need to rush to dismount.*

With hands nearly frozen from the cold, even with his thick gloves, Stiger began undoing the straps and ties that held him in place. Around him, Ruga's men and Eli were doing the same.

After a little bit of effort, some fumbling, Stiger gave up, drew his dagger, and simply cut himself free. He no longer had any need for the ties and straps. He stood on the dragon's back, his legs stiff and aching from remaining in the same position for such a long time. Stretching and pulling the scarf down about his neck, he gazed around, studying the area.

Both dragons had landed in a large field that clearly had been farmed. The field was covered with nearly a foot of snow, which looked to have freshly fallen. Little white waves followed the contour of the furrows from the field underneath. The stone walls bordering the field were also covered in snow. Only the boundary pattern gave away what they were.

The other dragon was sixty yards away. Ruga, Tiro, Restus, and the rest of the men on his back were undoing their fastenings or in the process of clambering down the side of the dragon.

Stiger turned full around, making sure to scan everything in view. The nearest buildings, about fifty yards to his right, were a good-sized barn with a small one-room farmhouse set right next to it. The house was rough-looking and run-down. Some poor tenant likely lived there, renting the land for a starvation wage … barely clearing enough to feed himself and his family. In reality, many land tenants were little more than slaves themselves, indebted to the landlord. All it would take was a bad harvest and they would lose everything, including their freedom, so that their obligation may be fulfilled.

The farm was set almost directly alongside the road, which Stiger now recognized as the Avianata Way. He could tell by one of the road markers, which had a large triangle carved into the top of the stone post. The wind had blown the top of the road marker clean.

Bleating sheep in a wooden pen next to the barn could be heard, as could the distant screams and shouts of alarm from along the road. Everyone and everything, including the animals, was in a panic.

Inex raised his head high, opened his mouth, and let out a roar. Startled, Stiger jumped. He clapped his hands to his ears, for the sound was earsplitting. The dragon shot a long jet of flame straight up into the air. The stream of fire went almost impossibly high before the dragon ceased the blast. Inex let loose another deafening roar, then lowered his head.

"Did you need to do that?" Stiger asked, for his ears were now ringing and likely would be for several hours to come. He gestured in the direction of the capital, which could be seen in the distance. "I think you might have woken up half the city."

I thought it best to announce the new emperor's arrival, Inex said, with not a little satisfaction. *When we go, we will fly high for all to see and make certain the entire city knows you are here.*

"The emperor who rode in on a dragon," Eli said, glancing up from untying his pack. "I sense a poetic song in there somewhere, a classic in the making."

"Right," Stiger said. "That's just what I need … bards and minstrels singing songs about me in the taverns."

"Something somewhat bawdry, no doubt," Eli said.

"You mean obscene." Stiger gave a slight shake of his head, disgusted by the mere thought.

"You've heard the songs your legionaries sing while they march," Eli said. "Those are hardly tame. It only stands to reason some enterprising fellow will come up with something clever, poetic too, no doubt."

"Great." Stiger shook his head. "Thanks for that cheerful thought."

Are you certain you do not wish us to remain a while longer? Inex asked.

We are uncomfortable just leaving you here, Tyven admitted, joining the conversation.

"No," Stiger said after a moment's consideration. He was worried about his army marching north and the lack of protection for it. "I would dearly love to keep you both close at hand but cannot afford to. You are needed back with the army, providing cover. Even with those legions over there"—Stiger gestured in the direction of his father's legions—"the enemy badly outnumbers us. I can't take the chance of the wyrms returning."

It is very unlikely the confederacy will send their wyrms to attack your army, Inex said. *They will not wish to risk their wyrms until they absolutely need to, for should they suffer another defeat in the air, we will gain the advantage over them, perhaps even a decisive one. They will be careful.*

"And if we're not careful, the same could happen to us as well," Stiger said. "We're spread thin at the moment. The army must be protected to the fullest extent possible. Both of those legions represent the best of the empire, not to mention our allies, the dwarves, elves, and gnomes. We cannot afford to lose them."

And if they send their wyrms here instead? Inex asked. *You will have no protection. What if they come to destroy this city? What then? Or how about that army that is marching off to the east? It has no protection.*

Stiger glanced eastward. He could no longer see his father's army, which was miles away from where they had landed. A stand of trees bordering the field and a small hill were in the way.

"That is certainly a risk," Stiger admitted, turning back. "I do not know why the legions are marching away from the city. If I am able, I will put a stop to it and have them return. Jeskix said that once he rejoined his people, he'd send a couple of your kind to Mal'Zeel for protection."

It could be a week or more before they arrive, Inex said. *There will be no protection until then.*

Stiger did not feel good about that, but he was still more concerned about his own army. He glanced in the direction of the city walls and felt leaving the capital unprotected was a risk he had to take. With the main body of the enemy so far from Mal'Zeel, he thought it unlikely they'd send their wyrms so far afield. "I know. We will have to construct bolt throwers, if they've not been built already, and take our chances."

Those will be of limited value, Inex said. *You know this… especially if the enemy throws all their wyrms at you all at once.*

You are set upon this course of action? Tyven asked.

"I am," Stiger said and felt a mental sigh of resignation from the dragon in response.

On our way back to the army, we can scout to the southeast, Tyven suggested, *fly near enough to the enemy that they might think we have established a presence to the north as well. It could keep them guessing as to our intentions.*

That could work, Inex said. *It might convince them to hold their wyrms close at hand for their own protection. They might believe we are probing for a strike against them.*

We can make it look quite convincing too, Tyven added.

"Is there risk?" Stiger asked. "It certainly sounds risky to me."

There is always risk, Tyven said with another mental shrug. *We will be careful. Neither of us wish to sacrifice ourselves needlessly.*

"Very well," Stiger said, not liking the idea of what they were going to attempt. However, if they were successful, it might buy time, a commodity Stiger was running out of. "Do it, but be safe about it, will you?"

We will give them a scare, Tyven said.

Stiger looked over at the other dragon, who was gazing his way. He wondered briefly what both had in mind.

We wish you luck, human, Inex said and looked away toward the city. Tyven glanced away as well. The conversation was clearly over.

Dagger still in hand, Stiger moved over to Dog, who had begun to try to squirm and wriggle out of the rope that held him securely in place. He cut the animal free and removed the blanket that had been wrapped around Dog for warmth.

Standing, Dog shook himself vigorously and then stretched. He looked up at Stiger, tail wagging madly, then leaped from the dragon's back and down to the snow-covered ground below. Stiger tossed the blanket after him. It fluttered to the ground.

"More snow," Eli said unhappily, without looking over at Stiger. He seemed to be speaking to himself. Stiger glanced over at his friend and saw he had unfastened his pack, which he hoisted onto his shoulder. His bow had been set aside. With a practiced ease, Eli began stringing it. Once done, he slung the bow over his back, then picked up a leather-wrapped bundle of arrows. He slung it over his shoulder too.

Stiger glanced around once more. Those who had fled down the road were far off now, most having gone from view. Some had even trekked into the surrounding fields, leaving only their tracks behind as evidence of their passage. He let out a long, unhappy breath. His arrival had terrified them.

It was not the auspicious beginning he had hoped for, but at the same time, not an unexpected outcome either. Dragons were dragons, after all. The manner of his arrival would not be forgotten. No matter what happened over the next few hours and days, it would be the talk of the city for years to come. That much was for certain. He just was not keen about the songs that would inevitably be made up about him.

Soon enough, though, the common people would know he was no threat to them. Treim and Aetius's agents had

had more than two days to go to work at stirring up the city. If everything had gone to plan, news should have preceded him. At least he hoped so. If something had happened to the messenger, he would have his work cut out for him.

"Lots of snow," Eli said, gazing down at the ground, this time speaking to Stiger. "It seems like we just left the mountains in Vrell. Know what I mean?"

"Not too cold though," Stiger said. "It's got to be just above freezing. The sun coming up should warm things nicely. It would not surprise me if much of this snow melts before day's end. It is, after all, only the beginning of winter. Besides, we've both seen deeper snow. It's really not as bad as it could be."

"True," Eli said, though he did not sound sold. "I've been thinking, if the confederacy continues north past the snow line, it will mean a winter campaign. We both know how difficult those can be."

Stiger had not considered that. It was an interesting line of thought. "Do you think the confederacy is prepared? They come from a warm land that I understand does not see snow. It's hard to imagine they are ready for such cold, let alone conducting large-scale operations under adverse conditions."

"They are a slave culture," Eli said, "more so than the empire. We know their religion to Valoor is bound up in it. Serve well and there is rebirth to a better class. Serve poorly and you suffer by being reborn to worse circumstances. I suppose, with such values, their respect for life is not equal to our own."

"As in they don't care as much about their own soldiers?" Stiger asked, considering his friend's words. "You are saying you expect they will push north into the snow, regardless of whether or not they are prepared to do so."

"I am," Eli said. "What might not be possible for another culture may be for them. If you recall during the battle ... before the real fighting began, their general threw a few thousand of their men against our entire line."

"I do." Stiger did remember. "They were unsupported."

At the time, it had made no sense to him. He had assumed there had been some reason for it, only he had never found one. His enemy had been simply throwing the lives of their men away.

"Good gods." Stiger rubbed his chin as the full implications of what Eli was suggesting hit him.

"Exactly," Eli said.

Stiger felt chilled. "Unprepared or not, the confederacy is coming."

"Despite their success in the south," Eli added, "I do not believe they will find a place to winter and wait for the snows to melt."

Stiger closed his eyes, thinking furiously. If the enemy pushed hard enough ... drove their men forward along the poor coastal roads ... "That means they could be here in a matter of weeks." Stiger opened his eyes. "A winter campaign is assured."

"You thought it might be a race to the capital," Eli said. "It looks like it will be."

"Our army might just arrive days before the enemy," Stiger breathed.

It seems you are running out of time, human, Inex said.

Stiger could not disagree.

If the enemy is pushing hard, Tyven said, *one of us will return to alert you.*

"I would appreciate that," Stiger said.

"Are you gonna climb down?" Therik asked from below, forestalling further conversation.

Stiger stepped up to the edge of the dragon's back and looked down. Therik was wearing the legionary armor that had been made for him. The orc had trekked his way across the field between the two dragons. His tracks made a straight line back to the other dragon. "I would think, as you say, you would want to get this show on the road. Maybe I'm wrong. Perhaps you just want to talk the day away with the elf."

"He's a little eager," Eli said to Stiger as he stepped up to the edge, "eager like a beaver."

Stiger felt a slight lightening of his mood.

"Eager? No. I am cold, tired, and hungry." Therik pointed toward the city with a thick green finger. "I am certain we can find food, real meat, and the comfort of a fire in there, drink too."

"No doubt," Stiger said, looking in the direction Therik had pointed. His thoughts strayed back to the enemy and what Eli had said. Though he felt Eli was correct in his estimation of the enemy's intentions, in a way, it was another what-if scenario. By worrying about what the enemy was up to, Stiger was getting ahead of himself. The more immediate issue lay a half mile away. He would deal with the enemy when they became a real problem again. Right now, he had to focus on the immediate future, the curule chair, the senate, his father, the empire, and the people. He turned his gaze back to Therik and felt a hunger pang. "I could go for something other than salt pork. A beef stew perhaps, with plenty of fresh bread for sopping."

"There are also people that need killing," Therik said. "At least there should be. We all know you bring out the best in people."

"Why does everyone think that?" Stiger asked, thoroughly amused.

"Because it's true," Therik said. "Do not bother denying it."

"You do, you know," Eli said. "There is just something about your personality. Like a moth to an open flame, you attract trouble. Perhaps that is what initially drew us together. Think of me as the moth."

"And I am the flame?" Stiger chuckled. He now knew why Eli had attached himself to Seventh Company all those years ago, the real reason. Shaking his head, he began climbing down before dropping the last two feet into the snow. His boots sank right down into the fresh powder. He almost fell, as his left boot went deeper than the other, sinking into the gap between furrows.

Therik gave an amused grunt.

Eli followed him down without issue, making it look easy.

"Sir." Ruga approached and saluted. The centurion was red-faced from the cold.

Stiger returned the salute and glanced around once again. A group of twenty of Ruga's men was spreading out around them protectively. A couple had gone off to scout the farmhouse and barn. The rest were still on the dragons' backs, untying shields and packs. Using ropes, they were lowering them to the ground.

"What are your orders, sir?" Ruga asked.

"Let's get the dragons fully unloaded," Stiger said, "then, when you are ready, form the men up on the road. We will march to the city gate and demand entry."

"What then, sir?" Ruga asked. "Once we gain access to the city, what are your intentions?"

Therik growled. Ruga's eyes flicked to the orc in question.

"He's getting impatient," Eli explained before Stiger could speak.

"The big bastard's likely hungry, is all," Ruga said. "It was a long flight and the food has not been the best of late, mostly salted meat."

"Centurion, you hit the nail right on the head," Eli laughed, while Therik threw a hard look to Ruga. The centurion only gave a knowing grunt in reply.

"Once inside the city, we will go to my family's house," Stiger said. "From there, it will depend upon what Senator Navaro has to say and of course the senate. I expect both will wish to see me. With any luck, things will go easily."

"And when has it ever gone easily?" Eli asked. "It always seems like we do things the hard way, just like at Fort Covenant, or Thresh, or dozens of other places we've been."

"Best get to it, Centurion," Stiger said, ignoring the elf. "We don't want to give those at the city gate too much time to think things through."

"Yes, sir," Ruga said. With a parting salute, the centurion moved away to hurry his men along, shouting at them as he went.

Rubbing his hands together for warmth, Stiger looked around again. A thin trail of smoke was emerging from the chimney of the farmhouse along the road. He gestured at it with a hand. "Let's go warm up while we wait. Shall we?"

Not waiting for an answer, Stiger started off. His feet crunched with each step as he began to make his way across the field toward the farmhouse. Dog, Eli, and Therik followed. The escort moved with them. A gust of wind blew across the field and kicked up a light spray of snow, which swirled about them before passing.

From the knees down, Stiger's legs were thoroughly wet by the time they reached the road. His feet were beginning to feel damp too. It was past time to replace his boots. He would have to make a point to get that done, and soon. They had been worn thin, almost to the point of completely wearing out. There were even a couple of small holes in the soles.

Stiger reached the road and discovered it had been rolled, which had packed the snow down, compacting it. The empire preferred rolling so that a road could be negotiated with little effort. In the city, the streets would have been shoveled clean and the snow tossed into the river. Out here, in the countryside, they just rolled it. There wasn't enough labor available to bother shoveling it all.

Wagon tracks and prints from steady traffic moving toward the city had already marked the road heavily. Manure from draft animals had also soiled the pristine white of the snow along the roadway.

There was no longer anyone in view, other than those in the city, a half mile distant. He could see hundreds standing on the walls, no doubt staring at the dragons. On a positive note, the city gate itself was still open. No one had yet to think to shut it. He suspected it would not remain that way for long.

Careful of where he stepped, Stiger crossed the road to the farmhouse. The door had been left partially open, likely from Ruga's men, who had scouted the farm. Stiger glanced in. There was no one present. Whoever had been here had fled when the dragons arrived.

The interior was dark, as the shutters were closed against the cold. The walls had been plastered over, though the plaster was cracked and crumbling. A low fire crackled in the hearth, providing the only light inside. Not even a candle or oil lamp had been lit.

Stiger made his way inside; the others filed in after. The house was humble and smelled of unwashed bodies. The floor was planked wood and had been recently swept clean.

There were very few possessions about, other than a table set aside for food prep, a large cot for two, and some pots, of which one had been suspended over the fire. It was slow-boiling water. Two medium trunks lay next to the far wall. Sacks were set against the same wall, as well as three knee-high casks. One had been labeled "flour." A soiled towel lay atop it.

Numerous onions and herbs had been suspended from the low ceiling. A loaf of half-eaten bread lay on the table. It looked somewhat hard, perhaps even stale. All in all, though hers had been superior to this, the farmhouse reminded Stiger strongly of Sarai's place. It evoked memories of warmth and a simpler time, one without too many worries—or so he'd thought.

Moving over to the fire, he forced such unwelcome and painful thoughts aside. Holding out his hands, Stiger removed his gloves and rubbed them together for added warmth. As feeling returned, his fingers began to ache painfully. Eli and Therik did the same.

Dog had not joined them. Stiger hoped the animal wasn't troubling the sheep. The people who lived in this house had little to begin with. Taking a sheep would hurt them financially and, from the looks of things, they could not afford that.

Through the open door, he could hear the guards take up position outside. They were speaking in low, hushed tones amongst themselves.

"Are you ready for this?" Therik asked suddenly. "Are you prepared for what lies ahead? For what happens when you step through that city gate?"

"We have come this far," Stiger said, suddenly amused. "We might as well see it through, find out what happens. Take things as they come, eh?"

Therik did not seem pleased by the answer, for his eyes narrowed. He picked at the tip of one of his sharpened tusks with a nail as he regarded Stiger.

"I am thinking most people are the same," Therik said, after a moment, "especially with those who crave power and what comes with it, whether they be orc or human. This is a time for you being utterly ruthless, offering no quarter. If you show even the slightest weakness, hesitate when you should not…your enemies will make your weakness their strength." Therik paused. "I know you know this…but it is best to be occasionally reminded, for once we go inside your city…once we step through that gate"—Therik jerked a thumb at the door—"things will get difficult. I am thinking this senate of yours will not want to give you the empire. You will need to prove your worth and take it by force if needed."

"The ride gave you some time to think, didn't it?" Eli asked with a grin thrown to the orc.

Therik growled at the elf. "I make no joke. I am deadly serious."

"I thought you were hungry," Stiger said, deciding to tease the orc a little, though he fully agreed with what Therik had said.

"That too," Therik admitted, growing grave. "But this is no joking matter. You must take this serious."

Stiger eyed the orc a long moment, then gave a slow nod as he pulled his gloves back on. "Therik, I've already come to that conclusion. There is a good chance we're going to end up doing this the hard way, and that will mean spilling blood."

The orc gave a pleased nod at the admission.

"I intend to be merciless and relentless in pursuing my objectives," Stiger said and felt his anger stir slightly. "I will let nothing stand in my way, for the High Father has given me a mandate and a job to do. I…we have come too far, done too much to stop now. I am committed and will not rest until I have accomplished all that I have set out to do. That is the vow I have made."

Stiger's hand came to rest on the sword hilt. He felt the tingle of the sword's bond rush up into him, before rapidly fading.

He took a deep breath, then let it out. "Any who stand in my way will regret doing so."

"Good." Therik's gaze was intense as he stared at Stiger. "Killing the opposition, allowing none to bar your way ... that is how I ultimately became king of my people, and how you will become emperor." Therik thumped his chest armor with a fist. "It will be my honor to be there every step of the journey to help you make that happen. I swear it so."

Stiger felt an immense rush of affection for the orc, his friend. He glanced to Eli. This would likely be the last time for a long while the three of them would be alone. Something needed saying and it was a long time coming.

"I want to thank you both for sticking with me and coming here," Stiger said. "I cannot fully express my gratitude for your friendship and likely will never be able to sufficiently thank you. I can't imagine anyone else I'd rather have by my side, especially when things get ugly ... Thank you."

Eli gave a slight hesitation and shared a look with Therik. "You know me, Ben. I would walk down the Seven Levels with you. And if you went without me, I would have followed after."

"Bah." Therik waved a meaty hand. "There is no need to thank. I told you, I will allow none other to kill you but me, which is why you will not leave me behind again."

Stiger grinned at that. It felt good to have such dedicated and steadfast friends with him. He was heartened by it. He only wished Taha'Leeth were here too. Then again, she likely was safer recovering with the legion and Venthus watching over her. The capital could be a very dangerous place.

"When this is all over," Therik said, "I may go find the orcs of this world and give them a true king."

"I wonder who that will be," Eli said.

Stiger had no doubts.

Therik grunted, turned away, and reached for the bread.

"Take nothing from whoever lives here," Stiger said to the orc. "They have little enough as it is. I would not beggar them further."

Therik looked unhappy at that but withdrew his hand. As he did, Stiger took out a silver talon. With a flick of his thumb, he flipped it up into the air and caught it. The silver flashed with reflected firelight. Such a sum was a fortune for whoever lived in this house. He tossed it onto the table, next to the bread, where it made a clunking noise before falling still.

"For allowing us to use your home and warm up, friend," Stiger said quietly to the absent tenant.

"Sir," Ruga said from the door, "my men are formed up and ready."

"Shall we do this?" Eli asked and clapped a hand upon Stiger's shoulder.

"As I've said, we've come this far"—Stiger threw a grin to Therik—"might as well see it all through, eh?"

Therik let loose a deep growling laugh. "We might as well, my friend."

Stiger moved for the door and stopped, a hand on the frame. He looked back at his two friends for a heartbeat. He gave a nod before turning away and stepping outside. It was time to do what he had come to do and get this show on the road.

CHAPTER SEVEN

"Well," Stiger said, blowing out a long breath that steamed in the cold air. The last vestiges of snow and ice lay scattered across the paved roadway around them. It had been shoveled into large piles to either side of the city gate. Sand had been thrown down to keep people from slipping. "This is certainly a switch."

"In that the gate is still open?" Eli, who was standing to Stiger's right, asked. "Or that they've not immediately tried to kill us?"

"How many times over the years," Stiger said, "have we had to either talk our way in or...?" He turned his gaze back to the gate, which was old and, unlike the other three city gates, plain and without ostentation. It was called the Mourning Gate. Along the road behind them were the tombs and gravesites of the expired.

"Force our way in?" Eli finished as Stiger trailed off.

The gate had two heavily reinforced doors that fit into its arched shape. Facing outward to the sides, both doors stood open. They had been constructed in layers of thick oaken planks that had been fitted together. The thickness of each door was about two feet. An enemy army attempting to force their way in would have a difficult time, especially with a determined and well-trained enemy defending the walls above.

"Might I remind you both, they've still not granted us entry," Tiro said from behind them.

Stiger glanced back at Tiro, who wore only his service tunic and not his legionary armor.

"You're just super helpful, aren't you?" Stiger said. "A real ray of sunshine."

"You know me, sir," Tiro said, suppressing a grin, "always trying to be helpful. I mean, what sergeant wouldn't want to be?"

"Right." Stiger turned back to the city gate ten yards before them. On his immediate left was Therik, who was clearly becoming impatient. The orc had been huffing and puffing. Ruga's century was formed up into a column of two that stretched out behind them along the road, which was hemmed in by a series of large, ancient tombs. These had been worn down by weather.

"He does have a point, sir," Ruga said. The centurion had positioned himself just behind Stiger and next to Tiro. Ruga had his shield up and ready. He was clearly uncomfortable with their proximity to the gate and concerned Stiger might become a target.

A formation of soldiers from the city stood just before the gate, barring their way into the city. None of those carried bows, but there were several up on the battlements above who did.

Stiger wasn't terribly concerned about them. The men with the bows would have to be really good to hit him from this distance, almost ranger good. He doubted any of those armed with bows and manning the walls were particularly skilled. Had they shown any hint of skill, they would have been assigned to an auxiliary cohort and likely be marching with his father's army.

"They usually close the gate on us," Eli said, before glancing back on Tiro. "Don't they?"

"They've done that a time or two," Tiro admitted. "Since we're speaking on gates, what was the name of that fort we found Lieutenant Hollux in? Remember that one, out in the forest? It was just before that shit show at Fort Covenant. The lieutenant didn't want to open that gate either. I seem to recall you pulling rank on him, sir."

"I did, didn't I?" Stiger chuckled at the memory, then almost immediately sobered. He had lost a lot of good men at Fort Covenant, including his first corporal, Varus.

Soon after that bloody ordeal, Hollux had become his executive officer and developed into a good one at that. Stiger could not have asked for a better second. Hollux had also become a friend, one as good as Captain Lepidus from the Tenth. All three of them, Eli included, had been through a great deal together. Stiger wondered how the lieutenant was doing under his new commanding officer. He hoped well.

"Perhaps they will let us in?" Tiro said. "Then again, you might have to pull rank, sir."

Stiger could only nod in agreement. He turned back to the gate, which towered above them. Men, women, and children by the hundreds lined the tops of the walls, all gazing down at them. Most of those above appeared to be civilians, but some were clearly armed soldiers, either from the city's garrison or militia. Stiger wasn't sure which. He scanned the battlements closely, looking between the civilians. A good number had bows, more than he'd initially thought. Maybe even as many as a hundred. With so many, they might not need skill. Still, he was not overly concerned and doubted it would come to that. After all, this was home, and Stiger was now the emperor. He turned his gaze back to the soldiers before the gate.

The formation to their front numbered over two hundred fifty men, which meant they were an overstrength company. They were formed up into five ranks and were armed with simple chain mail shirts, short swords, and rounded shields.

Studying them, Stiger figured they were city militia. Mal'Zeel's militia wasn't known for its fighting prowess. They were mainly toughs, recruited from the worst slums the city had to offer. They were generally expected to push civilians around during events and knock heads to keep order amongst the mob. Not much more was expected from them than that and any training they received was generally minimal. Along with the garrison and the praetorians, the militia helped to keep a lid on the seething discontent and misery of the urban poor.

This bunch did not appear highly disciplined, for there was much talking and jawing in the ranks. Were they a legionary company, such behavior would have been an unforgivable breach.

The formation was also not properly dressed, which gave their ranks a disordered appearance, as their alignment from one rank to the next was off. Had they been part of the standing garrison, he suspected they would have presented better, as the training would have been more intensive and thorough but still substandard when compared to the legion.

The militia company's equipment was not well maintained either. Stiger could easily spot rust marks on the chain mail of several of the soldiers. All of that reinforced Stiger's belief the men guarding the gate were poorly trained.

"You sent for their senior officer almost a half hour ago." Therik shifted his stance and crossed his arms. "Not only is this intolerable, it is an insult. I would be enraged were I you."

Stiger eyed the orc for a long moment but decided to say nothing. In the legions, one learned to wait. Usually it was hurry up, get to where you needed to be, and then wait on someone else to do their job, just so you could do yours. Serving the empire, if anything, taught one patience.

"What do you think the holdup is, sir?" Ruga asked. "Do you think they mean to cause us trouble?"

"I don't know," Stiger said and in truth he did not. He had announced himself and unexpectedly been denied entry by a fresh-faced lieutenant no less. The man had gone away to fetch his senior officer and had yet to return.

"Well," Therik said, "that group there won't stop us should we want in." Therik gestured at Ruga. "His legionaries will tear them apart."

"My boys would eat them for breakfast," Ruga agreed. There was no hint of pride in his tone. He'd said it only as a statement of fact. "They won't last a one hundred count in the press of the line. Heck"—he waved at the militia—"I don't think that bunch could manage to break up a rowdy tavern full of disorderly drunks. There is no doubt in my mind on this, sir. If you want in, just give the word. We'll shove them aside and send 'em running home to their mommas."

"Let's hope it doesn't come to that," Stiger said. He did not relish the idea of killing their own and would only give such an order if it became necessary. He did not want to begin his reign this way.

There was a ripple in the ranks of the militia company. Men moved aside as two officers made their way to the front.

The first was older, and his rank insignia told Stiger he was a captain, though he wore legionary armor. The armor was well maintained. The second was no more than a youth and his rank marked him as a lieutenant. Stiger had spoken with him before when they had arrived at the gate. He was too junior to have much experience and was essentially a nonentity in what was to come.

The captain hesitated, eyeing them. Stiger turned his full attention on the militia captain. The man's face was badly scarred from multiple cuts, likely taken in battle. One of the scars cut through his bottom lip. He was also missing his right eye and walked with a noticeable limp that was little more than a hobble.

He was clearly a disabled veteran, likely a former sergeant, who had been promoted to the command of a militia company. A noble would never have taken such a lowly position. This was the highest rank the man likely could gain. He may have even purchased his position with whatever retirement funds he'd managed to accumulate before being mustered out. Regardless, there was no question in Stiger's mind the man had seen hard action and knew the ugly realities of combat.

In general, Stiger disliked the system of selling commissions to senior military positions, for it frequently saw incompetent men rise to positions of power they had no business holding. Bastards like his first captain, Cethegus, Tribune Declin, or even Generals Lears, Mammot, and Kromen had all purchased their ranks. There had been many more such men he'd encountered over the years who had done the same. Hardly a one had started at a junior level and bothered to learn the ropes, gaining valuable experience before beginning the long climb up the ladder of command.

Each one of those bastards, and many more like them, had ultimately proven unsuited to leading men in battle or, for that matter, even commanding them. More often than not they had led their own men to the slaughter.

Many refused to listen to advice or outright spurned it. Even worse, having read a book or two on military tactics, they thought themselves brilliant tacticians and masters of the battlefield.

It took more than reading a few books to understand what was happening in the middle of a fight, let alone capitalize on it. It took training, study, and years of hard-earned experience, along with the ability to listen to veterans and get to know and understand the men under your command. And even then, one was not guaranteed to be victorious. Fortuna could be a real bitch when she wanted.

The militia officer scowled. He clearly understood Ruga's century were fighting men. There was no doubt in Stiger's mind about that. The officer glanced back as yet another man made his way through the ranks and joined them.

This newcomer wore a toga, highlighted on the fringes with imperial purple. It told Stiger, along with everyone else, that he served the emperor directly, or at least worked in the imperial household.

The newcomer turned what could only be described as hostile eyes upon Stiger and said something to the captain, who gave what appeared to be an irritated nod. Stiger had the suspicion the captain was far from pleased with whatever had passed between them.

"I sense trouble in the making," Therik said, looking over at Stiger. The orc checked to make certain his sword was loose in its scabbard. "At least the boredom is over. I hate being kept waiting."

"Don't we all," Ruga said, "don't we all."

"That is Sensetta," Restus wheezed before coughing lightly as he came up to stand with them. The paladin had been sitting on a fallen road marker a few yards away. Stiger looked over at him. The journey had not been kind to Restus. He was pale, with a sickly cast, and had developed a wracking cough. The cold and wind of their journey had clearly gotten the better of him.

"Are you all right?" Stiger asked. He was becoming concerned for the man's health. Restus was not a young man.

"Chilled is all," Restus said, "nothing a good fire and a hearty stew won't cure. Trust me, I've had worse."

Stiger wasn't so certain about the man's assurances, but he gave a nod just the same. Right now, he needed information.

"Who is this Sensetta?"

"He is from a smaller household, one in patronage to the imperial family," Restus said, "or really, to be more correct, Tioclesion's family. The Sensettas have been clients of theirs for dozens of years." Restus gave a light cough and took a wheezing breath. "He was the emperor's Keeper of the Palace."

"Keeper of the Palace," Stiger said. "You mean he is responsible for the administrative running of the palace, bossing the slaves, cooks, and such around?"

Restus gave a nod.

"What is he doing here, then?"

"I don't know." Restus coughed into his fist. "He was put into place by Tioclesion's father. His sense of his own importance is greater than those he serves. Be warned, he is a snake and loyal only to self-betterment."

"Trouble then." Therik cracked his knuckles. "And here I was worried we would not find any."

"Let's not get ahead of ourselves," Stiger cautioned and then looked over at Restus. "Do you know this militia captain or his lieutenant?"

"No." Restus cleared his throat before continuing. "When I left the city, the militia's ranks were being increased. Most of the regular garrison went with Tioclesion's army on campaign. If I recall, a few companies of regulars from the north were left in the capital to help the militia keep order."

Stiger recalled Treim telling him that. His old company, the Seventh, was among the regular formations that had been held behind. They were supposedly somewhere in the city, though he well knew they might be with his father's army by now.

The militia captain said something brusque to Sensetta, then waited for a reply. After it came, he gave a shrug and came forward, until he stood six paces from Stiger. The lieutenant, appearing nervous, followed. Sensetta advanced too and stopped at the militia captain's side.

There was a long moment of silence while each side sized the other up. The captain placed his hands upon his hips. His eyes moved to Eli, then lingered on Therik, before finally coming to rest on Stiger.

"Identify yourself and your reason for entry into the city," the captain said. His voice was deep and there was a natural confidence there, one born from years of hard service and leadership. Stiger easily recognized the man's type.

"I suspect you know who I am, Captain," Stiger said, deciding not to play the game, at least initially. "I told your lieutenant when I arrived."

"You came by dragon?" the captain said, his eyes looking beyond Stiger and out into the field.

"We did," Stiger said. "We flew here from Lorium."

"The stories working their way around the city must be true then," the captain said.

Sensetta stiffened slightly.

Stiger felt an immense wave of relief. Word had spread of what had happened in Lorium. That was incredibly good news... exceptional news. It meant the messenger had arrived.

"They are true," Stiger said. "I shattered the enemy army that was besieging Lorium."

"He lies," Sensetta said. "It is all one big lie. Do not believe it."

The captain spared the man a hard look, then turned his attention back to Stiger.

"It is all true," Restus said. "By the High Father, I swear it to be."

The militia captain's good eye narrowed as he studied the paladin. After a long moment, he looked at Stiger.

"I still have a duty to attend," the captain said, with an unhappy glance to Sensetta. "Your name, please, and the reason for entering the city. I need to hear it from your own lips." He jerked his head toward Sensetta. "He is requiring it."

"I am Bennulius Stiger." He spoke in a loud tone so the ranks of militia behind the captain could hear his words plainly and hopefully those up on the wall also. "And I have come to claim what is rightfully mine. I have returned home to save the empire from the Cyphan Confederacy."

Sensetta's expression became ugly, twisted. The militia in the ranks behind the two erupted into a riot of talking. Those up on the wall did as well. The captain looked back on his company with a seriously irate expression, one that promised punishment. None in the ranks seemed to notice the look or, for that matter, care.

"Let me guess," Stiger said, "this is a new command?"

"It is," the captain confirmed. His look was one born of frustration. Stiger knew that feeling too well. "They've not had time for discipline to be beaten into them, not like regulars in the legions. With the shortages of manpower in the city, we were posted right to duty on this gate, just days after forming. They've had little training. Give me a couple of weeks to get them into proper shape. Then they might begin to look like real soldiers."

"He doesn't need to know that," Sensetta hissed with acid. "Use your head, man."

The captain's jaw flexed, but he said nothing in reply.

"Well," Stiger said, "you know who I am and why I've come. Kindly stand aside and grant us entry."

"You are not permitted into the city," Sensetta said. "Like all legionaries under arms, you are to remain outside."

"Captain," Stiger said, deciding to ignore the functionary from the palace, "this is my personal guard. Shall we talk this through before things get, shall we say, heated?"

"There's nothing to talk about," Sensetta snapped and then looked to the militia captain. "You have your orders, Captain. I suggest you follow them."

The captain looked between Sensetta and Stiger, clearly uncertain, torn even.

"What is your name, Captain?" Stiger asked.

The captain hesitated a moment before answering.

"Harex, and this is my lieutenant, Aranam."

"Captain Harex," Stiger said, ignoring the lieutenant and Sensetta. "Do you doubt why I am here? Or, for that matter, who I am?"

"I do not, sir," Harex said. "I can see the dragons. I have no doubts."

Stiger noted Harex's use of the honorific for the first time. The two dragons were still out in the field where they had left them, a half mile away and quite visible. Both had their heads up and were watching what was going on. Should there prove to be trouble, Stiger knew they would come to his aid.

"Then you will let me and my guard enter the city," Stiger said. "It is your duty to do so."

Sensetta leaned toward Harex and said something that was no more than a hissing whisper. The captain turned and looked upon Sensetta for a prolonged moment. Stiger thought he detected disgust in the other man's expression.

Harex turned back to Stiger and said stiffly, almost formally, "I am afraid I cannot do that, sir."

"And why not?" Stiger asked, knowing that bad news would shortly follow.

Therik cracked his knuckles and growled deeply. Harex's eyes flicked to the orc a moment before returning to Stiger. The man had not shown any fear or worry. Stiger's respect for Harex increased. Sensetta and the lieutenant shifted nervously.

"I have my orders, sir," Harex said. "I am sure you can appreciate following one's orders."

Stiger did not like the answer. No one's orders should supersede his, unless they came directly from the senate. And for that to happen, it would have required extensive debate, followed by a vote. In the hour since he'd landed, Stiger deemed that unlikely. Something else was afoot, and that bothered him.

"Who gave these orders?" Stiger asked.

"The orders came directly from the emperor," Sensetta said, answering for Harex.

Stiger's heart plummeted at the revelation. It was as he had feared. They were intentionally denying him the curule chair and crown of wreaths.

Why?

He already knew the answer. After the civil war, most of his family's allies had been purged from the senate and city. It meant there were few friends, let alone allies, left in the senate, no one willing to speak up. They had made their move, preempting his return. Now, blood would be shed. That was a certainty. In fact, he had known before he'd even traveled home it would need to be.

"I am sorry, sir," Harex said. "I cannot permit you entrance into the city."

"And when did this happen?" Stiger asked in a deadly tone that was almost a whisper. If words could cut, his would. "The new emperor, I mean."

"The emperor was crowned last evening, sir," Harex said.

"Who is this emperor?" Stiger struggled to keep his tone calm. "Who has decided to steal my legitimate claim to the curule chair and crown of wreaths?"

"How dare you, sir?" Sensetta's face had gone red. "Your claim is no longer legitimate. The senate has spoken."

"Captain Harex," Stiger said, ignoring Sensetta, "who did the senate make emperor?"

Looking uncomfortable at the position he was in, Harex took a deep breath, and when he released it, he spoke.

"Emperor Lears, sir."

Stiger stiffened, not quite believing his ears. Lears? He blinked, thoroughly astonished. It was as if he'd been punched in the gut. His back began itching, almost painfully so. In fact, all these years later, Stiger could still feel the searing sting of the lash. Sometimes it even woke him up in the dead of night. He turned his gaze to Eli and they shared a meaningful look. Stiger could read the dreadful sorrow in his friend's eyes.

"Seven Levels," Tiro said in a strangled voice. "It had to be Lears. Fortuna just hates us. I swear, sir, there are days she bloody hates us."

"He was anointed by the High Priest before the senate," Sensetta added, almost gleefully. The man seemed to be enjoying Stiger's reaction. "I saw it happen myself, just before I willingly swore the new emperor my undying allegiance. It cannot be undone now. He is the emperor and you are not."

"The High Priest anointed him?" Restus asked in clear disbelief. The paladin began to cough uncontrollably. "He—the High—Priest..."

"Lehr Pompentius Lears?" Stiger spoke in a strangled whisper. He still could not believe what he had heard. No, not Lears. "He was made emperor?"

"Yes," Sensetta confirmed.

Stiger felt sick to his stomach. He sucked in a ragged breath and let it out slowly. As he exhaled, the shock of the news passed, almost abruptly. A wave of wintry calm descended over him.

"So be it," Stiger growled. In a way, the senate's selection made what he knew he had to do easier, more palatable. "They made their choice. So be it."

"And what does that mean?" Sensetta demanded.

In a flash, Stiger's anger kindled to a low burn, for the man that was now emperor was most assuredly his enemy and had been for years. Before his removal as commander of Third Legion, Lears had inflicted terrific pain and suffering upon Stiger personally. At his hands, Stiger had come close to death.

Without Eli, there was no doubt he would not be standing here this day. The elf had saved Stiger and nursed him back to health. Despite having saved Eli's life more than once, no matter how many years he lived, that was one debt Stiger knew he would never be able to fully pay. For all he had done, Stiger would be in Eli's debt 'til the day he died. There was nothing Stiger would not do for him, should he ever ask. And Eli had never asked for anything, other than friendship.

But Lears was a different matter. The man had even condemned two innocent men to death for crimes they had not committed. Stiger had been able to save one, but not the other. That death stung. The man's name had been Barbus, and it still haunted him to this day. At the time, Stiger had been unable to defend ... to save him. All he could do was promise a future reckoning. Well ... it seemed the time of reckoning had finally come.

"You will swear loyalty to Emperor Lears," Sensetta said, breaking in upon Stiger's thoughts.

"Not gonna happen," Stiger said, eyeing Sensetta with disgust. The man was nothing but Lears's creature. "And you are wrong. It can be undone. I made a promise long ago and I intend on fulfilling it. I will kill Lears and send him into the next life. That is a promise you can take back to your master for me."

Sensetta stared at him for a long moment in utter astonishment. He had clearly not expected the response he'd gotten. Stiger could almost read the cold calculation in the other man's eyes as astonishment passed rather quickly. Sensetta smiled. It was slow in forming, but the smile reminded Stiger of a cat who had caught a mouse and intended to play with it before dinner. Only, Sensetta did not understand Stiger was no mouse. He was a predator. He was the tiger and Sensetta was the mouse. So too was Lears and the senate.

"Captain," Sensetta said, almost triumphantly, "you may arrest him now."

There was a long moment where Harex did not move. He just stared at Sensetta as if he'd not understood the order.

"That is an order, Captain," Sensetta said. "He has refused to swear loyalty and promised violence against the emperor. That makes him a traitor, like his father was. He will be executed for it."

Harex did not respond.

Sensetta looked over at the captain. "You outnumber his men, even if yours are only half-trained. Do as I say, or I will find someone else to carry out my orders. Understand me?"

Harex looked at Stiger and then back at his men, who were still talking amongst themselves excitedly. He shared a looked with his lieutenant, who, despite his clear nervousness, gave a slow and deliberate nod.

"Form a line," Ruga barked in a voice well-accustomed to command. "I want two ranks, now. It's time to crack some skulls, boys. We're gonna show those militia over there how real men fight."

Ruga's overstrength century snapped to it, rapidly moving from a marching column to a battle formation. The militia company, which still had been talking amongst themselves excitedly, fell silent. They'd heard Ruga and suddenly appeared unsure, brittle. They seemed confused by what the legionaries were doing, but a battle line was a battle line. There was no mistaking that. A few in the rear even broke ranks to move several steps back through the gate in preparation to run for it.

"I think there must be some mistake," Restus said in a raspy tone. He coughed again. The paladin stepped forward, holding his hand up. It was almost a stagger. "Lears cannot be the emperor. The High Priest would never have anointed him."

"There is no mistake, old man," Sensetta said and turned his gaze from the paladin to Stiger. "A Stiger will never be emperor... never. The senate has decreed it and the church has seen to that by putting their holy stamp upon it." Sensetta pointed a finger at Stiger. "Tioclesion should have wiped out your entire family when he had the chance. It was a mistake not to. Now, we have a real emperor, one who is not afraid to do what must be done."

Stiger was on the verge of reaching out to teach the man manners.

"The church..." Restus seemed rocked by that statement. He coughed again.

"The church backs Emperor Lears, old man, not your pet Stiger. The High Priest himself presided over the ceremony. He gave it his *holy* blessing. As I said, it is done." Sensetta waved a hand at Stiger. "His claim means nothing now. The might of the empire backs the new emperor."

Restus looked to Stiger. The paladin had written directly to the High Priest. Stiger understood the other's thoughts, almost as if they were his own. There was clearly something rotten within the church, especially if the High Priest had acted after he had received Restus's letter. With the speed the senate had made Lears emperor, they must have known he was coming, gotten prior word. But how?

The paladin went into a terrible coughing fit. His legs suddenly failed him. Restus would have fallen had Ruga not stepped forward and gripped the man's arm, holding him upright. Ruga motioned to two of his men to take the pala-din from him.

Stiger had heard enough. He looked at Ruga's men, who had formed two ranks right behind him. The men were grim-faced, hard, and ready for action. So too were Therik and Eli. The orc's hand had come to rest upon the pommel of his sword. Eli had unslung his bow and nocked an arrow, though he wasn't aiming it. They were all a coiled spring, waiting for the tension to be released. All Stiger need do now was give the word and violence would be unleashed.

He had not wanted to be emperor, or the High Father's Champion, but he had come to terms with it. He had not wanted to leave Taha'Leeth's side, but he had. And he had not wanted to spill blood in claiming the curule chair, but the senate had made sure he would.

A cheer abruptly rang out from the battlements above. Stiger looked up. It started as a few, then all of those lining the wall were heartily cheering. From above, they could not sense the tension below. It was just like in Lorium. Navaro, along with Treim and Aetius's agents, had clearly done their job well.

Even though he had not been made emperor, the peo-ple were cheered by his presence. He knew it, felt it to be true, and as the realization came, Stiger understood all was not as bad as it could be.

He turned his gaze back to Harex. The captain's gaze had also gone to the wall. Stiger could see the captain understood too, only too well.

"Even the mob is against you," Sensetta said.

The man had misjudged, and badly.

"As I see it, Captain," Stiger said, drawing Harex's atten-tion and ignoring Sensetta, "you can stand aside and allow me to pass, or"—Stiger held out his hands to either side—"we will go through you. The choice is yours to make."

Grim-faced, Harex eyed Ruga's men. Stiger could read the hesitation in the man. He did not want to fight, not today, not here, not against Ruga's battle-hardened men. He knew what he faced. The outcome of such a contest was already a foregone conclusion. The legionaries would tear through his militia. Stiger could see it all in the man's scarred face, almost as if he could read Harex's thoughts.

"I said," Sensetta hissed, clearly becoming vexed, "arrest him. You outnumber him. Grow some balls, man."

Harex did not bother to look over at the palace functionary. His gaze had fixed upon Stiger. His jaw flexed again.

"No," Harex finally said in a strangled tone.

"What did you say?" Sensetta asked.

Harex drew himself up to a position of attention and saluted Stiger. His tone became firm, hard. "I will not arrest the rightful emperor."

Stiger felt a wave or relief wash over him. He would not have to kill Harex's men.

"You will be executed for this," Sensetta said, fairly seething with rage. "Lieutenant, relieve the captain."

The lieutenant did not move. Next to his captain, he too stood at attention and facing Stiger.

Sensetta looked to Ruga, still apparently not comprehending his situation. "Will you not support your emperor?"

"I know who my emperor is," Ruga said, "and it's not some asshole named Lears."

"I promise you," Sensetta said, malice dripping from his tongue, "you all will be executed for this—"

"Enough." Therik lunged forward, almost impossibly fast, and grabbed Sensetta by his neck. He lifted the man up into the air with one hand. Choking and gagging, Sensetta kicked wildly. He flailed about, batting at the orc's arms. Therik growled like an animal and drew Sensetta close until they were eye to eye.

"Stiger is the emperor, not Lears," Therik roared. "Before long, that shall be clear to all."

The orc shook Sensetta violently before throwing him, as if he were a mere child's doll, discarded in a momentary fit of anger. Sensetta landed hard, six feet from the orc. The back of his head impacted with the paving stones. There was a sickening thud. Sensetta did not get up. He did not even move, just lay, tangled up in his toga. Blood began pooling around his head and back on the paving stones. It stained the white of the man's cloth an ugly burgundy that looked garish against the imperial purple.

Silence reigned. Everyone had gone still, even the militia company. Those on the walls had stopped cheering. All were staring at Therik.

"He was beginning to bore me," Therik said to Stiger, looking over. "And you know I hate being bored and lectured too."

"Kind of ironic, coming from you," Ruga said. "You love lecturing everyone."

Therik gave a grunt.

Stiger turned to Harex. "Captain, order your men to stand aside. We do not want to have to go through you, but we will—if you force me."

"Yes, Imperator," Harex said, then shouted to his men. "Stand aside for the rightful emperor. Stand aside for Emperor Stiger."

Harex's men moved hastily aside, clearing a path into the city. Beyond them and through the open gate, thousands of civilians had gathered. Word had spread of his arrival. They had come out to see the victorious Stiger who had destroyed an army of the confederacy and been made Tioclesion's heir.

"Get your men back into a column," Stiger told Ruga. "I want to get moving."

"Yes, sir." Ruga turned to his men. "Reform into column and prepare to march."

Stiger turned to the paladin. The man had recovered a semblance of his strength and was standing on his own again. The two legionaries assigned to him stood within arm's reach.

"Are you able to travel?" Stiger asked.

"I am feeling sickly," Restus said, "but I can make it to your house. Still, my pride is not such that I am unafraid to admit I might need some help. After all, the High Father teaches that pride is a sin."

"Assist him if he needs it," Stiger told the two men. "I don't want him left behind, understand? If you have to carry him, do so."

"Yes, sir," both men said in unison.

Stiger turned back to Harex, who was now staring beyond them, out into the field. Behind them, there was a deep roar. It seemed to shake the paving stones under their feet. Stiger turned to look as another deep roar sounded.

Both dragons had taken to the air. Their massive wings gracefully carried them in a spiral up into the sky. Illuminated fully by the sun, they were magnificent, awesome in their majesty, and terribly fearsome all at the same time. The dragons roared again.

The people of Mal'Zeel had never seen a dragon, let alone two. Dragons had been mythical creatures, only inhabiting tales told in the epics. No one had seriously believed they actually existed, until today. Just as he had, the people of Mal'Zeel had learned the truth. Dragons were far from mythical creatures, and they had brought the true emperor home to the city.

As every eye watched, both creatures climbed high into the sky and flew directly over the city. Then they were gone from view, as the city wall blocked them from sight. A heart-beat later, there was another roar from the dragons, this one distant-sounding. A long moment of silence followed their passage. Harex recovered rapidly.

"Let me be the first to welcome you to Mal'Zeel, Imperator," the militia captain said.

"Thank you, Captain," Stiger said. "I can't tell you how good it is to be home." Stiger paused a moment, studying those ahead, before turning his gaze back to the captain. "Good luck with the new company. When next we meet, I expect they will be better disciplined and trained."

"They will be, Imperator," Harex said. "You have my word on that."

With that assurance, Stiger strode past the man and started through the city gate. Therik and Eli followed right behind him. Ruga's men came next.

"Look smart, boys," Ruga hollered to his men.

"A cheer for the emperor, boys," Harex shouted, and the militia responded heartily. "Long live Emperor Stiger!"

His men echoed his words in a massed shout. That seemed to break the paralysis of the civilians on the wall and in the street beyond the gate. They picked up the cheer too.

As Stiger passed through the gate, he was greeted enthusiastically by the thousands that waited. He continued forward and onto the main street that led deeper into the city from the gate. This, he thought as he gazed upon the multitudes that had turned out, was a homecoming.

The capital was the hub of trade for the empire and had been for years beyond counting. Riches almost beyond imagining flowed through its gates. Warehouses, leather makers, tanners, smithies, glass makers, woodworkers, clothing shops, home decorations stores...the list of businesses that crowded the main street beyond the gate went on and on.

Signs either hanging before the businesses or painted on the building walls proclaimed what they offered. Goods spilled out from the shops and onto the streets themselves as business owners attempted to capture the interest of passersby. Dozens of wagons, carts, and peddler stalls lined the streets.

None of the buildings had windows on the first floor. That was to discourage theft. Crime in Mal'Zeel was a problem. Many an emperor had tried to crack down on it without much success.

Stiger kept moving forward, down the street. The crowd drew back and away from him to allow him passage. He was afraid if he stopped and engaged those to either side, they would close in and movement would become difficult, if not impossible.

The real reason they drew away was not from his magnificence or stern countenance, but that Stiger walked boldly forward with a hulking orc with a nasty disposition on one side and an elven ranger carrying a nocked bow on the other. That and the entire century of heavily armed legionaries who followed close behind.

Before he had moved thirty yards down the street, six of Ruga's men went jogging past Stiger, three on each side. They fell into position just ahead of him, shields held to the front, eyes watching the crowd to either side. Another ten moved into position to either side. Ruga was creating a bubble of protection around him, Therik, and Eli.

He glanced back at Ruga. The centurion's attention was to either side, his head swiveling this way and that, scanning the cheering crowd as he moved. His men were doing the same. So focused was he on those around them that Ruga did not notice Stiger looking his way. The centurion was only performing his duty, as he should.

Stiger's thoughts shifted to his destination, his family's ancestral home. There he could regroup, send word to Senator Navaro and Aetius's people to get some additional armed men sent his way. Once that was done, he could begin planning with Navaro, Restus, Eli, and Therik. Whatever they decided between them, Stiger understood he could not wait long, for having gained entry to the city, he now had the initiative. And as in war, the initiative was something you did not want to give up.

The crowd seemed to swell in size the deeper they drew into the city. That only served to reinforce his decision to keep moving and maintain a quick pace.

The stone paving under their feet was dirty and bits of trash littered the street: an apple core, a piece of smoothed wood that had snapped off something, chicken bones, a partial wheel from a cart ... and numerous other items. That did not include the animal droppings all over the place. It was almost impossible to avoid stepping in nastiness.

He did not remember the main streets of the city being so dirty, but then again, he had been a teenager when he'd left for the army. Stiger ignored it all and kept going, moving forward.

As they left behind the city gate, Stiger noticed many of the buildings that hemmed in the street were now large, four-story tenements with shops occupying the first floor. The poor of the city had the misfortune of living within them and other similar apartment blocks scattered throughout the city. They were dens of pure misery.

Over the years, many of the men he led had come from such humble origins. They were some of the lucky ones. Through the legion, they had escaped the crushing poverty and misery.

In Mal'Zeel, those who were lucky enough to find available work did so. Those who could not survived however they could, but mostly relied upon the grain dole. The conditions in the worst of the slums were so bad that many turned to crime just to get by. Life for such people was short and hard. Stiger considered that, as emperor, he might be able to do something to make conditions better. At least, he could try. But that was a concern for another day.

"Once," Therik said, leaning close and drawing Stiger's attention. The orc had to shout to be heard over the noise of the crowd.

"What?" Stiger shouted back, cupping a hand to his ear. "What did you say?"

"You told me about something called a triumph," Therik hollered back at him. "Do you recall?"

Stiger turned his gaze to the cheering crowd. This was as close to a triumph as Mal'Zeel had seen for years, perhaps even centuries, for the emperors had not wanted to share the glory with victorious generals. The best one could hope for these days was an ovation in the senate.

It seemed like the entire city had come out to see him. He looked back at Therik and gave a nod. "I remember that conversation. We were riding up to Castle Vrell after a snowstorm."

"Good," Therik said, and snapped his fingers for effect, nearly in Stiger's face. "Good that you do remember our conversation."

After what had happened to Taha'Leeth, he was more than aware of being mortal. "My friend"—Stiger clapped Therik on the back—"I thank you for the reminder. Keep at it whenever you feel a reminder is required."

Therik gave a satisfied nod. Stiger turned his attention back to the crowd, which was continuing to cheer and scream madly. Stiger thought it all incredible, but at the same time he felt some unease. He had never seen so many people gathered so close together and all for him. It was more impressive than what he'd seen in Lorium. To them, he understood, he was more than the triumphant general returning home. He was their hope for the future, the man who would save them, deliver them from the confederacy.

They were showering their love upon him, their hope for the future, and not Lears. That told him he had the hearts of the people, the mob. It gave him power. The senate would learn of this and know fear. That would make the senators unpredictable and more dangerous than usual. He would have to be on his guard.

And yet, more concerning to him was the understanding that the mob's love was a fickle thing and could change in a heartbeat. One day they might cheer him wildly and the next curse him.

"Sir." Ruga had come up from behind. He pointed. "There's a fork ahead in the street. Which way do we go?"

"We're gonna turn right," Stiger said after studying the way ahead of them. He recognized the Massi Fountain at the end of the street. The fountain featured an incredible marble carving of several horses running through a field. Fresh water sprouted up into the air from behind the horses and down into a basin for people to collect.

"What then, sir?"

Stiger gestured with his hands. "Then, we will follow that street about a half mile before turning to the right once again. At that point we will begin climbing a hill, the Teritine, and make a series of turns along smaller streets before arriving at my family's house. The house occupies an entire block. You will need to post your men around it, not only to keep people back, but to look for assassins."

"I understand, sir," Ruga said.

"I will tell you when we need to make turns, okay?"

"Very good, sir," Ruga said and jogged ahead to his men leading the procession. And it *had* become a procession.

The centurion personally guided them onto the correct street. It was only at that moment that Stiger realized Dog had vanished. He looked around, and the big animal was nowhere to be seen. Stiger could not remember seeing him as they marched up to the gate. He felt a momentary pang of loss. But he knew Dog would return when he was ready. He had long since stopped wondering on where the animal went when he took off and was not overly concerned by his absence.

As they continued deeper into the city, the crowds swelled in size. People screamed madly at him, almost in a crazed fashion. Mothers held children out toward him, seeking a blessing. Grown men and women cried unabashedly and openly wept. It was overwhelming. Stiger had never much enjoyed this kind of thing, never craved or desired such adulation. And yet, time and again it was heaped upon his shoulders.

With his men, he had seen the necessity of putting up with a similar outpouring of emotion. They would fight better for it and be motivated by his example, their morale lifted. Now, he supposed it would become a regular thing, and that made him terribly uncomfortable. Though he had been greatly blessed by his god, he saw himself as but a man. But then again, Stiger would not refuse to use the madness of the people to his advantage to see his goals fulfilled. He often wondered if that, in the end, made him a bad person.

That the senate had acted to place another in the curule chair angered Stiger immensely. They had chosen a direct enemy of his family to occupy the throne and lead the empire. That surely had been done on purpose. The thought of it infuriated him.

Worse, they had chosen someone wholly unsuited for the position, someone who would bring the empire to ruin and death to tens of thousands. And what was his father doing while this had happened? Had he sworn loyalty to Lears? Stiger could not imagine such a thing happening. And yet, it might have … What complications would that bring?

Regardless of his father, to Stiger now fell the unenviable task of removing Lears. And that would not be easy. No, it never got any easier. It just didn't. Whenever he gained the crest of a hill, saw some success, a steeper, more challenging one waited behind it and another just beyond that one out of view. It seemed Fortuna loved placing obstacles in his path and screwing with him.

"Perhaps you should consider waving," Eli said, leaning in close. "Get them even more excited … put on a show. You look far grimmer than the dead on a battlefield the day after."

Stiger looked over at his friend and realized Eli was right. These were his people. An enemy more deadly than any the empire had ever faced was marching its way north and the people knew it. That was why they greeted him so warmly. They desperately wanted him to save them.

The mood in the city must have been grim, desperate even. The mob's turnout only proved that true. And all after another had just been made emperor. That was usually a cause for celebration.

The Stiger family name had recently been in disgrace, but at the same time, it ran deep in imperial minds. For hundreds of years, Stigers had been some of the foremost generals of the empire. If anyone was to save them from such a threat, a Stiger would do it, and the people clearly recognized that.

After he had been appointed to command the imperial army, had they cheered his father just as enthusiastically? He suspected they had done just that. How had Lears felt? Was he jealous? Had the new emperor replaced his father? Arrested him? Executed him? There was so much he did not know.

"Well?" Eli asked. "A wave might be a nice gesture. They did come out in the cold to see you."

Shooting Eli a look, he gave in and raised a hand, waving to the crowd. They fairly erupted, cheering much louder, and began to press in toward the procession. Ruga snapped an order to his men and the century closed up. The centurion sent more men moving forward and to the sides around Stiger for protection. Using their shields, they held those who got too eager back.

The going after that was slower, for the front of the procession had to nearly force their way forward through the gathering throng. It seemed with every passing heartbeat more people came out. Word had raced ahead.

"Bless my baby." A woman held out a blanket-wrapped bundle over the shields of the men. "Please, Imperator, bless my baby."

Stiger was reminded of the healing Father Thomas had performed on the infant back in Vrell. At a cost of some of his own life force, he had healed the child of a mortal illness. The vision struck him powerfully, as did the emotion of the moment. The paladin had sacrificed his life to save Stiger's. That was yet another debt he would be unable to repay.

He stumbled a step, recovered, and took a step nearer to see better. The child was no more than a newborn. A few strands of hair covered its head, and despite the noise of the crowd, it was asleep. Not knowing what else to do, he reached out a gloved hand and placed it atop the infant's head.

Unexpectedly, the power within him, his connection to the High Father, flared. Suddenly he felt warm all over. It was as if the chill of the winter day had been shoved away. He pulled his hand back, astonished, looking at it.

Something had happened.

What, he did not know, but it was clear the High Father had acted through him. He met the eyes of the mother, a young woman, a mere slip of a girl with long brown hair and rotten teeth. There were tears in her eyes. She had clearly felt the High Father's power too.

"Thank you, Imperator," she cried, "thank you, bless you."

The crowd pushed in, many holding out hands for him to grasp, and with that, she was swallowed up, pushed back, out of view.

"Best keep moving." Eli took his elbow and guided him onward. Still somewhat shaken, Stiger glanced back at where Father Restus was. The paladin had a sickly cast to him and seemed barely able to walk. He was being assisted by one of the legionaries. But his eyes were upon Stiger. There was a fierce light within them. He too had felt the High Father at work. The paladin gave him a pleased, though exhausted, nod.

A loose paving stone almost caused Stiger to trip. He was forced to watch where he was going. After several steps, he continued to wave. The path ahead would not be this easy. Lears would not make it so. Thoughts of the bastard who had scourged his back darkened his thoughts. The man would fight before he gave up the curule chair, and he likely had a small army within the city. Stiger had only Ruga's men and those that Treim, Aetius, and Navaro had prepositioned.

He would not be able to rely upon the mob to save him. This time, he would have to do it on his own. That meant he needed to strike before Lears got his act together. Striking quickly was the path to victory. Any delay meant defeat.

Each step brought the procession closer to Stiger's home, until finally, they began to climb Teritine Hill. As they did, the streets became narrower, cleaner, the crowds thinner, the way steeper. The buildings were finer, well maintained. There were no tenements in sight, no public housing projects. The street was also better paved and clean.

The people who now emerged from their businesses and homes had means and their cheering was not as enthusiastic as those who had preceded them. They were better educated and likely knew what was coming, a fight that might tear the city apart. The ensuing chaos could ruin their livelihoods. It might even cost them their lives. This was yet another reason to act quickly, before the battle lines could be fully drawn and Lears could secure more support. The man had not even been emperor for a day.

Stiger could read the worry in their eyes, the fear. And yet, still they seemed excited to see him. They cried out for him. Behind the procession, the street was packed with people from the lower reaches of the city, who were following after the common folk. How many followed, Stiger did not know, but it was a considerable number, thousands at least.

As they were about to turn onto the street that led directly to his home, something caught Stiger's nose, a familiar scent, and it triggered a strong memory. He looked around and almost smiled as he came to an abrupt halt, catching the nearest legionaries of his guard by surprise, Therik too.

He looked over at the orc and almost grinned. Despite all the worries and concerns about what lay ahead, it felt good to be home. And this street, the entire city, was home. After all these years and the painful memories of what he had left behind, it truly felt good to return.

"Are you still hungry?" Stiger asked Therik.

"What?" Therik looked at him strangely.

"I asked if you were still hungry."

The entire procession had now stopped. Ruga was looking back at him with concern. It was clear the centurion was wondering what was going on. After a moment, he began making his way back to Stiger.

"He's always hungry," Eli said.

Stiger turned and moved to the backs of the men who were keeping the crowd back with their shields.

"Step aside," Stiger ordered, and as they did, he stepped through his protective bubble. The crowd to his front parted, revealing a bakery and a rotund baker getting on in the years who had come out from behind the counter to watch. The baker wore a soiled smock.

The bakery was a large building, two stories in height, and was just as Stiger remembered. It serviced most of the homes of the hill—at least, it had when he'd lived here.

A marble counter separated the shop side from the bakery itself. Beyond the counter, Stiger could see dozens of men, most likely slaves. They had been working at making dough, checking ovens with long wooden spatulas, or stacking dozens of freshly baked loaves of bread upon wooden shelves set along the walls. They too had stopped to watch the procession move by.

The baker himself looked suddenly nervous as Stiger stepped up to him. The man offered a hasty yet respectful bow.

"How might I help you, sir?" the baker asked. Stiger saw a flicker of recognition in the man's eyes.

"Thetas," Stiger greeted, "it is good to see you again, truly good. Do you remember me?"

"It has been many years, but I do," Thetas said. "You are not the young Stiger I recall. Many years have passed since those days."

"Too many years, I think," Stiger said. Thetas had gone bald since he had last seen him. There were only a few isolated strands of gray hair left by his ears. He had also grown in girth and his face was lined with age.

"Too true," Thetas said, beginning to relax slightly.

"That is, Imperator," Ruga said from behind. The centurion had caught up with Stiger. He had brought several of his men. They began pushing the crowd back a few feet, giving them space. "Best show proper respect, baker."

Stiger held up a hand to Ruga. "There is no need for that."

"He needs to show more respect, sir," Ruga insisted, seeming to not want to yield an inch of ground. "You are the emperor after all, the true emperor."

"My apologies, Imperator," Thetas said, looking more nervous. Despite the cold, sweat began to bead his upper lip and forehead. He clasped his hands together before him and began wringing them. "I did not mean to cause offense. It's just the senate crowned another emperor last evening."

"Thetas is an old family friend," Stiger explained to Ruga, hardening his tone slightly. "His family are clients of ours and he should be treated with respect."

"Yes, sir," Ruga said, and relaxed a tad. "Understood, sir."

With that, the centurion turned his gaze to the crowd about them, clearly looking for threats.

"I assure you, there was no offense taken," Stiger said to Thetas. "As to the other emperor, I will sort that matter out soon enough." Stiger paused, running his gaze over the shelves and racks of the bakery, stacked with hundreds of loaves of fresh bread. The smell alone was almost divine. "Do you still supply my family with fresh, baked bread?"

"I do, Imperator," Thetas said. "Long has it by my honor and pleasure to do so."

"Great." Stiger clapped his hands together. "Then I want you to send enough fresh, baked bread for my men ... enough for a hundred and then some." Stiger jabbed a thumb at Therik. "The orc here is hungry too."

Thetas looked over at Therik, who stood several steps back, next to Eli. The baker paled as he realized Therik was not human. The hand-wringing began again.

"This had better be good bread," Therik rumbled darkly. "You know I want meat."

"It is the best," Stiger said and fished out a gold imperial talon. He tossed it to the baker, who caught it. "I think this should cover it."

"It does, Imperator," Thetas said. The coin rapidly disappeared into a pocket behind the smock he wore. "Thank you. I shall have your order delivered to your house within the hour."

"Very good," Stiger said. "I've been dreaming about your bread for years. I can't tell you how much of a treat this will be."

"I will not disappoint," Thetas said loudly, the nervousness having retreated, so that the nearest people in the crowd could follow. The crowd, which had pushed closer to hear what was transpiring, gave another cheer.

In the coming days, Thetas would be a busy man. Everyone and their brother would want to order from the emperor's baker. That was, if Stiger was still alive and actually sitting on the curule chair. It was only a matter of time before Lears came for him. And Stiger did not intend to give the man the chance. If he had anything to say about it, the initiative would remain firmly with him.

Stiger turned away toward Therik.

"We can undoubtedly find some beef at my family's house," Stiger said. "And if we can't find enough, I will send for more."

"That is acceptable," Therik said, then looked at Thetas. "I look forward to trying your bread, baker."

Thetas inclined his head.

"If we're lucky," Stiger said to Therik, "there will be some stew that we can use the bread for sopping ... butter too."

Therik perked up at that. "Now that, I like."

Stiger gave an amused grunt and stepped back onto the street. He resumed his trek up the hill, Ruga's protective bubble moving with him. The crowd had pushed closer around his guards but did not seem to want to push past them. There was just something about Ruga's men that kept them at bay, a certain grimness that was a warning in and of itself.

Stiger glanced around, spotted Tiro, and then motioned for the sergeant to join him. It was time to make the next move in the deadly game he was playing. And with any luck, it would keep the initiative firmly on his side.

"Sir," Tiro said, coming up.

"You know what to do?" Stiger asked. The centurion was only wearing his service tunic.

"I do, sir," Tiro said.

"No questions?"

"None, sir," Tiro said. "Ruga's already arranged for two men to join me. They fell out and have been following along with the crowd. Have no worries, sir. I'll find them if they're in the city. I will get it done, just as you want."

"I know you will," Stiger said. "Good luck."

Tiro fell back and Stiger resisted the urge to turn to watch. With any fortune, the sergeant would be able to slip away unnoticed into the crowd. He prayed Tiro's mission was successful and silently wished him well. For if Stiger's old sergeant failed, things would become difficult...perhaps even impossible.

Then again, Tiro had never failed him. Stiger took comfort in that. In the distance, he saw the outer wall of his ancestral home. It looked just as he'd left it...only there were guards posted about it...and if he was not mistaken, they were praetorians.

CHAPTER EIGHT

"Oh, now that's just bloody great," Stiger said as he came to a halt. He let out a frustrated breath and slapped his side. They were just twenty yards away from the entrance to his home. He placed his hands upon his hips as he gazed upon the praetorians.

"Halt," Ruga ordered and the guard came to a stop. "I don't believe it," Eli said. "Tell me that's not Corus?"

The elf was eying the officer who stood before the entrance to Stiger's home with a line of twenty praetorians just behind him. Each carried a shield and javelin, not to mention the short sword. Corus was in the armor and kit of a praetorian captain. There was no question in Stiger's mind who the man served. He had always been Lears's creature.

"And Lieutenant Yanulus too." Stiger felt the keen sting of anger mix with a sense of terrible frustration. Years had passed since he had seen either man, and now they stood before him, barring his path. "As the High Father wills it..."

"Who are they, sir?" Ruga asked, coming up.

Stiger did not respond. Instead, he studied Corus's men. Each man's armor and purple cape looked brand-new. There was no lived-in or used look to their kit, like one might see with a regular legionary after a few months of regular use. It was as if they had just received their kit, which, he considered, was quite likely. To his knowledge, all of the praetorians had gone with Tioclesion. Stiger had disbanded the survivors. Upon becoming emperor, Lears must have elevated and made new praetorians, specifically Corus and his company from Third Legion. This was yet another complication Stiger had not anticipated. How many more were there? How many men would he have to go through to get to Lears?

Behind the praetorians, the house itself was two stories in height and just as Stiger remembered it. The compound took up the entire block, which ran around three hundred yards in length. There were no windows on the ground floor, but several on the second. All had been shuttered, most likely against the cold.

The praetorians were posted around the house. From what he could see down the street, two stood below wherever there was a window. The captain, with twenty of his men, and his lieutenant had positioned themselves just before the double-doored entrance to his home. Both doors were open and led to a small, tiled courtyard. A timid slave, likely a footman, was peering nervously from around one of the open doors.

"It doesn't look like they were expecting us," Stiger said to Eli. "Otherwise his men would be with him, all of them, and they'd be formed up into a line of battle several ranks deep. Corus doesn't have a full-strength company present, at least from what we can see. There are likely a few more on the back side of the house, but I'd hazard only a handful."

"Who is he, sir?" Ruga asked again, pointing toward the praetorian captain.

"I would like to know that too," Therik said.

"He is a bastard from my past," Stiger said, looking between the two of them. "When I left for the south, he was the commander of Fourth Company, of Third Legion."

"Corus was and likely still is in Lears's pocket," Eli added. "Those are undoubtedly his men from the Fourth. In point of fact, I believe I recognize some of them."

"Me too," Stiger said. "They must be Lears's praetorians now, a reward for loyal service. And if they are his men from the Fourth, they're good fighters, some of the best Third Legion has to offer."

"Do you think it will come to blood, sir?" Ruga asked, studying the two praetorian officers and the twenty men of the scratch line Corus had created. "We do have superior numbers. It would be suicide for them to try to stand in our way."

"It will come to blood," Stiger said unhappily. He understood Corus would not go down without a fight. He would follow the orders he'd been given by Lears, even if it meant his own death. That was the type of soldier Corus was, loyal and determined. "And in truth, this meeting between us has been a long time coming."

"I will see that my men are ready for action, sir," Ruga said and stepped off to speak to his optio in low tones.

Stiger rubbed his jaw, feeling intense frustration mingle with his anger. "I'd been hoping to avoid any fighting until we went for Lears. Now, that seems unlikely."

"Oh," Therik said, looking over at him. "Did you really think claiming your throne would be that easy?"

"No," Stiger said. "I did not."

"They are standing watch over your father," Eli said. "Maybe even Max, too. Your father and elder brother might be inside."

Stiger had concluded the same. He'd not seen his elder brother since he'd left for the legions. They had once been close, but like everything else, the civil war had ended that. Max had gone off to serve and represent the family as a senator, while Stiger had been set to training for a military life. Over the years they had corresponded some, but not much more had passed between them than that. He understood Max had a wife and child. He looked over at the elf. "Do you mean guarding or keeping them as prisoners?"

"The latter," Eli said. "Lears might not be in a position to directly kill him. After all, the senate placed your father in command of the army protecting Mal'Zeel."

"Only now that army is marching away to the east," Stiger said. "And if what you say is correct, Lears must have put someone else in command, someone he feels he can trust."

"True," Eli said, "but with all that is going on, executing your father may play badly with the people—your mob. We saw how they acted in Lorium. The change in command might not be public knowledge yet. Lears might have even suppressed it."

Mention of the mob caused Stiger to glance about them. The people were still there, surrounding them, but much of the cheering had died off. They clearly understood a confrontation was likely. An eager mood, a sense of anticipation, was in the air. The mob loved games and contests of violence. This was just one more such game. Only it was a deadly one.

"You do have a point." Stiger grimaced, turning his gaze back to Corus and his praetorians. "I don't want to kill his men. No matter how detestable Corus is to me personally, they were … are our comrades."

"I told you to be ruthless," Therik said firmly. "You cannot think that way. Kill your enemies where they stand, murder them in the dead of night if you have to. Lay them low and do it as ruthlessly as possible. Only then will your enemies truly fear you. With that fear comes respect, respect of what you are capable of doing, and makes those standing on the sidelines think twice before pitting themselves against you."

Feeling his frustration mount, Stiger rubbed his jaw. He eyed the orc for several heartbeats. Ruling by fear was not how he envisioned things going. Then again, the orc frequently made a lot of sense. Therik knew what he was talking about. It was something he needed to consider, for fear was just another tool and one he should not disregard out of hand.

"What would you suggest I do?" Stiger asked Therik. "Send Ruga's men forward? We certainly outnumber them."

"That is one option," Therik said, then studied Corus briefly. He turned back to Stiger. "You two have history. It's bad, right?"

"Their history doesn't get any worse," Eli confirmed.

"I think I have made that plain," Stiger said.

"You people have honor fights, no?" Therik asked. "When there is bad blood, is there no way to satisfy that by personal combat?"

"You mean duels?" Stiger asked, turning his gaze back to Corus, suddenly seeing things in a new light. "Yes, we have duels, and that bastard has wanted a piece of me for as long as I can remember."

Corus, for his part, was gesturing at him and Eli, giving some sort of instruction to Yanulus. The lieutenant gave a vigorous nod, turned, and snapped an order. A heartbeat later, one of the captain's men went running off and away from them. He was clearly on his way to summon reinforcement.

Was the rest of Corus's company billeted in the nearby buildings? Stiger glanced again at Therik. Whatever he decided, Stiger understood he needed to do it quickly before the entirety of Corus's company arrived. Then, it would be they who were outnumbered.

"Challenge him to a duel," Therik said. "Play upon his honor if you have to, and just kill him. You chop the head off the snake and the body's not much of a problem after that."

"Corus is good," Stiger said. "He's an expert fighter and knows what he's doing with a sword. It will not be so easy as you think."

"Yes," Eli said, "Corus was always a superb fighter. It was his personality that was lacking."

"I can't disagree with that," Stiger said. "He's a bastard on the best of days. It's just in his nature."

"Challenge him," Therik urged.

The elf turned his gaze to Therik. "I thought you wanted to be the one to kill Ben?"

"After all of our sparring?" Therik said, ignoring Eli while sounding exasperated with Stiger. "Are you so blind? I doubt there is another who can beat you in one-on-one combat. You have become faster and more deadly than you were when we first began. If I had to wager money on a human in single combat, I would back you with my own coin."

"You have no money," Eli said.

"Exactly why I am not going to place a bet on the outcome of such a fight," Therik said. "Besides, even if I had some coin, no one here will bet on Corus. They've all seen Stiger fight."

Blowing out a breath, Stiger eyed Therik for a long moment. He turned his gaze back to Corus. The man was watching him, studying him. Their eyes locked. After all these years, Stiger still felt a gnawing dislike for the man, a hatred even. He knew it was mutual, for Stiger's father had killed Corus's father in personal combat back during the civil war. There was that and a lot more history between them. And all of it boiled down to a good deal of bad blood.

No matter what Therik said, Corus was very good with a short sword. He always had been. Like Stiger, Corus was a killer. Should they duel, there would be no mercy given, nor any asked for. It would be to the death.

"Some things," Stiger said after a moment, "you just need to do for yourself."

"Now," Therik said to Eli, "we get a little excitement."

"There is excitement," Eli said, "and then there is excitement. I thought you knew that?"

Therik shot the elf a frown.

Stiger started moving again. While they had been talking, Ruga had reformed his men into a small line just ahead of Stiger. It matched that of the praetorians. As Stiger moved, the centurion snapped an order to advance.

"Halt," Ruga called when Stiger came to a stop ten feet from Corus and his line. "Spread out. Push those civilians back. They are too close. I want our line extended, sharply now. Optio, give me two more lines, there and there."

"Too afraid to come out from behind your men and talk with me, Stiger?" Corus called. "Hiding behind your men—I should have expected as much, coming from you."

Even just the sound of Corus's voice irritated Stiger. With his time in the past, it had been years since he'd set eyes upon the man, and still his tone of voice and how he formed his words grated on Stiger's nerves. Stiger felt the patchwork of scars that stitched their way across his back begin to itch, almost painfully.

Here before him was one of his oldest enemies, a man he had long wanted to kill. And yet, Stiger had been specifically prohibited, ordered in fact, from taking his revenge. Now, nothing stood in his way but Corus himself.

Stiger felt the rage stir within his breast. It took effort, and force of will, to remain calm amidst the storm of emotion that assailed him. All of the history between them, the vitriol and animosity, was coming down to this very moment.

"Are you going to continue to hide behind your men?" Corus asked, disdain dripping from his tone. "Just like you hid all those years behind Treim and Aetius's skirts?"

"I like him already," Therik said with a sick chuckle. "He may be an enemy, but outnumbered, he has balls."

Pushing his way through the line, Stiger stepped out before his men. Yanulus was at his captain's side. Stiger could read the hatred in both their gazes.

Behind the two officers, Corus's men looked grim-faced and determined. Even outnumbered as they were, they would not run or break easily. These were well-trained and disciplined boys. Corus had always been a supreme asshole, but he had trained and run a first-rate company of fighters.

Eli stepped up to his side, as did Therik. Ruga, holding his shield, pushed his way past his men and stood off to the side a bit. Ready to draw steel, the centurion had his hand wrapped around the hilt of his sword. Ruga had also sent men down the side streets. These had formed a line in each direction, sealing them in, box-like, before the open double doors of Stiger's family home. The rest of his men had fallen into a second rank behind the first.

Corus's eyes flicked to Therik and then Eli before returning to Stiger.

"From the rumors flying about the city, I had heard Tioclesion named you his successor." Corus spat on the ground before Stiger. "I honestly don't know what he was thinking. A Stiger as emperor? Really? What madness is that? Your own father fought against Tioclesion's claim to the curule chair."

"What are you doing here?" Stiger asked, refusing to be baited. He was already angry and saw no need to lose his head to the madness of rage. In fact, that was the last thing he desired, for it was clearly what Corus wanted. To beat this man, Stiger understood he needed to remain calm, cool, and in control of his emotions. He had to be a ruthless killer. With Corus, that was the only way to win.

"Serving my emperor," Corus said, "the rightful emperor." He glanced back toward the house. "And ... keeping your father safe as a babe in her mother's arms."

"I don't suppose you will agree to let him go?" Stiger asked.

"Why pretend to care about your father?" Yanulus said. "Everyone in the Third knew you two did not get along."

"He is family," Stiger said simply. "I am sure even someone like you can understand that."

"He will be killed," Corus said, "if you try to go through me. I have two good men with him, and they have their orders. Even a Stiger should be able to understand that."

"We don't have to do this," Stiger said. "There is no need for bloodshed. You're outnumbered. You could just walk away."

"You are right," Corus said. "I could. So too could you. I suggest you do just that, because I am not moving."

"Go"—Yanulus waved a hand dismissively—"while you can."

"I think we know I won't be doing that," Stiger said.

"I figured not," Corus said. "Then what do you propose?"

"We have unfinished business between us," Stiger said, "especially after your actions in the north."

"What actions?" Corus said.

"You know of what I speak," Stiger said. "Do not play games with me."

Corus gave a shrug of his shoulders.

"If I am to be honest," Corus said, after a slight hesitation, "lashing you was one of the true pleasures of my life. It was a blessed day when Lears handed me that whip. I think on it often. I really do, and each time it brings on a smile of satisfaction, a job well done."

Stiger stilled. He kept his anger at a slow boil and reminded himself to remain in control, no matter how much rage and bile he wanted to direct at the man. What had been done was done. It was history now, and yet, it was his personal history, part of his own story.

"I enjoyed watching my captain discipline you," Yanulus added. There was a malicious note to his voice, a hint of the cruelty Stiger had seen the man exhibit in the past. "But he clearly went too easy on you. You still don't know your place."

Stiger regarded them for several heartbeats before he spoke.

"I should thank you both," Stiger said, in a near whisper. "You did me a great service."

"What do you mean?" Corus asked, scowling slightly. "What service? What are you talking about?"

"Lashing my back," Stiger said.

"What?" Corus asked.

"It made me stronger." The experience had shaped him in ways he had not fully understood 'til years later. But that did not mean a reckoning was not in order. It had taken Stiger more than a year before he had healed to the point where he could serve his empire again. That year had been filled with agony and pain. He had suffered almost beyond comprehension. It had been the ultimate struggle, and without Eli's help, he would not have survived. "Recovering taught me the meaning of strength, perseverance, and willpower."

There was a long moment of silence. Corus exchanged a glance with his lieutenant.

"If you say so," Corus said, sounding unconvinced. "I'll admit, I had hoped you'd die after being lashed. With the beating you took, any normal person would have perished. But you—you were just too stubborn to do that. You've always been too bloody stubborn."

"You and Lears gave me a reason to survive," Stiger said in reply.

"So, here we are," Corus said, "all those years later."

"Stop wasting my time," Stiger said, tiring of the game they were playing. He placed his hand upon the hilt of his sword. "Let's finish what's between us, once and for all."

"I've wanted to duel you for years." Corus slowly drew his sword so that it hissed coming out of the scabbard. "You can't hide from me, not anymore."

"I never did." Stiger said as he took off his bearskin cloak. He handed it to Eli. He shrugged his shoulders about to make sure his armor was comfortably positioned.

"We do this without shields," Corus said, "just blades."

"Fair enough," Stiger said and held out both hands.

"I am going to enjoy watching this," Therik rumbled.

"Your pig speaks." Yanulus gave an amused chuckle. "Like a pet dog, can it do tricks too? I've heard pigs can be smart like dogs."

Therik growled.

"Perhaps after my captain kills Stiger," Yanulus said to Therik, "we will have a roast. You will be invited, of course...as the main course." Yanulus laughed again. "I think I might enjoy that. Though who knows how orc tastes, eh? You might be stringy, like mule."

Therik turned his gaze full on the lieutenant, his eyes narrowing dangerously. He bared his teeth in a smile, showing his sharpened tusks. "After he's done with your captain, and cuts him down to size, I *am* going to kill you, little man. And I will enjoy that, oh so very much."

"Enough talk," Corus snapped, his gaze fixed upon Stiger. "I've been waiting for years for this chance."

Stiger exhaled a long breath through his nose. It steamed on the air as he pulled Rarokan out. He kept a tight lid on the door to the wizard's prison, locking the sword's power within. He wanted to beat Corus all on his own and without any help from the sword. He could feel Rarokan's irritation and hunger, for the mad wizard wanted the man's soul. Corus had the spark the sword sought.

"Sir," Ruga said, stepping nearer. Though he had seen Stiger fight on more than one occasion, the centurion was clearly uneasy about what was to come. "Are you sure about this? I can stand in for you. As emperor, you should not be fighting a duel."

"I am very sure," Stiger said. "Stand back and do not interfere."

Ruga looked torn between his duty to protect Stiger and obeying his orders. There was a moment where Stiger thought he might refuse. It passed and his face hardened.

"Yes, sir," Ruga said stiffly. The centurion stepped back, heated gaze fixating on Corus.

Stiger drew his dagger in his free hand. Corus watched him with what seemed like a grim eagerness. Stiger spun the dagger in his hand and then gestured at the captain with its blade.

"Corus," Stiger said, "this has been long in coming."

"Yes, it has." Corus gave a salute with his sword and then started forward. "I am going to enjoy gutting you like a fish."

Stiger did not reply but moved to meet his opponent. He knew there would be no more banter, no more goading.

The time for fighting was at hand. Two skilled and determined soldiers, the best the legions had to offer, were about to cross swords.

Corus feinted, causing Stiger to bring his blade up to block. He found only air as the man grinned, danced back a half step, then abruptly attacked, lunging out and stabbing straight for Stiger's hip. It was a fast strike, almost lightning quick. A lesser swordsman would have been caught by surprise and thrown off-balance. But Stiger had been ready. He had expected something like it, for Corus had always been one to make the first move, to lash out. He was aggressive and preferred being on the attack rather than on the defensive, waiting for an opening from his opponent. Corus preferred to batter his opponents into submission before beating them. Stiger did not intend to give him the chance.

He swung his blade downward to counter. The two swords met in a ringing clash. Stiger pushed his opponent's sword toward the ground and stepped into Corus's attack and bodily up against the man, almost hugging him.

The tip of Corus's sword struck the paving stone, causing sparks to fly as it grated along the ground. Corus struggled to bring the sword up, but Stiger had it firmly pinned, leaning against the man's sword arm with almost his whole body. Without giving his opponent time to breathe, Stiger, with his free hand, brought his dagger around and drove it up and under Corus's extended sword arm, right into the soft flesh of the armpit. The razor-sharp dagger drove inward, up to the hilt. Corus grunted from the impact.

The surprise in his opponent's eyes was plain, as was the pain...so too was the recognition that he had been hurt badly, even mortally. They stared at one another for a heartbeat. Corus seemed frozen in place. Stiger was not.

Shifting his sword around Corus's, Stiger stabbed the point into the captain's extended thigh and pushed hard. He felt the steel grate against the leg bone as the blade went deep before emerging out the other side, just above the back of the knee.

Corus gave another grunt of pure agony, then staggered as Stiger yanked the sword blade out. Blood fountained and flowed in a gush from the leg wound. Releasing hold of his dagger, Stiger left it embedded in his opponent and took a step back and away. Corus's injured leg gave out and he collapsed to the ground on his side. The man's sword clattered across the paving stones. He lay on his side for a long moment, then rolled onto his back. Blinking his eyes and panting like a dog, he stared up into the sky.

A stunned silence followed. The fight had taken no more than a span of heartbeats. Therik had been right. Their sparring sessions had made him faster, more deadly. The proof of it was his defeated opponent. The fight was over. It had ended before it had really begun.

There was a heavy *thwack*, followed by a gagging sound. Stiger looked around to see Yanulus staring at Therik in horror. The lieutenant had drawn his sword and had advanced toward Stiger. He stood, almost within arm's reach, sword poised and frozen in the act of stabbing at Stiger's exposed back. Yanulus dropped his weapon. His hands went to his throat, from which the hilt of Therik's dagger protruded. He pulled the dagger free with a single yank. In jets and spurts, blood flowed from the wound. Yanulus stared at the dagger, a dumbfounded look upon his face that was almost comical.

"There will be no roast, little man, not today," Therik growled, "but there will be two funerals."

MARC ALAN EDELHEIT

Blood spraying outward in ever increasing pulsing jets from his ruined throat, Yanulus slowly collapsed to his knees. He held his hands out toward Stiger, almost imploringly, for help. A moment later, his eyes rolled back, and he fell over onto his side, legs twitching. His lifeblood pooled around him as it continued to pump out onto the street.

"You've killed me," Corus gasped in pain, drawing Stiger's attention once again. The captain's head was turned toward Stiger, his pupils wide as he stared at his killer.

"I have."

Oddly, Stiger felt a sense of regret. Despite their mutual animosity, Corus had been a good officer and leader. Stiger could respect that.

"If anyone was to kill me," Corus said, drawing in a painful breath. Blood frothed to his lips. One of his lungs had clearly been punctured by the blade still embedded in his armpit. His speech was barely above a whisper. "I'd rather it be you. You are still a bastard."

Sucking in a breath, Stiger let it out slowly. "As are you."

"Good that we understand one another." Corus, with some effort, cleared his throat. "Now finish me, so I do not suffer. The pain is..." Corus gave a groan and did not finish his sentence. He recovered a moment later. "The only other thing I would ask of you... and I know I do not deserve it... spare my men. They are good boys and... I loved leading them. It was the best thing I ever did."

Stiger's eyes flicked to Corus's men. They were looking on, astonished by what had happened. Several pairs of nervous eyes met his. They did not appear on the verge of seeking vengeance for their captain's imminent death. Duels between nobles were generally respected, the outcomes honored. It was thought by many the gods had a say in such

202

contests. And despite how fast the fight had gone, it had been fairly fought.

"Well?" Corus cleared his throat, then hocked up some blood. "Will you spare my men?"

"I will." Stiger gave a nod. "They will have a choice, to enter my service or go on their way. Will that do?"

"Yes," Corus said. "It is quite generous. No matter how much it pains me, I thank you for that kindness. Now, finish me. End this thing between us."

Stiger stepped forward. The hate he felt for the man had evaporated. Now there was only pity, sadness, and oddly regret that it had come to this. Without hesitation, and with Corus firmly meeting his gaze, Stiger drove the point of his sword down into the other's throat, ripping it open. Hot blood shot out, spattering across Stiger's sword arm and his face. Corus choked once and convulsed violently before falling still. It was finished. Stiger withdrew his sword and stepped back. There was now one less enemy in the world to worry about.

Therik moved forward and retrieved his dagger. With a small towel, he calmly cleaned blood off, then sheathed it.

Stiger turned his gaze to the line of praetorians. They looked on stunned, but Stiger could also detect worry in their expressions. It was clear they were wondering if he would honor his word to their former captain. Stiger was, after all, a Stiger. He regarded them for a long moment before speaking.

"You know me," Stiger said finally. "Not too long ago, we were comrades in arms. Third Legion was our home." He pointed at Corus with his bloodied sword. "Your captain and I had unsettled business between us. It's done and over." Stiger paused to suck in a breath. "As I promised, I will give you a choice. You can leave now, walk away, and not look back. Or you can join us, serve me and the empire. There will be a place for all of you. On that, you have my word."

"If you let them leave," Therik said, "they will go to this Lears."

"I agreed to let them go and I will," Stiger said firmly to Therik. He turned to Corus's men. "Just so we understand one another, I will do to Lears what I did to Corus. And you all know from our time in the Third together... that no matter how difficult or impossible the task seems, I always get it done. Make no mistake. I will kill Lears and anyone who tries to stop me from doing it." Stiger paused to let that sink in. "The choice is yours. Make it now."

"I will serve you, sir." A sergeant immediately stepped forward and came crisply to attention. "It will be my honor, if you will have me."

"What is your name, Sergeant?"

"Sergeant Lanist, sir," the man said.

A heartbeat later, a second man joined his sergeant, then all of the men stepped forward. They too came to attention.

"It seems my men will serve you too, sir."

"Very good, Sergeant," Stiger said. "For the time being, you will be under Centurion Ruga's command."

"Yes, sir," the sergeant said. "I will follow the centurion's orders."

"Now, Sergeant," Stiger said, "would you kindly go and see that the men holding my father do not harm him? I would be irked were anything to happen to him."

"I will, sir," Lanist said. He saluted.

"Ruga," Stiger said, "take two men and go with him."

"Yes, sir," Ruga said and pointed to two of his men. "You both are with me."

They followed Lanist through the open doors and into the courtyard beyond.

"What is your name?" Stiger asked a corporal who was standing at attention with the others.

"Corporal Heben, sir."

"Go tell the rest of your men posted around my home what occurred here," Stiger said. "If they want to join me, they are welcome to do so. If not, they are free to go. Make them the same offer I made you, understand?"

"I do, sir."

"Get to it, man."

The corporal saluted and hastily left, almost running down the street.

Stiger turned his gaze back to Corus and breathed out an unhappy breath. One more enemy had been felled. The fight had not even left him winded. After all these years, their feud had finally ended in blood, just as he always thought it would.

"I knew you'd take him," Therik said, not with a little pride. He clapped Stiger on the shoulder armor. It was almost a body blow. "Fighting with me has made you better than good."

The orc handed Stiger his small towel. Stiger wiped the blood from his face and then cleaned the sword with the soiled towel. When Rarokan was clean, he sheathed it. As he handed the towel back to Therik, the crowd that had been watching gave a mighty cheer. Stiger glanced around, surprised. He had forgotten about them. The nearest must have heard his every word as he addressed Corus's men.

Stories would undoubtedly race throughout the city about how he had killed a praetorian captain in personal combat and spared the rest of the praetorians, who then pledged themselves to his service.

The tale, like so many others, would grow in the telling. In time, Corus would become a famous villain. He would be eight feet tall, thoroughly disreputable, and as skilled as they came with a sword, which in a way he had been ... just not eight feet tall. Stiger glanced at the orc. Therik had been right. Corus had not stood a chance.

With so many witnesses, Lears would shortly hear of what had happened. He hoped the man knew fear, for with a certainty, death would be coming for him soon enough.

"Right," Stiger said and looked toward the door to his home. "Let's go see my father."

"I am sure he will be just thrilled to meet Therik," Eli said. "Do you think he can behave himself in polite company?"

"Watch it, elf," Therik growled.

Stiger glanced once more at the orc and chuckled. "Let's go find out."

With that, he started forward. Corus's men moved aside for him. Stiger hesitated at the open doors and the entrance to the courtyard. He had stepped through these very doors over ten years before and started out on a journey of a lifetime, one he could never have imagined possible. Placing a hand on the doorframe, he patted it fondly, then stepped through and into the courtyard.

CHAPTER NINE

The courtyard was empty. There was not a soul in sight. The slave he had seen earlier was gone. Stiger looked around. He remembered the courtyard being bigger, nicer. He figured he was seeing it anew or really with an older pair of eyes. The space wasn't all that big. There were two raised stone garden beds to the right side. As it was winter, the plants had been removed. All that remained was the dirt.

In his youth, his mother had spent time gardening here, planting flowers and decorative plants. She took pride in her work and refused to let the slaves or servants help. As a child, he had even assisted her. Those had been good days, but they were long gone, lost to the mists of time and memory. Stiger blew out an unhappy breath at the sudden wash of memories. Some were fond, but most were painful.

The plastered walls of the courtyard had been painted into red and black patterns. Stiger had never learned the reason for it and had not thought to ask. The paint had long since faded. The plaster underneath was crumbling too. The entire courtyard had a decayed, neglected look to it.

On the left wall, rings had been mounted waist-high so that animals could be tethered when there were visitors or deliveries. Two of the six rings were missing. One of those remaining was hanging at an angle, clearly on the verge of falling off. Scowling, he surveyed the courtyard once again, wondering on the lack of basic maintenance. Why wasn't his father keeping up the home? It was a question he did not know the answer to.

He continued up to the main door, which was shut. Close behind, Eli and Therik followed. Tugging on the handle, Stiger found it unlocked. He pulled the heavy wooden door open. The hinges were well-oiled and barely made a sound as the door swung wide.

Stiger's home was a veritable fortress. The walls were thick and made of cemented brick covered over in plaster. There was only one main entrance and exit. This was it. The door, too, was thick and could be barred from the inside. It would take a heavy battering ram and team of determined men to even attempt to force it open.

Stiger peered into the near darkness that greeted them from the open doorway. Beyond was the grand hall, which was lined with beautifully crafted marble columns, each reaching up to the ceiling thirty feet above.

This hall was the family's public face, the central feature of the house, from which all rooms and passageways connected. It was the showcase that visitors were to be awed by, boldly proclaiming and displaying the family's grandeur, wealth, prestige, and power. The grand hall was also the venue where most guests were entertained. Few were permitted the privilege of venturing into the family's private quarters and suites.

But this too was not how Stiger recalled it. The hall was dim, almost completely dark, with only a handful of burning lamps scattered about. The large braziers placed next to each column had not been lit. These would normally keep the hall heated and the chill at bay. That and an overly large fire pit, which sat in the direct center of the hall. Directly above the fire pit was open sky.

When the house had been built, it had been constructed with a round hole set in the roof. This allowed the smoke to escape. Conversely, it also allowed the rain and weather in. The floor curved down slightly toward the fire pit. There were drains under it, so that when it rained, the water had somewhere to go, rather than pooling and flooding the home.

Without the opening in the roof and the light it provided, Stiger would have been able to see little of the grand hall. He hesitated a moment, glancing about, wondering if a trap had been laid. He saw no one hiding in the shadows.

"I don't see anyone either," Eli said, after scanning the hall. He had clearly had the same thought of ambush.

Stiger relaxed. Elven eyes were superior to a human's in the dark.

"Not exactly a warm homecoming," Eli said. "In fact, it's almost as cold in here as it is outside."

"No," Stiger agreed, "definitely not a welcome home. Then again, look who was waiting just outside when we arrived."

Stiger shifted his gaze back to the fire pit. It had been stacked with chopped logs, but the fire had yet to be lit. Basically, the stage had been set for a good fire. Arranged around the pit were chairs and a couch for reclining. A table with a pitcher and several cups had been set just off to the side. Beyond that, there were no other furnishings in the hall.

Stiger recalled the place of his youth as seemingly afire with light, as every lamp and candle available, along with the fireplace, had been lit. His mother and father had held lavish parties, entertaining guests by the dozens here. He could even remember his mother laughing and singing with guests as hired musicians played popular or catchy tunes.

She'd had a lovely voice. It was only a distant memory, and yet the sound of it seemed to still echo off the walls.

"This is your home?" Therik asked, sounding dubious. "Are you certain we are in the right place?"

"Corus being here did not convince you?" Stiger asked, looking over.

"You are a Stiger after all," Therik said. "Everyone we've come across seems to know your family." Therik held out both arms. "I just expected more."

"Me too," Stiger said as he ran his gaze about the room once more. Ever since his mother's death, the place had seemed cold, sterile, and without life. Now, it was worse.

Stiger started forward toward the unlit fire. Around the fire pit, a large mosaic had been laid. It told of the story of the Three Brothers—the High Father, Neptune, and Pluto—dividing up the world between them. The mosaic was a work of incredible art, one that Stiger as a child had not fully appreciated. Now, things were different.

Stiger stopped, studying the mosaic. He was the direct instrument, the weapon of one of the brothers, the most powerful of the three. The mosaic showed the High Father taking the heavens, Neptune the sea, and Pluto claiming the underworld. Beyond the columns, there were elaborate frescos telling more of the story in elaborate detail. In the darkness, Stiger could not fully see them.

With the struggle for this world, he wondered what Pluto and Neptune were doing. So far, he'd only seen the High Father, Thulla, Tanithe, and Divernus intercede to actively stop Castor and Valoor from gaining dominance. What were all of the other gods doing? Were they operating in the High Father's interest or against the great god? Were some working with Valoor? It was an interesting thought and one he'd not considered before. It was possible some might pose a threat. There was just so much he did not know.

He would have to ask Restus about it, at least when the man was better. Perhaps even speaking with Menos or Ogg would help. That was, if the opportunity presented itself. Both had abruptly left without word. Not for the first time did Stiger wonder on where they had gone. He found it incredibly frustrating.

His gaze traveled to his feet and the white marble tile that had been placed just before the mosaic. The normally polished tile was covered in a layer of dust. He moved his boot across the floor, shifting the dust aside. The place appeared to not have been cleaned in a long while. It needed a good, deep cleaning. He continued forward and stopped before the fire pit.

Eli stepped up to his side. "I must admit, I am disappointed."

"You and I both," Stiger said.

A door banged open and a slave appeared from a side passage to their left. That door led to the servants' quarters and the main kitchen. The slave approached and Stiger saw it was the same one he had spotted earlier, a boy, barely out of his teens. He bowed in respect, though in a somewhat awkward fashion. Blinking repeatedly, his eyes kept shifting between Eli and Therik, as if he could not believe he was seeing an elven ranger and orc in person. Then he seemed to remember himself.

"How … how …?" he stuttered as Therik's intense gaze turned on him. The boy almost stopped talking, then recovered. "How may I help you, masters?" The slave's tone cracked with the last and Stiger noticed his trembling hands, which he held tightly together before him.

"I am Bennulius Stiger. What is your name, son?"

The slave tore his gaze from Therik. His mouth fell slowly agape as his eyes widened. He made to speak, but no words came out.

Hoping to calm the boy, Stiger softened his tone. "What is your name, son? It is okay. I am a friend, and this is my home."

"Miso, master." The slave's expression went from one of shock to what Stiger took to be awe. The trembling became outright shaking.

"Where is everyone?" Stiger asked. "Where are the rest of the servants?"

"It is only me, the cook and—and—the two masters," Miso answered. "There is no one else and has not been for some years."

Stiger thought on that a moment. When he'd left for the legions, there had been more than a dozen slaves and servants to care for the home and the family's every need. "By the two masters, I take it you mean my father and brother?"

"I do, master," Miso said and gestured toward the far side of the hall. "Both are speaking with the soldiers that just came through here in the private receiving room."

"They will be out shortly, then," Eli said.

Stiger gave a nod. The private receiving room was a small space where Stiger's father could speak in private with close associates, important clients, or business partners.

"Do you know where Senator Navaro lives?" Stiger asked.

"I do, master," Miso said. His nervousness seemed to abruptly increase. "His home is two blocks away. It is not far—not far at all."

"Run there," Stiger said. "Fetch the senator. Tell him I require his presence as soon as humanly possible. I want him here. Got that?"

Miso gaped and did not move. He seemed suddenly fearful. Why, Stiger had no idea. He chalked it up to the boy's nerves of the moment.

"Did you misunderstand my instruction?" Stiger asked, wondering if the boy's nerves were getting the better of him.

"No, master," Miso said. "I just ... I just ... he ... that ..."

"As a slave, he's likely concerned about directly telling a senator anything," Eli said to Stiger and then addressed Miso. "Boy, pass this message on to one of the servants of Navaro. His emperor commands Senator Navaro's presence here and he's to hurry ... Emperor Stiger wants to see him. That should not be too difficult to accomplish and will be a mite easier for you to do."

"I do—but—I—he ..."

"No buts." Stiger gestured toward the door behind them. He had wasted enough time and wanted to see his father. "Go now."

Miso bowed hastily and left at a run, going out the way they had just come.

"Perhaps you should have sent someone with him," Eli said, after Miso had gone, "one or more of Ruga's men to make certain the message was communicated properly. He was a little nervous. It is possible the telling of it may come out jumbled. Navaro might think you are coming to see him."

Therik gave a low rumbling laugh. "That would be something."

Stiger looked over at Eli and shook his head. "Where was this sage advice a moment ago? You have great timing. You know that, right?"

Eli gave a slight shrug of his shoulders. "At the time, I did not think of it."

"Uh huh," Stiger said. "Hindsight is a bitch. Is that your excuse?"

"You forget," Eli said, "High Born never make excuses because we are never wrong."

"Is that so?" Stiger asked, turning to face Eli. "I seem to recall a few instances where you were most definitely wrong."

"I have absolutely no idea what you are talking about." Eli flashed him an innocent look.

"Uh huh," Stiger said.

"I think arguing with an elf is like arguing with a tree," Therik said. "It's a waste of time."

"You might be on to something there, Therik," Eli said, amusement dancing in his eyes as he gazed upon Stiger.

"You've gotten older," a familiar voice said. There was a hard edge to it and Stiger knew instantly to whom it belonged.

He turned to see his father standing at the far end of the hall by one of the few lamps that had been lit. With his time in the past, it had been more than a decade since he had set eyes on his father. Stiger remembered an imposing man, physically strong, full of life, powerful, demanding and expecting excellence in his sons. That is not what he saw now.

Marcus Stiger wore a simple tunic with sandals. He had gone completely bald and seemed worn down by age and worries too innumerable to count. And yet, just beneath the surface, there was still toughness there...Stiger could sense it in his manner. Or was it an unyielding stubbornness? That was something Stiger knew resided within him, an inability to quit, to surrender to what others might think inevitable. He had inherited it from this man. That was at least one thing to be grateful for.

Behind his father was Ruga, with his two men and the praetorians, as they filed through a doorway. Stiger's brother Maxentius came just after.

Max was older by four years. Wearing a tunic that matched his father's, he was fair-looking, tall and thin, also proud. He had never served in the legions, or for that matter any military command, but he had served the empire in the senate.

"You've aged too," Stiger shot back at his father.

Marcus gave an amused grunt as he started across the great hall toward them. He stopped halfway, hesitating for a heartbeat when Therik stepped out of the shadows and into the light of a lamp. He continued forward and stopped before them.

"Eli," Marcus greeted.

Eli inclined his head as Marcus looked to Therik. An unhappy scowl formed on his father's face. Therik did not back down, but stared intensely at Stiger's father, meeting his gaze as a challenge.

"You keep interesting company," Marcus said to his son after a moment.

"You have no idea," Eli said.

"Is it trained?" Marcus asked.

"Trained?" Therik bristled. "You had best not mean like an animal. I am a full-blooded warrior of the Tahani Clan, human." Therik took a step forward, balling his fists. "Because you are his father"—Therik pointed a finger at Stiger—"I will give you the benefit of doubt as to your meaning."

Eli gestured toward the orc. "May I be the first to introduce King Therik."

"King?" Marcus asked, looking at Therik more closely. "An orc king? Now, that is fascinating."

"I am king of nothing," Therik said. "My kingdom was snatched from me. What was left—your son shattered into pieces, like a broken child's toy."

Marcus turned his gaze to his youngest son. "Is he your servant then? A slave captured in battle?"

Therik sucked in an offended breath.

"He is my friend," Stiger said firmly before Therik could speak. "He and I have fought side by side. Like Eli, I trust him with my life." Stiger glanced at the orc. "I value Therik's counsel."

"I see," Marcus said.

"And how he came to be in my company is a long story," Stiger said. "One that is best told at another time."

"It is," Therik agreed, "you could say, history now."

"I did not mean to offend, King Therik," Marcus said. "You are the first orc I have met. It is my pleasure to welcome you to my home."

Therik inclined his head slightly, almost grudgingly. "I am honored to be here, Marcus Stiger."

Stiger breathed out a relieved breath, then glanced around before looking to Therik.

"The kitchen is that way." Stiger gestured toward the door that Miso had come through. "You might find some food in there."

"Food, right," Therik said and started toward the door. He grabbed Eli by the shoulder and quite deliberately steered him in the same direction. "Come on, elf. He wants privacy for his reunion."

There was a moment where Eli seemed like to protest. But then he gave in and allowed Therik to lead him away.

"I will keep him from eating the help," Eli said over his shoulder. A moment later, both were gone, the door banging closed behind them.

Stiger turned his attention to the sergeant. "Are there any more of your men in this house?"

"No, sir," Lanist said. "Just these two boys."

"Good," Stiger said and turned his attention to Ruga. "Take your men and the sergeant's outside. Put out sentries and look for trouble. I will call for you if I have need."

"Yes, sir," Ruga said and nodded to the men. "Let's go."

Stiger was about to address his father when another thought occurred to him.

"Oh and Ruga?" Stiger called after him.

Ruga stopped at the door, looking back. The others had filed out before him. The centurion turned. "Sir?"

"A Senator Navaro should be arriving shortly," Stiger said. "See that he's admitted the moment he shows."

"That will not be happening," Max said, speaking for the first time. "Lears had him executed last night. I believe it is not yet public knowledge. There were several senators who saw similar fates. Unfortunately, all were in a position to support Navaro."

"Some were also allies of ours," Marcus said. "Lears has started to purge from the senate any who may oppose his hold on the curule chair. Those who were lucky to escape have surely fled the city. They will be of no use to us."

"Until you arrived," Max said, "we were thinking we were next."

Stiger felt his heart plummet at that news. His list of friends and allies in the city was growing short, to the point of being nonexistent. He could no longer count on Navaro, Aetius, or Treim's agents' support. He wondered if the messenger, Lieutenant Kerrog, had suffered the same fate. The man had been General Treim's nephew and a good officer. He would have to think of something else, perhaps even send a runner to Treim's house. Aetius's wife, Desindra, might know too. He turned back to Ruga. "In that case, just wait outside for me."

"Yes, sir." Ruga saluted crisply. He eyed Stiger's father and brother for a long moment, almost speculatively, then spun on his heel and left.

"He seems like a good man," Marcus said, "a proper soldier."

"He is one of the best." Stiger turned back to his father and brother. Max stepped forward and embraced Stiger warmly, patting him on the back. Though Max had not served with the legions, he was physically fit and had received some training. The evidence of that were the small scars on his hands and forearms.

"I've missed you, little brother," Max said, then stepped back and glanced at his tunic and hands, looking back up. "Your blood?"

"No," Stiger said. "It's all Corus. I killed him just now in a duel."

"Like father like son, then," Marcus said, with a proud note. "His father thought he could best me. I showed him the error of his ways, in a permanent fashion. He was a real bastard of a man too and if anyone deserved an end by the sword, it was him. I tell you, I was very glad it was I who gave him the killing thrust and not some other."

Stiger did not say anything to that as his brother stepped back.

"We are more alike than you know," Marcus said.

"I very much doubt that," Stiger said.

"I see you are still holding a grudge." Marcus stepped over to the table with a pair of pitchers, along with several cups and mugs. Stiger chose to not answer as his father filled a mug with what was clearly wine.

Before him was the very reason for much of his suffering, the life he'd been forced to live. His father's poor choices had shaped his life, set him down the path he now walked. Stiger thought that somewhat ironic. In a way, he should be thanking the man. But Stiger could and would not do that.

"Of course you still blame me," Marcus said and took a sip as he regarded his son. He grimaced slightly. "I am responsible for everything that's happened to the family...including the deaths of your mother and sister. I do not deny any of it. Nor do I seek to hide from it. All that happened is the result of my choices alone, decisions I made." He paused and took another sip from the mug, his gaze becoming distant. "However, I very much blame myself."

"Do you?" Stiger asked, more savagely than he'd expected. This confrontation, very much like the one with Corus, was long in building. "Do you really?"

"More than you know," Marcus said.

"Somehow," Stiger said, "I find that difficult to believe."

"Ben," Max warned. "You are not being fair."

"Fair?" Stiger turned on his brother. "Are you kidding me? He chose the wrong side. It ruined our family, saw our mother and sister brutally cut down. I was there. I saw it happen. He betrayed the empire and led a civil war. Do you know what it was like for me all those years? Do you know what it's like to serve with peers who would rather you were dead? Imagine having to rely on fellow officers who feel you are not fit to serve the empire. And more than a few tried to end me."

"I do know what you endured," Marcus said, with sudden feeling. "Treim wrote me regularly. Your brother has also suffered. You are not the only one who suffers. So too do I."

"Please," Stiger said, "spare me."

"My decisions and actions haunt my nights," Marcus said. "They plague my dreams. They keep me up, sometimes until dawn. My sleep is fitful at best. You have suffered; so too has Max. I suffer as well."

Stiger suddenly thought his father looked incredibly frail, nothing like the pillar of granite he'd known growing up. But at the same time, Stiger's heart hardened. His father spoke of suffering. He might have received letters, but what did he really know of the true suffering his youngest son had endured? If he wasn't wearing armor, Stiger would have been tempted to show him his scarred back.

"I doubt that," Stiger said with bitterness, "very much."

"You blame me for all the wrongs in the world?" Marcus asked, his voice taking a hard tone. "Look at yourself, son. You should thank me for all that I have done, for all that I have sacrificed."

"I should thank you?" There had been a time when he had feared this man. Now, no more. Stiger could stand up for himself. "Thank you? That is bold, old man. I've cursed you more than once over the years. Thank you? That is rich, really rich."

"You think so?" Marcus suddenly laughed. It was a harsh sound and echoed around the hall. He gestured about them. "Look around, my son. Do you see wealth here? This monument to our great family that we call a home is crumbling. Most people in the city still think we have money tucked away, but it's all gone ... all because of you."

"Me?" Stiger asked. "How can you blame me for your mistakes, your poor choices in life?"

"My mistakes?" Marcus said. "You mean my greatest triumph, don't you?"

Stiger felt himself scowl, wondering where his father was going.

Marcus moved a half step closer. He gestured with his cup. "Even though it broke my heart, I started you down the road you follow, gave you the push you needed, the impetus." He tapped himself on the chest. "Me. I did it. I had you trained as a soldier. I paid for the best tutors, the finest weapons masters and instructors money could buy. Year after year, what was left of our family fortune was sunk into your education. Our coffers were all but empty by the time you left for Third Legion. All that remained of our income was the rent we received from the few land holdings Tioclesion left us, and that wasn't much … certainly not enough to maintain such a house as ours."

Stiger did not reply. He looked to his brother, who gave a nod that what his father said was true.

"Day after day," Marcus continued, "you were worked from sunup until sundown and then frequently beyond. It cost me our fortune and, let me tell you, I was pleased to spend it. You thought your brother, Maxentius, the blessed one? As firstborn, you believed him the favored son. With my disgrace, Max was destined for the senate and inheritance of little more than nothing. You thought him more loved, coddled even. But it was you who got everything. He got virtually nothing. You thought me a miser for only buying you a lieutenancy, resented me for it. That was all we could afford. Your allowance, a paltry sum, we could ill afford as well, but it was more than Max got. No, my son. It was you who got the best of everything from me. You were the favored one."

Stiger was silent as he considered his father. His eyes went to his brother, who was looking down at the ground, almost embarrassed.

"Do you realize you left this home better prepared to lead men in battle than anyone ever has been?" Marcus gestured with his cup again. "You were trained, hardened, and then sent on your way to complete your education through service to the empire. I gave you the best education in warfare money could buy. I supervised it, designed the instruction. How ungrateful are you? How selfish? How stupid? I spent everything we had left on you and you didn't even realize it."

Stiger thought back to all the long days and nights, the resentment he'd felt at being forced to relentlessly train and study until he was ready to drop. He had never thought to wonder on the family's money.

"Why would you do that?" Stiger asked, confused. "Why waste it all on me? What for? What purpose? Why not come out and tell me?"

"Was it wasted?" Marcus asked. He drained his cup, moved over to the table, and poured himself a refill. "I think not. You left this home trained, yes, a man … no. You were a sniveling boy who blamed me for every possible wrong. Yet your anger for me drove you on. Even if I'd told you the truth, you would not have believed me. Now … look at you. You are a man seasoned by combat, forged in the fires of war. You have led men in battle and against the odds, repeatedly won when you should have lost. You have faced certain death more than once, and cheated Fortuna as you did it. You have seen the horrors the world has to offer, just as I have, and been made stronger by it." Marcus paused, taking a deep breath. "And now, you are the conquering hero, returned home." He took another sip of wine. "I heard the people down in the city cheering and saw the dragons fly overhead. I knew without a doubt you had come. You, my son, are the future of this house. You always were. Blame me? Sure, go ahead. I would change nothing of what I have done ... even"—Marcus took a long pull at his drink and his tone softened, almost cracked—"even if I could get your mother and sister back. Long ago I made my choice, and by now, I am certain, you have made yours."

Stiger rubbed his jaw for a long moment as he considered his father. He stepped over to the table with the pitcher. He filled a cup of wine for himself and took a sip as he thought through what his father had just said, the actions he'd taken. The wine was poor quality, terrible really, and more than a little sour.

"Do you have nothing to say for yourself?" Marcus demanded.

Stiger turned back and regarded his father for several moments. A piece of the puzzle came together. He gestured with the mug at his father. "You knew. You bastard. You knew all along, didn't you?"

Marcus stilled. For a long moment, he said nothing. Then he gave a small nod.

"I did."

Though he had guessed, Stiger was rocked by the admission and actually took a step back.

"How?" Stiger asked. "How did you know the path I now walk?"

"When the emperor died, and I mean Tioclesion's father," Marcus said, "I was in command of six legions guarding the western frontier. All were positioned less than four hundred miles from the capital. Mine was the closest military command." Marcus fell silent for several heartbeats as he seemingly gathered his thoughts. "The civil war began when Tioclesion decided to seize the throne. He attempted to murder his older brother, Terhaulus ... well, to have his brother murdered at any rate. Tioclesion never liked to do the dirty work himself. You well know the two had long since despised one another. Their feud was destined to end in blood."

Stiger gave a nod of agreement. The two brothers had had a long-standing rivalry. As Tioclesion's friend, Stiger had disliked Terhaulus immensely. Terhaulus had also been a bully who had always been too full of himself.

"Anyway," Marcus continued, "the assassination was bungled and failed. With it, nearly half of the praetorians revolted, rallying around the emperor's older brother, who was popular amongst the ranks. The other half-backed Tioclesion because he bought them. Having lots of silver can be a handy thing, especially when you seize the treasury and spend it as if it's your own. Blood flowed liberally through the streets after that."

"It was an awful time," Max said in a distant tone, "terrible"

"It was," Marcus agreed. "Mal'Zeel became a battleground. The mob got involved, taking sides as well... rioting, killing indiscriminately. There was much death and destruction." Marcus fell silent again as he took a sip from his wine. "Both sides called upon me and the other generals to back them. They wanted me to bring my legions into the city to settle things, to put an end to the madness. By that point, it was not so easy a thing to do. There was fighting across the empire, with several cities declaring support for one side or another—even independence. Appeals for help were pouring into my headquarters from all quarters. Worse, a schism had formed, not just in the officer corps, but also in the ranks as well. Brother turned upon brother. As Max said, it was an awful time."

Stiger had been dealing with the fallout of his father's actions for years, but he had never known the why of it. He'd had his suspicions, of course, and had heard rumors, but he'd never heard the story from the source. It had never been spoken of and was a subject that had been expressly off limits.

"Intent on helping to restore order, and stop the bloodshed, I returned to the city with a strong escort. My legions were already on the move, marching to the city, but were days away. Unbeknownst to me at the time, so too were other generals. They had stolen the march on me and would arrive before the main body of my army." Marcus took a breath and let it out. "After arriving in the city and speaking with your mother, she and I decided upon throwing my support behind Tioclesion. At the time, he seemed the better of the two choices, for Terhaulus had begun to show a cruel streak. With that decided, I went to the first emperor's temple, to the gardens, to pray for guidance before heading to the palace." Marcus looked toward the door, his eyes suddenly distant. "You should really visit the place and pay your respects. All emperors should. It might remind them of their responsibility to the empire and a need to be just. Imagine that, a just emperor."

"I've never seen the temple," Max said quietly, sounding almost troubled as he gazed at his father. "He says it's hidden in the temple district."

"What happened while you were there?" Stiger asked, wanting to hear the rest of the story and not be diverted. He had never heard of the first emperor's temple either. "What made you change your mind and go against Tioclesion?"

"I was given a vision."

"A vision?" Stiger asked, suspecting the High Father's involvement.

Mine, the sword hissed in his mind. *He saw what he needed to see. I showed him the possibilities and direct consequences of his actions.*

Stiger went cold. For a moment, he had forgotten about Rarokan. The mad wizard had opened the prison door and had been following along, intently so.

You? Stiger could scarcely believe it.

Yes...

"A vision?" Stiger asked his father. He felt a headache coming on. "You were shown a vision?"

"Two actually." Marcus took another sip of wine. His look became haunted. "I was shown two possible futures. It was almost like I was at a fork in the road, a crossroads of my life. And I was left to make a choice between the two. One led to a future of indescribable greatness... the other... success, a happy and fulfilled life, but ultimately terrible destruction... the end of the empire... the world. My choice was obvious, and yet the personal price would be terrible. I was shown that as well, the true horror of what I must do. So—I chose and backed Terhaulus for the good of the empire, even though I and those I loved would suffer. It was the only real choice to make."

Stiger felt rocked to his core by not only what his father had said, but also Rarokan's admission. The implications of Rarokan's meddling were staggering. He turned his attention inward and to the mad wizard.

You?

Me, Rarokan said simply. *I did it.*

How? he demanded of the sword. *Why?*

Before I was locked within this prison... I was the master of time and space. It was I who set everything in motion. I alone have changed the course of the Last War. I made it possible for Romans and many others to leave their cradle world, to come to this one. I broke the ultimate rule, law, call it what you will, of interfering with a cradle world. I took action before it became too late... before another thought to make such a move, take such a gamble. Yes, I made the ultimate sacrifice for the future and I made it willingly. I forced the gods into engagement. I made them stir from their own self-imposed stagnation on Olimbus. I spurred them to action.

There was an exultant tone to the wizard's words.

Now, the worlds of strength and power are untouchable, inviolate. No more can be taken, moved, and transported away. No more can one who is not of a cradle world travel to such a place, not even a High Master. I alone made this possible. And it will change everything.

You think you control me with the tricks the noctalum taught you? I foresaw that too. Before this comes to an end, I promise—you will join with me in my great work. You will help me achieve all that I desire. And you will do it freely.

Stiger felt sick to his stomach. His anger sparked at all the mad wizard had done. Was it not enough that he had to fight the High Father's enemies?

I should have dropped you in a remote lake and left you for all eternity to the silt and mud.

You do not have the strength of will *to do that. The bond has been forged and cannot be broken.*

We can find out, Stiger said. *This city has plenty of sewers. I am tempted to go find one right now.*

Time to accept your fate, for we are one, as was always meant to be. You will not discard me, for you cannot. The High Father will not allow it.

The sword laughed maniacally in his mind. Stiger knew Rarokan's words to be true. He forced the mad wizard back into his box and closed the lid, sealing him in. It took more effort than he expected and almost left him panting. Even so, he could still hear the sword in his head, laughing madly away.

"Do you have nothing to say?" Marcus demanded.

Stiger looked up at his father and saw a sadness in the man's eyes he'd never seen before, or maybe never noticed. He suspected it had been there all along. He'd just been too blind to see. Marcus Stiger grieved for what he had done to his youngest son and his family. Marcus had suffered, and terribly too. Stiger saw that now, knew that very look, had keenly felt such loss himself. How could he have missed it?

And yet, Stiger was not ready to forgive him. Not yet.

"Excuse me, sir," Ruga said from the entrance. There was an urgent note to his voice. "I am sorry to bother you."

Stiger looked around, wondering what had gone wrong.

"Do you mind if we bring Father Restus inside?" Ruga asked. "I am afraid he's not doing so well, sir. He needs a fire and some warmth, maybe even a doctor."

"Bring him right in," Stiger said, then turned to his brother. "Can you get some blankets? He's sick with a cold."

"I can," Max said and left, heading back the way he had come.

Using a shield as a litter, two of Ruga's men bodily carried Father Restus inside. Restus was shivering uncontrollably and his teeth were chattering. The paladin's forehead was covered in a sheen of sweat. He seemed barely conscious and was mumbling incoherently.

"Place him in a chair by the fire pit," Stiger ordered. The men set the paladin by the fire, then moved him to a chair. As they worked, Stiger grabbed one of the unlit clay oil lamps. He shook it and heard the slosh of oil. Without hesitation, he threw it onto the stacked logs, where it shattered, dousing the wood in flammable oil. He grabbed another lamp, this one lit, and did the same. The logs flared to life, roaring into flame.

He stepped over to Restus and placed himself before the paladin's chair. Ruga's men moved aside for him. Restus was still mumbling to himself. Stiger pressed his palm against the paladin's head. The man was burning up. Max returned with two wool blankets that had seen far better days. He wrapped the paladin with both.

"He doesn't look so good," Max said, then gave a gasp. "If I'm not mistaken, this man is a paladin, right? He attends functions with the High Priest now and then."

"He is the head of his order," Marcus said, sounding troubled. "Part of the Old Order. That he is ill does not bode well for us. In the vision, he played a key part in what was to come."

Stiger glanced up at his father. He felt a terrible dread and looked back to the paladin. Restus was dying. Marcus knew it. Stiger was certain as well.

The fire was blazing and beginning to radiate heat, but Stiger knew it would not be enough. Restus's eyes suddenly opened and looked right at Stiger, then seemingly beyond, almost staring right through him. They had a distant, glassy cast to them. "I see the High Father waiting and the great river. The ferryman's on his way over to help me make the crossing. Can you believe it?" The paladin's voice was rapturous. "I have waited so long for this."

"It's not your time yet." Stiger took the man by both shoulders. He felt it to be true. Restus could not die. He was needed; there was still work for the man to do, good to be accomplished. "It's not your time yet. Come back to us."

"I don't want to," Restus said, his breathing becoming labored and barely more than a whisper. "Let me go— please. I have waited so long ... Let me join him."

Restus sagged in Stiger's hands, his eyes closing.

"Bloody stay with us," Stiger fairly shouted, hoping to get through. "Stay with me, man."

Restus gasped and opened his eyes wide. The pupils were unfocused.

"Ben." Max grabbed his shoulder forcefully and tried to pull Stiger back. "Let him rest. He needs it. We will send for a doctor."

"No." Stiger pulled his shoulder away. He could not allow Father Restus to die. Desperate, Stiger reached for the High Father's power within. He felt the warmth of the High Father's touch. In his mind's eye, the burning ball of light grew intense.

Will you give a little of your life force—sacrifice some—to help me save this faithful servant?

Stiger did not even hesitate, did not even need to question who was asking. He had heard his god speak before.

Yes.

The ball of light flared, becoming blazing hot, and it wasn't a soothing feeling either. Pain blasted through Stiger. From head to toe, everything seemed to be on fire. Through his hands holding the paladin's shoulders, power flowed outward and into Restus, much like a flood. Yet instead of water, it was a torrent of energy. Stiger almost screamed as the power roared through him, lancing and ripping away a measure of his soul, but he could not move. He was frozen to immobility.

There was a thunderous crack, followed by a bell tolling. The room exploded into white light. Though he could not move, Stiger saw his father and brother take a step back, as did Ruga and his men. The ground shook. Then, as abruptly as it came, it ceased. The god withdrew much of his power and the pain ended. Stiger felt a sense of calm settle over him. It soothed him, salved the wound within his soul. He took a deep breath and exhaled it as the High Father's power within continued to dim to what it had been moments before.

A moment later, it roared back. Stiger almost wept, for he felt his connection with his god like never before. It was as if he were standing before the High Father himself, basking in the god's august presence. He could feel the pure love, the trust from his god, and with it came a sense of calm and pure peace. He felt a tear run down his cheek at the wondrous joy of the moment. He was blessed, honored, and in a way felt rejuvenated.

My ability to directly intervene, influence events upon this world, will soon come to an end. So too will the other gods'. When it does, you will have all the tools you need to see my work and the effort of those who preceded you finished, completed.

The road before you will not be an easy one. It will be difficult and rocky. Do not doubt yourself… go forth, my son, with confidence and cunning and armed with faith.

A dark stain has fallen upon my house. Cleanse it and restore the faithful. You will also have to ultimately contend with Rarokan and the enemy. Heed your father's words and counsel well. He is wise and has suffered, just as you have. I grieve for you both.

All that is good in this world rests upon both your shoulders. Listen and heed my words, for there is a place you must go, a place you must visit, a person to honor, and a debt to be repaid.

I promised Karus and your people an empire without end. It will be up to you now, my Champion, to see that promise fulfilled. In you, I have placed my faith.

His task was before him.

"I will see it all through to the end," Stiger said as a whisper.

Thank you, my son.

The High Father withdrew, leaving Stiger feeling somewhat bereft. He still had the connection burning within, just not as intense as it had been a heartbeat before. Almost slowly, he became aware of his surroundings again. He found Restus looking into his eyes. Stiger blinked, suddenly feeling tired, terribly weary. For a moment, his vision swam. Then it cleared. He blinked again, not quite sure he believed his eyes.

The sickness had gone, but that was not all. Father Restus was no longer a decrepit old man at the end of his years. He was middle-aged, almost youthful, without even the trace of a wrinkle.

"It seems the High Father is not done with me yet," Restus said, his voice strong and far from raspy. There was a trace of a sad smile upon his face. "You have given some of your life force. I can feel it within. It is a gift I do not feel worthy of receiving." The paladin paused to suck in a shuddering breath. "The High Father has given me even more—a second chance to serve, a new opportunity to make a difference. I swear to you and our god, I shall not waste this wondrous gift you both have bestowed upon me."

Stiger straightened and took a stumbling half step back. He felt no different, other than being a little more tired and weary.

Restus gazed down at his hands in pure amazement, turning them over, flexing his joints. He moved his neck around.

"No pain," Restus said to himself, "no more ache. The stiffness in my joints is gone." Then the paladin looked at Stiger and he sobered. "One day, my time will come to cross over the great river. After today, it is clear I have much work left to do. Though it will be difficult, I will be patient, for when my journey finally ends, my god will be waiting with open arms."

"Blessed gods," Max breathed, "a true miracle. You have healed him."

Stiger looked around at his brother and father, who were staring at him in wonder.

"Gods blessed, is more like it," Ruga said. "He is the Champion of the High Father and my emperor."

Marcus clapped his hands together with a clear sense of triumph. "I would not change anything that I've done. For this is the choice I made, the future I chose for you, my son, favored of the gods and—an empire without end."

Stiger stared at his father, not quite knowing what to say. His father stood himself to attention and saluted in the old style, with his arm extended.

"Hail Emperor Stiger and Champion of the High Father, defender of the empire. I pledge my loyalty to you and that of my house, Imperator. In the High Father's name, I swear it so."

CHAPTER TEN

Stiger rubbed at his eyes as he lowered himself into a chair by the fire. It creaked as it took his armored weight. He felt terribly weary and spent, exhausted even. The warmth of the fire felt good, for the hall was cold, almost frigid.

A door banged open. Stiger looked, as did everyone else. Empty-handed, Eli and Therik emerged from the door that led to the kitchen. The door banged closed after them as they made their way across the hall toward the fire. As they approached the last few feet, both slowed, eyeing Restus warily.

"What did we just miss?" Eli asked, looking between Stiger and Restus several times in rapid succession. His gaze finally settled on Stiger as he came to a stop next to the fire.

Stiger let out a long breath that was more sigh than anything else. He did not feel like explaining. He just wanted to sit in the chair, recover, and enjoy the warmth of the fire.

"Why do you assume it was me?"

Eli tilted his head to the side and gave him a long look. "Seriously?"

Therik's gaze was fixed on the paladin. He gestured at the man. "He is Restus, right? He's wearing the same armor and looks kind of like him, only younger—a lot younger."

Stiger glanced over at the paladin. Restus's armor and kit looked ill-fitting. It was clearly too tight for the man, who now looked to be in the prime years of his life, powerfully muscled and broad-shouldered. He even appeared slightly taller. The transformation was truly astonishing. Even Stiger had to admit that, and he'd had a hand in it.

The paladin had been working at untying the leather straps on the left side of his armor. He had already removed his sword and harness, setting both on a chair. Restus paused, looking up directly at Therik, then glanced down at himself and back up again. The paladin grinned at the orc.

"It's me. I would love to see a mirror right now." Restus returned to working on the strap. "I really would."

"You are no longer old," Therik said simply.

Stiger continued rubbing at his eyes. The weary feeling intensified, as did a reluctance to talk about what had just happened. He yawned mightily. With the fire shedding its warmth, a nap sounded good about now.

"What did you do?" Eli asked again, clearly refusing to be put off. "Tell me."

Stiger looked up at his friend. The fire cracked loudly, with smoke swirling toward the hole in the ceiling. For some reason, he found himself hesitating. "How to explain …?"

"It is simple," Eli said. "You start at the beginning and move on from there until you come to the end of the story."

Still, Stiger found himself reluctant. It was almost as if he was being prohibited from talking about what had just happened. Feeling suddenly helpless, he looked toward Restus.

"With the High Father's help, he healed me," Restus said, coming to Stiger's rescue. "Sometimes after such work, it is difficult to speak on such things. It has been speculated that the High Father does not want us boasting about what has been done. At least that is what some paladins have come to believe. But no one really knows for sure why it happens."

"He healed you?" Eli seemed as if he did not quite believe what the paladin said. He pointed at Stiger. "It looks to me like he did a little more than that."

Restus gave a nod of affirmation. "With the High Father's help, of course. It is a great honor, one which I do not feel worthy of receiving. I will do my utmost to repay this blessing through service."

"Sickness I can understand," Eli breathed, "but I've never ever heard of anyone being cured of aging. Not even amongst elves have I heard tell of such a thing, and we have long memories. Some of my people have searched their entire lives for a fountain of life or youth—whatever you want to call it. No one has ever found one." The elf took a step nearer Restus, studying him intently. The elf reached out a finger and poked at Restus's arm, as if making sure he was real. "This is truly astounding, astonishing."

"I thought your people were immortal." Therik looked over at Eli. "Elves live forever. At least that is what I've always thought, what people say."

"Though many of our elders would like to think so"—Eli glanced over at the orc before returning his gaze to the paladin—"like any other, we are mortal beings, just long-lived."

"Huh," Therik said. "Isn't that something."

"Though it may be shocking to you both, the High Father simply saw fit to give me more time upon this world," Restus said. "There is additional work for me to do, good to be done."

Eli stared at the paladin for a protracted moment. "Incredible, just incredible."

"It is only the *Will* of my god," Restus said, "nothing more. Having faith brings one many rewards and sometimes"—he glanced down at his unblemished hands—"sometimes, there are gifts that prove to be wholly unexpected."

Shaking his head, Eli walked over to the table with the pitcher. He poured himself a mug of the bitter wine. He turned back and stared at Restus for several heartbeats before downing the wine in one swallow. He put the mug down on the table, a little too hard. The clay mug made an audible clunking sound. Stiger was surprised it did not break. "Just incredible."

Therik, for his part, gave a grunt, followed up by a shrug of his shoulders. He turned toward the fire and held out his hands for warmth. "My people have a saying: The gods will do what the gods will do."

"We missed a miracle, Therik," Eli said. "Don't you think it would have been something to see?"

"It happened," Therik said, suddenly sounding bored. "Accept it."

"It happened?" Eli asked, incredulous, his voice rising in pitch. "Accept it? Is that all you have to say?"

"At the moment, I am famished," Therik replied. "I could do with something to eat, preferably some roasted beef or even the bread that was promised. There was nothing in that kitchen worth eating, nothing cooked anyway."

"You're still thinking about food?" Eli was aghast. "Seriously? At a time like this? Unbelievable. Ben ... where exactly did you find him again?"

"This is not the first time I have seen such a thing," Therik said.

"Oh really?" Eli sounded dubious. "You've known another who has been rejuvenated?"

"A priest I knew was restored to his youth by Castor," Therik said with a sour note. "That and the medicine the priest could wield almost cost me everything."

"His name was Cetrite," Stiger said, in a near whisper. "Father Thomas killed him."

"Yes, he did." Therik bared his tusks. "That was a good day—a very fine day. Not only did I kill my traitorous son, but Thomas took that bastard priest's head from his body. It was a beautiful killing. I wish I had thought to save the skull to fashion a drinking mug. Still, Cetrite had more than earned what he got. Had he survived, I would have shared a drink with Thomas and toasted him. I was saddened by his passing."

"Me too," Stiger breathed.

"He made the ultimate sacrifice for the future," Therik said.

Stiger recalled that day quite vividly. It had seen him mortally wounded and dying, his soul on the verge of crossing over the great river. Father Thomas had given his life to save Stiger's. He still felt terribly guilty about that. Stiger put a hand to his chest, where the minion's blade had pierced him. Despite the healing and Father Thomas's sacrifice, the wound had never healed quite right. When it rained or snowed, he still felt some discomfort, and sometimes it even throbbed painfully.

Marcus cleared his throat loudly. "Miracles aside, as impressive as that was, we need to begin thinking about Lears and how we're going to deal with him. The sooner the better."

"Agreed," Max said as he moved over to the table and poured himself a drink. "We either need to go after him now or leave the city."

"You mean flee?" Stiger asked, looking up. His weariness retreated at the suggestion. He felt a stab of anger.

"We are running out of time," Max said, taking a sip of his wine. "The longer we remain here talking, the more time Lears has to react to your presence."

Stiger regarded his brother for a long moment. "I did not come all this way to run. Besides, I have an old score to settle with Lears. He has wronged me, and I am not in a forgiving mood."

"How many men did you bring?" Marcus asked as he too took a chair next to Stiger's.

"One hundred," Stiger said. "I don't know how many of Corus's company came over, maybe thirty—give or take a few. The rest of my army hasn't even left Lorium yet. By foot, they are weeks away at best."

"And the dragons?" Marcus asked. "By the High Father, they were impressive beasts. What of them?"

"They are gone," Stiger said plainly.

"What do you mean gone?" Max took a step closer. "Where did they go?"

"I sent them back to the army," Stiger said.

"Whatever for?" Max asked, clearly dismayed. "Why would you send them away?"

"They are needed here." Marcus's disapproval was plain. "You could have used them as leverage to unseat Lears. Just the mere threat of using them would have proved incredibly valuable. Explain to me your thinking."

"I can't afford to have what happened to Tioclesion's army happen to mine," Stiger said. "It was a risk even using them to come north. You have to understand, I must pro-tect the army, and that includes our allies, from the enemy's wyrms."

"Wyrms," Max said, "what are they?"

"Think of slightly smaller dragons," Eli said, "but no less deadly."

"There are different types of dragons?" Max asked.

"Oh yes," Eli said. "Some are friendly and others ... not so much."

"And the Cyphan have more dragons than we do." Stiger paused. "At least, that's what we believe. Besides, the city is not the place to bring such creatures into. Were I to do that, things could go badly, and very quickly too. They breathe fire and will not hesitate to defend themselves if attacked. I think we can all agree that Mal'Zeel must not burn."

"This is not good," Max said, looking over at his father. He began to pace. "Not good."

"No," Marcus agreed, "it is not. A little more than a hundred men against what Lears has. We are at a serious disadvantage."

"How many men does he have in the city?" Eli asked. "Do you know?"

"Several hundred legionaries," Marcus answered. "Likely a few hundred more irregulars and auxiliaries. He also has great numbers of militia spread throughout the city. They're barely trained, and their loyalty is questionable, but when you have numbers—sometimes quality does not matter all that much. Not counting the militia, I'd say he probably has about a thousand good men. Though Lears is a fool in my opinion, even he won't wait long before he comes for us."

"Especially after he learns about what happened with Corus and his praetorians," Max said. "And now, your one good deterrent, the dragons, are gone."

Stiger did not respond. It might have been a mistake, but he had made his decision and now he had to live with it. He simply could not afford to lose the army that would soon be marching up to Lorium. At the moment, they needed the two dragons more than he did. And soon enough, he would need every available sword to counter the enemy's numerical advantage.

"A threat is a threat, and the best way to deal with it is to end it," Marcus said.

All of the straps undone, Father Restus lifted his armor over his head and set it against one of the nearby pillars. All he wore underneath was a simple gray tunic and his sandals. He picked his sword harness up from the chair and slung it over his head and shoulder, settling it into place.

"Now, that is much better," the paladin said, regarding his armor for a long moment. "I will need to get it adjusted, perhaps even remade."

"No doubt." Stiger blew out a long breath as he turned to his father. "And I am the threat you were referring to?"

"Lears will want to deal with you as quickly as possible and set an example that others cannot mistake," Max said, drawing Stiger's attention back, "before there are any more defections from amongst his ranks."

"Navaro, Treim, and Aetius were to have a few hundred men waiting," Stiger said. "Do you know how to contact them?"

"No," Marcus said. "I don't. With any luck, they might find us. But I would not hold out hope. Lears has been arresting and executing people who might pose a threat to him and his new position. Any potential allies may very well have gone into hiding. That is, if they are still breathing."

"Do you have anyone we can rely upon in the city?" Stiger asked.

"No," Marcus said. "Most of our clients have long since left us."

"What of your army?" Stiger asked, looking at his father. "We saw them marching east."

"It's not my army." Marcus breathed out a heavy breath. "Not anymore. I was summoned by Lears late last night, just after his installation. He relieved me of my command. I was marched here"—Marcus held his arms out—"where I found Max already under guard and the house surrounded by Corus and his men. I wasn't manacled, but I was told if I resisted or attempted to escape, I would be summarily executed. Corus made that clear enough."

"Do you know who took over command?" Stiger asked. "Who replaced you as commander of the army?"

"Lears said that Mechlehnus would have that honor. Do you know him?"

Stiger thought for a moment, trying the recall the name, then shook his head. "I am afraid I do not."

"That's not surprising. He's in his late seventies," Marcus said, "and led men in battle long before you were born."

"He's an equestrian," Max added, after taking a sip from his wine. "It is likely another reason you've not heard of his family."

"And Lears put him in command?" Stiger asked, both astounded and intrigued at the same time. "Why not a noble, someone from the senatorial class? Why would the senate agree to this? An eques commanding the entire army? A legion I can understand, but the army... that's unheard of."

"If I had to guess, he needed someone with experience acceptable to the senate," Max said. "Mechlehnus is it. He was once of senatorial rank."

"He was?" Stiger asked.

"Mounting debts and declining income saw his fall to the equites," Max said. "From what I understand, he was also unable to produce any children, from which an advantageous union with another senatorial family might have been made."

Stiger gave a nod of understanding. It was rare, but not unheard of, for families to occasionally come and go from senatorial rank. There were even equestrians who were incredibly wealthy but did not want to pay for the fee for admission into the senate. Or they did not want to deal with the problems that came with being a senator. They were content to remain equestrian. In a way, there was more freedom in that. He looked back over at his father as something occurred to him.

"How were we able to maintain our senatorial rank? From what you have told me, as a family, we are dead broke. Surely the senate would demand an accounting. How were you able to hide our lack of wealth from them?"

"We weren't," Marcus said unhappily.

"Surprisingly, Tioclesion provided cover for us," Max said. "He had several prominent lenders provide us tablets of credit to show the senate auditors. Of course, we were not permitted to draw upon the money. It was only for show. But appearing to have access to lines of credit totaling millions of imperial talons was more than enough to satisfy our fellow senators and even our enemies."

"We have no idea why he did that," Marcus said.

"Or why we were spared from the purges that followed after the civil war," Max said.

Stiger tapped the arm of his chair with a finger. He knew the answer. Recalling what the paladin had told him about showing the emperor a vision, he turned his gaze to Restus, who gave him a nod in reply.

"I saw to that," Restus admitted to Marcus. "You weren't the only one given a vision. Tioclesion had one as well."

"It is why, on his deathbed, he named Ben emperor," Eli said. "Tioclesion had known for years that Ben was going to be his successor and the empire's hope in a dark time."

Marcus leaned back in his chair and gazed up at the ceiling. It was clear all the pieces of the puzzle were finally falling into place for him.

"The gods move in mysterious ways," Marcus said, more to himself than anyone else.

"Mechlehnus," Stiger said, wanting to move things along, "does he know what he's doing? Can he effectively lead an army? Or is he as incompetent as Lears?"

"He may be old," Marcus said, "but he's a soldier through and through. Much like you did, Mechlehnus worked his way up through the ranks. He commanded a legion and even managed to beat a small Castol army on the frontier. He did not just simply beat them; he crushed them. It gave the Castol something to think about. His action likely ended a bloody and protracted war before it could even begin."

"But that was years ago," Stiger said. "Do you think he's missed a step with age?"

"That might be a dangerous assumption for anyone to make," Marcus said.

Stiger gave a nod. He had long since learned making assumptions without evidence was not a wise process.

"He's loyal to Lears, then?" Stiger asked. "One of his clients?"

"No, not a client," Marcus said. "Even before he became an eques, Mechlehnus was too proud to accept patronage. My father—your grandfather—respected him greatly, just as I do."

Stiger's father rarely, if ever, spoke of his own father, Edelus. Stiger knew Edelus had commanded a legion in the field, but not much more than that. Still, Stiger understood the message. His father was telling him to respect Mechlehnus's skills as a leader and field commander. And anyone Marcus Stiger respected was dangerous in the field.

"He must be loyal to Lears," Stiger said, "especially after being given such an important command."

"I am not so certain of that." Marcus stood and grabbed an iron poker from next to the fire. He poked at the logs, creating a shower of sparks that swirled upward toward the hole in the ceiling. Apparently satisfied with his work, he returned the poker to its original position and sat back down. He was silent for a long moment before he spoke. "No. I do not think so. Mechlehnus is his own man."

"Are you certain of that?" Therik asked. "We might end up wagering our lives upon it."

"He has a very strong sense of honor," Max said to Therik as he returned his empty mug to the table. "At least, we believe he does. He's been married to his wife for more than forty years. She was unable to produce an heir for him, let alone any children whatsoever that managed to survive beyond the cradle. He could have simply divorced her, but he chose not to. Had he done so, he might have remarried into a more powerful family, or snared a wealthy widow, thereby rescuing his financial situation. Instead, he kept his wife, remained true to her, and gave up his senatorial rank."

"So," Stiger said, "he has character, then, if not an affinity for making money. I am already beginning to like him."

"Once he has made a commitment, he lives by it," Marcus said, "no matter how disagreeable a position it puts him in."

"That sounds familiar," Eli said to Therik, "doesn't it?"

Therik gave a grunt of amusement.

Ignoring the elf and orc, Stiger looked over at his father. It seemed so unreal to be sitting next to the man. Especially after all the time they had spent apart. Stiger had come to not only resent him, but hate the man he had once loved. And in truth, he did not now know how he really felt. It seemed like whenever he got an understanding of what was going on, there was a new twist waiting just around the corner. He decided it would need some thinking on, for he was not yet ready to forgive. Regardless, they were family, and that was that. In imperial households, it all came down to family in the end.

"His wife's family, who are they?" Stiger needed to know more. The weary and exhausted feeling had thoroughly passed. In its place he had begun to feel a mounting sense of urgency, or really a nudge to get moving, to take the fight to Lears. Before he could do that, he needed to know the ground he'd be fighting over. It was why he had come home in the first place.

"You would not know them. They are equestrian also," Marcus said. "He married below his station, a common merchant's daughter. Though she was a beauty beyond compare, it was quite a scandal at the time."

"I see," Stiger said, staring at the flames dancing in the fire for a long moment as he thought on all he had learned. "Will he send men back to the city to secure Lears's hold on the curule chair?"

"If Lears ordered him?" Marcus asked, to which Stiger nodded. "I suspect he will follow Lears's orders until there is no more breath in the emperor's lungs."

"How well do you know him?" Stiger asked. "There are some officers who think quite highly of you, even to this day."

"You want to know if he is one of them?" Marcus asked. "I do."

Marcus turned his gaze to the fire again and held out his hands for warmth. He rubbed them together. "Mechlehnus served before my time. For whatever reason, he did not participate in the civil war. We have only ever exchanged the occasional polite word in passing, but not much more. His family was never an outright enemy of ours. Nor were they friends."

Stiger ran a hand over his jaw, feeling the stubble.

"When I was younger," Restus said, drawing their attention, "a paladin on one of my first quests, our paths crossed.

Mechlehnus struck me as a good man, religious, a little stiff, formal even, and loyal to the empire. More recently, I recall him a frequent visitor to the High Father's temple during the High Holy Days. Many think him a pious man. He is known as a patron of the church and honors the Old Order."

"Just like our family," Marcus said.

"That is my understanding," Restus said.

"It's something," Marcus said. "At least he's not an absolutist."

"So, if ordered by Lears," Stiger said, "do you also think he'd likely answer the man's call?"

"Like your father, I believe he will do what his emperor tells him to do," Restus said. "He is bound by his oath."

"And if ordered by Emperor Stiger?" Therik rumbled. "Who was, after all, made heir by the last emperor."

"I suspect," Restus said, "that since the senate and High Priest confirmed Lears, there is a strong chance he'd respond to Lears and ignore you."

"If he receives two sets of orders, from both Lears and you," Marcus said to Stiger, "he may also just decide to sit things out ... to see what happens. Mechlehnus is not stupid. Really, there is simply just no way to tell how he will react given such a situation."

Stiger turned his gaze back to the fire. A moment later, he looked at his father. "And your command structure, your senior officers, will they prove loyal to you or Mechlehnus?"

"Now that is a good question," Marcus said. "I was in command of the army for a few weeks. It was enough time to put some of my own people, former clients and associates, into senior positions, men I had served with or believed could be relied upon. Many I specifically called out of retirement."

"That's what I thought," Stiger said. It was something to potentially work with.

"Remember," Marcus said, "Mechlehnus just assumed command last night. I doubt Lears has even managed to swear the legions to loyalty before they marched. I believe, if I wrote them, most of my senior officers would come over to our side and support your claim." Marcus paused. "I must caution you, though. Taking such action will split the army and see brother fighting brother again. I've had enough of that sort of thing to last me a lifetime."

"I don't want that either." Stiger leaned back in his chair and stretched his legs out before the fire, enjoying the warmth. At that moment, he wished he had his pipe. He had left it back with the army. Stiger had always found smoking a pipe calming to the mind.

He looked back over at his father. "If anything, turning the army upon itself must be avoided. No, I will deal with Lears, the senate, and the High Priest as soon as possible. Mechlehnus will come later."

"The High Priest?" Max seemed surprised by that. "What's he done?"

"The High Priest anointed Lears," Stiger said.

"But that doesn't mean he's an enemy," Max said.

"He's not a friend either," Stiger said. "Restus wrote him about me and he still sided with Lears."

"Something is not quite right within the church," Restus added. "I can feel it, and that troubles me greatly. There is a foul stench on the wind."

Stiger could feel it too, sense it, now that he thought on it. The High Father had told him a dark stain had fallen upon his house. He was to cleanse it and restore the faithful. How exactly he was to accomplish that, he was not so sure. However, his immediate problem was Lears. That man had to be his focus, his objective. Securing the curule chair and crown of wreaths came first. Everything else could wait and be dealt with afterwards.

"There can only be one emperor," Stiger said firmly. "When I'm the last man standing, only then will I issue an order to Mechlehnus."

"And what of reaching out to my officers?" Marcus asked. "I think we should consider that—alert them to a potential need to act."

"No, I will do nothing to upset Mechlehnus," Stiger said firmly. "I don't want word or even a hint of such an effort to reach him. He might prove a valuable ally after we sort things out with Lears."

"If it gets difficult for us," Therik said, "you might not want to rule out that option so fast."

"As if they could get any more difficult," Eli said.

"Knowing him," Therik said, pointing at Stiger with a thick green finger, "it will."

"I agree with Therik," Marcus said. "My people could stop Mechlehnus from using the army against us. I urge you to reconsider."

"My mind is made up," Stiger said. "The last thing we need right now is another civil war tearing the empire apart. I will not risk that unless I have no other choice. If anything, we must end this business as soon as possible. Lears needs to go, and now."

The room fell silent for a long moment. The fire cracked loudly, sparking and spitting, as Stiger turned his gaze into its depths.

"Why is the army marching?" Stiger asked after several moments, looking back over. "Do you know?"

Marcus turned grim. "Yes. The Castol have invaded from the north."

"The Castol?" Stiger asked, surprised. He sat up straight. He had not expected that. The Castol were almost as dangerous as the Rivan had been. They were a hardy people living in the far and remote north.

"Tioclesion withdrew the northern legions to deal with the Cyphan," Max said. "The Castol took advantage of the empire's weakness and lack of security on the border. They struck southward, easily overrunning the province of Han. The stories coming out of there are horrendous."

"They basically walked into Han unopposed," Marcus said, "then pushed on to the city of Tiber, which is now under siege. Two weeks ago, in Tioclesion's absence, the senate, with infinite wisdom, ordered me to prepare to march north, break the siege, and throw the Castol back."

Stiger closed his eyes. His problems were mounting. The Castol, just like the Rivan, were hard fighters. And Stiger had fought against them in the north. He had no desire to do so again. Now, his hand had been forced. Once he secured his throne, he would be forced to contend with two powerful enemies. He would soon enough have a real fight on his hands, likely the fight of his life.

"When it rains, it pours," Stiger said after a prolonged moment.

"At least it isn't too late to recall the army," Marcus said. "As you said, we just need to deal with Lears first."

"Why are they marching east?" Therik asked. "That I do not understand. The Castol are to the north, yes?"

"With an army as large as ours," Marcus explained, "and in winter, good roads are a necessity. There are two paved highways along the coast that move northward. More importantly, both highways are relatively close together, only a few miles apart, and in excellent condition. They will facilitate a rapid march and movement, especially for a large army.

The more direct roads toward Tiber are isolated and travel through rugged lands, with several places that can be easily blocked by a small force, such as river crossings, potentially holding up the advance. That is something that must be avoided at all costs."

"I see." Therik gave a nod. "The two roads along the coast also allow the army to basically move almost as one. If an enemy threatens one of the columns of march, the other can maneuver to assist."

"That was the general idea," Marcus said, "or it was, when the senate approved my plan. There is no telling if Mechlehnus has altered anything."

"And the enemy are watching the roads that go directly north from Mal'Zeel, aren't they?" Therik asked.

"They are," Marcus confirmed. "Their scouts have yet to reach the roads along the coast, meaning it may be possible to execute a rapid march into the north without detection."

"What about the confederacy?" Eli asked. "If the imperial army moves north, it leaves the door to Mal'Zeel open to their army coming up from the south."

"That is why I argued against the senate's orders," Marcus said, frustration plain in his voice. "They would not listen to me or consider any other strategies, especially after the last word on the confederacy's position."

"Where are they?" Stiger asked.

"From all indications," Marcus continued, "the enemy has halted their advance around Asti. Why, we're not sure, but we think it is supply-related. We already know they are living off the land and bringing supply in by sea. But their army is so large that, even with what they're able to scrounge, they may not have sufficient ships hauling in food to meet their needs. So their inaction is more of a strategic pause than anything else."

Stiger wasn't so sure about that. The enemy had planned well to this point and were up to something. He felt it in his bones. What that was, he had no idea. Yet he was also certain they were coordinating with the Castol. And the Castol were not simply taking advantage of an unguarded border as Max had suggested. He had to assume that, together, the Castol and the Cyphan were working mutually toward the destruction of their foe, the empire. That meant they had a unified and coordinated plan.

"Given sufficient time," Stiger said, "they will move north, most probably after our army is long gone and the road to Mal'Zeel is open. They likely have spies and scouts watching the roads."

"I thought that a very real possibility," Marcus said. "By the time word reaches us of their movement north, we may not be able to march back in time to stop them from reaching the capital."

"You should know I received word they landed a second army, a smaller one, far to the south," Stiger said.

Marcus blew out an unhappy breath. "Between the Castol and the confederacy, we will soon be in a difficult position."

"After the senate gave you your marching orders," Stiger said, "I am guessing your plan was to strike first against the Castol, fast and hard, then turn as quickly as you could and march back to face the confederacy when they move up from the south. Do I have that right?"

Marcus gave a nod. "I was intending on force marching north. In winter, it will not be an easy undertaking, but we greatly outnumber the Castol and I believe we can achieve surprise. Most of the cavalry left well before the army began marching. I sent them farther north, with orders to swing around and behind the enemy, with an aim toward severing supply lines and communications. With any luck, after they get to work, the Castol will use their cavalry to attempt to drive ours off."

"Interesting," Stiger said with approval.

"As it's winter," Marcus said, "even a little disruption in supply is a big problem. An army will eat themselves hungry if the supply trains cease coming or even if a few are eliminated. There is also the added benefit of forcing their cavalry to react to ours. It steals their long-range eyes, further blinding them to my approach with the main body of the army. I was hoping to close with theirs before they became aware of us."

Stiger took a few heartbeats to think it through. "It's a good plan," he admitted.

"I believe it has a fair chance of working," Marcus said. "Out of their forests and on the plains around the city of Tiber, the Castol are exposed. They are not accustomed to our style of fighting. With our numbers, and even with the army being half-trained, I was confident of the end result. However, if they choose flight over fight, they would be forced to flee back through a land they themselves pillaged, one stripped of food and in the throes of winter. The effect would be the same as me defeating them directly in battle. At that point, I would be free to march back to the capital, on more direct roads."

"It seems as if Lears is sticking with the plan," Eli said.

"He would not want to upset the senate," Max put in, "at least at this stage."

"I have even prepositioned stocks of food along our route of march," Marcus added. "Moving supply in winter is a bitch and changing the plan at this point would be foolish. No, Mechlehnus and Lears are committed. They must follow through with everything I have set in motion."

"Do we have any idea on the size of the army the Castol have brought south?" Stiger asked.

"At least a hundred thousand men," Marcus said.

"That many?" Stiger whistled, shaking his head. Even with superior numbers, that was still a large force. And much of the imperial army were composed of fresh troops, wet behind the ears recruits.

"Maybe more," Marcus said. "They have a lot of cavalry and our advance scouts have had difficulty determining their exact numbers."

"Over a hundred thousand, then." Stiger felt sick to his stomach. If the Castol and Cyphan were able to unite their two armies, things would become very difficult for the empire. Such a thing could not be allowed to happen. Onc way or another, as his father had said, the imperial army would have to continue north and deal with the Castol. The risks of doing that were huge, especially with a half-trained army. Worse, the army might not be able to return to Mal'Zeel before the confederacy arrived, especially after having removed his father from command.

"That all sounds like a challenge to me," Therik said.

"Does it?" Stiger looked over and shook his head again before turning back to his father. "Okay—one problem at a time. Lears comes first. We tackle that little problem, then everything else after."

"Little problem?" Max asked.

Therik turned to Marcus and Max. "Do either of you know where Lears is in the city?"

"I'd guess he's taken up residence at the palace," Max said.

"But we cannot be certain of that," Marcus said. "Though he was there last night, he may not be there now."

"We should strike before he can concentrate his soldiers." Therik punched a fist into his open palm. "Hit him now, before he is prepared."

"He could be anywhere in the city," Eli said. "We don't know for sure he's there in the palace."

"He's there," Stiger said. "Knowing Lears, I don't think he'd give up the palace. Not willingly."

"The moment you entered the city," Max said, "he might have surrounded the palace with a ring of steel."

Eli looked to Stiger. "After he lashed your back, you did sort of tell him you would kill him. It would be like him to do that, let others fight his battles for him."

"There was no 'sort of' about it," Stiger said. "I made him a promise and I aim to keep it."

He had already delayed long enough. If he marched to the palace and Lears wasn't there, or worse, he fled, Stiger would be in a difficult position. Lears would have the leisure time to consolidate his men and even recall Mechlehnus. That wouldn't be good. Time was not on Stiger's side. He was outnumbered, and badly.

Stiger stared into the flames of the fire that cracked and popped before him, sending sparks and embers toward the hole in the ceiling. The urge to get moving was becoming very strong. There was no point in delaying any longer. He had learned all he could of the political landscape. Navaro was dead and he had no way of contacting Treim and Aetius's agents. That was, if they were even alive. They might have fled the city.

It was time to act. He clapped his hands together and stood, looking around. "I see no other option than go directly to the palace. We strike before Lears can get organized."

"And if he runs?" Eli asked. "He did that once before."

"I well remember," Stiger said as he gave his answer some thought. "If he runs this time, he weakens his position and strengthens ours."

"That won't mean a thing," Marcus said, "if he's able to rally enough men to his side. He can rebuild his reputation later, after he deals with us. It is frequently the victors that pen the history."

"We will just have to make sure we are the victors," Stiger said.

"On our way, we should stop by the temple district," Father Restus said. "There may be some of my order present who can assist us. I can order the temple guards to join us as well. That will add considerably to our numbers."

"Very good." Stiger liked the idea. That said, he did not feel good about what they were going to attempt. There were too many things that could go wrong, too many unknowns. But at the same time, he felt compelled to act. "Let's push this show onto the palace."

"Do you think I can find a good meal there?" Therik asked.

Stiger patted the orc on the back as he turned toward the door. "Of that, I am certain, my friend."

As Stiger started for the door, Ruga came in at a run. The centurion stopped and came to a position of attention.

"Sir," Ruga said. "The civilians are leaving, and in a hurry. There are soldiers coming up the hill too, and not just a few."

Stiger felt his heart sink at the news. He had waited too long to act. Now it would cost him potentially everything.

"Get your men formed up in front of the building," Stiger ordered. "Any who are out watching, or on sentry duty, pull them back immediately. If need be, we can withdraw into the house and bar the door. This place is a fortress. Got that?"

"Yes, sir." Ruga turned and, armor chinking, jogged back out the way he'd come.

"I'm going to need a sword," Marcus said. "Mine was taken."

"You can have Corus's," Stiger said. "He's won't be needing it."

"I suppose not," Marcus said.

Stiger started for the door, knowing his position had become desperate. Lears had gotten the jump on him.

CHAPTER ELEVEN

Ruga's men had begun forming up into the ranks, hastily dressing themselves next to one another as Stiger stepped out of the courtyard and back onto the street and small square before his house.

There were four ranks, with those men from Corus's company comprising the last line. Moving amongst the ranks, Ruga's optio was busy making sure the men continued to form up and prepare for action.

"Stand aside," Stiger ordered. "Make a hole."

The men, glancing back, made room for him, stepping aside and moving their shields out of the way. He quickly passed through the ranks and joined Ruga, who was standing at the head of the formation. The centurion was staring down the street they had recently come up. There were still a few civilians about in the square, but these were ducking into nearby shops, hastily moving away on side streets, or disappearing into alleys. In Stiger's experience, that was never a good sign. They well knew trouble was in the offing.

Ruga glanced over at Stiger before pointing ahead of them. "There, sir. There they are."

Stiger expelled an unhappy breath. What looked like an entire company in a marching column was working their way up the hill toward them. Worse still, these were not militia, but legionaries. He'd not be able to bluff his way by them. These men would do their duty, just like he would were he in their place.

"And more coming up that side street there." Ruga pointed to their right. "We're gonna be badly outnumbered in a moment or two, sir. They have us boxed in nicely."

"Right," Stiger said sourly as he looked. There was yet another company of legionaries approaching from the direction of the temple district.

"It seems as if we won't have to go that far to find a fight," Therik said as he joined them. Eli, Restus, and Marcus came through the ranks a moment later, with Max trailing just behind. "They are coming to us."

Stiger eyed Therik for a long moment. He felt sick to his stomach, for he had waited too long. Stiger cursed himself again for that. And yet he knew he had needed intelligence, to learn the lay of the land before going for Lears. He slapped his thigh. There was no point in second-guessing his decisions, not now. Lears had simply reacted before he could. That was all.

"It is what it is," Stiger said.

"That's right," Therik agreed, "and now we will fight."

Stiger looked around and spotted his father. He turned to Ruga. "My father needs a sword. What did you do with the one Corus was using?"

"It's over there, with the body, sir." Ruga nodded off to the side of the formation. Both Corus and Yanulus had been dragged out of the way and placed against the wall of Stiger's house. "I gave orders that the bodies were not to be rifled. I did not want the men of Corus's company to become incensed."

"Good thinking," Stiger said.

"Both men were also officers and legionaries," Ruga added. "They deserve some respect, sir."

"I agree." Stiger turned to his father. "There's a sword over there for you."

Marcus gave a nod and moved off.

"Some more javelins than the handful Corus's men have would be nice, sir," Ruga mused as he turned back to watching the legionary company approach. "I'd have liked to whittle their numbers down a bit before the real action begins and our lines meet."

"They don't have javelins either," Therik pointed out.

"So?" Ruga asked. "What is your point?"

"Would you like me to run out to the city armory?" Eli asked Ruga. "I could fetch a few javelins for you."

"Would you? That is, if you wouldn't terribly mind." Ruga turned to Stiger. "For a while now, I've been wondering on something, sir."

"Oh?" Stiger asked, glancing over.

"Where exactly did you find him, sir?" Ruga asked.

"He sort of found me," Stiger said, glancing over at Eli. The elf had attached himself to Seventh Company, Stiger's first command, years ago. "It's a long story, a very long story."

"I can only imagine, sir," Ruga said and then looked at the elf. "Do you want me to bind and gag him until this is all over, sir? That way, we might die in peace."

"Bind and gag me?" Eli turned a scandalized look upon the centurion. "You would not dare!"

"Try me," Ruga said. "It would be my pleasure."

"I am beginning to revise my opinion of you, Centurion," Eli said.

Stiger's gaze returned to the first company, which had reached the small square before Stiger's home. The red-caped legionaries with their shields, armor, and sheathed swords looked smart and deadly.

"Company, halt," an officer shouted from somewhere amongst the column of march. The company ground to a halt at the edge of the square. "Sergeant, form three ranks. I want a battle line, yesterday, if you please."

"Yes, sir," a sergeant at the head of the column replied in a gruff tone. He turned to face the men. "You heard the captain and you know the drill. Find your places. Get a move on."

The company began redeploying, just thirty yards from them. It was quickly done and well executed. A sudden thrill of excitement washed over Stiger at the display of professionalism, that and of the company itself. Before him was the epitome of what a legionary company should be, and he felt a stab of pride.

The officer stepped out before his men. Stiger did not know the man, but that did not much matter. A handful of heartbeats later, the second company off to the right marched into the square before coming to a halt. After a brusque order, they too began to deploy into a battle formation next to the first company. They were putting on a show of strength.

Beyond them, yet a third company was coming up the street to the right. In the small square, there would be no room for another company, which made these newcomers effectively a reserve. His excitement fading, Stiger blew out a long breath. He estimated there were six hundred men against Ruga's command, which numbered just over a hundred.

A growl close at hand caused Stiger to jump slightly.

"Bloody gods," Ruga exclaimed, having jumped. "Fucking dog nearly made me shit myself."

Dog was sitting by his side, between him and Ruga. Where he had come from or, for that matter, when he had arrived, Stiger had no idea. Ears up and hair standing on end, the animal's attention was completely focused on the legionary companies before them. Dog had his teeth bared and was growling deeply.

"And just where have you been?" Stiger asked the animal. "And how did you find us?"

The growling ceased. Dog looked up at him with brown, watery eyes. He tilted his head to the side, ears flopping over, and his tail gave a half wag.

"Well?" Stiger demanded, though he knew he would never get an answer.

"He's here now, sir," Ruga said, having recovered. "I think that's all that matters. To be honest, even though we're badly outnumbered, I am comforted by it."

Dog's tail gave another wag, this one clearly of approval, as he looked at Ruga and then to Stiger. His tongue hung crazily out of his mouth.

"Me too," Stiger agreed, and he was, for he felt better having the animal by his side. He reached down and patted the dog's head.

"That is the largest dog I've ever seen," Marcus said as he returned with Corus's sword in its sheath and holding the man's sword harness. He raised the strap over his head and settled the leather harness into place on his shoulder and sword at his side. "He's yours, I take it? I never figured you for keeping pets."

"Dog is his own master," Stiger said, "and he is most definitely not a pet. He comes and goes when he pleases."

The animal's tail began wagging as he stood and turned about to face Marcus. The wagging became more vigorous, to the point where the tail shook the entire animal.

"You named your dog Dog?" Marcus asked. "You could not come up with something more creative?"

Tail still wagging wildly, Dog approached and nosed Marcus's hand, licking it with a long pink tongue. Marcus scowled. Stiger knew his father had never been overly affectionate with dogs, other than those that could hunt, but that did not stop him from rubbing the top of the shaggy animal's head, which came up to chest level.

"I was told to name him," Stiger said simply. He'd had the conversation before, not just once, but a few times. He did not feel like explaining more, for he was suddenly reminded of Theo, one more friend he had left behind. "So, I named him."

"He is a killer," Therik said, eyeing the dog warily. "Don't let his looks fool you."

Marcus spared the orc a disbelieving look. "He doesn't look like he could chase down a rabbit. I don't even think he'd be good for the hunt."

"Ben's been busy. Not only did he get himself a dog," Eli put in, "but he also got married too."

"What?" Marcus's hand froze on the dog's head. He turned a shocked gaze to his son. "Tell me I did not hear that correctly. Is what Eli says true?"

Stiger closed his eyes at that. He did not need this right now.

"You heard me right," Eli said. "Your son now has a wife, and a beautiful one at that. Yes, she is a real looker."

"You married?" Max said to Stiger. "You took a wife?"

Shaking his head, Stiger opened his eyes before shooting a heated look at Eli. At the same time, he felt a stab of anguish at the thought of having left Taha'Leeth behind with the army. The feeling was replaced rapidly with one of irritation. "Eli, do you really think this is the time for that conversation?"

"Well"—Eli gestured toward the legionaries to their front, who were still forming up—"we're badly outnumbered.

I will pose a counterquestion. If not now, when? I mean, you should really thank me for breaking the ice with your father. You were going to have to tell him anyway. I've just helped you get it out of the way, is all."

Stiger just shook his head, the feeling of frustration only growing more intense. There were days he wondered on Eli and this was one of them.

"You married?" Marcus asked again, disbelief plain in his tone. There was anger mixed in there too. "That is a family matter and, as head of house, I should have been consulted. You should know that."

Stiger did not want to have this conversation, not here and especially not now, with all the ears around. He spared his father a long look, then blew out a resigned breath. "It seemed like the right thing to do at the time."

Marcus did not appear pleased with his answer. He raised his chin. "Whom did you marry?"

"She's not exactly what you will be expecting in a wife." Stiger sucked in a deep breath. "Taha'Leeth became my wife a few weeks back."

"What kind of a name is that?" Marcus demanded. "It's not imperial. That's for certain."

"Elven." Eli almost bounced on his toes as he said it, his eyes dancing with his amusement. "Your son married into the High Born."

Marcus turned his gaze squarely on Stiger in what could only be described as utter disbelief.

Stiger shot Eli a warning look. His friend was purposely avoiding his gaze. It was clear he was thoroughly enjoying himself and the moment. Stiger stared at the ground before his feet, then looked up at his friend.

"You always love to poke the bear."

"I can still bind and gag him should you wish it, sir," Ruga said.

"I should have taken you up on it when you first offered," Stiger said. "Maybe I still should."

"You married an elf?" Max appeared as if he could not quite believe what he was hearing. He was looking between Stiger and Eli. "Really? An elf? He's jesting, right?"

"You both can relax," Eli said. "It's not like Ben married my sister."

"You don't have a sister," Stiger said, his frustration with his friend reaching whole new levels.

"That's my point," Eli said to Stiger's father. "Think of her as not just anyone, but a princess of her people. Your son married as high as one could go. She is the ruler of her people."

Stiger let out a heavy sigh. He pointed at Eli. "We're going to talk later, you and I. We're past due for a good talk."

"I look forward to it." Eli shot him a close-mouthed grin. "You know, what with you being married, I've been feeling a little neglected of late. It's almost as if you've had your mind on other things."

"We're going to definitely have that talk," Stiger promised.

"Stand ready," a voice shouted across the way, abruptly ending the conversation before it could continue. Stiger was grateful for that. He would rather face an action at that moment than be questioned further by his father on his marriage.

He turned his gaze back to the two legionary companies that had formed up to their front. The sun had come out from behind a cloud and bathed them all in bright light. The legionaries facing him looked good. Their equipment was well maintained, with a used look, and their ranks ordered.

These were trained and battle-hardened men. They were not conscripts, fresh to the legions.

As a cold wind whipped across the square, ruffling cloaks, four officers emerged from the ranks of both companies, two captains and their lieutenants. They eyed Stiger and Ruga's men for a long moment. Then, they walked toward each other and began speaking amongst themselves. The conference lasted only a few moments before the officers turned and moved a few yards forward, then stopped halfway between the formed-up companies and Stiger's men. All eyes were focused upon Stiger, but he did notice them flicking to Therik with curiosity.

Stiger's heart began beating faster. He shared a look with Eli and resisted a smile.

"This is turning out to be quite an interesting day," Eli said, "don't you think, Ben?"

"My thoughts exactly," Stiger said with a slow nod.

"I don't suppose we stand a chance against such force," Max said.

Stiger glanced back at his brother, contemplated saying something, then disregarded the idea. He turned back to the officers. They were waiting for him.

"These are not good odds," Marcus said to his eldest. "They want to talk, only to demand our surrender."

"Like that is going to happen," Therik growled. "I'll not surrender. I'd rather die first."

"If they want us, they are going to have to come and get us," Ruga said, tone grim and hard. "And we're not going to go down easily."

Stiger clapped his hands together. "Eli, Therik, Ruga, and you, Father, you are all with me. Right then, let's go see what they have to say."

He started forward. Eli, Therik, Ruga, and Marcus followed. They stopped six feet from the delegation of officers. Max and Restus remained behind with Dog.

The captain from the first company to arrive stepped out before the others. He was short, standing just under five feet. His armor seemed somewhat ill-fitting. He struck Stiger as more clerk-like, someone better suited to being a minor magistrate than a man of action and leader of men in battle. He puffed out his chest before speaking.

"You must be Stiger." The man's voice was nasally, almost as if he spoke through his nose instead of his mouth.

"That's Imperator to you, sonny." Ruga's hand slipped to the hilt of his sword. "Show respect or I will teach you manners."

The captain's gaze shifted to the centurion. He raised an eyebrow.

"Stand down, Ruga." Stiger held up a hand to forestall the centurion before more words could be exchanged. Ruga hesitated a moment before relaxing. He removed his hand from the hilt as Stiger turned his attention to the captain. "I am Bennulius Stiger."

"I've heard a lot about you." The officer glanced back behind him at the ordered ranks of men. "More than enough, actually."

From the man's look of distaste, it did not seem as if what he had heard he had much enjoyed. Over the years, Stiger had become more than accustomed to such sentiments, even from minor nobility, like the man before him. Or was he of the equites class? Regardless of the man's station, such attitudes did not bother him as they once had. He had accepted who he was and that was that.

"And who, sir, are you?" Stiger asked in a firm but polite tone. He would play the man's game, at least for a time.

"Ikuus, commanding Seventh Company, Third Legion," the captain said, self-importantly. He turned to his fellow officers. "And these men, I believe you know: my executive officer, Lieutenant Hollux, and Captain Lepidus of Tenth Company, along with his lieutenant, Spiro."

"I know them," Stiger said, and it came out more as a growl than anything else. "And more importantly, they know me."

"Know you? Is that all you have to say? After all those years serving together?" Hollux broke into a wide grin. "It's good to see you again, sir."

The lieutenant stepped forward toward Stiger. Therik's and Ruga's hands went for their swords, prepared to draw them. Hollux hesitated, eyeing them warily as he held his hands out before him to show he meant no harm.

"It's all right," Stiger said. "He is a friend. Hollux can be trusted."

Both relaxed. Eyes still on the two, Hollux slowly extended his hand. Stiger took it and shook warmly.

"It's good to see you well, Lieutenant," Stiger said. "I'd expected you to make captain by now and have your own company."

"Bah," Hollux said. "Sadly, I could not afford the price of the commission. Besides, I did not want to pull from my pension and beggar myself. I would like to retire with some land to my name." He jerked a thumb at his captain. "He got command of the company instead."

"Lieutenant," Ikuus said in a scandalized tone. "This is quite improper. Improper, I say, not to mention disrespectful."

Hollux glanced back at his commanding officer, his face a schooled mask of control. "Improper or not, sir, I owe this man my life, and more than once too. He commands my respect."

Ikuus scowled at that, for the implication in the lieutenant's words was plain.

"The south has been rough on you," Lepidus said, stepping forward as Hollux moved back. The captain of the Tenth offered his arm, which Stiger clasped. Lepidus pulled him into a bear hug and patted his back warmly. "You look older, my brother, and it's only been a few months since we last saw one another."

"A lot has happened," Stiger said as they disengaged. "A great deal, actually."

"He's gotten married," Eli said.

"Not that again," Stiger groaned.

"Really?" Lepidus said, perking up. "You took a bride?"

Stiger gave a reluctant nod, desperately wishing the elf had dropped it. He pictured Taha'Leeth in his mind, not pale and still as he had last seen her, but full of life. He remembered her vibrant hair, her exquisite face, the gleam in her eye that spoke of her intelligence and spirit. She was a fighter and he had to believe she'd pull through.

"Congratulations, old boy," Lepidus said. "I can't wait to meet the lucky woman who'd take a tough old bastard like you."

"She's gonna be just thrilled to meet you," Eli said, "especially after she finds out all the trouble you've gotten her husband into over the years."

"Eli, I see you are still doing your best to drive him nuts." Lepidus jerked his chin at Stiger. "Any luck with that?"

"You know I am." Eli glanced over at Stiger, his amusement plain. "It is my lifelong ambition, and with each passing day I grow one step closer to unseating him mentally."

Lepidus gave a chuckle and offered a hand, which the elf took. "It is good to see you again too. The legion hasn't been the same without you, Eli."

"I am certain of that," Eli said, then leaned forward, almost conspiratorially, and lowered his voice, though they could all still hear him. "I can't begin to express how delighted I am that it's you who came to greet us instead of someone else."

Lepidus gave a grunt at that. Hollux and Eli shook warmly next.

"Spiro," Stiger said, "good to see you, son."

"You too, sir," Spiro replied. "When we heard about the fate of the southern legions, we were all worried for you and Eli."

Stiger was touched by the concern.

"Well," Eli said, "you know me—can't keep a good elf down. And I do my best to keep Ben out of trouble."

"Uh huh," Spiro said, sounding far from convinced.

Lepidus turned his attention back to Stiger. "I have a couple bottles of the good stuff back in my quarters. After this is over and things are settled, you can tell me what happened over a few drinks. I want to hear all about how Tioclesion named you his successor. In fact"—Lepidus chuckled—"I am certain there is one heck of a story in there and I am really looking forward to hearing it."

"We have our orders," Ikuus said. "As senior officer and in command of this expedition, you can't disobey them."

Lepidus spared the captain of Seventh Company a patient look.

"Lepidus," Stiger said and glanced at the two companies formed up behind the four officers, "we're not going to do this, are we? You are not going to make me fight you."

"Of course not," Lepidus scoffed, waving a hand. "I consider you a brother. A disreputable one at that, but I'd never raise my sword against you, especially now that you're imperator—my emperor."

"Are you mad?" Ikuus asked. "We have our orders. We could be executed for this. It's treason to support him. Do you understand that?"

Lepidus let out an impatient breath as he turned to face the captain of the Seventh. He studied the man for a prolonged moment before speaking.

"Do you really believe your men, those of Seventh Company, will follow orders to go against their former captain? Seriously, man, think things through. Your company is the best in the legion and it's all because of him." Lepidus gestured toward Stiger with a hand. "You might not realize it, but most of your boys see him as a father figure. By the gods, my men love him too, and he's not even their captain. I am."

"I," Ikuus spluttered, "I—but—he..." The captain of Seventh Company trailed off with a clear sense of defeat. His shoulders slumped in resignation.

"Now," Marcus said, "things are really getting interesting."

"You can say that again," Therik said. "Only moments ago, I thought it would come to blood. I was convinced of it."

"We were short on men," Stiger said, "and Lears was kind enough to send us some."

"That was very generous of him," Marcus agreed. "We will have to make certain we thank him properly."

"Gentlemen," Stiger said, "may I introduce my father, Marcus Stiger."

"It is an honor, General," Lepidus said and stepped forward. He shook hands, then stepped back. "I have had the pleasure of fighting alongside your son and his company. I do not know of a finer soldier or combat leader in the empire. You must be very proud."

"More than you know," Marcus said, "more than even he realizes."

Stiger felt himself frown as he glanced over at his father.

"I am pleased to meet you as well, sir," Hollux said and bowed slightly. "Your son has not only resurrected my career, one I thought failed, but has helped make me into the man I am today. I can never repay all that he has done for me."

The scar on Stiger's cheek pulling taut, he felt himself scowl slightly. He was uncomfortable with praise and always had been.

"You are giving me too much credit," Stiger said. "The leader you are was always in there. You just needed a chance to find him."

"Regardless, sir," Hollux said, "I am in your debt."

"I have long wanted to meet you, General," Spiro said. "My father fought under your command at Lake Harrand. Growing up, I heard a great deal about that action."

"Did he now?" Marcus said. "Deateas Spiro was your father?"

"He is, sir."

"He was a fine officer," Marcus said. "I was sorry to see him injured. How is he doing these days?"

"Well, sir," Spiro said. "He bought a farm—well, really a plantation—just outside the city. It started as a small operation, but now... the gods have blessed him. The plantation has grown and turned quite profitable. He has over three hundred slaves."

"Does he now? That's good to hear," Marcus said. "When you see him next, please pass along my regards."

"I will, sir," Spiro said. "He will be pleased you recall him."

Stiger noticed Ikuus staring at them. He could readily read the man's fear and worry at what was transpiring. He understood he'd lost control. That was plain. Stiger himself had had such feelings in the past and could sympathize with him.

"And this is Therik," Stiger said. "He and I have been through a lot together. I consider him my friend."

Lepidus and Hollux turned their gazes to Therik, who had crossed his muscular arms and was regarding them with a not-so-friendly look. It was more of a challenge than anything else. They seemed hesitant at first, then Lepidus stepped forward and extended his hand.

"Any friend of Ben's is a friend of mine," Lepidus said. "And I mean that. I really do."

Therik unwound his arms, took the offered hand, and shook. Lepidus held it a moment, then stepped back. Hollux offered his hand next, which Therik shook as well. Spiro simply gave Therik a nod and seemed content to remain where he was. Ikuus stayed rooted to his spot. Dog came nosing his way forward, sniffing.

"He's with me also," Stiger said as Dog jumped up on Lepidus and began licking at his face. The captain of the Tenth staggered under the large animal's sudden weight.

"It seems Dog has no taste in people," Eli said.

"My, he's a big boy," Lepidus said, laughing. After some effort, he was able to push Dog back down.

"Go ahead, Therik," Eli said. "Tell him what a killer that shaggy thing is."

"I think you just did for him," Stiger said.

"This loveable boy?" Lepidus asked, rubbing Dog's head with both hands. "I seriously doubt that. I've always loved dogs. It's cats I can't stand."

"Why does everyone assume Dog is just a lovable, shaggy ball of fur?" Therik asked Stiger.

"Because he is," Stiger said, "to those he likes."

Therik did not appear quite convinced.

"Who's got the other company?" Stiger gestured back up the road to the right. That company was still formed up in a column of march. Stiger could not see her captain. "Who is commanding the reserve?"

"Spatz," Lepidus said, straightening up and stepping away from Dog.

"Second Company's here too?" Stiger asked, surprised. "I thought they were with the Third."

"They are," Lepidus said. "Spatz was reassigned after we arrived in the capital and given a new company from the Eighteenth. Those men of his are trained recruits who have yet to see action."

"Is he going to be a problem?" Stiger asked, looking again toward Spatz's company. "He and I never much got along. We did not see eye to eye."

"A problem?" Lepidus followed Stiger's gaze to the other company. "No. He hates Lears more than he does you. So I think it's all good. At least he says so, and we both know his word can be trusted."

Stiger nodded. Spatz was a pain, but he was as good as his word. If he said he would do something, you could count on him to do it. Stiger and Spatz respected each other professionally; they just disliked each other.

Ikuus was looking between Stiger and Lepidus. His worry had mixed plainly with the shock at how quickly things had changed for him.

"Before we marched down here from the palace, we conferred," Lepidus explained. "We decided that we were going to back you."

"You did?" Ikuus asked, seeming to snap out of his shock. His face colored with anger. "And you did not think to include me?"

"It's all right," Lepidus said and placed a hand on Ikuus's shoulder. "You're with us now. Trust me, you don't want to serve Lears. Let's just say he's lacking in character and leave it at that."

"I..." Ikuus shrugged off Lepidus's hand.

"Unless you want to go against us?" Hollux asked his captain, with a hard edge. "I would not recommend doing that, sir. It might... ah, prove unhealthy for you."

Ikuus did not respond as he looked over at his lieutenant. The color drained from his face. A moment later, he turned his gaze to Stiger, his mouth working.

"Whose side are you on?" Therik demanded, taking a menacing step forward. The orc's gaze bored into Ikuus. "Decide now."

The man took a half-step back before steadying himself.

"If you choose to support Lears," Stiger said, "you will be detaincd until we've resolved things and then allowed to leave, unharmed."

Ikuus's jaw flexed as he turned back to Stiger. There was a long moment as he thought things through. He took a deep breath and drew himself to a position of attention.

"In the last few months, I have come to know Lepidus, Spatz, and Hollux. All three are good men with years of experience behind them. They say you are too and have spoken highly of you. I ask to serve, Imperator. If you will grant me that honor, I will pledge my loyalty to your service." Ikuus paused. "Unfortunately, I cannot pledge the loyalty of my house, as I am the youngest son. If you accept me, you will have mine."

Stiger studied the man for a long moment. He certainly seemed sincere enough. He sensed no deceit in Ikuus's manner, even with Hollux's recent threat and Therik's intimidating behavior. He might not be all that quick, but Stiger decided to give him the benefit of the doubt. Everyone deserved a chance to prove themselves, and he would give Ikuus such an opportunity.

"Your service is accepted," Stiger said.

"Thank you, Imperator," Ikuus said.

Stiger turned his gaze to Lepidus. "I take it Tiro found you?"

"He did," Lepidus said. "Just before we received our orders."

"Where is he?" Stiger asked, looking around, for he did not see his old, wily sergeant. Stiger had been worried for his safety after sending him off.

"Back with Spatz," Hollux said and glanced over at Ikuus. "We did not think it wise to give away our intentions ahead of time."

Stiger felt an immense wave of relief that Tiro was all right. He glanced in the direction of the Palatheum Hill. Sitting upon its crest, the palace could be seen from their current position. "Do you know where Lears is?"

"He's holed up in the palace, with that bastard tribune watching over him like a mother hen," Lepidus said.

"What tribune?" Stiger asked, turning back.

"Handi," Lepidus said. "Do you know him?"

"Handi?" Stiger growled, feeling an intense stab of anger at the mention of the man's name. He also felt a wave of deep disgust. Then the wheels turned. It all made sense now. Handi had not just fled Lorium, he had ridden straight through and likely had arrived just before Treim's messenger. As an officer, he would have had access to the courier stations and a change of mount. He would not have been questioned.

The bastard had gotten to the senate first. The senators had acted, and swiftly too, which was unlike them. Who knew what lies the man had told them.

"I know him," Stiger said. "He is a snake."

"He seems to be the one really giving the orders," Lepidus said. "He passed ours along to me personally. I don't even think he conferred with Lears first."

"And what exactly were your orders?" Stiger asked.

"We were to demand your surrender, with an assurance that you would not be harmed," Hollux said, suddenly looking uncomfortable. "Once you turned yourself over, you were to be executed on the spot." Hollux paused. "I couldn't believe it when Lepidus shared the orders. Neither could Spatz."

Stiger glanced in the direction of the other company and saw Spatz walking across the square toward them.

Therik growled. "There is no honor in such behavior."

"Honestly, I think Lears is frightened that you are in the city," Lepidus said. "He's hiding somewhere in the palace and seems content to be letting Handi run things. And"— the captain of the Tenth glanced around at his men and those of Seventh Company—"that worked to our favor."

Stiger thought it odd that Handi had been able to worm his way into not only Tioclesion's confidence, but now Lears's too. He had the feeling that something else was at play here. He just did not know what that was.

Lepidus held his hands out about them and chuckled as Spatz joined them. "It seems Handi did not know our history, or that you commanded the Seventh prior to heading south. He sent the best he had on hand, hard-charging veteran legionaries, to deal with you."

"Thank the gods for the man's ignorance," Marcus said.

"I love it," Stiger said, then turned to face the other captain. Spatz was Stiger's height, fit, and a hard-looking man. He had a scar on the base of his chin and his eyes were brown and intense. "Spatz, it's good to see you."

"You're still an asshole," Spatz replied, then softened his tone. "Did you really liberate Lorium and crush an army of the confederacy? We all know what rumors are like. They spread like wildfire and get embellished in the telling. There's even some bullshit about you being the High Father's chosen one. Is any of it true?"

"Yes," Eli said, before Stiger could answer, "I can confirm, he is an asshole."

"I'm seriously thinking of having Ruga gag you," Stiger said to Eli. Then he turned to Spatz. "It's true, I found the Thirteenth Legion and, with the help of allies, liberated Lorium and crushed two enemy armies. There's more, but yes"—Stiger glanced at Eli—"like you, I am an asshole."

"I guess it takes one to know one." Spatz gave an amused grunt. "So, we're gonna really do this and kill that bastard Lears? We're going to commit treason against the empire?"

"It's only treason if we lose," Marcus said. "The victors get the privilege of writing the history."

"With your help, we can get it done," Stiger said.

"Well," Spatz said, "Lears screwed up in a major way commanding the Third and got a lot of our comrades killed, including half of my company." He fell silent for a heartbeat. When he spoke next, his tone was grim and low. "I can only imagine what a shit show it would become with him in command of the empire, especially with the confederacy knocking on our door."

"Agreed," Stiger said.

"You," Spatz said to Stiger, "I think, are the better choice."

"Again we are in agreement," Stiger said.

"Then, Imperator"—Spatz pulled himself to a position of attention—"I pledge myself and my company to you and ending Lears's reign."

Stiger took a step forward, studying the captain. He extended his hand. Spatz regarded it for a long moment, almost with distaste, then with a shrug of his shoulders took it and shook.

"I accept," Stiger said and took a step back. He looked at Lepidus, who was the most senior of the officers present. "Tell me, do you know how many men Lears and Handi have guarding the palace?"

"About a thousand," Lepidus said, "a mixed bag of militia and auxiliaries. There is one light company of legionaries, from the Thirtieth. I understand Handi, late last night, sent word for several companies from the army to be recalled."

"When we left the palace," Spatz said, "they had not yet arrived."

Stiger glanced around, thinking. He would have to send word to Treim's household and Aetius's wife, Desindra, in the event they could still manage to assemble the men that were promised. That said, there was no real time to wait for them. He would move against Lears with what he had on hand, which was a considerable force.

"We now have three full companies of legionaries and Ruga's overstrength century, with Corus's praetorians," Stiger said. "Say, a little over seven hundred men of good quality. Though, Spatz, Lepidus tells me your men are untested. Is that a correct assessment?"

"That's true," Spatz replied, "but they will hold their own. On that, you have my word. I've worked them hard to get them into shape."

Stiger gave a nod. "Good. It's enough to take the fight to Lears."

Lepidus gestured with his chin. "Is that Corus over there?"

"It is." Stiger turned and regarded the two bodies for a moment. "I killed him in personal combat."

"Good." Hollux spat on the ground. "He had it coming, especially after Lears had him lash you. I swear the bastard enjoyed that."

"I never much liked him either," Spatz said to Stiger. "What was done to you by Lears and Corus was very ungentlemanly. It should never have come to pass."

"All right," Stiger said, not wanting to bring up old wounds. He wanted to move things along. "What's happened is firmly in the past. We must focus on what is before us. We're going to march on the palace. Once there, we will surround it, so that none can escape, and demand their surrender. Anyone who lays down their arms is to be spared."

"And if they don't surrender?" Marcus asked.

"Then we go through them. We make sure we kill both Lears and Handi," Stiger said. There was a long moment of silence. "They cannot be permitted to escape. Any questions?"

"No, sir," Lepidus said.

"None," Hollux said.

"I am with you, sir," Ikuus said firmly.

"Let's go kill Lears," Spatz said.

Stiger gave a nod, then looked over at Seventh Company. "Captain Ikuus, with your permission, I'd like to spend a moment with your men, my old company. They are good boys and I've missed them."

"Of course, Imperator," Ikuus said and stepped aside. "They are yours."

Stiger stepped past the officers toward his old company. He felt a wave of emotion roll over him as he took in the faces of the men of the Seventh. There was a moment of hesitation and then, with a cheer, the men broke ranks and gathered around him, shouting and patting him on the back. Stiger felt not only a lump in his throat, but the prick of tears in his eyes. He had trained these men and fought with them, bled with them, suffered through terrible privation, and together they had mourned fallen comrades. When he had not had a home, they had given him one.

He abruptly found himself hoisted up into the air, with the men shouting.

"STIGER...STIGER...STIGER..."

The other two companies joined in and the chant became thunderous. He caught a glimpse of the palace off in the distance and knew that within a short time, he would be there. Death was coming for Lears and Handi, along with everyone else who stood in his way.

CHAPTER TWELVE

Stiger looked first up and then down the column of legionaries. Sentries had been put out to the sides and rear of the line of march. Runners had also been sent forward to keep watch. Stiger had ordered a halt to the march in the middle of the temple district a short while before so that Father Restus could round up the temple guard to help swell their numbers. The paladin was also going to see if any of his order were around. An extra paladin or two would be more than welcome.

To either side of the wide paved street, massive marble-faced temples honoring the gods crowded in upon one another. The buildings themselves were grand, imposing structures, each with dozens of broad steps that led up to the entrances of the temples themselves. Marble columns by the dozens, each wider than the largest tree Stiger had ever seen, ran completely around the temples. These columns were engineered to hold up and support the orange–and-red-tiled roofs. Several of the more important temples were five to six stories in height, with the High Father's being the largest and grandest of them all.

The temples were designed to awe the average person, to make them feel small, insignificant when compared with the divine. They were also meant to celebrate the majesty of the gods. And Stiger felt himself dutifully awed by the grandeur. He was humbled by the effort and will it had taken to build them. Every time he had come here, whether it had been as a boy, teen, or young man, he had been deeply impressed and moved. This time was no different.

Unseen from the outside, within each temple resided a grand statue to the god the structure was meant to honor. It was the public face where the civilians were permitted to gather, make their offerings or devotions, and simply pray. The temple was the home for the god's spirit and a place for worshippers to connect directly with their divine god.

To his right was the temple to Fortuna, one of the smaller temples in the district, though it was still incredibly large. The temple itself reminded him of Castor's temple back in Forkham's Valley, the one he had ordered torn down. It was eerily similar in its design and construction. That brought on uncomfortable and dark thoughts.

Before Castor's temple, as his men had gone to work on demolishing that monument honoring the dark god, he had almost been dominated by Rarokan. The mad wizard had nearly escaped from his prison and taken control of Stiger's body. Without Father Thomas's intervention and assistance, Stiger might have ended up imprisoned within the sword for eternity. Had that happened, his cause and all he had worked toward would have been lost. It was a chilling thought.

Stiger eyed Fortuna's temple warily. Over the years, he had cursed her more than once. She had done her best to complicate his life, frequently throwing up roadblocks and obstacles that others would think impassable or impossible to overcome. Would she continue to work against him as he went for Lears? It was certainly something to be concerned about.

At the far end of the temple district, farther upslope and directly on the summit of the broad hill, sat the High

Father's temple, the place on Istros where the great god's spirit could always be found. Or so the priests taught. Stiger had found it within himself. He did not have to travel to a temple to discover his god or, for that matter, pray for him. It had been years since he'd visited the great god's temple.

It was really a complex, a series of several buildings, with the main one being the largest, set aside specifically for worship. The temple itself dwarfed the others in the district. And topping it all, instead of clay, the roof was plated in gold tiles. Under the light of the sun, the golden tiles gleamed and flashed brilliantly.

Stiger reflected that it must have cost a fortune. Legend told that when the legionaries from Rome had taken this region, they had seized so much plunder, a portion of it had been set aside to make the gold-plated tiles. It had been their way of thanking the great god for not only their deliverance, but success in finding a new home. He did not know if the story was true, but the empire had grown rich and powerful beyond compare. It might have simply been the citizens' way of honoring their patron god. Or more likely, in Stiger's mind, the church was wealthy and simply wanted everyone to know it.

Other than his legionaries, there were few people in view, and those had drawn away from the legionaries. It seemed as if the entire city knew they were coming. All along the route to the palace, civilians had made themselves scarce. They knew fighting was soon to break out and wanted to be far from it. He would not be getting help from the mob this time. Stiger did not begrudge them that. In war, it always seemed that the civilians, those stuck in the path between two sides, suffered the most.

Stiger himself was positioned halfway down the column of heavy infantry, with Ruga's century his escort. Lepidus's company was in the vanguard. Spatz's boys came next, while Seventh Company brought up the rear.

Therik was a few yards up, standing with Eli. The elf was pointing something out to the orc. Therik seemed fascinated by the grand temples, intently listening to Eli.

"How long will we be here, sir?" Ruga asked, coming up.

"As long as it takes," Marcus said, sounding suddenly grumpy. "You should know the legion's unofficial motto by now, Centurion."

Stiger glanced over at his father. Was he feeling impatient too? Stiger suspected his father was, only, like Stiger, he was good at hiding it.

"Hurry up and wait?" Ruga said, sourly. "Is that what you were getting at, sir?"

"That's it," Marcus said.

Stiger spared his father a sour look. Max was standing with them too. His elder brother had not said much since they'd stopped. Stiger could sense his unease.

"Father Restus said it would take about half an hour to assemble the temple guard," Stiger said.

"In my experience, nothing takes a half hour, sir," Ruga said. "It's gonna be more like a full hour, maybe even closer to an hour and a half before we get going. It all depends upon how motivated this guard is and how quickly they fall in."

Stiger himself felt frustrated by the delay. He had almost given the order to continue forward and have the temple guard, when they assembled, play catch-up. But after consulting his father, he had made the decision to wait until the guard was ready to march. It would be much better to arrive at the palace with a complete and as large a force as possible. Besides, Stiger did not want someone else coming along in his absence and offering the guard a better deal in support of Lears. No, he would take them with him when he marched.

"How many men are we talking?" Ruga asked.

"Around four hundred," Stiger said.

"And all they do is guard these temples?" Ruga asked, looking around.

"That's correct," Marcus said.

"From what?" Ruga asked. "Worshippers? Must be boring duty, sir."

"Boring?" Marcus asked. "No, not at all. The temple district is usually a very busy place. There is a lot of money that changes hands around here. Most legitimate lenders operate under the supervision and protection of the church. Then there are those selling sacrifices, or bringing valuables and coin as offerings. The temple guard keeps thieves, pickpockets, and the riffraff away."

"They also serve to keep the peace," Stiger said. "Factions of one god or another have been known to stir up trouble and fight with each other. Between hundreds, if not thousands, of fanatical worshippers, things can get heated and easily turn violent."

"They do a good job of keeping the order and peace here." Marcus tapped his foot on the ground. "Over the years, full-on battles have been fought on these bloodsoaked streets. It's the temple guard who work to keep a lid on it all."

"Can they fight?" Ruga asked. "I mean not against maddened worshippers, but stand in the line, so to speak?"

"They can hold a sword and shield," Marcus said, "face off an irate mob or stop a riot. However, I don't think they were ever intended to truly fight as a legionary does."

"I see," Ruga said. There was a lot of meaning conveyed in those two words, most of which was disappointment.

"That doesn't mean they can't be useful in helping to seal off the palace," Stiger said. "We cannot afford having Lears or Handi escaping. When we get there, they will help make certain that does not happen."

"If you say so, sir," Ruga said, clearly not wholly convinced on the temple guard's virtues.

Stiger felt himself scowl. It was possible Lears would flee the palace. That said, Stiger did not believe he would. To do so might fatally weaken his position and strengthen Stiger's hand. No, Lears had more men. He would stay and wait. The man knew he had additional reinforcement coming and it was only a matter of time until they arrived. Mechlehnus was sending several companies. Lears would remain and do everything he could to hold out until help arrived. That meant Stiger had to finish things before that relief arrived.

"Have the men stand at ease," Stiger said, feeling a stab of irritation. He had already made his decision and now had to live with it. There was no point in rehashing things further, agonizing over the wait to get moving again.

"Yes, sir." Ruga saluted and moved off.

"You said he's a good man?" Marcus asked of Ruga.

"I did," Stiger said, "but he can also be a pain in my ass." "Some of the best officers I've known have been," Marcus said. "A pain in the ass is not a bad thing, as long as he does his job well."

"I encourage my officers to speak their mind," Stiger said. "Ruga is a good example of that."

"It's a good practice," Marcus said. "The last thing any leader wants or needs are men who will only tell you what you want to hear. You need to guard against that."

A whining drew their attention off to the left. Dog was nosing around an old iron gate that stood open. It was half rusted and in need of being replaced. Beyond the gate and sandwiched between two temples was what looked like some type of a garden surrounded by a chest-high wrought iron fence. The fence also was badly rusted. On the inside were thick green shrubs. Beyond that, Stiger could see little of the garden, for the shrubs shielded most of everything from view.

A square brick building, only a single story in height, stood farther back in the garden, about fifty yards away. It looked old. Stiger had not really noticed the building. In fact, he could not ever recall seeing it before. Unlike the other grand temples, this one was plain, to the point of being ugly. The building and gardens seemed out of place, and he assumed he'd just overlooked it as a result. Was it a maintenance building? Or did it have some other purpose?

Dog looked back at him, and their eyes met. The animal gave a clipped bark and looked back at the gate. Oddly, there was something about the gardens that seemed to speak to Stiger, almost beckoning him forward. There was a power exerting its influence upon him. In the past, he would not have understood what was happening or that he was being influenced. Now, things were different. After the training he'd received from Menos, he recognized it for what it was: a use of *will*, and a powerful one too.

"That, my son"—Marcus stepped closer to Stiger and lowed his voice slightly—"is the temple to the first emperor. It was there that I had my vision."

Stiger glanced over at his father. Their eyes met.

"Do you feel it?" Marcus asked, with an eager note. "Do you feel the pull? We are expected, welcomed even."

Is this your doing? Stiger asked of Rarokan.

Even if it was, the mad wizard replied, *would you believe me if I told you no?*

Far from satisfied with the answer, Stiger turned his gaze back toward the garden and temple. Dog had sat down and was facing him. The animal seemed to be telling him to hurry, to get moving. At the same time, he felt an internal nudge. It came from the power that resided within, the High Father. Stiger's god wanted him to go in there, for something was waiting for him.

This is not me, Rarokan said.

He glanced around at the men that had been allowed to relax. Some were rooting around in haversacks. Others had sat down. A few even had pulled out dice and had gotten a game going. Most appeared bored.

His gaze shifted to the temples themselves. Most of the gods were honored here. Even Valoor and Castor. There were no priests to those gods, but temples honoring the deities had been built just the same.

Stiger felt no sense or pull from the other temples, even the High Father's own, at the far end of the street. He turned back to the first emperor's temple. His father was right. They were expected. That thought concerned him. Who was anticipating their arrival? Stiger sucked in a breath and blew it out slowly.

"Shall we go?" Stiger asked his father, looking over.

"Go where?" Max asked, looking around. "What are you both talking about?"

"You don't see it?" Marcus asked, surprised, and pointed.

"The alleyway between temples?" Max asked. "What about it?"

Stiger and his father shared a look.

"Ruga," Stiger called, "join me for a moment, would you?"

The centurion came back to them.

"How can I help you, sir?" Ruga asked.

"Do you see Dog?" Stiger asked, lowering his voice and stepping closer to the centurion.

"Yes, sir." The centurion nodded toward the animal. "I do."

"What do you see beyond him?"

"An alley between the temples, sir." Ruga's brows drew together. He looked at Stiger with a confused expression. "There's nothing else there, sir."

"You are wrong," Stiger said, recalling how the dwarves had concealed the entrance to Old City. "There's something hidden in plain sight, likely through magical means."

"Magic?" Ruga said, looking in Dog's direction. "What is it? What's there?"

"A temple to the first emperor," Stiger said.

"Father, you've mentioned this," Max said, "but I've never heard of such a place, nor seen it. I even went looking for it. After all these years, I did not quite believe it real. There is no record of such a temple being constructed any-where in the city. I always believed it was part of the vision you received. There was no other explanation until now."

Marcus turned his gaze upon his eldest son, and there was sadness in his look. "Over the long years, I have visited this place from time to time, my son. I find it calming of the mind and a restorative to my faith, reinforcing the hard decisions I've made for our family. It is a shame you did not have the faith to believe me."

"I am sorry I doubted you, Father," Max said. "Truly."

"I am too."

"Karus has his own temple?" Ruga asked, sounding intrigued. "This is my first time in the capital, sir."

"It seems he does," Stiger said. "My father and I are going in."

"Are you sure, sir?" Ruga asked. "I don't like the idea of you entering a place no one else can see, sir. If you will give me a moment, I will organize an escort for you. I think I'd also like to see such a temple myself."

"No," Stiger said, for he felt a strong sense of wrongness with the suggestion. "My father and I are going alone. We're expected."

"You're expected?" Ruga's gaze slipped back toward Dog. His face hardened before looking back at Stiger. "I don't like it, sir, not one bit. Would you reconsider? I could send a couple of men with you as an escort instead of a full detail."

"I don't like this either," Max said.

"It will be all right," Stiger said. "We will be back shortly." Stiger paused a moment. "Ruga, I don't fully understand the power of that place. No one is to follow us. That is an order. It could be dangerous for anyone who tries. No matter how long we take, do not come for us. Got that?"

"Yes, sir," Ruga said. "I don't like it much, but I understand."

"Shall we go find out what's waiting?" Stiger asked his father. "I figure we don't have much time before Restus gets the temple guard rousted."

Marcus gave a curt nod, and with that, they both started off, with Ruga and Max trailing just behind.

"Remember," Stiger said, "no one is to follow us in."

"Yes, sir," Ruga said. "I will make sure of that."

Stiger took another couple steps up to the open gate and stopped next to Dog. He looked down at the animal and hesitated. The draw to move forward was becoming nearly impossible to resist. Dog stood and nudged the back of Stiger's leg.

"All right, boy, I am going." Stiger stepped through the gate. He felt a funny tingling sensation, as if he were passing through some sort of an energy barrier. It pushed against him slightly, then gave way and he was through. He slowed to a stop just inside as the tingling passed.

"Isn't it wonderful?" Marcus asked, stepping around him. "Just beautiful. I come here whenever I can. This is where I find peace and solace."

Blinking in surprise, Stiger could only nod. It was as if they had stepped into a warm and well-insulated room. But it wasn't a room. They were still outdoors. In fact, it seemed like a spring day had dawned and the garden around them was in full bloom, bursting with life. Birds flitted about and butterflies fluttered through the sunlight. Even the air was fresh. There was no city stink.

The garden was well manicured and cared for. Beyond the shrubs that ran along the inside of the iron fence was thick forest. The other temples were no longer in view.

Had he and his father been transported to some other place? Stiger considered that a distinct possibility. Ogg had once magically transported him from a battlefield to the World Gate, so he knew it was possible.

And yet, deep within, he understood he had not been transported anywhere. They were still in the temple district. How he knew this, he wasn't quite sure, but he could feel it was so. There was some sort of magical bubble that kept the garden warm and in a perpetual state of spring. A grass path led through the middle of the garden and up to the temple itself, which was rather plain and stood in stark contrast to the beauty that surrounded it. The path wound its way around a fountain just before the temple.

Dog nosed his way past Stiger and into the garden. His tail was wagging as he sniffed intently at the grass, as if on the hunt for prey.

In the center of the fountain stood a life-sized statue of a man with a sheathed sword and his hands on his hips. He was gazing outward, as if looking upon something with satisfaction, perhaps a life's work well done. The statue wore legionary armor, of a type that had not been worn in centuries. It had been intricately and expertly carved and was so detailed the statue looked almost lifelike. Stiger suspected he was gazing upon a likeness of Karus, and the sword was Rarokan.

You are correct, the sword hissed in his mind. *That is Karus.*

Stiger abruptly froze, not at the sword's words. There was a hooded, white-robed figure standing on the bottom step that led up into the temple. It was small, barely the size of a four-year-old child. Stiger knew without a doubt it was not human. The small creature slowly pulled the hood of the robe back and Stiger sucked in a breath. In his wildest imaginings, he had not expected this. How could he have? He looked around. Where there was one, there were always more. He did not see any others about.

"What kind of a creature is that?" Marcus asked in a hushed voice.

"A gnome," Stiger said unhappily.

"What is a gnome?"

"A mean-tempered bastard that you never want to take your eyes off of," Stiger said as he started forward. It was time to find out what was going on, what game the gnome was playing. Marcus followed. Dog padded up next to Stiger and sat down. The gnome gave Dog a respectful nod before turning its attention squarely on Stiger.

"Welcome, Champion," the gnome said in a high-pitched and squeaky voice. Like the rest of its race, the creature spoke incredibly quickly. "We pleased you come. We pleased you accepted our welcome invite."

Stiger studied the gnome for a long moment. A large iron key hung on a chain about his neck. The little creature's robe was pure white, as the freshest of snows. A silver lightning bolt ran down the side of the robe, one of the High Father's symbols. That, Stiger found quite a surprise.

"You are a priest?" Stiger surmised.

The gnome gave a grave nod and folded its hands before its chest. The fingers seemed in constant motion and the creature fidgeted, as if incredibly anxious. Stiger knew that was just the nature of the race. They seemed barely able to contain the energy within.

"A priest of the High Father." Now that he had said it, he could sense and feel the *will* radiating from the gnome. He found it not only unexpected, but unsettling.

"I am so blessed," the gnome confirmed. "So blessed. It is great honor."

"I did not know your kind followed the High Father," Stiger said. "I don't even know which deity your people mostly keep." Gnomes, for the most, part were a mystery to him.

"Saclaw, Castor, Thulla, Neptune, Seetah—" the priest said, its pupil-less and unblinking gaze fixated on Stiger. "Many gods. There is not just one."

"And now the High Father," Stiger said.

"Some follow," the gnome said, "some don't. High Father gives each free will of choice."

"And this is the temple to the first emperor?" Stiger asked, looking up at the brick building. "Do I have that right?"

"Yes, yes," the gnome said, seeming to suddenly become excited. "His shade resides here, waits in peaceful place. He remained behind, waits for you—has always waited."

"Me?" Stiger said, studying the temple. The wooden door was closed. There was a lock on the door. "Who waits? Karus?"

"You follow." The gnome turned and made its way quickly up the steps. It stopped at the door and pulled the key from around its neck. It looked back on Stiger, excitement in its manner, before inserting it into the lock and turning the key. There was the sound of gears turning. The door, as if of its own will, swung inward, revealing a brightly lit interior. The gnome turned back again, this time looking expectantly at Stiger.

"You come," the gnome beckoned. "He waits."

"I never went inside." Marcus indicated the gnome. "The door has always been locked. And he wasn't here the last time. The garden is as far as I have ever gotten."

"Well, we've been invited. Might as well go find out who wants to see us." Stiger started up the steps. At the top, he stopped before the gnome. He sensed no danger or malice from the creature. The entire garden and palace seemed to exude a peaceful sensation.

"You go," the gnome said. "Go, go."

Stiger moved inside, his father a step behind. Dog padded in after them and sat down on his haunches by Stiger's side. The interior of the brick building was plain and nothing at all like any other temple he had ever seen. There was no statue inside for people to worship. The floor was red brick, the walls plastered over in white. There was not a spot of dust anywhere. It was all very plain, utilitarian. A shelf ran along all four walls about waist-high. Hundreds of fat candles had been placed on the shelf. These provided the light to see by. There were no other rooms or doors that could be seen. The temple consisted solely of one large room.

A stone altar lay in the exact center. Stiger moved toward it. Upon its surface lay a set of armor. The armor was old, ancient, and archaic-looking, the original lorica segmentata, what was seen now only in carvings and mosaics. It was the same kind the statue in the fountain had been wearing. The armor had a used look to it. He could see scrapes and dents. At the same time, someone had lovingly looked after it. The armor had been polished to a high sheen and reflected the candlelight.

"I think this might have been Karus's armor," Marcus said, moving several steps closer, almost up to the altar itself. He seemed thoroughly awed.

"It might very well be," Stiger said, then looked around for the priest to ask. The gnome was nowhere to be seen. "He's gone."

"Maybe he went back outside," Marcus suggested.

Few visit this place, a voice hissed.

Stiger spun around and, with his father, took a step back. A glowing figure, a specter of light, stood before them. The image was that of a man, an officer, wearing the trappings of a camp prefect. The specter wavered before their eyes, as if he were made of a glowing fog. Stiger realized he could see right through the specter. The man looked exactly like the statue. Stiger had no doubt on the specter's identity. He felt a moment of pure shock wash over him, for he was standing in the first emperor's presence, the man who had brought the Ninth Legion from Rome to Mal'Zeel and founded the empire.

Dog stood, shook himself, and moved forward, around the altar. The specter gazed down upon Dog and smiled.

He held forth a hand. The big animal's tail began wagging as he leaned forward and sniffed at the glowing hand.

These days, few visit with me, the specter said sadly, *other than the gnomes.*

"Only my father and I could see the temple, and Dog," Stiger said. "I would assume that's why you don't get many visitors."

That was intended. The spirit moved toward them, walking through the altar. *As was your coming.*

"You know who I am?" Stiger asked.

I know what you represent. The spirit stopped just before them. *An end to what was begun long ago—and a new beginning. You are all that I, and so many others, worked toward.*

Stiger did not know what to say.

I wanted to meet you, the spirit said, *to wish you well, before I join my wife in eternal rest. That is why I have waited, lingered in this pleasant place, this refuge, all these long years, to see the fulfillment of my work.*

"Is that all?" Marcus asked. "Is that the only reason you waited?"

No, the spirit admitted and held out a hand toward the altar, while his gaze shifted to Stiger. *I give you a gift of Rome, something personal.*

"You are giving me your armor?" Stiger guessed.

I am, the specter said. *You are a warrior, a leader of men in battle. Now, you must become a warrior emperor, a leader of the empire and her people.* The specter's gaze slipped back to the lorica. *This armor served me well. Wearing it will mostly be symbolic, something to help solidify your rule in the minds of the people. And yet, it is also so much more.*

Stiger did not know what to say. He shared a look with his father.

The gnomes promised to keep it safe and care for it until the day you came. I am pleased by their faith and that they have kept their word, for some of their race cannot and should not be trusted.

"You will bear the first emperor's own armor, my son," Marcus breathed. "There is no greater honor."

And that is where you are wrong, Marcus Stiger, the spirit said. *There are greater honors. Well, you should know. Being a father is such a one. You have sacrificed much for a destiny not of your choosing, nor your offspring's. Now is the time to make amends for that, to repair the rift that has grown, to mend things before the end.*

Marcus had gone still. He glanced over at his son and gave a nod filled with emotion. "I will make amends the best way I am able—to both of my children."

The specter turned his ethereal gaze back to Stiger. *Wear this armor with pride and know that, at the end, when all seems lost, I will be with you in spirit and more importantly—will. Do this and you will please me greatly.*

"I will take up your armor," Stiger replied. "I will wear it with pride. Thank you for this fine gift."

It is but little, the spirit said. *In truth, I grieve, and terribly so. You bear a heavy burden and curse not of your making.* The specter's tone hardened. *And yet, as my descendent, Roman blood flows through your veins, and with it comes strength. Use that strength, the will you have been given, and complete the work I began. Give our people what they so deserve, an empire without end.*

"I will," Stiger said.

Support your son, the spirit said to Marcus, *for he will need your help as he walks the lonely path ahead.*

"It shall be done," Marcus said. "I shall be the father I wanted to be, but could not."

The spirit seemed pleased by the answer, for he gave a nod, then shifted his attention back to Stiger. *Watch Rarokan, for he will do all in his power to meet his own end. If he succeeds, all we have worked toward will not come to pass.* The spirit began to fade before their eyes. *And now, finally, I go to cross the great river. I go to rest—with my beloved. Good fortune to you both—you will need it.*

And then the spirit was gone. They were left alone. Stiger offered up a prayer to the High Father, asking that the crossing of the great river be an easy one for Karus.

Prayer complete, he rubbed his jaw as he regarded the armor for several heartbeats. The gift was, in Stiger's estimation, priceless. He untied the strap to his helmet and placed the heavy thing upon the stone altar. He began hastily unbuckling and untying his armor. As he did it, he looked over at his father.

"You can have mine," Stiger said. "It was Delvaris's, from the Thirteenth Legion. It may be a little big, but we're going into a fight. I think you will find its protection welcome."

"Really?" Marcus said, intrigued. "How did you find it?"

"In his tomb," Stiger said as he continued to untie the straps that held the armor in place.

"You robbed his tomb?" Marcus seemed shocked.

"It wasn't like that," Stiger said. "The armor was a gift. Everything we knew about him was wrong. He knowingly sacrificed so much so that we could have a chance. When we have some time, I will tell you what I know."

"There is a lot to tell, then?" Marcus asked.

"You have no idea." Stiger shrugged out of his armor and found himself hesitating. He had worn this armor so long he was reluctant to part with it. Still, it was time. He handed it over to his father. In a way, it felt like he was losing an old friend. Then again, he would be wearing armor that the first emperor wore, Karus's own. He felt incredibly honored by it. He picked the lorica up and found it lighter than expected. He examined the interior. The leather pads and straps all seemed new. Someone had replaced them, likely the gnomes.

Slipping it on, he began the tedious job of lacing it up, tying each strap tight. It was only then he noticed the phalera, the distinguished honors the previous wearer had won for bravery. One even had the face of the High Father emblazoned on it. He did a double take, for he thought the face was glowing. He attributed it to a trick of the candlelight.

Carefully, Stiger untied each and removed them. He left the phalera on the stone altar. It would not be right to wear the honors of another. Besides, he felt they belonged here in this forgotten and hidden temple. Once they were removed, he continued putting the armor on. Within a short time, he had it secured, pulling the last of the laces tight and tying them off into knots that would not come loose.

He shrugged his shoulders about, settling the leather pads into place. It was a surprisingly good fit. He glanced over at his father as he slung his sword harness over his shoulder and settled Rarokan into place. Marcus had finished putting on Delvaris's armor. Stiger picked up his helmet.

"Are you almost ready?" Stiger asked. He placed the helmet upon his head and tied the strap tight, to the point where it pulled painfully at the skin on his neck.

"I am," Marcus said. He glanced down at himself. "Not bad—a little loose. I can have it adjusted later."

"There's no need," Stiger said. "That armor is enchanted. Give it some time. It will fit you like it was made for you."

"Enchanted, you say?" Marcus looked down at the armor again, marveling. After a moment, Marcus looked up at him. "Shall we go kill Lears and win you an empire?"

Stiger clipped his ragged and tattered blue cape onto the rings set into the armor. He pulled on the bearskin cloak next.

"Right now, that sounds like an excellent idea." Stiger started for the exit and stopped at the doorway. He glanced back at the empty altar. He had a flash of Delvaris's tomb. "Rest easy and thank you."

There was no answer. He had not really expected one. Having crossed the great river, Karus's specter was gone, no longer to haunt this temple. He was with his wife, the High Priestess, in eternal rest. For a moment, he felt a flicker of envy. Stiger glanced around and spotted Dog. The animal was sitting in the spot where he'd greeted Karus.

"Dog," Stiger called, "come."

He turned away and stepped back outside. Dog emerged a moment later. The gnome was nowhere to be seen. Stiger wondered where the little creature had gone.

He made his way rapidly back up the path and to the gate. His father followed after. As Stiger stepped through the gate, the temple district materialized around them. With it, the cold of winter was a harsh slap in the face. He found Ruga, Eli, and Therik waiting for them. So too was Restus. They looked immensely relieved as he appeared with his father.

"I see you found the first emperor's temple," Restus said, "and his armor too. It was meant for you."

"Karus gave it to me himself," Stiger said, tapping the armor with his knuckles. "Well, his spirit anyway." He looked around. The column was still halted.

"You spoke with the spirit of the first emperor?" Eli asked.

"Really, sir?" Ruga asked.

"He did," Marcus said. "It was the first emperor and that, I can attest, is Karus's armor."

"And I missed it." Eli seemed crestfallen.

"Amazing, sir," Ruga said. "You are truly gods blessed."

"Some days," Stiger said, "it seems too much so."

"You can never be too blessed," Ruga said.

"You could have taken me along," Eli said. "I would have loved to see Karus's ghost."

"Is the temple guard ready?" Stiger asked Restus. He was eager to be off.

"They are," Restus said, "what's left of them at any rate."

"What do you mean?" Stiger asked, warning bells sounding in his head.

"The High Priest took most of the guard with him." Restus clenched a fist. "When I get my hands on him, there will be a reckoning."

"He did what?" Stiger asked.

"He's gone," Marcus said. "You mean he fled?"

"Yes," Restus said.

"He probably joined Lears in the palace," Marcus said.

"We can only hope," Stiger said, "for given the chance, I intend to have a word with him as well."

"That's not the worst of it," Restus said. "He took the temple's treasury with him. The priests he left behind confirmed that. They also had the impression he was intending on leaving the city."

The temple treasury was effectively the empire's treasury. Guarding it was the temple guard's primary mission. That it was gone was a catastrophe, especially if he could not get it back.

"Well," Marcus said, "if they went to the palace, it won't matter much. We just need to break the men Lears has and simply take it back."

"And if they didn't?" Eli asked. "What if they fled the city, like the paladin said?"

"In that case," Marcus said, "after we deal with Lears, we won't be able to pay the army."

"That's a big problem," Max said. "You can't run an empire without money, something with which to grease the wheels."

"They will have to be hunted down then," Therik said. "It's a shame Hux isn't with us, along with several troops of cavalry."

"I don't even want to think about that right now," Stiger said. This was yet another problem to work on later. "There are too many problems before us. We focus on one at a time. The immediate problem is Lears. He comes first." Stiger turned back to Restus. "How many of the guard did you manage to round up?"

"Less than twenty," Restus said unhappily.

"Out of a complement of four hundred?" Stiger felt a stab of frustration. His gaze went to Fortuna's temple. She was screwing with him again. That was for certain.

"Any paladins?" Stiger asked, hopefully.

Restus shook his head. "Just me. The rest must be on quest."

"So be it." Stiger glanced up and down the column of men. He had over seven hundred men of good quality. Yes, they were outnumbered, but they were legionaries, and he was confident in their quality. He told himself it would be enough. They had to be, for he did not want to contemplate them not being sufficient.

"Seven Levels," Ruga exclaimed. "Seven bloody Levels. It just can't be."

Stiger turned and saw the centurion staring back toward where the first emperor's temple was located. Led by the priest, gnomes were emerging in single file from the gate. They wore what looked like miniature legionary armor, much like Karus's. Each had a white cloak. They were armed with a shield and a small sword. Stiger could not believe what he was seeing. Gnome legionaries? Could the little bastards have taught themselves discipline and formation tactics? Was such a thing possible?

"This day is just getting more interesting by the moment," Eli said.

"I don't know if I would call it that," Therik said quietly.

The priest marched right up to Stiger.

"Champion." The priest looked up at Stiger, black eyes glittering under the sunlight. "We come to fight. We kill enemies together, yes?"

A gnome officer, denoted by his centurion's crest, began shouting at the gnome legionaries in their own language, with the clear intention of forming them up into a column alongside Ruga's men. The legionaries who had been standing about looked on in fascination.

"How many gnomes are there?" Stiger asked, looking at the growing formation, who were jumping to follow their officer's orders without complaint. Coming from them, it was a surprising show of alacrity and discipline.

"Three hundred," the priest said. "They good fighters. Give enemy hard time."

"And all follow the High Father's teachings?" Stiger asked. "They all worship our god?"

"We are of Anderri," the priest said, with a fierce pride. The name meant nothing to Stiger. "We follow High Father."

"The army already includes gnomes. They do not follow the High Father. Will this present a problem for you and your boys?" Stiger could already imagine how Cragg would respond to these gnomes and a priest with power and the *will* to use it.

"Maybe, maybe not," the gnome said with a shrug of its tiny shoulders. "We shall see. Not big problem in my eyes. No problem at all."

Stiger wasn't so sure about that.

"You can trust them," Restus said to Stiger. "Their faith is true."

"This is a bad idea," Therik said with a horrified tinge to his voice. "More gnomes?"

The priest turned its gaze to the orc and simply stared at him before slowly smiling. It was a smile devoid of warmth.

"It is the High Father's will," Stiger said, eyeing Therik, whose hand had found the hilt of his sword as he returned the priest's gaze.

"Yes, it is," the priest said. "We fight along you and allies, including him." The gnome pointed at Therik. "We fight with your pet orc."

"Pet?" Therik growled.

"Very well," Stiger said, wondering what other future problems this arrangement might cause. "You are welcome to join us."

"We kill enemies, yes?" the priest said.

"Yes, we will," Stiger said.

Stiger looked up the column of march. He could see Lepidus at the front, gazing back at him. Stiger raised his hand and pointed it forward in an exaggerated manner that could not be misunderstood. Lepidus got the message.

"Fall in," Lepidus shouted. That call was taken up by the officers of the entire column. "Tenth Company, fall in. Hurry now."

"What is your name?" Stiger asked the priest.

"Sehet, Champion," the priest said. "I am called Sehet."

"Forward," came the shout from Lepidus at the front of the column, "march."

Lepidus's company began moving out. Stiger watched as the Tenth continued up the street toward the High Father's temple in the direction of the emperor's palace.

"March," Spatz shouted a few moments later, and his company began moving, with a gap of ten yards between the Tenth.

Stiger started forward, moving along the column, as Ruga snapped an order and his century stepped off. Eli fell in at Stiger's side, as did Dog. Marcus started walking with Max at his side. The two quickly fell into conversation about what had just occurred in the first emperor's temple.

"Found some more friends, I see," Eli commented dryly, drawing Stiger's attention.

"It seems that way," Stiger said as he spotted Dog nosing around the gate to the first emperor's temple. The gate had been closed.

"I wonder what the rest of our gnomes will think of your new friends," Eli said.

"That's what I am afraid of," Stiger said, sharing a long look with Eli. He turned his gaze forward as the palace came into view ahead of them and up the hill. It was time to focus on the job at hand. "Dog, come."

CHAPTER THIRTEEN

"What do you think?" Stiger asked Lepidus and Spatz as a cold wind blew by, fluttering cloaks. Eli, Therik, Marcus, Spatz, and Ikuus stood gathered around him on the street. Snow had been shoveled to the side and off the paving stones.

The snowbanks rose three feet to either side. Restus was there too, along with Sehet and the officer who commanded the company of gnomes. His name was Wast, and from what Stiger had learned already, his personality was intense and focused, almost single-mindedly so. As if he had something to prove, Wast took his job incredibly seriously.

The column had once again come to a halt. This time, thankfully, they were finally on the edge of the palace district. A small arched gate stood before them. It was open. The plastered wall that surrounded the palace grounds was decorative and had never been meant to defend against a determined force. Ivy had grown up over portions of the wall and most of the gate.

At best, both the wall and gate were meant to keep the curious out. The Praetorian Guard had been the real deterrent, and they, for the most part, no longer existed. Most of the guard had died with Tioclesion, and Stiger had disbanded the rest in Lorium. Corus's company had been the only one Lears had made into new praetorians. At least, according to Lepidus and Spatz.

The entry gate into the palace grounds stood about twelve feet in height and the wall eight. Under the ivy, the stone face of the gate was intricately carved with a relief of the story of Karus. It told the legend surrounding how the Ninth Legion had come to this world and, more importantly, how Karus had led them to their new home.

Under the mass of ivy, which had yet to fully lose its leaves, the carvings could hardly be seen. The leaves, for the most part, had turned a reddish brown. Like much of ancient imperial history, in a way, the story of Karus had been lost to the mists of time.

The events surrounding the Ninth and the founding of the empire were now considered by most imperials to be simply legend and myth. And in truth, Stiger had never really given it much thought. But now, he found himself looking at it differently, for he knew the tale of Karus was anything but fanciful storytelling. Karus had been real and so too had the Ninth Roman Legion.

There was around twenty yards of open space between the wall and the nearest residential buildings. Stiger recalled that cut grass normally grew in the cleared space. It was now covered in a layer of fresh snow crisscrossed by numerous footprints. There was even a snowman some children had made.

At Stiger's question, Lepidus and Spatz turned their gazes through the gate, clearly thinking on it before voicing an answer. No one could be seen in the area beyond. The street past the gate was empty. Open snow-covered gardens could be seen to either side, as could several large buildings, the first of which was located to the right side of the gate. Stiger knew that structure to be a stable for the emperor's horses. The barracks for the Praetorian Guard were set farther back and in plain view. It was an ostentatious, multi-storied building and almost as large as the palace. It was enough to house more than five thousand men.

Neither Lepidus nor Spatz immediately answered. Stiger glanced over at them and raised an eyebrow.

"Gentlemen, I'd have your thoughts," Stiger said.

"I think this is the perfect spot for an ambush," the captain of the Tenth said, "especially with that large building right by the gate."

"I agree," Therik said. "It is too quiet. And there is no one about. Everyone out in the city has fled the area."

"If I knew we were coming," Spatz added, "I'd try to stop us at the gate."

Stiger pointed. "That building just to the right is a stable. The emperor keeps his horses there, as do the officers of the Praetorian Guard. If an ambush is planned, the stable could be holding a company-sized group of men, more if they pack themselves in closely enough and move the horses out."

"That building is only twenty yards inside the gate," Marcus said, "which creates a perfect chokepoint or funnel. We have to be careful as we move through the gate and assume they are watching us even now."

Stiger gave a nod. There was no doubt in his mind that they were being watched.

"There also could be men hidden just on the other side of the wall," Spatz said, "though that would give any larger ambush away, especially if we sent scouts forward."

"If there are men on the other side of the wall," Marcus said, "it wouldn't be a wise move on their part. All it would take would be one pair of eyes to sound the alarm and the element of surprise would be lost."

"There are ambushes, and then there are ambushes," Eli said.

Marcus scowled as he shot Eli a look.

"We will be sending scouts forward," Stiger said, ignoring Eli. "We won't be walking in there blindly."

"That wall's not all that high," Ruga put in. "If the gate becomes a chokepoint, we could easily flank by moving to the right or left and sending a company or two over the wall. Heck, in basic training, as a recruit, we had to figure out how to overcome walls taller than that one."

"True, but if their entire force is at the gate…what then?" Spatz asked. "They outnumber us. We could lose more men forcing our way in than we would otherwise. It would end up being a bloody affair."

"That is a serious concern," Stiger said, "and I want to limit our casualties. I'd rather bleed them than us. Do not forget, we have the quality advantage. I expect that to give us a serious edge in what is to come. If anyone doubts that, I want to hear from you now."

"I don't bloody doubt it," Spatz said. "I know it. I will take a legionary over an auxiliary or militiaman any day."

"And our men are mostly veterans," Lepidus pointed out.

No one else said anything for a long moment.

"You've been here before," Therik said. "Is there another gate?"

"There is," Stiger said and pointed. "This road cuts straight through the palace district. The Sectari Gate is on the other side and looks just like the one before us. We will need to send men to secure it"—Stiger gestured to their sides—"and also, during an assault, to watch the walls so Lears and Handi cannot escape. We need to create a net to catch anyone coming over the wall with a mind to flee."

"That effort is going to drain our strength for a direct assault," Lepidus said unhappily. "As it is, we've already established that we're outnumbered."

"No doubt," Stiger said, "but it is a necessity. Lears ran from me once. I will not allow him to escape again. There can only be one emperor. This ends here today."

"Yes, sir," Lepidus said and shifted his stance slightly. "Then I'd recommend having the scouts check the stables before we move the main body forward."

"I have a better idea," Spatz said, looking to Stiger. He gave a nasty chuckle. "We have to assume there are men waiting in the stables, right? Heck, I would put a force in there. So, we send the scouts forward to make certain that there are none waiting on the other side of the wall. We intentionally order them not to check the stables. Once they confirm that there is no one outside of the stables and lying in wait by the walls, we send two companies forward at the double, in a street fighting formation." Spatz waved toward the stables. "If they're in there, the enemy will think their ambush is working and they're going to catch us by surprise. Only we won't be marching steadily in but moving on the double."

"I see," Lepidus said, "the idea is to get as many men through the gate as possible, before they spring their ambush. Is that what you are saying?"

"Correct," Spatz said. "If we can manage to get a substantial enough force through the gate and into the palace grounds, we might be able to turn things around on them."

"I like it," Marcus said.

Stiger turned his gaze back toward the gate. He felt there was a strong chance an ambush waited ahead. Like Therik said, it was too quiet. Lears and Handi were up to something. Besides, the nearest buildings outside the walls were empty. The wealthy civilians who lived here had gone. The slaves had even vanished.

"As I see it," Spatz said, "the only other explanation is that they're holed up in the palace and are going to fight room by room, or that they've all fled. Though, I don't think that likely."

"They have not gone." Stiger sucked in a breath of the cold winter air and let it out slowly as he regarded the gate. If Spatz's plan was unsuccessful, and the enemy managed to cut up Stiger's legionaries, they would be able to increase their numerical advantage, perhaps even in a decisive manner, over him. If the enemy had put a good number of men in the stables and more in the praetorian barracks, just a hundred yards away, it could and likely would mean a brutal fight.

He shifted his gaze back to Spatz. Despite their mutual distaste, like Stiger, Spatz was a professional soldier. The plan was not all that bad. More importantly, it was better than anything Stiger could think of, and it might just turn the ambush around on the enemy. That was, if there was an ambush, and Stiger had to remind himself there might not be one.

Stiger gave Spatz a nod. "I think your plan is as good a plan as any, and it is what we will do."

"I want honor lead attack," a small voice to Stiger's right said.

Spatz gave an amused grunt at Wast's request. "This is no place for children playing at war."

"We no children," Wast said, insistently. There was strong indignation in his tone. "We legionaries. I show you." The gnome waved back at his company with a tiny hand. "We—we all show—you, you big man."

"I think I'd like to see that," Spatz said, having clearly become thoroughly amused. He gave a laugh. "I really would."

"Be careful what you wish for," Therik warned quietly.

"He's no stronger than a child," Spatz said incredulously as he waved a hand at Wast. "I could take him with one hand tied behind my back, perhaps even both."

"You think so, big man?" Wast asked, taking a step toward the captain. There was clear menace in his manner. "I show you." Wast looked meaningfully at the man's crotch and rested a hand upon his sword hilt. "Perhaps I cut something off. Then you show respect."

Spatz's amusement left his manner and he took a step forward toward the gnome. "Was that a threat?"

"I make no threats," Wast said, not backing down.

"I would advise caution," Eli said slowly to Spatz as he stepped between the two. "You might want to reconsider challenging Wast—that is, if you want to see the next day's dawn."

Spatz shot Eli a scowl that was filled with incredulity.

"My people fear theirs," Therik said, "and as much as it pains me to admit, myself included, I think it is better to respect them than disparage." Therik glanced at Eli. "And healthier too."

"Are you serious?" Hollux asked, speaking up for the first time and looking between Therik and Wast. "They're smaller than most eight-year-old children."

"I am very serious," Therik said, his gaze turning to the lieutenant. "Gnomes are hard fighters and"—he looked over at Wast—"no end of trouble."

"We no trouble," Wast said, rapping his chest armor with a little fist. "We legionaries. We show you."

"Enough of this," Stiger snapped, drawing everyone's attention. "Spatz, I ask you to accept that gnomes are competent fighters. We're lucky to have them, and more importantly, I've seen them in battle. I would not want to go against them." Stiger paused as he glanced around at those gathered and hardened his tone. "To get through this"—he waved a hand toward the gate—"we need to work together. Sowing strife amongst ourselves is counterproductive at best. We're all professionals here; let's act like it. Is that understood?"

Stiger looked at those gathered around him. There were nods from everyone, excluding Spatz and Wast, who were staring at one another. Stiger stopped on Spatz, locking eyes with the man.

"Well?" Stiger asked Spatz.

"It is understood, sir," Spatz said after a brief hesitation. "Wast, I meant no offense. I did not know of your people until today. I ask that you excuse my ignorance."

Stiger turned to the gnome, who was staring at Spatz but had not replied. "Wast?"

The gnome tore his gaze from the captain. "I understand, *sir.*" The sir was said with a grudging attitude. "I not kill for such speak—no cut him. I rather kill enemy than—*friend.*" The last word was filled with resentment. "Good?"

"Good," Stiger said, and with that, the tension on the air eased as Wast and Spatz took a step back to their original positions.

Tiro hustled up, wearing his armor and carrying a shield. In the cold, the old veteran's cheeks and nose were flushed.

"Sir," Tiro said, coming to a position of attention. "Reporting as ordered. It took me a bit to get my kit on."

"At ease and no worries," Stiger said. "You're reassigned back to Ikuus's company for the duration of the assault."

"Yes, sir," Tiro said, without any hint of disappointment. He turned his gaze back to Ikuus, who stood next to Hollux. "It's good to be back home with the Seventh, sir."

"Welcome back, Sergeant," Ikuus replied and seemed genuine in the sentiment.

"Ikuus," Stiger said, "do me a favor and listen to Hollux and Tiro. Both have years of hard experience under their belts. I myself have heeded their advice on more than one occasion and found it of great value. Being new to the army is nothing to be ashamed of. We all were where you are now."

"That's right," Spatz said, turning his gaze to Ikuus. "I was a shitty officer when I first joined the legion. Having been trained by my family's tutors, I thought I knew everything. I can plainly tell you I was wrong. It took me some time before I began listening to my sergeants and men. That's when I began to grow into my position. Like I was, you still have a lot to learn and"—Spatz nodded toward Hollux and Tiro—"they will be happy to help educate you. Listening and then making an informed decision will help you grow into a competent officer."

Lepidus shifted uncomfortably, as did Hollux and Tiro.

"That's right," Stiger said, somewhat surprised by Spatz's admission, which had clearly made the other officers uncomfortable. He decided to reinforce it. "If they suggest something, I strongly advise you listen. Is that understood?"

"It is, sir," Ikuus said. Stiger couldn't detect any sign that he felt disrespected. His estimation of the man increased. Perhaps there was hope for him. After all that they had been through over the years, the Seventh deserved a competent officer.

"All right," Stiger said, "this is the plan. Tenth will lead. Spatz will follow up."

"Hopefully," Spatz said with a trace of a grin thrown to Lepidus, "I won't be picking up the pieces."

"Not a chance," Lepidus said. "You won't ever find yourself carrying my water."

"Wast's company," Stiger continued, looking to the gnome, "will advance after the first two companies are inside the gate. Ikuus will send one hundred men around to the other side of the gate and secure it. He will lead that force personally. The rest of the Seventh will be divided evenly between Hollux and Tiro. Spatz, I want you to take one hundred men and assign them to the Seventh to bolster Hollux and Tiro's force."

"Sir," Ikuus said, "I'd like to go in with the main force."

"You are needed to keep anyone attempting escape," Stiger said. "Once we secure the grounds and have the palace itself surrounded, I will send a runner and have you move up. When the entire force is together, then you will get in on the action as we assault the palace as a cohesive and unified force."

"Yes, sir," Ikuus said. "I understand, sir." He glanced at Hollux and Tiro. "We won't let you down, sir. No one will escape our net."

"Right then," Stiger said. "The main assault will push through the gate, as Spatz suggested, double-timing it so that we get the maximum amount of men out into the palace grounds as possible. We will deal with any sort of ambush as it comes. Lepidus, I know your men will be ready for whatever is thrown at them."

"They will be ready, sir," Lepidus said. "Have no fear of that. The enemy will not get the jump on us."

"Good," Stiger said. "Once the ambush is dealt with, if there is one, we will move up to the palace itself and surround it, forming a ring of steel. At the same time, we will also need to clear out the rest of the palace district, searching every building. Take the initiative and order any structure you come upon to be thoroughly searched and cleared. Once done, Seventh will be called in, and when we're ready, the palace will become our main focus for assault. Does everyone have that?" Stiger paused to draw in a breath. "Are there any questions before we move out?"

"What about me, sir?" Ruga asked. "Where do you want my boys?"

"You and your men are coming with us," Stiger said, then turned to Wast. "Does your company have a name or designation?"

"Sixth Company," Wast said.

"Ruga," Stiger said, "you will follow the Sixth."

"Yes, sir," Ruga said.

Stiger looked over at the gnome as something occurred to him. "If your company is the Sixth, that sort of implies there are more companies. Do I have that right?"

The gnome gave a nod.

"How many?" Stiger asked, curious.

"A light legion," Sehet answered for Wast. "Ten companies, totaling twenty-two hundred gnomes."

Stiger blinked, surprised by the answer. Therik shifted uncomfortably. It was clear he had gotten accustomed to the idea of gnomes being in the army they had left around Lorium. Now, he was learning more were about to join it, and not just a few.

"And"—Therik glanced around, as if he expected them to sprout from the ground or emerge from the nearest buildings—"where are the rest of them?"

"Outside city," Wast answered. "In deep dark."

"So," Eli said, "not here."

"Unfortunately, no," Sehet said. "We only have Sixth Company in city. They honor guard for temple."

"How far outside the city?" Therik asked.

"Two days' walk," Wast said, "through deep dark."

"There are underground roads in and out of the city?" Stiger asked, recalling the dwarven roads in Vrell. "Gnome roads?"

"Yes," Wast said.

"Our people have lived here," Sehet said plainly, "since Karus and Ninth came."

Stiger eyed both gnomes for a long moment before sharing a look with Eli. The gnomes had been living right under the empire's feet and no one had known it. He blew out an unhappy breath as he considered this new information. He would have to see these roads for himself and make sure the enemy either did not learn of them or simply could not use them. But that was yet a problem to handle for another day.

Stiger looked over at Sixth Company. He had seen gnomes fight. He could not imagine how brutal it would be to face disciplined and trained gnomes who could fight as a cohesive and organized unit. Still, he only had one company of the little buggers at hand and had to be content with that.

"Okay," Stiger said, "we go as planned then." He clapped his hands together. "Gentlemen, let's get to it."

The officers moved out, shouting to their commands as they went. Stiger watched them go with mixed feelings. He had once again committed himself to action. Now, he would see it through.

"I fear this will be ugly," Eli said as he unslung his bow from his shoulder. He set his leather-wrapped bundle of arrows on the ground, untied it, and pulled out a dozen arrows, holding them in his left hand with the shaft of the bow. He turned his gaze toward the palace and was silent for several heartbeats. "I think very ugly."

"If they are still in there, it isn't going to be pretty," Stiger said, "that's for sure. And if they're all hiding in the palace, we will have to dig them out."

"You be careful," Therik said to Stiger.

"Me?" Stiger asked, looking over at Therik in surprise.

"Yes, you," Therik growled. "You have a tendency to take unnecessary risks." The orc tapped Stiger on the chest with a thick finger. "Remember, I am the one who will kill you. That is why I will be close, to make sure none other gets the chance."

"Uh huh," Stiger said and almost grinned as he looked between Therik and Eli. It felt good to have friends close at hand during such times. He was comforted by it.

"There is darkness that way," Sehet said, looking toward the palace. "We must find it."

"I can sense the darkness too," Restus said, "something ugly and black hearted is nearby."

Stiger glanced in the direction of the palace. Now that the gnome had mentioned it, he too felt the darkness. It was an ominous feeling. He felt cold, and he didn't think it was just the wintery chill of the day. There was evil about, another god's presence, one opposed to their own.

Stiger turned to Max. "I think it best if you remain here and out of the way when the action begins. I know you can use a weapon, but do me a favor and leave this to the professionals." Stiger placed a hand on his older brother's shoulder as he made to protest. "When this is all settled, I will need your help with the senate and the political battles to come. Killing Lears does not end this. The senate will need to confirm me as emperor. I can't afford to lose you."

Max did not immediately answer.

"Do I need to assign a man to watch you?" Stiger asked, hardening his tone.

"All right," Max said, sounding none too happy. "I will do as you ask and hang back. You have my word on this."

"There will be plenty of swords available soon enough," Stiger said. "Make sure you arm yourself with one, just the same."

Max gave a nod.

"Where do you want me?" Marcus asked.

Stiger looked over at his father. He had already decided what he wanted his father to do. But he had not wanted to embarrass Ikuus further, at least publicly.

"Take command of Ikuus and the men outside the walls," Stiger said. "Coordinate things. Ikuus doesn't have a lot of experience, but there may be some hope for him as an officer. Kindly make sure he does not do anything stupid."

"And if I catch Lears or Handi?" Marcus asked. "What do you want me to do with them? Hold them?"

Stiger thought for a heartbeat.

"Kill them, immediately," he said. "Do not wait for me. Dead in this instance is dead. These are two enemies who cannot be left standing."

"It is good that you understand the harsh world in which we live." Marcus started to turn away, then looked back. His gaze was intense. "I will see you when this is all over."

"You too." Stiger oddly felt a lump in his throat. With that, Marcus stepped off toward Ikuus, who was moving with his men over the snowbank to the left. Hollux, with a group of fifty men, was already farther out ahead of them.

Seventh Company and part of Spatz's boys were already in motion too, spreading out to the right and left of the gate, tramping through the snow as they moved to surround the palace district.

Tenth Company was deploying from a marching column of four into a city fighting formation of six ranks. The rest of Spatz's company, just behind them, was doing the same. The gnomes were falling into the same formation. Ruga was organizing his century behind the three companies.

More than six hundred men and gnomes were about to storm their way into the palace district. If they got through the chokepoint of the gate, and there was no ambush, it would likely mean fighting in the palace itself.

Clearing a large and determined force from confined spaces, even a building as large as the palace, would be a difficult venture. A room-to-room struggle was not something Stiger wanted, for it was grim, ugly work and extremely dangerous. It might even see his qualitative advantage negated.

Four men approached from Ruga's company. They snapped to attention as one of their number stepped forward. "Centurion Ruga sent us. We're your personal escort, sir."

"Very well." Stiger gave them a nod, then glanced at Eli, Therik, Restus, and Sehet, who were still standing around him. Dog was sitting nearby, watching. As he turned his eyes upon the animal, Dog's tail gave an encouraging wag.

Stiger glanced toward the gate and started off. It was time. "Let's go."

He moved up along the line of grim-faced men and gnomes, who were preparing for the assault, and joined Lepidus. The captain of Tenth Company was watching a team of four scouts move cautiously forward toward the gate. The men had their swords drawn and held their shields before them. Their job was a dangerous one, for if the enemy had men lying in wait behind the walls and around the gate, they would be most at risk.

"High Father," Stiger said, bowing his head, "give us the strength to see this through to the end. Spare as many of our men as possible and see us victorious upon the field of battle." Stiger finished by silently commending his spirit into the High Father's loving embrace.

"Amen," Lepidus said.

"Well spoken," Restus said. "And so," Therik said eagerly, rubbing his hands together, "it finally begins."

Lepidus looked over at the orc, his brows knitting together, before returning his attention to his scouts, who had reached the gate ten yards ahead. Two were on each side of the gate. One peeked around the corner, his head swiveling to the right and then left. He looked back at Lepidus and, holding his sword, gave a thumbs-up, before the four of them moved through the gate and into the grounds beyond.

"Sir." Lepidus looked over. "Do I have your permission to bring my company through the gate?"

"You do," Stiger said, his gaze going to the stables. He felt sure there was a surprise waiting for them there.

"Tenth Company," Lepidus said, in a voice not too terribly loud. It was just enough for his men to hear as he drew his own sword. "Draw swords." The swords hissed out. "At the double—march."

Armor jingling and chinking, with Lepidus at their head and setting the pace, the company stepped off in a good jog toward the gate. A moment later, Spatz gave the same order for his reduced company. Stiger made to jog with them, but Therik reached out a restraining hand, gripping his arm.

"I think it wise," Therik said, "to let them go first. Don't you? There is no reason for the emperor to be near the tip of the spear. Not if an ambush is waiting for us."

Stiger felt a stab of frustration at not going with the men, shirking from sharing their danger and risk.

"You've already proven yourself brave and fearless." Therik still gripped his arm. Though it wasn't tight, the orc had a firm hold. "No need to keep doing that. Let your people do their job. Get involved only when it's absolutely needed. You are their leader."

Stiger almost jerked his arm free, then stopped himself.

"You are correct," Stiger said. "My job is to command. We will go in after Spatz's company, and before the gnomes. Is that good?"

Therik released him and gave a satisfied nod.

Eli nocked an arrow as the last of the Tenth, still in a tight block-like formation, jogged by them. Spatz's company was close on their heels. Stiger watched as the first of Lepidus's men made the gate and then began passing through.

Stiger started moving with the tail end of Spatz's company, jogging after them. Eli, Therik, Restus, and Sehet kept up with him. The gnome had to run in a near sprint. Dog and the escort moved just behind them.

"Company, halt," Lepidus shouted abruptly, and his formation ground to a stop. The tail end of his company had not made it completely through the gate. Though he could not see it, beyond the wall and gate, Stiger immediately knew there was trouble.

"Right face," Lepidus shouted at his men. "Wheel left, two steps. Very good. Halt. Pull yourselves together, boys. Dress the line. Shields up, shields up, boys."

The shields came up, locking together with a solid-sounding *thunk*. There was a tremendous shout that sounded from beyond Lepidus's company and just out of view. A bolt of concern shot through Stiger, for he could not see what was happening. But it was clear there had indeed been an enemy force concealed in the stables.

"Stand ready, boys, brace yourselves, brace yourselves, now," Lepidus hollered again as he positioned himself behind the left portion of his formation, which had gotten through the gate. "Remember, we are the legion." The sound of charging feet could be heard. "What are we, boys?"

"Legion!" the men of the Tenth shouted.

A heartbeat later, a mass of men appeared in view and began slamming into the Tenth's shield wall. The clash of contact was loud, almost earsplitting, as was the shouting from the enemy. From what Stiger could see, they appeared to be militia, and there were a lot of them. The first rank of the Tenth was pushed back in some places a step, in others two or more. Under the pressure of the attack, Lepidus's line bent, before the men were able to hold firm.

Most of Tenth Company had made it through the gate to face the enemy. But there was no room for Spatz's boys to get by them. Spatz and his men, like Stiger, had become spectators watching the struggle play out before them.

"Spatz!" Stiger shouted.

The captain looked over at him.

Stiger pointed to their left. "Move your men to the left of the gate and get them over the wall and into action."

"Yes, sir," Spatz shouted and, waving his sword in the air so his men could see, turned to face them. "This way, boys, this way. Follow me." He led them over the snowbank and off the street.

"Ruga." Stiger turned to look back at the centurion and pointed to the right. "Get your men to the right. Send them over the wall. See if you can flank the bastards."

"Aye, sir," Ruga shouted back and, with a curt order, led his men off to the right.

Stiger looked around for the gnomes and moved back to them.

"Wast," Stiger said, stepping over to the gnome, who was watching the fight ahead with great interest. Wast pulled his gaze away from the action. Stiger pointed toward the gate. "There is a small gap on the left side of the Tenth, between their last rank and the gate itself. It isn't large enough to move men through, but a gnome might just make it. Can you feed your gnomes in there and get them formed up inside palace grounds, before going into action?"

"Yes, yes," the gnome said with sudden excitement. "Yes, yes. I do, I do. We do—now."

Wast turned to his gnomes and gave a series of orders in his own language. Within heartbeats, Sixth Company was in motion, moving forward.

Stiger watched them. The gnomes began moving around behind the human legionaries, going single file through the small gap. The legionaries there glanced around as the gnomes moved by in a steady stream.

Satisfied, Stiger started after Spatz's company, who were at the wall and already in the process of going over it. Several men stood on the top and held out hands to help others up and over. Spatz was nowhere to be seen, which meant he was already on the other side.

Stiger lined up with the rest and waited patiently. The fighting at the gate seemed intense. He was impatient to get over, to get a better picture of what was going on inside the grounds. He forced himself to remain calm and wait with a patient air. He had to set the example for others to follow. He also had to show confidence in his own officers to do their jobs and fight their own companies. Besides, it was more important that the bulk of Spatz's men made it over the wall first and got into the action.

Then, finally, it was his turn. He gripped the hand that was offered and scrambled up and onto the top of the wall. To his side, Therik and Eli did the same. At the top, the orc, like Stiger, hesitated, looking over the field of battle for a long moment to get a sense for what was going on.

"Help up."

Therik turned, reached down, and offered a hand to Sehet, who took it. With ease, the orc hauled the gnome up and then literally dropped him over the other side to the snow below before jumping down himself. Stiger jumped down too, his boots sinking into the fresh snow.

"Form up!" Spatz was shouting a few yards from them. "Form up. Two ranks, now. Hurry, boys. Come on. Get a move on. We need to get our act together before we can join the fun."

Stiger looked around, studying the action. He could see Tenth Company engaged with light infantry, militia, just off to the right, by the gate. The large doors of the stables had been thrown wide open. The militia were still coming out. Watching for a long moment, he estimated there were nearly four hundred of them. It was more than he had expected.

To his left was open space, snow-covered gardens. Farther up the street that led from the gate, toward the praetorian barracks, Stiger took in a sight that made his heart freeze. Pouring out of the barracks were auxiliaries. They were forming up into what looked like two full cohorts. Farther to the left was the palace. Another cohort was in the process of pulling themselves together there before starting forward.

"We're outnumbered," Therik said as he drew his sword. "And badly."

Stiger could not disagree. Worse, he had sent a good chunk of his combat power away to create a net around the district. He now understood that decision might have been a mistake. The enemy was not looking to run, but to fight.

"What's done is done," he said to himself. For better or worse, he had to live with his choices. Such was the heavy burden of command. Decide wrong and there was always a price to pay. That said, Stiger was not ready to give up. This was battle. Stiger had faced worst odds and come out on top.

Eli nocked his bow, aimed toward the praetorian barracks, and loosed. It was a long shot, but his arrow flew true and struck an auxiliary officer in the back, punching right through the armor. The man had been exhorting his men to fall into formation. The force of the missile strike drove him forward and into the first rank of men. The auxiliaries stepped aside in horror as the officer fell to his knees amongst them before collapsing face first into the snow. He did not stir.

"Nice shot," Therik said.

"Keep it up," Stiger said.

Without replying, Eli took several steps forward, went down to a knee in the snow, and loosed another arrow in the same direction.

Stiger turned to Spatz, who was still in the process of organizing his half company, working to get them into a coherent line.

"Captain," Stiger shouted over the noise of the fight just yards away.

"Sir," Spatz said, looking over.

"Once you are formed and your ranks ordered," Stiger hollered, pointing toward the two auxiliary cohorts, "move your men forward to meet those cohorts by the barracks. I need you to keep them from flanking the Tenth. Got that?"

"Sir," Spatz replied, "I don't have enough men to hold them for long."

"I know," Stiger replied. "I will get the gnomes to help. You only need to hold long enough for Lepidus to break those militia before him. Then, he too will come to your aid. Ruga's also moving around the side to the right."

Spatz glanced toward the gnomes. Stiger could see the doubt in the captain's expression. "They better be good, or we're screwed."

"They are," Stiger said. "Trust me on that."

"You're still an asshole," Spatz said, then added with a grin, "sir."

"You got that right," Stiger said, and then turned away. He moved toward the gnomes, who were forming up behind the Tenth. Attempting to be heard over the noise of the fight, Wast was screaming at his little legionaries, clearly encouraging them to fall in quicker.

The gnomes were still emerging through the gate in the gap behind the Tenth. Stiger understood from personal experience, when it came to reforming and maneuvering large formations, things did not happen immediately or, for that matter, quickly. Anything done right generally took time. Only there was not much time.

"Wast," Stiger said, and when he had the gnome's attention, he pointed at the auxiliaries getting themselves organized outside the barracks. "Spatz and his boys are moving to block those bastards over there and keep them off the Tenth's back. Needless to say, he and his boys will shortly be outnumbered. Once the Sixth is formed up, move your company to assist Spatz."

The gnome studied the auxiliaries for a long moment with black eyes that glittered darkly in reflected sunlight. He looked back up at Stiger. There was an eager look in his gaze, a near hunger, one Stiger found chilling.

"Kill, yes?" the gnome asked. "We kill?"

"Tear them apart," Stiger said.

"We kill them all," the gnome hissed in a whisper to himself and then turned away, shouting with more intensity at his gnomes in his own language.

Stiger took several steps back to give the gnomes room. Therik, Sehet, and Restus joined him. Dog sat down at his side in the snow. The animal's attention was on the fighting.

"Those humans are in trouble," Therik said.

Stiger glanced back at the orc and could only agree. He turned his gaze to the Tenth and the fighting raging just feet away. Lepidus had finally managed to get most of his entire company through the gate by moving the last two ranks out of the way. He was repositioning them to the side, his left extending his line up the street a few yards to keep the militia from swarming around his flank. His front rank seemed to be holding against the massed press of the enemy. Satisfied with what he saw, Stiger glanced toward the auxiliaries.

The enemy had clearly used their militia, their least trained men, as shock troops to disrupt the legionaries moving into the district. Stiger understood what they were trying to do. The auxiliaries would be the second phase of the ambush. The militia were acting as the anvil, and the auxiliaries, the better trained and disciplined soldiers, were the hammer. They were intending to slam into the legionaries' flank while they were pinned by the militia at the gate, the chokepoint. It was a clever strategy and, facing another commander, might have worked.

Only Stiger had gotten more of his combat power over and around the wall than the enemy had anticipated, and in moments, Spatz would be moving into a blocking position to keep the hammer from falling. Though the palace gardens were large and expansive, the actual space where most of the fighting would take place would be a rather small, almost confined area. He could see it in his head, as if it had already happened.

Still, the enemy had more than enough men to eventually overwhelm Spatz's half company, but they would pay a steep price doing it. And yet, that did not take into account his gnome company, or Ruga's men, who Stiger could not see. He assumed they were somewhere behind the stables, getting organized.

Stiger stepped over to Lepidus, who was standing off to the side, shouting encouragement at his men, who were engaged in the first rank. Lieutenant Spiro was off to the left, getting the extension of the line into position and better organized as they joined the fight.

"Lepidus." Stiger leaned toward the captain's ear. "How are you doing?"

"It was touchy at first," Lepidus said, looking back. "They came at us something fierce. But we're holding now, sir. I figure I am facing around four hundred militia." He waved a hand toward his front. "My men are butchering them something good."

"Excellent," Stiger said.

"I think we can keep this up all day, sir," Lepidus added. "I want to bleed them a bit more before we begin pushing at them."

"Listen," Stiger said, "I am going to need you to end this as soon as possible."

"I was hoping you weren't going to ask that of me," Lepidus said.

Stiger pointed to their left. "There are three auxiliary cohorts over there that will shortly join the action."

Lepidus looked in the direction Stiger indicated. The captain's eyes narrowed as he took in the enemy. His focus had been on fighting his company. By his reaction, he'd clearly not seen them.

"Spatz and Wast," Stiger continued, "are going to move into a blocking position to screen you, but when they become fully engaged, they will be badly outnumbered."

Lepidus gave an understanding nod. "Shall I give these bastards to my front a shove or two? It will cost me more casualties but I have no doubt we can break them."

"Do it," Stiger said. "Once you've broken them, reform, turn, and join the fight as you see fit."

"Yes, sir," Lepidus said and waved toward the militia. "And what about prisoners after I've broken them? I will need to detail men to guard them."

Stiger felt himself scowl as he considered the problem. "Only hold the officers and sergeants. Those are the ones that matter. Send the rank and file through the gate and on their way. Without their leaders, I seriously doubt they will reform on their own and come back at us, especially after you've beat them up something good."

"That works," Lepidus said. "I've got this."

"I know you do." Stiger took several steps back and away to allow Lepidus to get back to the fight.

"Lieutenant Spiro," Lepidus called, "on me. We've got some work to do."

"This is going to get tricky," Therik said.

"Agreed," Stiger said, glancing in the direction of the cohorts. "It all depends upon how aggressive and determined the auxiliaries become."

"Prepare to push," Lepidus shouted, and hesitated a long moment, his head moving slowly from the left side of his formation to the right. He pulled a wooden whistle out from a chain that hung about his neck. "Push." Lepidus blew the whistle.

The legionaries of Tenth Company took a half step forward, shoving with their shields, pushing the enemy back. The Tenth gave a massed grunt as they made the effort. The movement caught the militia by surprise. A heartbeat later, the legionary shields scraped aside, and the deadly short swords stabbed out. Men by the dozens screamed as sword points found purchase.

"The auxiliaries are moving," Restus said, calling Stiger's attention.

Sure enough, one of the auxiliary companies had finished forming and was advancing down the street toward the Tenth. Spatz's half company was in motion too, moving across a series of snow-covered garden beds to intercept them. Stiger looked around for Wast's boys. Though they were almost ready, the gnomes were still forming up into four ranks just behind the Tenth but were angled toward the praetorian barracks and the oncoming enemy. It was only a matter of time until Sixth Company got moving.

"Again!" Lepidus roared, drawing Stiger's attention. He blew his whistle and through the side of his mouth shouted, "Push!"

The front line of the Tenth gave another mighty effort, shoving the militia back several steps. The legionaries stepped over the bodies of men they had just felled. Most were still alive but injured. Men in the second rank stabbed down. Efficiently and without thought to mercy, they finished the enemy's wounded off so that they would not be a threat to the front rank.

After shoving them back a step, once again, the shields scraped aside and the swords stabbed out. Screams and cries of agony followed as dozens of men were wounded and fell. Stiger ran his gaze over the Tenth one last time to make sure things were well in hand, then turned toward Spatz's line and started over to them.

The cohort that had been advancing down the street toward the Tenth had altered their advance and were now closing on Spatz's company. As the two formations neared contact, the enemy cohort abruptly halted. Each man was carrying a javelin. A series of orders was snapped. The front rank took two steps forward, while the rear rank took four back. The entire formation was spreading out for a massed toss. Stiger came to a stop to watch.

"Halt," Spatz ordered and joined the line. "Stand ready to receive missiles. Shields up. Stand ready, boys. Lock your shields."

The legionaries held their shields over their heads, locking them together for added protection. An order to release was shouted by an officer in the enemy cohort, just yards away. A heartbeat later, a wave of javelins flew up into the air, toward Spatz's half company. The deadly missiles seemed to hang for a prolonged moment before falling downward in a steel-tipped rain of death.

The missiles crashed into the raised shields, making a terrible clatter. A number of men screamed or cried out as the heavy javelins punched through the shields, injuring or outright killing the men behind. A dozen fell out of the formation or collapsed to the ground. More than a dozen more men tossed aside ruined shields that had been pierced by the javelins. It was almost impossible to quickly remove a javelin.

All in all, Stiger decided the toss had been poorly made, with many of the missiles having fallen short or to the sides of Spatz's formation. Spatz lowered his shield and looked over the results of the toss.

"Let's make them pay for that, boys. Shields, front!" Spatz roared. "Shields front! Advance!"

The enemy formation began adjusting their lines, closing up their ranks from their javelin toss. Stiger started forward again. Before he arrived, the auxiliaries and legionary lines met with a loud crash.

Spatz had formed his half company up into two ranks of fifty men each. The auxiliary cohort was organized into a solid block of equal length. Stiger counted eight ranks of men, which told him the enemy's strength was at least four hundred men.

He looked beyond the fighting and studied the auxiliary cohort still in the process of forming before the barracks and the third enemy cohort by the palace. Between the militia and the three auxiliary cohorts, he estimated the enemy had more than twelve hundred men on the field. And Stiger still did not see the legionary light company. That told him that his understanding of the combat strength Lears could field had been incorrect and woefully underestimated. How many more men did he have?

He wondered where Lears's legionaries were. Was the man holding them in reserve? Were they guarding him in the palace, keeping the emperor safe? If he had been in Lears's sandals, he would have deployed them with the auxiliaries to add backbone to the ambush.

"Hold steady, hold!" Spatz was shouting. The captain was pacing behind the line. "Hold them, boys. Use your shields, block them. Remember your training. Stab. Stab them, jab them. You are doing a fine job. Keep up the good work. Keep it up."

Stiger came to a stop a few yards from the fight. He glanced back at the gnomes. They had finally formed up and were moving forward, angling to the left of Spatz's line. Wast was in front of his boys, pointing with his sword, as he guided them toward the fight.

The gnomes held their shields, which were half the size of a legionary's and nearly too large for them, forward. Swords were positioned at the ready. As they worked their way almost slowly across the field, they began humming. It was something Stiger had heard once before. He found it somewhat unnerving.

"I don't ever want to hear that sound again," Therik said.

Stiger glanced over and gave a nod.

An indistinct shout over the fighting farther back caught his attention. The second auxiliary cohort by the barracks had begun moving forward. Stiger knew it was about to get ugly. Worse, the auxiliaries already engaged with Spatz had begun extending their line to the left with the clear intention of wrapping around to flank.

"Spatz … you need to extend your line," Stiger hollered, "before you are flanked."

"I am already on it, sir," Spatz said, and Stiger saw that he was shifting ten men from the second rank over, only they would not arrive in time. The enemy would get there first.

Stiger clenched his fists. In his mind he could see the line being flanked and rolled up, as if it had already happened. He could not allow that. He glanced around at his escort. They were closer than Spatz's men, who were being repositioned. Instinctively, Stiger knew he had to buy time for Spatz to get his men into position to block the flanking effort.

Opening the wizard's prison, Stiger drew Rarokan. The energy flowed into him and, like a tidal wave, slammed home. The day brightened and, with it, Stiger felt an intense surge of warmth. The cold of the winter day retreated. Any tiredness he had felt vanished instantly. Stiger was invigorated, alive, energized, as if he had downed three mugs of fresh coffee in rapid succession.

He felt a terrible spike of anger. A matching rage at what was going on gripped him. He and his men were killing their fellow soldiers, who in another place and time would have been comrades in arms. And it was happening when the empire desperately needed every sword. It was a bloody waste, and the tragedy of it all tore at Stiger's heart. That fired his rage even further.

Handi and Lears had brought them to this. They had caused this. Stiger understood he had to bring the killing to an end. For that to happen, Lears and Handi would die this day. That was the only way to stop it from spreading and consuming the empire.

"It is time to join the fight," Therik said to him, for he had clearly seen the same thing. "We must throw ourselves into the line."

"You men, join the line at the end there," Stiger ordered his escort and pointed. His sword flared into life, burning with blue fire. The men jumped into action and rapidly moved up to the end of Spatz's line. The four legionaries brought their shields up to face ten auxiliaries who were moving into position opposite. Another ten men were behind those. They had only moments now.

Stiger did not have a shield. He looked around for one, but a spare was not close at hand. He gave a mental shrug and stepped forward, next to the last legionary of his escort. Therik joined him on his right.

The orc bared his teeth at the enemy falling into position and closing on them. Therik gave a roar that set the hair on the back of Stiger's neck on edge. Eyes upon the large orc, those nearest auxiliaries hesitated, making the oncoming line abruptly uneven.

Something flashed between Stiger and Therik, hissing as it passed. He felt the wind of its passing against his cheek. It was followed by a crack as an arrow slammed through the chest armor of one of the auxiliaries. The stricken man rocked unsteadily for a moment, then collapsed to his knees. A heartbeat later, he fell onto his side into the trampled snow. Stiger did not need to look. He knew who had shot the arrow.

There was another hiss, followed by a crack. A second auxiliary went down, and with that, Therik sprinted forward, throwing himself at the enemy's broken line. The move caught not only Stiger by surprise, but the auxiliaries too. Stiger went forward, after the orc. So too did his escort.

The sounds of the fighting faded around him as his vision narrowed down to his opponent, as an auxiliary stood in his path and brought his round shield up to block Stiger's attack. Stiger lunged over it, hammering down with the blade. There was a solid-sounding *clunk* as the steel of his blade bit into the rim of the shield. Stiger got a flash of the auxiliary's terrified face. Before his opponent could react, he lashed out with his fist and hammered the auxiliary in the cheek guard of the helmet, as hard as he could.

As the man's head snapped back from the strike, pain exploded through Stiger's hand. Dazed, the auxiliary fell backward, stumbling away and dropping his shield and sword into the snow at their feet.

Stiger spun and jabbed at an auxiliary directly to his left, taking him in the side. The sword went in easily and grew warm in his hand as it took the man's life force.

Dog flashed by him, shooting through the air. The animal took a man who had been about to strike at Stiger to the ground. Growling, Dog stood upon the man's chest, seized upon his sword arm, bit deeply, and in one powerful motion, ripped the arm free from the socket. As if in a death grip, the hand still clenched the sword tightly. Dog dropped the arm and then, snarling, tore out the screaming man's throat.

Stiger caught a glimpse of Therik stabbing a man through the stomach with so much force it picked his opponent up and off the ground. Then Eli was by Stiger's side, bow strapped to his back and daggers out, moving with a deadly gracefulness that would have made the best dancer envious. Eli killed two men in quick succession and then engaged a third as he went spinning away from Stiger in what could only be described as a blur of motion.

Stiger attacked the next man, stabbing him in the thigh. This one screamed as the sword went in. He fell to a knee and dropped his sword. Stiger threw him aside and stepped past, intent on the next man, only feet away.

His anger had grown to a terrible fury. All that was on his mind was kill, kill, kill, and the sword was loving every moment of it, feeding him additional rage and energy. Rarokan blazed like a sun as he swung the dread weapon again and again, taking one life after another. Stiger lost track of time as he fought with a fury.

Abruptly, a legionary bashed the man Stiger was going after next with a shield, knocking him violently to the ground. A blinding flash snapped Stiger back and out of his rage. He glanced over to the right, from whence it had come. Father Restus had his hands out. In each were glowing balls of white light. A man lay in a heap at his feet.

"Forgive me, my son," Father Restus said. There were tears in his eyes as he raised his hand toward another auxiliary three feet to his front who had raised a sword to strike at the paladin. Before the auxiliary could react or bring his sword down on the paladin, a beam of white light shot out from Restus's left hand. It encased the man, and as it did, he went rigid. When the beam ceased, he fell limply into the snow. Stiger knew, without knowing how, that the man's soul had been torn from its body and sent back to the High Father.

A sword swung for Stiger's head. Having been distracted, he barely managed to catch it and block the strike. The two blades met in a powerful clang that, in the cold air, set Stiger's hand tingling and sparks flying through the air.

The auxiliary slammed his round shield into Stiger's side, knocking him painfully back. Stiger staggered, almost tripping and falling over a body. The auxiliary brought his sword around and lunged. The tip punched into the armor over Stiger's stomach.

Stiger gave a grunt, as the armor absorbed much of the blow, but not all. As the pain registered, the rage returned, and shouting incoherently, he lunged forward, stabbing with his sword at the arm of his tormentor. The sword slid into the arm. Hot blood sprayed into the air and over Stiger as the steel nicked an artery. The auxiliary, arm ruined, still clutching the sword in fingers that had gone stiff, attempted to fall back.

Stiger pushed forward and stabbed again, this time in the man's collar, just above where the armor ended. It was only a glancing strike, but it was enough to take him down. Thoroughly enraged and hurting from the blow he'd taken, Stiger made for a finishing strike, but was abruptly knocked aside by Therik as the orc stabbed another auxiliary who had gone for Stiger's exposed back.

Before Stiger could recover, the men Spatz had sent to extend the line arrived and, rushing forward, moved before them, shoving violently at the confused auxiliaries with their shields in a unified line. Within heartbeats, the auxiliaries were roughly forced back and away.

Breathing heavily from the exertion, Stiger felt bruised from where the shield had hit him. His stomach hurt too, as did his hand. His anger and rage once again began to drain away as the legionaries before him solidified their line and thoroughly blocked what remained of the enemy's attempt to flank.

"Kindly let my men do the bloody fighting," Spatz called over to him, "and try not to be killed before we win you that throne. You're supposed to be the emperor, for gods' sake."

Stiger blinked, and as he did it, reason fully returned. Spatz was right. He had a battle to fight. He looked up and around. Spatz's men were holding. They were actually doing better than holding. They were beginning to drive the auxiliary cohort back, one difficult step after another. It was a testament to the toughness of the legions, for Spatz's company was outnumbered. The auxiliary cohort had far more reserves and were able to swap out the front rank at a more rapid pace with fresh men. And still, the heavy infantry of the legions was managing to shove them backward.

There was a thunderous clash. The gnomes had struck home against the second auxiliary cohort. From his current vantage point, Stiger could not see the action clearly, for Spatz's men were between him and the gnomes. He was about to move to a position to see better when a mass groan from behind caused him to turn.

The Tenth had broken the militia. Dozens were dropping their weapons and holding their hands up in surrender. The rest were running for their lives, fleeing in nearly every direction. A few who were attempting to surrender were cut down in the heat of the moment before Lepidus and Spiro, both shouting, got the men back under control.

"Ben." Eli pointed. "Look."

Stiger followed Eli's finger. He saw Handi behind the two auxiliary formations with another officer, a legionary. Both were studying the action. Ten legionaries stood guard around the tribune and officer. Stiger felt his anger return in a heated rush.

"Can you hit him from here?" Stiger asked.

Eli shook his head. His bow was strapped across his back. "I am out of arrows."

Frustrated, Stiger could see no easy way to get to the tribune. That pissed him off, and fiercely too. He had to win the battle. That was the only way to get to Handi. He looked around again. Spatz was fully engaged with the auxiliaries. So too were the gnomes, but he did not have a good sense for how that struggle was going. Lepidus's men were now disorganized. He moved his gaze away and spied Ruga's men, with the centurion, coming around the stables in battle formation. Ruga walked before his battle line. They were late to the party, but more than a welcome sight. He now had reinforcements to feed into the fight.

Stiger jogged over, with Therik and Eli following.

"Ruga," Stiger said.

"Sir?"

"Drive into the side of the formation Spatz is fighting. Kindly roll them up, if you would."

"Yes, sir," Ruga said.

Stiger stood back as the centurion led his men by. Shouting orders, Ruga adjusted his line of attack, maneuvering it into the optimal position. Incredibly, the enemy officer commanding the auxiliary cohort seemed oblivious to the approaching threat. He made no move whatsoever to counter it. This might have been because his men were beginning to give ground at an increased pace and he was struggling to check that, for it meant the cohort was close to breaking. Like rats fleeing a sinking ship, there were already stragglers streaming back and away from the fight, along with some wounded.

The dead and injured were also beginning to add up. The trampled snow had been stained burgundy. Bodies, both friend and foe, littered the ground, more so of the later. It tore at Stiger to see the men on both sides injured or lying dead on the snow. In a way, they were all his boys now that he was emperor.

Ruga's men closed to ten feet, five, then his line struck home, hammering into the side of the enemy cohort. The intensity of the fight immediately increased. Ruga's men continued to push their way forward, driving into the side of the cohort's formation. The fight lasted no more than a sixty count before the auxiliary formation, under incredible pressure from two sides, began to crumble. It was not an immediate collapse, and that, Stiger thought, was a testament to their discipline and training.

"Fall back!" an officer began shouting. "Fall back. Maintain formation. Fall back."

"Break them, boys!" Spatz shouted. "Push 'em. They're breaking. Keep on them."

Spatz's men redoubled their efforts and, a heartbeat later, the enemy formation completely and thoroughly fell apart. It was suddenly a mass of confusion as both Spatz's and Ruga's men surged forward, cutting down, without any thought to mercy, whoever they caught. As they rushed after the fleeing auxiliaries, Stiger could finally see the gnome formation.

The gnomes, holding their shields at an upward angle, pressed forward against the cohort they faced. The auxiliaries had to awkwardly angle their rounded shields downward, as the gnomes were striking at exposed legs and feet. It seemed they were having difficulty handling their smaller foes.

Shockingly, the gnomes were driving the cohort before them, forcing them back, one rugged step at a time. Already the little bastards had taken out dozens of auxiliaries, who lay in the bloodied snow twenty yards behind the fight. That was how far the gnomes had driven the auxiliaries, and the pace was accelerating by the moment.

There was a high-pitched whistle. The front rank of the gnome company stepped back as the second rank moved forward and brought their shields up. They immediately went into the attack and, like regular legionaries, they used their shields for cover as they stabbed with proper technique at their enemy. Stiger was impressed with the change in ranks. It had been done efficiently, in a practiced manner that demonstrated the gnomes' training and professionalism. They were indeed legionaries.

The auxiliaries, seeing their fellow cohort fleeing the field in disorder and pressed tightly by the gnomes, suddenly seemed to lose heart, for the formation fell apart. Like angry ants, the gnomes swarmed after them, slaughtering with apparent glee all they managed to catch.

Stiger felt an immense wave of relief. All three of the enemy cohorts that had been engaged had been broken, and rapidly too. Despite being outnumbered, he was master of this field of battle.

Stiger looked for Handi. Amongst the confusion, it took a moment to find him. Handi had moved and was with the last formation of men, the one by the palace. That cohort had been advancing to engage. Now, they were withdrawing toward the palace in good order. He spotted a man with Handi and his blood ran cold. Stiger felt an intense wave of disgust roll over him.

"Veers," Stiger breathed.

"What?" Eli asked. "Where?"

"The dark paladin?" Therik asked, following Stiger's gaze.

"There." Stiger pointed. "He's with Handi."

Veers suddenly came to a stop and turned, as if he sensed Stiger looking at him. Handi stopped too. Absurdly, Veers raised a hand in greeting and waved at Stiger before starting up the dozens of marble steps toward the palace.

Give him to me, the sword hissed. *I want Veers.*

"You can have him when we catch him," Stiger said. "Both parts of his soul."

"Did you see him?" Restus came up and pointed toward the palace where Veers had disappeared with Handi. "The dark paladin. Did you see him?"

"I did," Stiger said. "His name is Veers and he's a paladin of Valoor."

"This is not good that he's here," Therik said, "not good."

"I agree," Stiger said and then looked around. They had to not only secure the grounds but seal off the palace. "We're going in after them." He paused and raised his voice. "Spatz, Lepidus, Wast, Ruga, reform. Reform your boys. We've got more work to do."

CHAPTER FOURTEEN

The palace towered over Stiger and the men, in parts rising to a height of five stories. Even by imperial standards, Stiger felt the building lacked any semblance of grace or elegance. He had always thought it ugly, unworthy of the grandeur of the empire, and yet the people loved it no less.

Stiger doubted that any real thought or preplanning had gone into the palace's construction, at least past whatever the original structure had been. It was also doubtful that anyone, even the historians, knew what the original layout of the palace had looked like.

This was the result of successive emperors, each adding to the building in their own way, so that the additions and renovations looked almost discordant, perhaps even incompatible with one another. Gazing upon the palace, Stiger thought it was as if an architect, in a fit, had gone thoroughly mad.

Despite all that, the emperor's palace was a terribly imposing structure, so much so that standing in its shadow made one seem small and insignificant, perhaps even a little humble. The only other structure in the empire that was larger, besides the High Father's temple, was the colosseum down in the city.

On the south side of the palace, where the family residence was located, there were covered walkways that led out to the palace gardens and grounds. These were lined with intricately shaped and carved columns. Each column reportedly came from a different part of the empire. They had been installed by Tioclesion's father, who had also renovated the palace grounds. The walkways were covered with arched and tiled roofs. Benches had been strategically placed at points for those enjoying the views of not only the city, but of the grounds too.

Stiger considered that the imperial palace was not just the emperor's home and personal residence but the administrative center for the empire. It represented the beating heart, and as the empire had grown, so too had the palace to meet the needs of the bureaucracy.

On the north side, where he was standing now, there were administrative offices of all types. It was there that much of the bureaucracy worked to keep the gears of the empire functioning and well-lubricated. Without those people, the bureaucrats and administrators, the empire simply would not function. They could be inefficient, sometimes incompetent, but they were a necessity.

Slave and servant quarters, guestrooms and suites, kitchens, receiving and banquet rooms were spread throughout the rest of the palace. The throne room, with the curule chair, was at the heart of it all.

The portion of the palace the emperor and his family occupied was quite small by way of comparison to the rest of the palace. If Stiger recalled correctly, it was perhaps even smaller than his own family home.

Stiger gazed on the palace with a sour feeling. He had always disliked the palace and now more so. It struck him not just as ugly, but also as cold, sterile, and thoroughly unwelcoming. With Lears and Handi in possession of the place, as well as Veers, he felt the irrational desire to tear it down to the ground, just as he had done with Castor's temple in Forkham's Valley.

He pulled his gaze from the palace and looked around. His men had thoroughly surrounded the building. Almost an hour had been consumed searching and clearing the buildings within the palace grounds, along with bringing Ikuus and Seventh Company up and getting them positioned. The rest of Spatz's men had rejoined their company as well.

Stiger and his officers had surveyed the outside of the building, studying it. A conference had followed and a plan of assault, which struck at multiple points simultaneously, had been worked out. Shortly thereafter, each unit had begun moving into their jump-off positions for an assault. That was what he was waiting for now, the last of the units settling into position. Then, the hard work could begin: the assault and clearing of the palace.

Across the gardens and behind him, the dead and wounded littered the grounds. No serious effort had been made to care for the injured or even collect them. That, sadly, included friendlies. Only a handful of men, walking wounded mostly, had been assigned to the task. It tore at his heart, delaying care, but he had to focus on the task at hand, successfully storming the palace and limiting further casualties. Stiger was mindful that Lears had sent for reinforcements from the army. It was only a matter of time until they arrived, which left him impatient to get things going. But Stiger had long since learned that to do something right took time. And so, he outwardly remained patient.

"Imperator," Lepidus said, coming up. The captain of Tenth Company saluted. "My company is in position."

Stiger returned the salute. He considered Lepidus not only a friend, but an equal. He was not sure he would ever get used to being saluted by the man. With Lepidus was Stiger's father. The Tenth had been the last unit to report their readiness. Stiger had sent his father to check the positioning of each company and confirm all was in readiness. Eli and Therik stood a few feet away, discussing something amongst themselves. Dog was sitting patiently by Stiger's side.

"I believe the assault is ready, sir," Lepidus said.

"I agree," Marcus said. "We await your order, Imperator."

Stiger looked at his father and resisted a scowl. He considered replying, but instead gave a nod, accepting the report. He was not looking forward to this next part. Not in the slightest. The fighting would be hard, brutal, as he expected the defenders to prove not only stubborn but determined.

Inside the palace, Stiger knew there were at least an entire cohort of auxiliaries and a light company of legionaries. There might even be more. Perhaps as many as five or six hundred defenders waited.

"We've been friends for what, ten years?" Lepidus asked. "It seems like just yesterday you took command of Seventh Company."

Stiger looked over at the captain of the Tenth, wondering what was coming. Lepidus appeared somewhat uncomfortable.

"Yes, that's right," Stiger said. "I value our friendship too."

"Then, may I offer the emperor some advice?" Lepidus asked.

"You know your advice is always welcome," Stiger said. "Don't stop speaking your mind now."

His gaze tracking to the palace, Lepidus gave a nod. He hesitated before he spoke, then looked back over at Stiger.

"Hang back for this next part," Lepidus said. "You are now our emperor. There is no need to put your safety at risk."

"He's right, my son. You should not risk yourself unduly," Marcus said.

Stiger did not say anything as his gaze shifted back to the palace as well. He sucked in a long breath and let it out slowly. The breath steamed on the cold air. He found it a difficult thing letting others do the dirty work for him. It never got easier, whether that be in command of an army on the battlefield or here, when he was so close to taking his throne.

They wanted him to remain away from the fighting, safe and protected. Only, as the High Father's Champion, he knew he could not do that, not completely. Risks had to be taken, danger faced, and Stiger suspected in the near future he would be putting himself once again in harm's way. He was the High Father's weapon—and weapons were meant to be used.

"I can't talk you out of this?" Lepidus said. "Can I?"

"Staying out of the assault?" Stiger looked back over.

Lepidus gave a nod.

"No," Stiger said. "But I will hang back, allow the men to go in before me. However, if it comes to it and the need is there, I will fight. Sometimes, examples need to be set for others to follow, hearts need to be hardened and courage reinforced."

"I still don't like it, though," Lepidus said. "We can handle what's to come. You well know that."

"How can you ask me to let others do all the fighting?" Stiger asked them, looking between Lepidus and his father. Now he understood why Lepidus had come to report personally the readiness of his company. The two had talked beforehand. "You'd have me stand back and simply watch? You both understand how tough the fighting in there is going to get, the casualties we are likely to take. I have experience with this sort of thing."

"And so too do your officers, for the most part," Lepidus said.

"Were something to happen to you," Marcus said, "and Lears survive, each one of the officers supporting you would be summarily put to death, perhaps even the men themselves. At the very least, examples would be made. Risking your own skin needlessly is selfish."

Stiger eyed his father for a long moment. He knew his father's point was fair—more than fair, actually. Marcus was right. His time of fighting in the line was over. Going forward, he understood, he would have to be more careful. Though he well knew there were battles ahead only he would be able to fight.

"There are some things I must do for myself," Stiger said simply, "and you both can rest easy. I will not risk my life needlessly. I care for it too much. Besides, the High Father gave me a task to complete, a job to do. I intend to see that through to the end."

A legionary jogged up to Stiger, ending the conversation, to Stiger's relief. He came to attention and offered Stiger a salute.

"Captain Spatz requests your presence, Imperator," the legionary said. "There is a delegation that wishes to talk at the south entrance. My captain would like to speak with you before accepting their offer to talk."

"Tell Captain Spatz I will be right there," Stiger said.

"Yes, sir." The legionary saluted, turned, and jogged off the way he'd come.

"This is an interesting development," Lepidus remarked. "I wonder what they want to talk about."

"Whatever it is," Marcus said, "I seriously doubt they want to surrender."

Stiger agreed. He turned to Lepidus. "I will hear them out. When they're done, I intend to give the order for the assault to commence. Be prepared for it when it arrives."

"Yes, sir." Lepidus saluted and left, working his way through the snow and back to his company.

Stiger looked over at his father. "Would you care to join me for this?"

"I wouldn't miss it," Marcus said. "Shall we go?"

With that, Stiger, along with his father, began moving toward the south side of the palace. His escort of four legionaries assigned by Ruga moved with him. They had created a small bubble of protection. Dog stood, shook himself, and padded along behind them.

They passed men positioned in assault groups, prepared to make the final attack. They had been permitted to relax. Some sat on the ground in the snow and rested while they waited. Others leaned upon their shields. Though they had just been through a fight, they looked more than ready for another. Legionaries were a tough breed and Stiger loved them. As he passed close, the men stood and came to a position of attention. A few even offered salutes. Stiger returned them whenever they were offered.

He found Spatz standing a short distance from one of the covered walkways that was lined with columns. Ten of the captain's men stood behind him in a line. They had been permitted to stand at ease but were clearly ready for action. A few yards away, under the nearest walkway, stood a legionary officer, a lieutenant. He was not one of Stiger's men.

"Sir," Spatz said as Stiger came up to him. The captain offered a salute, then gestured at the lieutenant. "He wants to talk, or really Lears's representative does. They sent him out to arrange terms to speak. I don't think there is much of a chance they will surrender, and he pretty much admitted it to me."

"He did?" Stiger asked, wondering what Lears's game was.

"Sir," Spatz said, "I don't think he is too happy to be in there, either. Do you want to speak with their representative? It seems like a waste of time to me."

Stiger agreed with that assessment and considered refusing the offer to talk. But after he glanced about at Spatz's men, who had already given him so much this day, he knew he had to make the effort. If there was even a remote chance of a negotiated deal ending things, he had to give it a shot. The alternative was more blood, a currency Stiger did not wish to spend, unless he had to.

"I think you should talk with them," Marcus said. "Not only does it give them potentially a way out, but we might find out vital intelligence before we send our men in. Whoever their representative is might slip and give something of value away."

That sealed it. He turned back to Spatz.

"I will speak with their representative," Stiger said, "but out here. They come to us, not the other way around."

"Right, sir," Spatz said. "I will be right back."

The captain stepped off to speak with the lieutenant, who was staring at Stiger with unmasked curiosity mixed with an intense nervousness. Or was it worry?

"Waste of time," said a small voice.

Stiger glanced down. Sehet was standing there next to him. The gnome had come up without Stiger noticing, which was an impressive feat, especially considering that Eli had trained Stiger.

"Maybe," Stiger said, with a glance at his father, "maybe not."

"Time will tell truth of that," Sehet said. "You want make effort? Stop killing, yes?"

"I do," Stiger said and glanced in the direction of the palace. He felt a sense of unease that seemed to be growing by the moment. "I do not enjoy the idea of wasting the lives of my men or, for that matter, your gnomes."

The gnome gave a tiny nod. He turned his gaze in the direction of the palace and was silent for a long moment. "Darkness at play. I feel it. You too?" Sehet looked back up at him expectantly. "You feel it, don't you?"

Stiger did not immediately answer. He did indeed feel the darkness in the direction of the palace, just yards distant. It made him cold on the inside. Something clearly was not right.

"You do, yes?" the gnome pressed.

"What does he mean?" Marcus asked, brows drawing together. "What do you feel?"

Stiger gave a nod of affirmation to the gnome, then turned to his father. "As Champion, I have a connection with the High Father. It allows me to sense evil, at least those who can do priestly magic or devices that have been imbued with such magic."

"And there is evil in there?" Marcus asked, glancing toward the palace. "In the palace?"

"Yes," Sehet said. "Evil is about. Is why we are here. We end it."

"That is why we are here." Stiger's gaze shifted to Spatz and the lieutenant. They spoke for a few moments, then the lieutenant drew himself to a position of attention and gave a crisp salute. Stiger watched the enemy lieutenant as he turned on his heel and walked up the covered walkway toward the palace and disappeared inside a door. Spatz returned to Stiger.

"I have guaranteed their representatives safety, sir," Spatz said, "at least for the duration of the talks. There will be two of them and a small protective escort. I expect that will not prove to be an issue?"

"That's fair enough." Stiger's sense of unease increased. There was almost a menace on the air. He glanced back down at Sehet for a long moment before turning back to Spatz. "Get your men ready. Send runners to the other companies. I do not expect these talks to bear fruit. As soon as they are done, we will make the assault, understand?"

"I do, sir. I will see that it is taken care of," Spatz said and stepped away. "Lieutenant Darius, I need three runners."

"You left us," Therik said as he and Eli approached. Restus was with them too. "We turned around and were surprised you were gone."

"I seriously doubt that," Stiger said. "Eli always has his eye on me."

"I do," the elf admitted. "We decided to follow."

"If I am not missing my mark, something, I believe, is afoot," Restus said.

"What's going on?" Therik asked. "We saw that enemy officer speaking with Spatz."

Stiger was about to explain when two men, along with four legionaries as an escort, emerged from the same side door the lieutenant had disappeared into. Handi was one of the two men. Stiger's sense of unease increased, as did his anger, which immediately began to boil. He now wished he had listened to the sword back in Lorium.

Dog started growling. The animal's hair was standing on end.

Power, the sword hissed, startling Stiger. *There is power here. Be on guard.*

Stiger could sense it himself, feel it on the air. The sensation was so strong, he could almost taste it, as was the feeling of terrible menace. He studied the two carefully as they approached. The power was radiating not from Handi, but from the man who walked calmly at his side. There was nothing remarkable about him. His face was an ordinary one, plain even. His hair was short and his tunic was brown, cut in imperial style. He was not armed and wore civilian sandals. In a crowd, he would not have stood out. Then, Stiger saw it: a thin steel collar about the neck.

He recognized it, for he had seen similar ones, back before Vrell and during the aftermath of the battle a few miles from Lorium. The elite slave soldiers of the confederacy had worn them. Only, this man was no slave soldier, but something else. There was no doubt in Stiger's mind he was incredibly dangerous. Stiger glanced over at Sehet and Restus. Both had gone still. Their gazes were fixed upon the man, which only confirmed Stiger's suspicion. He knew without a doubt this was why Restus had been called to travel with him to Mal'Zeel.

The talks would most assuredly end in blood. Stiger drew Rarokan, which immediately got Therik and Eli's attention. The orc drew his sword.

The two men and their escort stopped at that, just seven yards distant. Handi's escort drew their own swords and raised their shields in response, moving before their charges. The tribune seemed amused and waved them back. When they did not move, he spoke harshly in a strange, guttural tone. The men responded and stepped away. It was then that Stiger noticed the legionary escort wore collars themselves.

They were not imperials, but soldiers of the confederacy, here in the heart of the empire.

How had it come to this?

The man with Handi had been eyeing them coolly. His gaze traveled from Stiger, to Restus, then Sehet, before finally moving on to Therik, Eli, and Marcus. Stiger got the sense they were being sized up. He did not like it, not one bit, for his sense of unease and menace increased with the man's proximity. There was a darkness to the man's soul that was utterly repugnant to Stiger.

"Swords?" Handi scoffed. "Is that how you greet an old friend? Seriously, you disappoint me, old boy."

Stiger pulled his gaze from the man radiating power and shifted it to Handi. Everything about the tribune, from his teeth to his hair, seemed perfect, almost too much so. Stiger had never seen a man better groomed and his armor maintained to such a high degree. Speaking of the armor, it had clearly been made by a master smith and likely, along with his cloak and boots, had cost a fortune.

When Stiger had first met Handi, he had seemed a fop, a fool, a player of camp politics. It was clear he was much more than that. He was dangerous. Both men standing before Stiger were dangerous.

"I don't know where you got the absurd idea we were friends," Stiger said.

"Come now," Handi said, "we're old comrades. We should be friends."

"Where's Lears?" Stiger asked, deciding to get right to the point. He did not enjoy being toyed with.

"Where I left him, cowering on his throne in abject fear," Handi said, sounding thoroughly disgusted. "He's really afraid of you, terrified even."

"He should be," Stiger said. "He and I have a score to settle."

Handi glanced over at his companion. "I think the proper word is gibbering mad. Lears is truly a disgrace. The sight of him sickens me. Though I must say, he served his purpose admirably." Handi turned his gaze to his companion again. "Wouldn't you agree, Ferdol?"

Ferdol, for his part, shot the tribune an unhappy look but said nothing. Stiger got the feeling Ferdol tolerated Handi because he had to, maybe even was forced to.

"What do you want?" Stiger asked, having seriously tired of the game. "Speak your mind and let us end this farce. You are not going to surrender. So stop wasting my time. Tell me what you came to say and be gone."

"All right, if you insist," Handi said. "I wanted you to know who it was that engineered all this ruin." Handi held his arms out wide. "I wanted you to know who was responsible for everything, including the collapse of the empire you so hold dear."

"Oh—oh. Let me guess," Eli said, his tone dripping with sarcasm. "It wouldn't be you, would it?"

"Funny elf," Handi said.

"The empire is far from collapse," Stiger said, not liking Handi's choice of words.

"Are you so sure?" Handi asked. "You may kill us all this day, but I've already done what I've come to do. The empire is done, finished. You just don't know it yet. But you will get to watch it happen. That, I think, is the best part, knowing what you will witness."

Stiger was silent for several moments as he considered the tribune. Handi had been in the south with Mammot and Kromen, then with Tioclesion, and finally here, with Lears. In all three instances, he had been in a key position to do harm, to manipulate events, critical to the damaging and weakening of the empire.

"It was all your doing," Stiger said as the full realization and horror hit him. "You were responsible for what happened to the southern legions." It was only a guess, but even as he voiced it, the words rang true to Stiger. "And Tioclesion as well...you made all that happen. I don't know how you did it, but you're also responsible for Lears becoming emperor."

Handi's eyes flickered ever so slightly. Beyond that, the man covered his surprise well. After a moment, he smiled slightly and then gave a shrug of his shoulders.

"Sure, why not," Handi said lightly. "I wasn't specifically speaking about that. But I will not deny my work, not now. There is no longer any point to conceal who I am."

"You take orders from Veers," Stiger said, the pieces of the puzzle continuing to come together. "You always have."

"Willingly." Handi's smile grew wider. "The confederacy represents the new order of things. You and this empire of yours will soon be nothing more than a memory, and a bad one at that. All that will remain of this city will be ruins when it's all said and done. Three hundred years from now, maybe four hundred—people will wander the ruins and wonder who lived here. That is how complete your destruction shall be. In the end, Valoor will reign supreme."

"I don't think so," Stiger said, his head spinning at the implications of what he was learning. The confederacy had engineered so much, actively worked toward their invasion of the empire for years, perhaps even decades. "We've already won here, and I've destroyed two of your armies. Give me some time. I assure you, I'm just getting started."

"Believe what you will," Handi said. "It matters little at this point. We're winning and you are losing, have already lost, actually." Handi glanced around them, at Spatz's men. "I have done everything that was asked of me and then some. There is no doubt in my mind I shall be rewarded for it, given a new life. And when it comes to time itself... well, you are already too late. What's done is done and time is the fire in which we all burn. You cannot stop it from burning, not now, not after the inferno I've set." Handi paused and his smile grew. "And yes, as you guessed, I am responsible for the demise of the southern legions. It was I who bankrolled those incompetents, Kromen and Mammot. I owned those two degenerates. They were so far in debt they would have done anything to dig their way out." Handi gave a chuckle. "And they did. Yes, I gave them the money to buy their positions, like I did so many others, and in return, they led your legions to disaster and ruin, with my help and nudging here and there, of course."

"And with the confederacy's money," Stiger said, "no doubt."

"Of course," Handi said. "Gold and silver don't grow on trees."

Stiger remained silent as he thought on all the planning that must have gone into everything Handi had done. At the same time, his rage was growing.

"And I bought the praetorians too, and blackmailed when needed," Handi admitted. "They were the ones who really owned Tioclesion. Your childhood friend was so frightened of Nouma that it really did not take much effort on the prefect's part to encourage him to march his army south, to be the imperial hero he always wanted to be. Nouma promised Tioclesion the praetorians would keep him safe as a babe on her mother's teat as he faced off against the confederacy."

"You bastard," Marcus said.

Handi gave a shrug of his shoulders.

"And," Stiger said, "the praetorians saw to it that Tioclesion was made vulnerable to attack during the fighting that followed."

"Correct again," Handi said, with an exaggerated sigh. "It's a crying shame Nouma was too stupid to simply leave him on the battlefield to die. Had he done that, we would not be here now, and you would not be seeking the curule chair and crown of wreaths. Things would have gone easier for us."

Stiger was not so sure about that, especially after he had met Karus's specter. One way or another, he was certain he would have ended up here. But he did not voice that to Handi.

"Back in Lorium, you knew I'd never agree to your terms," Stiger said. "The plan was to kill me regardless."

"Correct again." Handi clapped his hands together lightly. "Bravo. You are not as thick as the average soldier tends to be or some of your enemies would like me to think. I could not even get Nouma to do that job properly and kill you. He insisted on doing things his way. He was just too incompetent and messed it up as well in the end, which is why we are here now. Of course, if you'd had the good grace to die in Vrell, as I had originally intended, things would have been so much simpler. At that point, you were a minor headache, at best a spy sent by the senate, an inconvenience to be dealt with. But no, there I was wrong. I admit it. The gods move around you, don't they? At least Veers and Ferdol tell me so. At the time, they did not even know what you were destined to be, could not even guess. I guess it was a lack of foresight."

Ferdol shot Handi a warning glance.

Stiger's rage was roiling within. It was barely under control now. This man was responsible for so much death and suffering that it was almost incalculable, inconceivable even. Two entire imperial armies had been destroyed because of him. Cities and towns had been razed, their populations put to the sword. Stiger vividly recalled the civilians of Aeda, who had been tortured and nailed to crosses along the roadside leading north. Even children had not been spared. Rarokan began to glow.

Handi gave a shake of his head. "Had they known what you were, or really what you would become, they would have sent more to Vrell."

"You talk too much," Ferdol said to Handi, his gaze fixed on Stiger and Rarokan. "He doesn't need to know that, you fool."

Handi shot Ferdol an unhappy look. "Does it really matter now?"

Ferdol said nothing.

"And Veers?" Stiger asked, almost through gritted teeth. "What of him? Is he hiding too? Like Lears, afraid to face me?"

"Oh, he's left," Handi said, "gone, vanished. He stopped by to check in, patted both of us on the head, and then left. He tends to do that when his business is concluded— leave, that is. And I don't think he fears anyone or anything, except perhaps failing in his mission."

"Enough of this," Ferdol said. "I grow tired of your talking."

"What?" Handi asked in sudden surprise, looking over at his companion. "This isn't what we discussed. Wait—"

Ferdol had already raised his hands, from which fire sprang. Handi took several steps back. Sehet rushed forward before Stiger, his little hands up in the air. At the gnome's side was Restus. Time suddenly seemed to slow, if not stop altogether. Stiger could feel the *will* being unleashed. It seemed to crackle on the air all around. Stiger worked desperately to bring his sword up, but it moved ever so slowly. The fire in Ferdol's hands began to grow and expand toward Stiger and the rest.

There was a concussive blast. Stiger found himself on his back, looking up at the sky, blinking. His ears were ringing painfully. His vision swam for a moment and then cleared. Wondering how he'd gotten here, he rolled to his side and saw Therik was down too. As was everyone else, including Eli and Marcus. Even Spatz and his men had been knocked from their feet.

What had happened?

He looked around and spotted the man with the burning hands. He was surrounded by a sphere of pure white light. Stiger could see Sehet, his little hands still up in the air in the middle of it all. Energy flowed from the gnome to the sphere. Restus and Ferdol were the only other ones inside it.

Light and lightning flashed from each man as they battled one another, releasing incredible torrents of energy that snapped and cracked violently against the walls of the sphere of light. Stiger got the sense the protective sphere was barely managing to contain the battle raging within.

Stiger suddenly understood what had happened. Sehet had saved them. The little gnome, with his power, had knocked them away and created the sphere, raising it with the High Father's help, and in doing so, locked the combatants within. The gnome had saved him, possibly all of them.

Groaning, Stiger picked himself up onto his hands and knees. His entire body ached something fierce. He figured Sehet's actions had thrown him at least ten feet from where he had been originally standing. He looked up and around, searching. Handi was on his feet and staggering back toward the palace.

Stiger felt a wave of nausea wash over him as he pulled himself to his feet. Seeing Handi, his anger spiked, and with it, Rarokan fed him a surge of energy. It was then, he realized, he was still holding onto the sword.

Kill him, the sword encouraged. *He must die.*

Stiger wanted nothing more than that. But he stopped himself and turned around, looking.

"Spatz," Stiger called. It came out as a gasp. He tried again, this time in a stronger tone. "Spatz."

Looking shaken, Spatz was pulling himself to his feet. So too were his men. Those standing farther away seemed not as badly affected. All eyes were on the sphere and the battle raging within.

"Sir?" Spatz managed, sounding strangled.

"Give the order to go in," Stiger snapped as he began to stagger after Handi. "Send word to the others to begin the assault."

"Yes, sir," Spatz said. "Company—fall in."

Stiger turned back, looking for Handi, and began moving. It was time to get him. With each step, Stiger's footing and sense of balance became better, more certain. As he was passing the sphere, he could feel the energy within bleeding outward.

One of Handi's escorts, who was staggering backward toward the relative safety of the palace, spied Stiger, checked his progress, and raised his sword to strike. He seemed somewhat dazed still, and Stiger, having gained momentum, did not give him the chance to recover or strike. He lunged and stabbed with Rarokan. The tip took him in the sword arm, just above the elbow. Gasping in pain, the slave soldier disguised as a legionary dropped his sword, and as he did, Stiger shoved him roughly aside and out of the way.

Handi was just ahead. Another member of the man's bodyguard attacked Stiger. The man had lost his shield but he came on anyway. Stiger blocked the strike, pushing it forcefully away. The slave soldier took two steps backward to gain room for another attack. He brought his sword back up as Stiger gave a tentative stab. The move was easily blocked.

The man was trained well and clearly competent, one who knew his sword work. Stiger lunged, launching a flurry of attacks, and immediately the slave soldier found himself on the defense. After blocking three attacks, the soldier missed the fourth, which slipped in and stabbed him in the chest. The sword cut straight through the armor, as if it weren't there. The life rapidly faded from the man's eyes as the sword took it. He fell stiffly backward and to the ground.

Another slave soldier, dressed as a legionary, stepped in his way, blocking his pursuit of Handi. Before Stiger could react, Dog was there. Snarling savagely, the animal took the man down in a single bound. Stiger did not pause. He kept going, moving forward, chasing after Handi. Behind him, Therik attacked and killed the last of the guard. Handi was ahead, full-on running down the walkway now, toward the entrance to the palace. An auxiliary stood there, waving him on.

Stiger could think of nothing other than catching the traitorous tribune. Behind Stiger, there was an incredible snapping sound, followed by a violent tremble. The ground under Stiger's feet cracked, then seemed to jump up. He found himself crashing painfully to the ground. Still gripping Rarokan, he picked himself up again and looked back.

The sphere was gone. Ferdol lay on the ground, his corpse smoking. Sehet wavered on his feet, then toppled over onto his side and lay still. Restus fell to his hands and knees. The paladin looked up and their eyes met.

"Go!" Restus shouted. "Get him. He cannot escape."

Stiger glanced around and spotted Handi. He too had fallen. The tribune picked himself up and started once again toward the auxiliary at the door. Stiger dragged himself to his feet and sprinted after Handi.

The tribune reached the door and disappeared inside. Stiger pushed for all he was worth. The auxiliary at the door, seeing Stiger, began to close it. Stiger threw his shoulder into the heavy door, just as it was closing the last few inches. He hammered into it, his momentum carrying him forward and throwing the door wide open. The auxiliary was sent sprawling to the floor. Stiger himself barely managed to keep his feet, stumbling several steps before bringing himself to a stop. Having hit the wall, the door banged back closed behind him and the latch clicked as it locked.

Stiger glanced around and found himself in a small foyer. It was a side entrance from the gardens, the kind primarily used by servants. There were half a dozen armed auxiliaries in the room with him. They seemed startled by his abrupt arrival, frozen into immobility. Stiger glanced at the locked door behind him and suddenly recalled Lepidus warning him to take fewer risks.

Gritting his teeth, Stiger knew there was nothing else to do but attack. He lunged for the nearest man, slicing downward and opening his thigh to the bone. The auxiliary screamed horribly as he fell back. That shattered the moment of indecision. A man made to attack. However, the door seemed to explode inward with such force that the lock snapped free and flew across the room, hammering into the far wall. The top hinge of the door was ripped off the wall and the door hung at an angle.

Therik stood framed in the doorway, hulking and menacing. He took a step into the room and roared, baring his teeth at the enemy. The sound of the roar in the small room was utterly deafening. Sword swinging, he surged forward, attacking the nearest man, nearly cleaving his head from his shoulders with a single slash. A heartbeat later, the man's body slammed to the floor, blood gushing out onto the polished white marble. There was a moment's hesitation but that was all. The rest of the auxiliaries in the foyer lost heart and fled.

Stiger punched out and stabbed a man in the leg as he was passing by. He fell to the floor in a tumble of arms and legs. Roaring, Therik pursued after the fleeing auxiliaries. Stiger was about to follow, but Dog burst into the room, saw Stiger, gave an enthusiastic bark, and then dashed after Therik.

Eli was next to appear in the doorway. The elf seemed relieved to see Stiger. He was followed by Marcus. They looked around at the carnage and the two injured auxiliaries on the ground moaning. One gripped his wounded leg as he rocked on the floor. They turned their attention to Stiger.

"You don't have to kill everyone yourself, you know," the elf said.

"I should have known," Marcus said, "you'd not listen to my advice about letting others take the risks."

"Where a Stiger goes, death follows," Stiger said to his father.

"Don't give me that horseshit," Marcus said. "Who do you think made that line up?"

"I wanted to get Handi," Stiger said, somewhat sheepishly. "He has much to answer for."

In the direction Therik and Dog had gone, screams sounded. Therik roared with what Stiger thought was satisfaction from a kill. Snarling and barking could be heard as it echoed back down the hallway to the foyer.

"Then," Marcus said with a heavy breath, hefting his sword, "let's go find him."

Stiger gave his father a nod and followed after Therik and Dog. Behind them, Spatz's legionaries began pouring into the room. Stiger found himself in a narrow hallway designed for servants. No one could be seen, but he could hear the fight as Therik and Dog pursued the fleeing auxiliaries, somewhere ahead.

Ten feet in, he found himself stepping over the body of an auxiliary who had been brutally cut down from behind. Blood was all over the floor and walls. A door to the left was open. Stiger peeked in and saw an empty storeroom.

He continued on. Thirty feet in, he came to a junction with a hallway turning left and another continuing forward. A blood trail led forward and he followed it. He rounded a bend and saw Therik, twenty yards ahead, in the middle of what looked like a larger room. Singlehandedly, the orc was battling two auxiliaries. Picking up the pace, Stiger continued in that direction.

He emerged into what appeared to be a banquet or hosting hall. Wooden tables had been pushed against the walls, along with stools and benches. These had been stacked upon each other. As Stiger, Eli, and Marcus entered, fifteen more auxiliaries came from another door to the left. Off to the side, Dog had just taken a man down and was standing on his chest as he tore out the man's throat.

Therik sliced his sword neatly across the neck of one of his opponents. Blood spurting into the air, the man staggered backward, his free hand going to his ruined neck.

Stiger moved forward and attacked the new arrivals. Eli was at his side, daggers out. Marcus came too. The fight was brutal, hard. The harsh clash of weapons rang out, echoing almost painfully off the walls. Blood sprayed through the air. Men screamed, called out war cries, sobbed, moaned, grunted. Therik continually roared through it all, while Dog snarled and barked as he fought.

Then Spatz's men spilled into the room and, within moments, overwhelmed the defenders. The last of the auxiliaries turned and fled, with the legionaries hot on their heels.

Blood ran freely across the floor, making the marble incredibly slick. Stiger almost slipped as he stepped aside to allow a legionary to pass. Men continued to stream by them, following the fight or heading through the two other doors that led off from the room. Stiger felt himself frown as reason returned. He knew not which way Handi had gone.

Feeling frustrated and breathing heavily from his exertions, he glanced around. He realized he knew this place…well, this banquet hall specifically. He remembered it as a child. He had played hide-and-seek here with Tioclesion.

There was a window to the left that was shuttered. It led out into a small courtyard with a garden. Stiger recalled it had been an herb garden for one of the kitchens. He moved over to it and opened the shutter, looking out. There was no one out there. The courtyard and garden were filled with fresh snow. There weren't even footprints. He had a sudden idea and looked back at the others.

"If we cut across the courtyard," Stiger said, "there is a shortcut through the back hallways of the palace. It leads directly to the throne room. We might be able to surprise Lears."

"I like it," Therik said.

Stiger looked to his father. Marcus seemed to hesitate a moment, then gave a reluctant nod.

"It sounds exciting," Eli said.

Stiger glanced around. Dog had gone after the defenders. There was no telling where in the palace he was now, though he could be heard barking off in the distance.

Stiger climbed through the window and dropped down into the garden below, his feet sinking into the fresh snow. Across the way was another shuttered window. If he recalled correctly, that led to a kitchen, and from there they could follow servants' passages directly to the throne room. They might even be able to avoid the defenders, as the passages he was thinking of traveled through the interior of the palace and were sort of out of the way.

Eli dropped down after him and then Therik followed. Marcus came next.

"I am getting too old for this sort of thing," Marcus said.

Stiger glanced back at his father, amused. Marcus's sword was splattered with blood, as was his sword arm, armor, and face.

"I've had that feeling a time or two myself," Stiger said, then turned and made his way swiftly across the courtyard to the window. He tried the shutters. They were locked from the inside. Fighting could be heard from every direction now, as his men seemed to be storming the palace. He decided that the assault might work in their favor, as the defenders would rush to throw the attackers back.

Stiger pulled on the shutters with no luck. He was about to use his sword to pry them open when Therik, growling with irritation, shoved him roughly aside. The orc full-on punched one side of the shutters, driving his large green fist right through wooden frame. The orc took hold of the inside of the shutter and ripped it open.

"I guess that's one way to open a shutter," Eli said.

"It is the quick way," Therik said as he looked inside. He gave a satisfied grunt. A moment later, he climbed through the window, which wasn't as easy as it sounded. The window was on the smaller side and the orc wasn't. Therik had to squirm a bit to get through.

"You may want to try eating a salad or two," Eli quipped to the orc as Therik looked back at them from inside the kitchen. "You are getting a little pudgy around the center."

Therik grinned at the elf, for his stomach was all muscle.

"I am still waiting for that meal that was promised," Therik growled and then turned away.

Stiger climbed through the window after the orc and found himself in a large kitchen. Eli followed a moment later and then gave a hand to Marcus to help him up and through.

The kitchen was warm, hot even. The smell of burning bread was strong on the air. It was clear the cooks had fled and left the loaves to burn. Therik was at the door, which was open. He looked out and then turned back.

"The hallway is empty," Therik said. "Which way do we go?"

"Left leads in the direction of the throne room," Stiger said.

"Are you sure?" Therik asked. "You told me you were last here when you were a child. I am thinking a lot of time has passed since then."

"I am not that old," Stiger said. "And I have an excellent memory. We're going left."

"Do you really think we will find Lears there?" Eli asked.

"I hope so," Stiger said. "Handi said he was in the throne room. I don't think he was lying about that. At least I hope not."

Therik stepped out into the hallway, which was very narrow, and turned to the left. Stiger followed him out. The hallway was almost too small for the orc and had been made specifically for servants to use. Doors lined the hallway on both sides ahead.

"This is the servants' section of the palace," Stiger said.

"You mean slaves," Eli said as he stepped out into the hall.

"That's right," Stiger said, glancing back. "Though not everyone who is a servant in the palace is a slave. Many are freedmen and women. This is where they live. That kitchen we passed through is for them."

Therik began moving down the hallway. He opened each door they passed and looked in. The fighting throughout the palace had become quite loud. Stiger found it almost surreal that they were moving through the very heart of the palace without bumping into active opposition. And fighting seemed to be raging all around them.

Therik opened yet another door ahead and several screams issued forth. The orc paused a moment, bared his tusks at whoever was inside, and continued on. Stiger looked in and saw three middle-aged women, all slaves, huddled in the corner. They screamed again, this time at the sight of him. Stiger realized for the first time that he was covered in blood and gore, much of it dried, from the earlier fight in the palace grounds. He held his finger up to his lips and the women quieted. Stiger continued on.

Ahead, they were coming to the end of the hallway. It opened to a broad corridor with polished marble floors. Several legionaries went charging by to the left. Each held a javelin. Stiger wondered if they were real legionaries or the confederacy's slave soldiers in disguise.

"Those are the enemy," Stiger whispered to Therik.

"How can you tell?" Therik looked back at him. He had been about to lean out when the men had gone by. Thankfully, they had not been seen coming down the side passage.

"The javelins," Stiger said. "Our men don't have them."

Therik grunted.

"The throne room should be to the right a few yards," Stiger said.

"It is," Marcus agreed. "I know this place."

Therik peeked out into the corridor, looking left and then right. He pulled his head back rapidly.

"Six men to the right," Therik said. "Standing before a big door that's closed. Thirty yards away."

"Let's go," Stiger said, "before more show up and we find ourselves at a disadvantage."

Therik stepped out into the hallway. Stiger and Eli joined him. The men at the door to the throne room were standing in a circle and talking. A shout of alarm sounded a heartbeat later as Stiger and his party were spotted.

"Javelins," a sergeant ordered. They leveled their javelins. None had shields.

Stiger began moving down the corridor, with Eli and Therik by his side. Stiger's father brought up the rear. As he drew close, Stiger came to a halt.

"Lay down your arms and you can go," Stiger said. He did not see any slave collars, which meant they were likely from the light company. "My quarrel is not with you. It's with Lears."

"Piss off," a sergeant said. "You are outnumbered."

"I am Bennulius Stiger, the rightful emperor. You know what follows me."

"Death," one of the men gasped. His hand holding the javelin began to tremble.

"That's right," Stiger said, taking several steps forward. His sword was still glowing. The men were looking between it and Therik, even Eli. He could see their will begin to waver. Stiger did not want to kill them. There had already been too much of that, and from the sounds of things, the battle still raging throughout the palace, there would be much more death before things were settled.

There was a deep, guttural growling that almost caused Stiger to jump. Dog had joined them. The animal took several steps forward, moving between Therik and Eli, stopping before Stiger. His hair along his back was standing on end and his teeth were bared. Bloodied drool dripped to the marble flooring. Dog's fur was covered in blood, as if he had bathed in it. The men with the sergeant stared in what was clearly horror at the large dog.

"Hold fast," the sergeant ordered, though his voice wavered slightly. "Don't listen to him."

"I've spent my life in the legion," Stiger said. "I don't want to kill you. Don't make me. I've done enough of that already today to last me a lifetime."

"Boys," Marcus said, "it's time to go, while you still can."

One of the men threw down his javelin. It clattered loudly against the marble floor. He drew his sword and dropped it as well. Another man dropped his javelin.

"I ain't fighting for the bastard hiding in that throne room," one of the men said.

"I said hold fast," the sergeant barked. "That's an order, damn you."

"Sergeant," Stiger said, softening his tone as he drew another step closer. "Let it go. Walk away. This is no longer your fight, not anymore. It's mine."

The rest of the men dropped their weapons. The sergeant looked disgusted with his men, but at the same time also with himself. Stiger could read it in his eyes. He wanted to leave too. He did not want to fight for Lears or, more likely, what now appeared to be a losing cause. After another moment, he dropped his javelin and held his hands up.

"I surrender, sir," the sergeant said.

"Go," Stiger said and pointed with his sword in the direction they had just come. "Surrender to the first of my men you come across and you will be spared."

"Yes, sir," the sergeant said.

The men moved past, almost edging their way by, looking quite nervous, as if Stiger would turn on them and kill them all. He watched them for a moment, then stepped forward and, one-handed, opened the throne room door, which swung open easily and almost without sound. He stepped back, lest there was someone waiting on the other side.

There were no defenders lying in wait. The throne room beyond was empty and as he remembered it. Rectangular-shaped, the room was wide and long enough that the emperor could hold court for three or four hundred petitioners. Thick marble columns supported the roof thirty feet above. Chandeliers with dozens of fat tallow candles hung from crossbeams. None were lit. Windows provided much of the light. These had been set high above near the ceiling.

The throne room was sparse. There was no furniture, no seats or benches, other than the curule chair. It was standing room only and that was intentional. The floors were polished black marble, the walls white marble.

At the end of the throne room, set against the far wall, was the curule chair. It sat upon a raised dais. A large mosaic of an eagle in flight took up the entire wall behind the chair. It was a representation of the divine spirit.

Stiger could see a man sitting slumped forward in the chair and what looked like a woman sprawled at his feet and unmoving, tangled up in a dress. The man was wearing a toga. He also wore a crown of wreaths. It was Lears.

The hobnails on Stiger's worn boots clacked loudly against the marble as he walked slowly toward the throne. He stopped just before it and gazed upon Lears.

Lears looked slowly up at him, blinking. He held a cup in a hand that shook violently. His eyes were wide, and he was sweating profusely. The expression on his face was a strained one, filled with intense pain. Stiger blew out an unhappy breath, thoroughly disgusted by the man before him.

"Lehr Arsenus Pompentius Lears," Stiger said, "we meet again at last."

Eli stepped forward and grabbed the cup from Lears's hand. He sniffed at it and then grimaced.

"Poison." The elf dropped the cup, as if it had burned his hand. The contents spilled out onto the marble. "I don't believe he drank all of it."

Lears spoke with a hoarse voice. "I couldn't. I wanted to," he sobbed, "but I couldn't. I thought I could, but dead is dead." A heartbeat later, he groaned and grabbed at his stomach with a hand. "The pain. It hurts. I don't want to die."

Stiger felt dull, empty. He had been looking forward to this reunion for years and it was not going the way he had hoped. He had wanted his revenge, but this, watching a man die slowly from poison, was not it, not what he had envisioned.

Lears looked up at Stiger and his face twisted. "I should have killed you when I had the chance."

"Yes," Stiger agreed, "you should have."

Kill the coward, Rarokan hissed.

Stiger did not move. He just stared at Lears, feeling the scars upon his back like never before. He had hated this man, loathed him. Now, he pitied him.

"I wanted to be emperor," Lears gasped. "I wanted it so bad. I should have killed you. Why do you always stand in my way? Why can't you for once leave well enough alone? I deserve this."

Stiger said nothing.

Lears went to speak again. Instead, he doubled over in his chair, grunting in agony. Stiger looked on the man who had so wronged him and felt a wave of sadness. The sadness wasn't for Lears, but for what had been done to him and so many others. Lears was not just a disgrace, but he had been a tool of the confederacy. The man had disgraced not only himself, but his entire family. They would live with the shame of that for years to come, just as Stiger had lived under the cloud his father had made.

"I—" Lears began coughing. Blood frothed to his lips. It was clear he was suffering tremendously and the end was near. Stiger had thought seeing the man suffer would bring him joy. It did nothing of the kind. Lears looked up and motioned him closer, clearly losing the ability to speak.

Stiger took a step and leaned forward, and as he did, Lears jumped from his chair, a dagger in hand, looking to plunge it deep. The blade swept toward Stiger's neck. Stiger grabbed Lears's forearm, stopping the point a hairsbreadth from his skin.

Locking eyes with his nemesis, he held Lears's forearm in an iron grip and then squeezed. Lears cried out and the dagger fell to the floor, clattering upon the marble. Stiger released his grip and stepped back, down from the dais. Lears collapsed back into the curule chair, breathing heavily, cradling his arm.

"Once again," Stiger said, "you have failed to kill me."

"Screw you," Lears rasped as a wave of pain wracked him.

"Dog," Stiger said. The animal growled as he stepped forward and around Stiger's leg. Dog bared his canines at Lears, whose eyes had gone to the big, menacing animal. Lears began to tremble violently as Dog drew near.

His gaze on Lears, Stiger hesitated a moment.

"Take him."

Dog lunged forward, jaws closing around Lears's throat. There was a strangled cry and then Dog tore open the would-be emperor's throat. Lears spasmed, his legs kicking violently underneath the animal. Then he fell still as his lifeblood flowed in a torrent down his toga and onto the polished marble.

Dog returned to Stiger's side and sat down, looking up at him.

"Good boy," Stiger said and patted the animal's head fondly. "You are a good dog."

Dog's tail gave a wag.

There was a long moment of silence. Therik broke it as he turned to Marcus.

"See, I told you he was a killer."

Marcus gave a nod, his eyes warily on the big animal. A moment later, they shifted to the woman at the foot of the dais.

"That is Martella," Marcus said, with a sad note, "Lears's wife. Despite who she was married to, I knew her to be a kindly woman. It was an arranged marriage and I do not think she derived much happiness from it."

"I'm guessing he took the easy way out."

Stiger spun. Dog barked and then growled. Handi was at the entrance of the hall and he was alone. His sword was out, and he started walking toward them, his polished boots clicking against the floor.

"Not quite," Stiger said.

"As I told you earlier, my mission is complete," Handi said. "I could have left with Veers, but I decided to stay, to serve my god even further. Through service comes rebirth to a higher station in life."

"You are a traitor to your people," Stiger growled. "A good-for-nothing traitor."

"Not to my god." Handi swung his bloodied sword around with the ease of a trained and confident swordsman. "When I was younger, I found myself drawn to Valoor's temple. I never felt the High Father's appeal or pull. I was repulsed by his priests, the regular devotions, the festivals my mother forced me to attend. Name it, nothing about your god appealed to me. It took me years to understand that I was a man reborn and sent here for a purpose, for a cause. You see, I learned I had given good service in a previous life. Valoor rewarded me with an elevated station in this life and—" Handi paused and glanced around the throne room—"well, let's just say, with this opportunity. Valoor's priests opened my eyes and I was graced with becoming acquainted with my past lives." Handi's gaze returned to Stiger. "Now I have an opportunity to perform an even greater service. That is, if you have the balls to fight me. Will you face me one-on-one? Are you man enough? Or do I have to go through them to get to you?"

"If you faced me," Therik said, "I'd make you suffer terribly for your crimes." The orc lowered his sword, placing it point-first down on the floor and almost leaning on it as he glanced over at Stiger. He turned back to Handi, his tongue caressing one of his sharpened tusks as he considered the tribune. "I am disappointed, actually, that I will not be the one you will be fighting. Still, I will get to watch an entertaining fight, even if it will be one-sided."

"Son," Marcus said and reached out an arm, "there is no need to fight him. The palace is falling. Our men should be here shortly."

Stiger glanced down at Lears's body before looking over at his father. "I disagree. For all that he's done, he has earned what's coming. I intend to deliver justice, my way."

"Justice?" Handi laughed. The sound of it was harsh as it echoed off the marble-faced walls of the throne room. "Are you serious? Only Valoor delivers true justice."

"All right then," Marcus said, glancing at Handi. His face hardened. "Send the bastard on to his god for judgment."

Dog's growl intensified.

"Dog," Stiger snapped. "This one is mine."

Dog ceased his growling and sat down in an obedient manner.

Stiger faced Handi.

The tribune shot him a pleased smile filled with perfect teeth. "I plan to do great service this day."

"Make it quick," Eli said in Elven. "Yes, he's done great harm, but don't play with him, at least not too much."

Stiger gave a nod and studied Handi for a long moment. He sensed no power within the man. He doubted that Handi could use or manipulate *will*. He could sense no implements or devices of evil on his person either. Over the long years stuck in the past, Stiger had learned to sense those. There was nothing that might mark Handi as a servant of a dark god. That was what had made the man such a deadly agent. He had been able to slip into the background, play a fop, a pampered fool from a wealthy family, and not be noticed by the paladins. It bore thinking on, for how many more were out there like him?

Handi stepped forward, raising his sword before himself in mock salute.

Stiger closed off the energy flow from Rarokan and the sword's glow vanished. Just in case he was wrong about the man's ability to use *will*, he left the door open to the wizard's prison.

Handi gave a practice swing and then adopted a fighting stance. Long gone was the foppish attitude Stiger had first seen back in the south. It had all been a façade. Before him was a killer, and Stiger had no doubt the tribune was well trained in the use of the sword he carried.

Handi struck first. His attack was fast. Stiger blocked. Their swords met with a clang that echoed off the marble-faced walls. Handi danced back before Stiger could counterattack. The tribune flashed another infuriating smile his way.

Stiger studied his opponent a heartbeat and then moved to the side. Handi moved opposite. They circled each other for half a turn before Handi lunged forward again, striking out. Stiger batted his sword away with a ringing clang. Then he jabbed, aiming for Handi's extended leg. The tribune danced back again and away.

Handi attacked, and once more, Stiger blocked. The tribune moved nimbly back again before stepping forward and launching a furious attack, attempting to land a series of blows and strikes. Stiger blocked each one.

As the tribune went to pull back, Stiger went over to the offensive himself, lashing out with his sword. He cut a deep slice along Handi's forearm. The tribune hissed with pain and stepped back three steps. Stiger was about to follow when Handi immediately lunged back for another attack.

Stiger blocked and this time Handi came away with a slice on the cheek that bled freely.

"Sorry to mar your looks," Stiger said.

"Bastard," Handi hissed as he touched his face wound with his free hand and then looked at the blood. "You are a bastard."

"I can be," Stiger agreed.

Grim-faced, Handi came forward on full attack. Stiger blocked each lunge, parrying them away. Handi received several more wounds in the process and, Stiger noted, was becoming winded.

The tribune danced back several steps, eying Stiger warily. With every movement, he was dripping blood onto the marble. Sweat beaded his forehead and mixed with the blood running down his cheek. There was no fear of death in the man's eyes, but Stiger saw now that Handi understood this fight would end with him losing. That would make him dangerous, for a cornered man might try anything.

"It is time for you to die," Stiger said.

Handi lunged for a killing strike. The attack was desperately made and a tad slower than his previous tries. Stiger danced to the side, and as he did, he reached out with his free hand and gripped his opponent's sword arm. Stiger pulled hard, yanking Handi forward and off balance, while at the same time ramming his own blade deep into Handi's right thigh.

The sword bit deep and Handi collapsed to a knee, gasping in pain. Stiger yanked the sword out and raised it to strike again. The tribune deliberately dropped his sword and turned to look up at Stiger.

"Finish it," Handi said. "I would look upon the face of my god and be reborn. Maybe—one day—we shall meet again." Handi grinned up at him. "I think I'd like that."

"No," Stiger said firmly. "There will be no rebirth for you. This ends here, for I will be taking your soul."

Handi's eyes widened as Stiger's sword began to glow once more, blue flames licking along the blade's edge. Stiger saw comprehension dawn on the tribune's eyes.

Gripping his sword with both hands, Stiger fed it a little power, then sliced downward with all his might. Rarokan neatly carved through Handi's neck, severing the head from the body. The hilt grew warm in his hands as Rarokan took both sides of the soul. The sword said nothing, but he could feel the mad wizard's satisfaction.

Slightly winded, Stiger straightened. It was over. He reached down and picked up Handi's head by the hair and regarded his enemy for a long moment. The tribune's eyes were lifeless and unmoving. Holding the head, he turned and walked back to the curule chair, stepping by Eli and Therik, who moved aside for him. Marcus simply watched, saying nothing. At the throne, Stiger held up the lifeless head and looked into the face of the dead man.

"Your service to your dark god," Stiger said, "is done."

With that, he tossed the head aside. There was a commotion at the end of the hall. Stiger turned to see Ikuus and Hollux entering, along with a dozen legionaries. Tiro was with them.

They spotted him and walked up to the throne.

"We've won, Imperator," Ikuus said in an exultant tone. The man's armor was covered in blood and his sword was stained by it too. "We are victorious."

"The last of the resistance is being mopped up," Hollux added. "As far as we can tell, most of the defenders are surrendering."

Stiger felt an intense wave of relief. Lears and Handi were dead, finished. The empire was his, or it would be when the senate confirmed him. He could not imagine the senators refusing him after this—then again, they were professional politicians. So who knew what they might do in the end.

"What happened here?" Tiro asked, looking at Handi's head lying upon the dais before the throne.

"He lost his head," Eli said and pointed at Handi's headless body. "Surely you can see that."

Feeling sour once again, Stiger turned his gaze to Lears. He reached forward and removed the crown of wreaths. Turning back around and facing everyone, he placed it upon his own head. He gazed at those before him for a moment, then turned back to Lears. With a hand, Stiger reached out and yanked his former enemy from the curule chair, the emperor's ultimate symbol of imperium. Lears's body rolled limply down the dais steps, where it came to a stop next to his deceased wife.

Stiger sat down. The chair, though padded, was uncomfortable and hard. Stiger supposed that was, in a way, a sign in and of itself. Emperors should never become too comfortable with their imperium. Or it could simply be that the chair, with all its finery, trim, and gold paint, was just too ostentatious to be comfortable.

Tail wagging, Dog padded up and sat down next to the throne and Stiger. More of his legionaries had entered the hall, crowding it, including Ruga and Lepidus. Both men grinned broadly at Stiger.

"Long live the emperor!" Ruga shouted.

"Long live the emperor!" came the massed shout, which echoed about the hall. "Long live the emperor!"

Stiger had won the curule chair and an empire. He knew he should feel exultant, satisfied, proud, and—as Ikuus had said—victorious. Instead, he was angry, for he was awash in a sea of blood with no end in sight and the war for the empire and Istros was only just beginning.

Stiger looked up at the men standing before his throne. They were silently watching him. He stood, raised his sword up into the air, and held it there a moment. He spied his father amongst them. They made eye contact for a heartbeat. His father gave a curt nod of what Stiger took to be approval.

"An empire without end!" Stiger shouted.

There was a moment of silence as the sound of his shout echoed off the walls.

"An empire without end," came the massed reply. It seemed to shake the very air of the throne room. "An empire without end. An empire without end... An empire without end!"

Epilogue

It was the third day after the assault on the palace. Stiger was back in his family home, sitting before the large circular fire with his father and Max. Dog lay by the fire on his side, enjoying the heat and sleeping away, occasionally snoring.

After the fight, Stiger had not wanted to stay in the palace, not for a heartbeat. He really did not want to go back either, but knew he would need to... eventually. It wasn't home, not yet. That was, if the empire managed to survive the next few days. Handi had damaged it, possibly beyond repair.

Outside, like in Lorium, vast crowds had gathered, praying, chanting, and singing the day away. It seemed as if the entire city was rejoicing, celebrating. Stiger had been told the people were treating his ascension to the throne like a holiday. The city was one great big drunken party.

Unlike the people, Stiger did not feel like celebrating. After the news he had received over the last two days, he felt dreadful. More had just arrived at his doorstep. It made him sick to his stomach. Stiger glanced down at his mug of mulled wine. He swirled the contents about before looking up at his brother.

"They are all gone?" Stiger asked. "You are sure?"

"Almost, the entire senate," Max confirmed.

"How many remained?" Stiger asked.

"Six senators," Max answered. "The rest fled the city. The gods only know where they are now."

Stiger rubbed at his tired eyes. The news, it seemed, was continuing to get worse, not better.

"Most of those who stayed are the weakest of the bunch, the least influential," Max said. "They are looking for some advantage to be gained by pledging their loyalty to you."

"Can they be trusted?" Stiger asked.

"They are politicians," Marcus scoffed. "Of course they can't be trusted."

"Well," Stiger said, "it is a start, I guess."

"But it's not a quorum," Marcus said. "The senate needs to officially confirm you as emperor. Until that happens…"

"I know," Stiger said.

"We will have to find ways to tie these six senators closer to us," Max said.

"I imagine that will be the least of our problems," Marcus said.

"I suppose we could elevate new families to the senate," Stiger said.

"A few, yes," Max said. "Creating an entirely new senate—that would be unwise. Those currently serving in the senate have vast holdings throughout the empire, not to mention wealth. They exert control and power over the provinces where they have holdings. I think you will agree, we need that influence, especially now."

Stiger gave an unhappy nod. "No word on the treasury either, I suppose?"

Marcus shook his head. "We know the High Priest fled the city with it. Where he went, we have no idea. We don't even have cavalry to run them down either."

"I'll wager he's taking the treasury to the confederacy," Stiger said.

Neither Stiger's father nor brother said anything to that, which told him they believed the same.

"And Mechlehnus has not replied either?" Stiger asked.

"Not yet," Marcus said. "It is possible we could receive his messenger sometime today or tomorrow. At least the reinforcements he sent to the city pledged themselves to you."

"Three legionary companies and four auxiliary cohorts," Stiger said. That was one of the few bright spots of the day. "At least we now have the largest military force in the city."

"It's also possible," Max said, "that the senate fled to Mechlehnus, along with the High Priest. They might offer him the empire for his protection."

"Let's hope not," Stiger said and leaned back in his chair. He took a sip of the wine. It tasted like ash in his mouth.

"If he does not respond," Marcus said, "you should let me write to the men I put in place."

"That could lead to more bloodshed," Stiger said.

"Yes, it could," Marcus said. "There may be no way to avoid it."

"I've seen enough of that," Stiger said, becoming heated. "We need to bring the empire together, not drive it further apart." Stiger paused and took a sip of the wine. "Still, if it becomes necessary, and Mechlehnus rebuffs us, we will do it and see if we can limit the bloodshed."

The door that led to the kitchen opened and Therik walked in. The orc held a steaming bowl of stew in one hand and a loaf of bread in the other. It was clear he had been using the bread to sop up the stew. The entire house seemed to smell of the stew the cook had made.

"You were right," Therik said as he came up. He shook the loaf, dripping droplets of stew onto the floor. "This is really good bread, and I mean good."

"I am pleased you approve," Stiger said.

"You should get some, before it is all gone." Therik took a large bite and chewed with his mouth open. "Ruga's men are devouring it. They eat like a pack of wolves that's not seen a kill in a month."

"I've lost my appetite," Stiger said. His headaches seemed to be mounting by the moment. Food just did not sound appealing.

"What's wrong with him?" Therik asked, looking to Max and Marcus.

"He has an empire to manage," Marcus said.

"Some minor problems, then," Therik said, and took another bite.

"Minor problems?" Stiger exclaimed, sitting up in the chair. "The senate's fled, the treasury is gone, Mechlehnus has yet to respond to my orders. Worse, I've just learned Handi has murdered the bureaucrats and administrators that worked in the palace. The entire High Command has been killed. Most of the tax collectors have seen the same fate, as have nearly all of the treasury accounting officials. We don't think that even the lowliest of clerks survived from amongst them. It's either that, or anyone who survived ran for the hills. They may never come back. He also had most of the records destroyed."

"So," Therik said, "get new clerks, make new reports. You legionaries seem too fond of written reports. I've seen what Ruga is required to do and it's a lot, too much."

Stiger closed his eyes and leaned back in his chair. On top of all of these problems, which seemed to be mounting by the moment, he still had to find the Key to the World Gate before the enemy did.

"It is not as simple as that," Marcus said.

"No?" Therik asked.

"No," Marcus said.

"Explain it to me, then." Therik seemed thoroughly unconcerned. He took another large bite and chewed rather noisily.

"Without the trained administrators," Marcus said, "the clerks, and the records, we lack basic information about the empire, which is huge in scope. We don't know who the provincial officials are, who's been given grants of imperium, let alone the magistrates, local tax collectors, amounts owed to contractors, the list continues. We're not even sure what military forces and assets are where, besides those with Mechlehnus's army. And when it comes to those formations that are left, the records that were kept in relation to pay and retirement funds have been lost, as have those of the general pensions and disability funds across the government. And even if we had them, there is no way to pay, as the treasury is gone. A good portion of those people out there in the city, who are currently celebrating the new emperor, will turn on us soon enough if they find out. See the problem?"

Therik had stopped chewing as he looked between Marcus and Max.

"Almost everything that was used to manage the empire," Max added, "has been destroyed or is lost to us. The most concerning thing to me, at the moment, is the grain dole. Those records are gone too. We have vast stores of grain, but don't know who's entitled, or for that matter who is a citizen and who is not. If the mob goes hungry because of it, we will lose everything in a heartbeat. The city will consume itself in an orgy of rioting and destruction."

Therik resumed his chewing, before swallowing. He was silent for a long moment.

"I see a challenge ahead," Therik said. "I am not worried in the slightest."

"A challenge?" Max exclaimed. "It's more than that. I fear the road ahead is not just rocky, but an impossible one."

Therik laughed. It was harsh and grating. He pointed a finger at Stiger. "He pulls off the impossible every day."

"This may be too much, for even me, my friend," Stiger said to Therik.

"We'll see," Therik said, "we'll see."

The door to the hall opened. Ruga strode in and snapped to attention.

"Sir," Ruga said. "There are visitors here to see you."

"I left orders not to be disturbed," Stiger said, feeling irritated at the interruption. It seemed everyone in the city who felt they were even moderately important wanted an audience. "Add them to the list."

"I am sorry, sir, I can't do that."

Stiger felt his anger rise as Ruga stepped aside.

In walked Currose, followed by Venthus and then, as impossible as it seemed, Taha'Leeth. Stiger froze in his chair, his anger draining away. He stood, dropping his mug of wine onto the floor, where it shattered. Taha'Leeth seemed pale and very frail. She moved slowly too, not like her normal graceful self.

Dog leaped to his feet and, like a missile, ran over to her. She laughed as he greeted her. Stiger had missed her laugh. The animal was gentle and did not jump up, but licked her hand as she patted him. He seemed to sense she was recovering. Taha'Leeth bent down very slowly and kissed him on the head.

She looked up and straightened. Her gaze swept the room and stopped on him. Their eyes met. In them, Stiger saw love, hope, and dreams of what could be. Everyone else in the room seemed to vanish in an instant, but for her.

Taha'Leeth walked slowly across the hall to him, limping slightly. He just stood there, staring at her almost stupidly, as if she were not real. Her beauty stole his breath away.

She slapped him hard across the face. The blow was strong enough that it brought tears to his eyes. It also broke the moment of shock.

"I think I deserved that," Stiger said, reaching up a hand to his cheek, which stung painfully.

"You left me behind," she said firmly. "You will not make that mistake again, husband."

She grabbed him by the tunic and pulled him close. Their lips met and suddenly Stiger was lost in her kiss. He started to pull her tight. She gave a pained grunt and pulled away, grimacing.

"Easy," Taha'Leeth said and touched her side. "I am still healing. You need to be gentle."

"And the baby?" Stiger asked hopefully, glancing down at her belly, which was still flat. There was a bulge under her tunic, where she was clearly bandaged.

"Still there too," Taha'Leeth said with a slight smile, her eyes glistening. "Currose assured me of that. The baby is well."

"Thank the High Father," Stiger said and pulled her close again. He reached up and grabbed her face, kissing her hard. All of his worries faded. With Taha'Leeth at his side, he could face anything, accomplish the impossible. That included rebuilding a crumbling and destitute empire.

"I hate to rain on your lovely picnic," Currose said, "and reunion, but I am afraid I am the bearer of bad news."

Stiger felt his mood shift as he turned his gaze to the noctalum. Taha'Leeth looked as well. It was clear she did not know what was coming.

"What bad news?" Stiger asked. He'd gotten more than enough already. He did not need any more.

"My mate and that frustrating wizard, Ogg, went to find the sertalum," Currose said.

"They did what?" Stiger asked and closed his eyes in frustration. He'd been wondering where Menos and Ogg had gone off to without word. He had thought they'd done something not only stupid, but dangerous. That they'd gone to find the noctalum's sister race and ancestral enemy was madness in the extreme.

He took a deep breath, let it out slowly, and opened his eyes, turning his gaze back to Currose, who had not replied.

"They went to bargain," Stiger surmised. "They look to enlist her in our fight against the confederacy. In return, they are planning on giving her access to the World Gate, aren't they?"

"And now," Currose said, "they are in deep, deep trouble and need our help."

"Our help?" Stiger asked. "Against the sertalum?"

"If only it were that simple," Currose said. "No, there are gnomes involved." She heaved a heavy, almost weary sigh. "And a particular volcano that you and my mate are *very* familiar with."

Stiger stared at her for several long moments, not quite believing what he was hearing. "The volcano?"

Currose gave a slow nod. "The very one."

"Seven Levels." Stiger just shook his head. He had hoped never to go back there. "Bloody gnomes. This day just keeps getting better and better."

The End

Stiger's journey will continue in The Tiger's Fight, Book 7 of the Stiger Chronicles series.

Important: If you have not yet given my other series—Tales of the Seventh or The Karus Saga—or The Way of the Legend a shot, I strongly recommend you do. All three series are linked and set in the same universe. There are hints, clues, and Easter eggs sprinkled throughout the series.

Give them a shot and hit me up on Facebook to let me know what you think!

CONNECT WITH MARC

Marc works very hard on his writing. He aims to create high quality books to be not only enjoyed but devoured by the reader. Late into the night he writes with a drink at his side, usually a whiskey, gin and tonic (Aviation), or beer.

It helps fuel the creativity ... *If you think he deserves one, you can help to encourage the creativity. Think of it as a tip for an entertaining experience!*
Cheers!

Go to www.maenovels.com and scroll down to the bottom of the page!

Patreon Legion: Consider supporting Marc as an author and get special access. Follow the link below to learn more about the benefits of joining the legion.
www.patreon.com/marcalanedelheit

Facebook: Make sure you visit Marc's Author Page and smash that like button. He is very active on Facebook. Marc Edelheit Author

Facebook Group: MAE Fantasy & SciFi Lounge is a group he created where members can come together to share a love for Fantasy and Sci-Fi.

Twitter: Marc Edelheit Author

Instagram: Marc Edelheit Author

Author Central: You can follow Marc Edelheit Author on **Amazon**. Smash that follow button under his picture and you will be notified by Amazon when he has a new release.

Newsletter: You may wish to sign up to Marc's newsletter by visiting www.maenovels.com to get notifications on preorders, contests, and new releases. **In fact, he recommends it!** We do not spam subscribers.

Reviews keep Marc motivated and also help to drive sales. He makes a point to read each and every one, so please continue to post them.

Made in the USA
Las Vegas, NV
24 September 2023

78044223R00239